The Lost Minyan

The Lost Minyan

David M. Gitlitz

UNIVERSITY OF NEW MEXICO PRESS | ALBUQUERQUE

© 2010 by David M. Gitlitz
All rights reserved. Published 2010
Printed in the United States of America
15 14 13 12 11 10   1 2 3 4 5 6

Library of Congress Cataloging-in-Publication Data

Gitlitz, David M.
  The lost Minyan / David M. Gitlitz.
      p. cm.
  "The Lost Minyan is historical fiction."—Introduction.
  Includes bibliographical references.
  ISBN 978-0-8263-4973-6 (cloth : alk. paper)
  1. Crypto Jews—Fiction. 2. Marranos—Fiction. 3. Jews—Spain—Fiction.
  4. Spain—Ethnic relations—Fiction. I. Title.
  PS3607.I63L67 2010
  813'.6—dc22
                                    2010020379

For Daniel Carpenter, without whose courageous gift of half his liver this book would not have been possible

Contents

Introduction   ix

1. Beatriz Núñez   1

2. The Arias Dávila Clan   45

3. The Doctor's Daughters   81

4. The Rojas and Torres Women   113

5. The Miners Fonseca   127

6. Francisco Gutiérrez: A Man of Three Faiths   179

7. Jerónimo Salgado   193

8. Diego Pérez de Alburquerque   219

9. The Barajas Women   261

10. Carlos Mendes: Turkish Jew, Spanish Christian   291

Notes and Sources   305

Introduction

Prior to the anti-Jewish riots of 1391 Spain's Jewish community was the largest in Europe. Over the next hundred years, a substantial portion of that community converted to Catholicism. Many of the conversions were voluntary. Some were physically coerced. Others were psychologically coerced by the proselytizing campaigns of Franciscan and Dominican preachers or by staged public debates such as the 1413–14 Disputation of Tortosa. Another large group, forced by King Fernando and Queen Isabel in 1492 to choose between conversion or exile, opted to become Christian and to remain. By August 1492 Spain held the largest single community of former Jews in the postbiblical history of Judaism.

While the converts who had been coerced, the ones whom the Jews called *anousim*, observed the Sabbath at home and went grudgingly to mass on Sunday, other *conversos* determined to break cleanly with their Jewish past. But even the most eager new-Christians found it difficult to close the door on their heritage. Their Jewish relatives still incorporated them into family events. The rhythms of the holidays, the echoes of familiar tunes, the smells of traditional dishes emanating from the kitchens of their Jewish neighbors—all these flooded them with memories. Habits of prayer, rituals of cleanliness, culinary preferences, and philosophical commitment to the oneness of God impeded their assimilation. They found it difficult to shake their long-ingrained mistrust of clergy and disdain for images.

By the 1470s pressure mounted in Spain to come up with a way to ensure the former Jews' exclusive adherence to Christian practices. The Church believed itself mandated to compel strict Catholic orthodoxy and touted the medieval papal Inquisition as a model. The old-Christian middle class feared competition from literate, ambitious conversos who were establishing businesses and moving aggressively into municipal and fiscal administration, and they thought it scandalous that some of the neophytes still hung on to their Jewish practices. The monarchs and the nobility welcomed the prosperity that seemed to accompany a thriving Jewish/converso community but also saw the advantage in strict controls. In 1478 the papacy approved Fernando and Isabel's request to establish an Inquisition in Spain and to entrust its organization and administration to the Dominican monk Tomás de Torquemada.

The Holy Office, as the Inquisition was called, functioned in Spain until 1834. In the Spanish colonies tribunals operated from the 1570s through their independence from Spain in the early nineteenth century. In Portugal, to which the majority of Spanish Jews fled when they were expelled from Spain in 1492, and where they were forcibly converted en masse in 1497, the Inquisition operated from 1539 to 1821.

The Inquisition's twin goals were to save souls by inducing individuals to recant their heretical beliefs and behaviors in order to commit themselves to wholly orthodox Christian practices and to encourage everyone to behave and believe appropriately by making the punishment of sinners a public, exemplary event. In the early decades, and sporadically over the next two hundred years, the Inquisition focused on Judaizers, as the unassimilated former Jews were called. But during its long history the Inquisition also concerned itself with secret Muslims, certain mystics, Protestants, blasphemers, bigamists, fornicators, Masons, freethinkers, and priests who sexually abused their male and female parishioners.

In Spain the Inquisition operated from twelve regional centers. In the New World there were three: Lima, Cartagena, and Mexico City, which also had jurisdiction over Spain's Asian colonies. Over them sat the Supreme Council, which determined the policies, set the rules, and heard the rare appeal. While the Suprema's authority derived from the pope, its marching orders came from Spain's monarchs. The Inquisition's bureaucracy was vast: inquisitors, secretaries, scribes, comptrollers, accountants, masters of confiscated property, jailors, bailiffs, doctors, and torturers. It dispatched visiting committees to ferret out heresy and moral laxity in the provinces. It deputized local clergy and salaried commissioners to take depositions from witnesses. It supported a network of informants, both paid and unpaid, called *familiares*.

Inquisitors began by inviting testimony in a publicly read Edict of Grace, which required anyone who had committed any act of heresy (which the edicts enumerated and described, in great detail) to so inform the inquisitors within a specified period and thus receive the Church's grace. Eventually the carrot of grace was removed; in the new Edicts of Faith the dire consequences of not denouncing oneself, or of not informing on one's acquaintances, were spelled out in detail. Files grew fat with the depositions of neighbors, friends, business associates, and relatives of the accused. When enough evidence had been amassed to conclude probable cause, and when this was endorsed by a committee of theologians and high-ranking clergy, the accused was arrested and all of his or her earthly possessions were confiscated. Imprisonment and interrogation could last for days or years. Because arrests were predicated on the accumulation of sufficient evidence, the inquisitors presumed guilt. The purpose of their interrogation was to elicit confession, atonement, and acceptance of any penance that the Church might impose. If the inquisitors thought a witness was lying or withholding the entire truth, they could order torture, which they did far less frequently than the civil or episcopal courts of the era. Speed-writing scribes attended each interview, whether in the audience room or the torture chamber, to make note of every word spoken by the accused.

Most *procesos* (the Inquisition's term for the interrogation process) followed a set format. Without disclosing the nature of the charges, the inquisitors first admonished the accused three times to explain why they thought they had been brought to prison. Eventually, sometimes after months, a summary list of charges was read aloud to them, and they were charged, on the spot, to respond. Then inquisitors asked them to produce a complete genealogy of their families (names, dates of birth, places of residence, professions; grandparents, parents, siblings, spouse, spouse's family, and children). They followed by asking the prisoners to narrate fully the events of their lives. At some later moment they presented the accused with detailed summaries of the individual testimonies against them, without, of course, divulging the identity of the witnesses.

From the reading of the edicts through arrest and interrogation, the Inquisition's principal tool was fear: fear for one's soul; of the loose tongues of one's neighbors and family; of torture; of financial ruin; of public shaming; of the effect on one's family. The entire process was designed to break down an individual's will to resist. Defense was difficult but not impossible.

A defense attorney, usually an Inquisition employee, was provided to assist the accused. The anonymity of testimony was a problem. Accusations might be inaccurate or outright lies motivated by some personal, political, or economic grudge. The accused could attempt to discredit the testimony of the anonymous witnesses by naming all the people who might hold a grudge against them, explaining why they were enemies and naming credible witnesses to that enmity. Under pressure, family members hoping for leniency or a clear conscience might have confessed untruths or half-truths. Even self-denunciations required careful corroboration. It was in the conflicting interest of both the inquisitors and the accused to verify dates, pin down facts, and clarify motives. In a way they resembled today's historians, who must carefully sift the accumulated evidence to determine what is true, what is probable, and what is false and must be discarded.

At the end of the process, the committee of Inquisitors, theologians, and distinguished clerics voted on the case. They had three options: to exonerate or to suspend the investigation; to conclude guilt, remorse, and the possibility of recovery; or to conclude irremediable guilt. In the first case the accused were set free, though their files always remained open to receive new evidence, and they were very likely to have been bankrupted and publicly shamed during the long months of imprisonment. The convicted were liable to a range of punishments: being shamed by being forced to abjure their sins in a public act of faith (*auto-de-fé*) while dressed in a yellow penitential garment (*sambenito*), fines, public flogging, imprisonment, banishment, or rowing in the king's galleys. For the third group, those who were repeat offenders or who refused to repent, who over the course of time appear to have amounted to less than 4 percent of those tried for heresy, the sentence could be death.

Those are the cold facts, laid out by hundreds of scholars over the past century, including such pioneers as Henry Charles Lea, Yitzhak Baer, Henry Kamen, Gustav Henningsen, and Benzion Netanyahu. But behind these facts are real people who wrestled on a daily basis with questions of identity, religion, and survival. How did they manage in a society determined to coerce them into conformity? How did they navigate their choices? How did they negotiate the emotional maelstrom of their lives?

And we, today, how do we sustain the heritage of our Italian or Vietnamese or Jewish ancestors, providing we choose to do so? With a few exceptions—France's prohibiting public wearing of the burka, Switzerland's banning the minaret—we struggle not against coercion but against seduction, against the easy homogeneity of today's mass-culture, melting-pot world. What do these long-vanished conversos have to say to us?

Until the 1480s a substantial number of conversos—we will never know precisely how many or what percent—behaved as if they were still Jews. There were risks, but the Inquisition had not yet come, and the danger was relatively minor. But after 1480 the Inquisition began to persecute Judaizers with terrifying vigor. The cursory show trials of this early period and the public execution by burning of hundreds of Judaizing conversos sharpened the issue for all the rest. Should they leave Spain to seek a haven in France, the Low Countries, Italy, or Turkey? Should they remain where they were, educate their children exclusively as Christians and try to avoid exposing them to Jewish customs? Should they marry them to old-Christians to facilitate their total integration into the mainstream? Should they teach them the ways of Judaism in hopes of preserving the family traditions? Should they, by their own example, show their children how to observe one Law at home and another in the street? When the parents died, did they want their children to recite Kaddish, the Jewish prayer for the dead, or to commission masses for the salvation of their souls? For that matter, how could they ensure that their grandchildren would even know what the Kaddish was?

A substantial number of conversos—again, we cannot know precisely how many or what percent—opted to observe aspects of both religions. Prior to the coming of the Inquisition, the danger was relatively minor; but to Judaize after 1480 incurred mortal risk. Observance was driven into hiding. Judaizing conversos became crypto-Jews, learning to mask their Sabbath preparations, disguise how they koshered their meat, and pray in their hearts rather than with their lips.

Because they were public Catholics, and had to educate their children as Catholics, they soon began to couch their Judaism in Christian terms, holding, for example, that it was essential for them to believe in Moses, or the Law of Moses, for their souls to be saved. The Jewish education of their children—once they were old enough to be trusted not to blab the family secrets to their neighbors—tended to occur at home, with mothers and aunts the principal teachers. As time went on, women assumed larger roles in communal religious observances, sometimes even leading their communities in prayer. Traditional Judaism requires a minyan, a quorum of ten adult men, to conduct certain rituals; among crypto-Jews any group of men and women praying together deemed itself sufficient.

Old-Christian pamphleteers of the late fifteenth century sometimes likened conversos to Muhammad's mythical steed Al-Buraq, which was part mule, part woman, part peacock, and part eagle. The implication was that the converts were hypocrites, taking whatever public shape and color might minimize their personal risk and maximize their acceptability to their old-Christian neighbors. A better metaphor might have been Janus, the two-faced Roman god of changing seasons; for the conversos' apparent changeability stemmed from simultaneously looking back at the Jews they had been and forward toward the Christian world they had committed to join.

By the beginning of the eighteenth century, with a few notable exceptions, the Judaizing culture of the first generations of converts had diffused into the great Catholic sea of the Iberian world. The Inquisition was finding few Judaizers, and the dossiers of their cases suggest that most of those accused had only sketchy knowledge of Judaism, and only the thinnest traces of orthodox Jewish practice. The remnants who have emerged in recent years in the American Southwest, Latin America, and the Iberian Peninsula ascribe their ancestry to those long-ago Spaniards and Portuguese who struggled to retain their sense of Jewish identity. In memory of their ancestors they call themselves *anousim*. They are insightfully portrayed in several recent studies, perhaps most notably in Seth Kunin's *Juggling Identities: Identity and Authenticity among the Crypto-Jews* (New York: Columbia University Press, 2009).

The Lost Minyan is historical fiction. Fiction, in that many of the details and conversations of these lives are imagined. Historical, in that the backbone of fact in each story is real, documented in eyewitness accounts, contemporary chronicles, and the dossiers of Inquisition trials in the archives of Spain and Mexico.

These are the stories of the in-betweens, the poor souls picked up by the thought police on their way from the synagogue to the church. Theirs are accounts of courage and betrayal, of mismatched spouses and alienated teenagers, of housewives and bishops, grifters and financiers, peddlers and miners, of thoughtful seekers of truth and unschooled working people trying to survive while juggling their conflicting religious loyalties. Those who failed left a paper trail.

✼

Heartfelt thanks are due to the Memorial Foundation for Jewish Culture and the University of Rhode Island's Center for the Humanities for material support, to the Fundación Valparaíso for providing space and a period of tranquility in which to develop the narrative style for this project, and to the University of Rhode Island for granting me a research sabbatical. I give thanks, too, to the many friends and colleagues who read and criticized early drafts of some of these chapters, in particular, my longtime collaborator Linda Davidson, whose sensitivity to language and insight into character were a constant inspiration.

Introduction

Yo vine aqui a Guadalupe casada con mi marido; e como yo era estrangera e non conosçia a ninguno desta tierra, non sabia a quien me descobrir; e mirando los trabajos de mi marido e perdida de su fasienda e temiendo non me viniesen mas trabajos e perdidas, non osava faser las cosas asy como en Villa Real segund las tenia en el coraçon.

—AHN Inq. Leg. 164, Exp. 2: 2r

1

Beatriz Núñez
GUADALUPE, JUNE 1485

The minutes pass so slowly and the weeks are like years. I stand; I sit; I press my shoulders against the wall. I pick a louse from my hair. Twice a day they bring me something to eat. Now and then I hear the monks chanting upstairs. Sometimes I catch fragments of prayers and moans of other prisoners, fewer every day. No light. Nothing to work at with my hands to help the time pass. There's nothing to fill the hours but my thoughts.

People say I'm not very sharp. Maybe not. I have no schooling, not like Fernán. But I keep my eyes and my ears open and I've seen a lot. I've heard laughter and I've seen too many tears. Shed them, too. Oh yes, I know what I know.

I haven't had such a bad life. I have—well, I used to have—a family. Some are dead. Some have turned against me. Others . . . who knows where they are? Oh, my children, my children! God keep you from this place!

Most of the time here in the dark I talk to myself, remembering the days when my life seemed simple, when my second husband—God rest his soul— and I made a life together. Who will remember this old woman? Who will know I had happy moments, beautiful babies, a man—two men—to warm my bed, food to fill my stomach. *Sueños malos, sueños buenos, todos sueños.* If only the dreams I dreamed when I was a child had not turned to ashes. As I will soon, I suppose.

Speak these words out loud? The friars and their spies would use them all against me. Better I should think them into the empty air. Maybe my words will hang there, like the angels that we can't see but know are all around us. The angels will gather them up and whisper them into the ears of the people who follow us on this earth in a hundred years, or five hundred, or a thousand. Until then my words will live on as dreams, as visions. May Jesus Christ and his Blessed Mother, may the God of Abraham, Isaac, and Jacob, hear the thoughts of this old woman. Help the angels remember my words.

Frío hace, no me place. These walls trap the cold air. No meat on my bones anymore to keep away the chill. And the damp. It's colder here than in the winters in Ciudad Real where I grew up. Happy days, those. Wrapped up close in the arms of my mother or aunt Úrsula, wool blankets pulled tight around us. We kept a fire going, too, all day long. In the evenings, when my father closed up his lace shop and came scurrying home, the first thing he'd do is break up some more sticks and pile them on the fire. It didn't matter what my mother was cooking there. She'd just have to slide the olla to the edge of the hearth or swing the iron crane holding the kettle to one side.

I remember seeing King Juan once as he passed through Ciudad Real on his way to Andalucía. Of course it was still called Villa Real in those days. A grand train of knights rode with the king, their dress armor glinting in the sun like jewels. The pennants they carried, the banners in the red and gold of Castilla! The king wasn't tall, but he had a radiance about him, a way of squaring his shoulders and carrying his head, that made people look up to him. The whole city turned out to see him that day, so many people in the Calle de Toledo that we could barely move. Trumpets sounded a fanfare to announce his approach, and we all craned our necks to get a glimpse of him. The mayor and the governor of the citadel welcomed him and handed him the keys to the city gates. Every balcony in Ciudad Real was draped with tablecloths, rugs, blankets, whatever the owners could muster. We—my parents, my husband, Bernardo, our son, Gonzalo, and I—managed to find a place to stand at the corner where the Calle del Barrionuevo enters the main thoroughfare. Bernardo held Gonzalvico high in the air. Not that he would remember this day, he was far too young for that, but we could tell him when he grew up: "You were there; we held you up, and the king looked right at you."

The crowds pressed us against Santo Domingo Church; the Jewish neighborhood was behind us, the Muslim streets in front. The odors of couscous, ground lamb patties, roasted eggplant slices, cloves, and hot honeyed fritters mingled in the air above the crowd. Ciudad Real's Christians went wild over Jewish and Muslim festival foods, so we knew there would be brisk business that night in the food stalls of the *morería* and the *judería*. Even here in Guadalupe the smell of lamb and honeyed fritters brings back that moment. How everyone seemed happy, smiling; on the face of it we were all standing together—Christians, Jews, conversos, Muslims—to honor our king. How empty those hopes seem now.

I wonder if father knew what was coming. I certainly didn't. Mother . . . she didn't talk much about those things. But Papa loved to tell us stories about when he was little. He said that when he was a child and his own father was still a young man there had been a great preaching against the Jews all over Castilla. Father remembered how one day mobs of old-Christians swarmed into the city armed with knives and clubs to hunt down the Jews. He would tell my brother Pedro, my sister Isabel, and me that my grandfather had a jagged scar on his left cheek where a farmer from Miguelturra stabbed him with a pitchfork. Grandfather tried to run away, but they caught him just before he reached the Puerta de la Mata. They made him kneel in the street so a priest could sprinkle some holy water on him and make him a Christian. They told Grandfather they would kill him if he didn't bring the rest of his family to the square in front of the Great Synagogue to be baptized, so that's what he did. Father used to say that though he was only six or seven when it happened, he never forgot the smell of burning houses in the judería or the wailing of the women kneeling there in the street.

Father said that before the mob came in 1391 Ciudad Real was a different sort of place. About half the people in Ciudad Real were Jews. Wealthy Jews, too: exporting Castilian wool, farming taxes, accountants keeping the books in the great houses of the nobles and the Calatrava knights. Back in those days the Jews could live the Law of Moses as freely and as publicly as they liked. Jews even carried their Torahs in procession every year to pray for rain for the wheat just the way the Christians paraded their crosses and the statues of their saints. The Ciudad Real community built the largest and most beautiful synagogue in all Castilla. There were rabbis, lots of them well known, and poets, like most of the Cota family. Sometimes, my father said, you could even hear Hebrew spoken in the streets. We had schools, too, for the boys, and ritual baths for the women. A Jewish slaughterhouse and a half dozen kosher butcher shops.

That was before they turned most of the Jews into Christians, just by sprinkling water on them. After that, everything changed: one day this, the next day that. Changed like my life after the friars took Fernán away that first time.

Father loved to tell us how brave his parents had been. "Your grandfather," Father would say, "went right back to the very same house he had lived in before the mobs came. It was on a new street, though. They had changed its name to 'Calle del Barrionuevo' after the riot. People used to joke about the name because there was nothing new about it. Your grandmother swept out the broken crockery and the torn curtains; they bought new furniture. Your grandfather had the walls painted and the door repaired, and he and your grandmother went on about the business of raising me and your aunt Úrsula and your uncle Tomás to be good Jews. Just as we are raising you."

So Father and Mother taught us that we were Jews. The only difference between us and their friends who had to pin a yellow circle to their coats when they went out in the street was that we were conversos. Baptized Christians. Every day they told us how important that was, to be Jews. It was how our souls would be saved. It was how our family would prosper, how Ciudad Real would prosper, because God favored the Jews. A few Jews survived the riots unbaptized, and a few more moved into our city from Toledo or Andalucía as the wool business grew more profitable. We bought our meat from the one remaining kosher butcher. We didn't have an oven at home: it wasn't allowed in Ciudad Real because of the threat of fire. So we took our dough to be baked at one of the Jewish bakeries. They sold trays of almond and honey pastries there, too. Mother would buy them for us when we went to pick up our bread. The Jews fixed up a small house as a new synagogue, a shabby, two-room affair that wouldn't attract too much attention. Pedro sometimes went there with Father.

We also went to mass when we had to; dipped our fingers into the holy water; repeated the Paternoster; celebrated the saints' days; didn't eat meat on the Church's fast days, at least not in public.

Pedro, my sister Isabel, and I trembled at that story about our grandparents and the riots. It frightened us at the same time it made us feel special, and proud. Proud to have remained faithful to the Law of Moses in spite of the swords and the pitchforks and the priests' holy water. Frightened at the thought of the faceless mobs that we knew in our children's hearts were still out there, crouched and waiting.

By the time I was seven or eight, I had the run of our street as far as the corner. I used to play tag or hopscotch with the other converso children in the neighborhood. My best friend was a girl named Costanza who was my age and lived only three houses away. Her family was churchy, but they still lived in their old house in the judería. Costanza taught me handclapping games and we would stand in front of each other for hours beating out the rhythms. "Whén I'm lóvely ás can bé, a hándsome prínce will cóme for mé."

That's when I wasn't helping Mother with her chores. "*Niña ociosa, no vale cosa,*" she would say to me, and then set me another task. My main job was to keep an eye on Pedro and Isabel while Mother gossiped with her best friend, Francisca González, and my aunt Úrsula as their drop spindles turned wool into thread. Isabel was easy: she would sit on the floor and talk to her stick dolls for hours on end. But Pedro was a handful, always running and jumping, knocking over chairs, making a mess of things. I had to help clean, too. My father bought me a toy broom so that I could sweep along behind mother as she readied the house on Friday afternoons. I would take my little clay jug and follow her the two blocks to our fountain to fetch water for the house. And I helped cook, too. What I liked best was stirring the stewpot. When they were on the hearth our iron skillets and ollas were at my knee level, so when Mother lifted up their lids it was my job to stir with a wooden spoon whatever it was we were going to have for dinner. She also had me put our table knives and spoons back in their box when they were clean. We only had two forks then, long-handled ones with two tines. "We'll buy more when business improves," my father would always say, though it never did. His one little store, the one my grandfather had started, sold lace that he used to buy from the farmwomen in Almagro and Daimiel. Papa was always complaining that the tailors weren't buying as much as they used to, that the styles were changing. I suppose that's why we only had two forks. My parents gave them a lot of use, though, spearing chunks of beef and vegetables from our olla onto the slices of bread that covered our plates. It makes my mouth water just to think of it. What I wouldn't give for a plate of Mother's Sabbath stew right now!

She taught me how to mix and knead the bread dough, too, how to set it on a wooden board to rise, covered with a towel. When the *masa* was just the right height we carried the boards to the bakeshop around the corner where the dough was baked to a golden brown. For the holidays some of the neighborhood mothers made sweet pastries, but we always bought ours, since Mother said she didn't "have the hand" for those things. The one exception was matza in the spring: we always made that together. She would sprinkle out the flour onto a board, add a few drops of water, and quickly pat it into a flat cake. Then I got to poke a dozen holes in the top of the cake with a twig so that it wouldn't rise before she baked it in a frying pan over the fire, three minutes to a side. Mother taught me about herbs, too. A half-dozen different ones hung in bunches from the rafters. I would stand on a chair and Mother would tell me which sprigs to cut for the afternoon meal. "Rosemary," she would say; "two sprigs." Or "Just three mustard leaves, that's enough." We didn't have many spices, just a few threads of saffron, pepper, cloves, and cinnamon, and these she kept in a small locked box on a shelf near the window. When she was going to use one she always made a great show of opening the box, taking a bit of the spice on the tip of her knife blade, and sprinkling it into the cook pot.

I must have thought then that I was playing at being a mommy. Though now that I've raised some children of my own, I can see that the kitchen was my school and I was learning my life's work.

When Pedro was five, my parents sent him to Isaac Melamed with the other boys his age to learn his Hebrew letters. When Mother's friends came to the house she would always brag about how quick he was. And I could see how my father beamed whenever Pedro chimed in with a Hebrew phrase while my father was praying. Nothing that I did made him light up like that.

But as they say, *No hay nada segura, ni bien que dura.* The very next winter both Pedro and Isabel were swept off by a fever. Three days they coughed and fretted, three days I ran to the fountain every few minutes to bring cold water to bathe their foreheads. Then they were gone, just like that. Pedro's Hebrew tutor came to our house to tell us how sorry he was to lose such a bright pupil. He didn't say one word about my sister Isabel's death, though. Outside the house girls don't count. I learned that lesson early.

Inside the house we were all in tears. Papa, too. I'd never seen anyone die before. We cried ourselves to sleep for nights. Aunt Úrsula helped Mother prepare their bodies for burial. She was so sad. She had always come to our house to spin or sew with my mother or help her in the kitchen. But what she had liked best was to play games like ring toss or cat's cradle with the three of us children, or to tell us fantastic stories of knights and princesses, ogres and dragons. She'd tell us that since she didn't have any kids of her own, we would have to listen to her stories. Once in a while she would bring a book and read to us the adventures of Amadis of Gaul. We would squeal in mock terror at the battles and shiver with delight at the love scenes. Thinking back on it now, I realize that Aunt Úrsula was the only woman I knew who knew how to read. I can't imagine where she learned, or where she got that book.

Afterward, after Isabel and Pedro died, it was all different. No games. Not so many stories. Lots of tears. Aunt Úrsula still came, and Francisca González. They gossiped and worked at their spinning, but when they talked with me their only subject was how to keep a Jewish home. I told them I had already heard those things a hundred times. But they'd remind me how I was the only child left, so now everything was up to me. So I kept my ears open, and once in a while there was something new. Aunt Úrsula and Francisca knew as much about keeping a Jewish home as my mother did, and the three of them together taught me what I needed to know.

"You have to start your sweeping early on Friday," Francisca would say, "so that you'll be sure to finish before the sun sets. It's a sin to work after sundown."

"You have to wash the table and dust things down first," Aunt Úrsula would add, "or all that dirt will just settle back on the floor."

"And make sure you keep your clean clothes out of the way, or they'll get soiled, too," my mother would butt in. "Clean first, then wash yourself, then put on your Sabbath dress."

"By then your cooking should be done, and the olla bubbling in the fire. Don't let it splatter your dress, though." Francisca again.

"That's why you have to cover yourself with an apron until just before the stars come out. Then you can bank your olla with coals and take your apron off." Mother always had to have the last word.

Cleaning, cooking, when the festivals were and how to prepare for them, what to do with my fingernail parings, which blessings a woman had to recite along with the men, and which ones she could only listen to . . . No subject escaped the attention of those women. By the time I got to be nine or ten I knew what they were going to say even before they opened their mouths. Just because I didn't talk much they thought I would forget things if they didn't constantly remind me. But they were wrong: I have a good mind and a good memory. I hear something once and I know it forever, no matter how long it is or how complicated.

I was getting taller. I found myself eager to go out, to try new things. I didn't know how to put that into words, except to nag my mother all day long: "Can't I go to the fountain by myself? Why don't you let me take that thread over to Aunt Úrsula's house? It's only a couple of onions: can't I go buy them? Please?"

Mother always answered the same way: "All right. Be careful."

The old-Christians didn't like us much, but we kids could live with that if we took care, as long as we stuck to our own neighborhood. If we strayed very far, though, the old-Christian kids would throw stones at us and call us Christ-killers. They said we smelled bad. If we tried to answer back, we risked a beating. So I was careful when I went out alone.

In the spring of 1449 I was thirteen. There were all kinds of rumors going around. Every day Mother brought home gossip and Father picked up news from his friends. How some madman named Sarmiento was whipping Toledo into a frenzy against the conversos. How there had been riots. How soldiers had fought with the mobs in the street. How some of the ringleaders had been hung from the city gates. Every night I heard Mother asking, "Are we going to be all right? What are we going to do?" And Father would say, "It's too far away to worry about; there haven't been any problems in Ciudad Real in a long time."

But he was wrong. The mob did come to Ciudad Real. When Father heard the shouting in the street, he swept Mother and me into a closet that he had built behind our chimney. There was just enough room for the two of us to stand close together, and just enough air for us to be able to breathe. For two days we stood there, not moving. There was nothing to eat, nothing to drink. When the pressure on our bladders grew too great we had to pee on the floor.

We were among the lucky ones. When Mother and I came out of our hiding place, we found Father bruised and battered; Uncle Tomás, dead; and Aunt Lucía, moaning, lying in a corner. Mother said later that Aunt Lucía had been raped. I didn't yet know what "rape" meant. I was sure it was something horrible, like being scorched by the fiery breath of a dragon from that Amadís book that Aunt Úrsula used to read to us. I can still picture Aunt Lucía: from then on she was always dressed in black, eyes cast down, never smiling even when we tried to cheer her up by telling some funny story. I haven't seen or heard from her since I moved away from Ciudad Real nearly twenty years ago. I wonder if she ever remarried, if she's still alive.

Much of the judería was burned to the ground, including father's store. Sarmiento murdered Alonso de Cota, the richest converso in Ciudad Real. Our house was spared the torch, but all our furniture was chopped to pieces and anything we had that was valuable disappeared: Mother's candlesticks, our tableware, Father's best coat and shoes. Even my dead sister's dolls that Mother had been saving. For her grandchildren, she said. We cleaned up the house; Father found some other furniture, and we went about putting our lives back together.

The rioters took away my childhood, too, my easy laughter, my love of play. My delight in each new day with never a thought of tomorrow. The only thing the mob left behind was bitter memories and corpses to be buried. And one linen sheet from my hope chest that for some reason I had hidden deep under my bed in a dark corner of the room. For a long time I didn't go out unless Mother ordered me to run some errand or other. Before the riots I used to know which were the safer streets, but now nowhere seemed safe. It all smelled of burnt wood, just like Father used to say he remembered from his own childhood.

Later that year my breasts started to swell and my monthly flux began. By then the games that Costanza and I used to spend so many happy hours playing seemed childish and silly. I didn't have to beg to go to the fountain now; it was one of my chores, three times a day. The boys who passed by me on the street began to tease me less, and I started looking at them not with scorn but with curiosity. In the mornings I combed my hair and scrubbed my teeth with a willow twig without even being asked. I didn't think my parents noticed, but now that I have had teenage children of my own, I feel certain they did. Then one Thursday afternoon, a year and a month after the riots, my mother and father told me they had found me a husband.

I shouldn't have been surprised, since that is the way of the world. Even though I was already fourteen, I hadn't thought it would happen so soon. Since the riots I'd only managed to embroider two more linens for my hope chest. My parents expected me to be excited and grateful, so as an obedient daughter I put on a happy face. Bernardo wasn't a total stranger. A couple of times he had come to our house to pray with my father's minyan. But I never paid him any particular attention. I had never spoken to him. The night my parents told me I was to be his wife, I soaked my pillow with tears of apprehension before at last I drifted into a fitful sleep.

Bernardo was everything my father wanted for his daughter: hardworking, dependable, and a strict follower of Moses who would raise his grandchildren in the Law. Bernardo had come to Ciudad Real two years earlier because he thought the economic prospects were better there than in Madrid. He bought sheets of leather from the tannery, and then with his wooden lasts, his shears and needle, his hammer and tacks, he fashioned them into shoes. Although he was a newcomer to Ciudad Real, in two years he built up a list of clients, mostly for his boots, which were known for being sturdy and long lasting. His workshop—little more than a cubbyhole, actually, tucked between two houses on a side street on the far edge of the Magdalena district—escaped the notice of the rioters, so, unlike my father, he came through the troubles pretty much unscathed. Father was confident he could support me.

If I had had a choice, I'd have turned the match down. But of course I was not given any voice in the matter, so I smiled, and said that I was honored, and put an "X" on the Hebrew wedding contract next to where my father signed my name.

Bernardo, Bernardo. A full beard almost as black as his eyes. Soft spoken, eventempered; never shouting, never cursing. Never, for that matter, even laughing out loud. He was tall, too, but a little stoop-shouldered from bending over his lasts. His hands were the color of walnuts. If his fingers smelled of leather, his breath was sweet. He was only twice my age. I could have done worse.

The wedding—I should say weddings—took place less than a month later. We decorated our largest room with spring flowers chained into garlands. I wore my finest shift, one that with mother's help I had stitched and trimmed with Almagro lace. I put on new shoes, a wedding gift from Bernardo. There weren't many guests: Uncle Juan Falcón and Aunt Úrsula, and Francisca González, the councilman's wife. I wanted to invite my best friend, Costanza, but for some reason my mother wouldn't hear of it. Ysaac Melamed, the schoolteacher, was rabbi. Uncle Juan and Francisca stretched my father's prayer shawl over our heads as Bernardo and I exchanged small gold rings and recited the words that made us man and wife. Father blessed the wine, we all took a few sips and then cleansed our mouths with a few bites of anise-flavored pastry. After that Bernardo and I took off our rings and we all trooped to the parish church where Father Juan Pablo was waiting for us. We knelt at the altar as he recited the words of the nuptial mass. Bernardo signed the Church papers, I marked my X, and we received the priest's blessing and went back to my parents' house for our wedding feast, which we began by replacing the rings on our fingers and reciting again the *beracha* over the wine.

After the dinner, and the singing, and the speeches—none of which I listened to— they escorted us to the bedroom that Mother had laid out with the sheets from my bridal chest. The door closed. Bernardo laid me in the bed, took my virginity, and fell asleep with his head on my shoulder. My most vivid memory of that sleepless night, beyond the pain and the newness of it all, was how afraid I was of making any noise that might tell my parents in the next room what we were doing. I talked to you, angels, that night. I told you how miserable I was. How frightened I was about having to be a wife.

What a ninny! I knew that real marriages are like my parents': neverending routine, every day the same as the last, the woman at home, the man out and about. But my head was still addled by the stories Aunt Úrsula had read me when I was a child, so at first the fact that there was nothing like that fiery love in my marriage disappointed me. Yet Bernardo was kind and gentle, always asking what I needed. A good man. And if he did not make me sigh with rapture, still, I came to like him well enough. Before we got married Bernardo slept in his workshop and took his meals at one of the taverns in our neighborhood that catered to the converso bachelors. Now father gave us a room in his house while Bernardo saved money for a home of our own. We all of us ate together; I still went to the fountain three times a day; I still helped mother with the cooking. If it were not for the fact that I now shared a bed with a man, at first my life didn't change very much.

And then it did. My mother knew was happening to me the first time I ran crying from the kitchen and threw up my breakfast. When she told me what it was I was terrified. Terrified and happy both. I remember how I thought that each new change to my body was a kind of miracle: when my breasts grew tender; when my apron strings did not hang down as far as they used to. The first time I felt the baby kick inside me, I thought my heart would burst with joy.

Gonzalo was born almost exactly a year after our marriage. Father Juan Pablo baptized him as he baptized all the converso children in our parish, welcoming him into the communion of Christ with a sad smile and a mumbled prayer. After the church ceremony we whisked Gonzalvico home, scrubbed off the oily residue of the baptismal chrism, and watched with pride as the *mohel*—a real rabbi, not a converted Jew—circumcised him and welcomed him into the tribe of Abraham, Isaac, and Jacob. Gonzalvico's cries could be heard halfway down the block, but in our neighborhood that didn't matter much.

Fifteen years Bernardo and I lived as husband and wife, the first four of them in my parents' house. When we finally moved, it was to an apartment in a house only a few doors away, so naturally we all continued to eat most of our meals together. I still spent most of every day at my mother's house. Mother doted on Gonzalvico, cradling him in her arms, bouncing him on her knee, fretting about his every cough and sniffle. About the only time I got to hold my son was when I was nursing him, and within two years that had stopped. It seemed like Mother and I were always competing for Gonzalvico's attention, and since she was more forceful than I am, and since, like a good daughter, I had to defer to her out of respect, to tell the truth I sometimes felt more like Gonzalo's aunt or older sister than like his mother.

Well, I thought, I would have more children. I would fill my house with babies. I would nurse them, I would hold them when they cried, and teach them the ways of the Law of Moses. They would be mine, not Mother's. Another dream. The years passed, and no babies came.

Baby Gonzalo began to talk, and once he started he never seemed to stop. Whoever came to the house, for whatever reason, Gonzalvico was their friend. Since there were no other children in the house, he looked to the grownups for entertainment. His sweet temper made people smile. And the questions! Mother's friends said he would grow up to be a magistrate or a lawyer. People were always bringing him presents: a pastry from the market, a braided rope ring for tossing, a stick with a carved head to be his horse. He almost never cried, but when he did, he always ran to my mother for comforting. Or in the evenings, when we had gone back to our apartment, to Bernardo. When Gonzalo turned five I took him each morning to master Ysaac to learn his letters. There were five or six other boys in his class, children from our neighborhood—Ernesto Ramírez, Samuel Cordovero were the ones whose names I knew—and they soon became Gonzalo's friends. Sometimes in the afternoon he would go to their houses to play. I would have liked them to come to our apartment, too; but it was on the third floor and small, and I still spent most days at my mother's. So I never worked up the courage to invite them. By the time Gonzalo was nine there was little time for play anyway: most of the boys were spending their days with their fathers, learning the family trades. Gonzalo was soon adept at buffing a boot, or filing the rough edges from a leather sole, but what he liked most was to talk with his father's customers. Bernardo used to complain to me in the evenings how Gonzalo never finished anything because he couldn't talk and work with his hands at the same time. He didn't see much future for him in the shoemaking trade.

Life had a certain rhythm to it, and that carried me along from one week, one year, to the next. The rituals of the kitchen, of prayer, of candle lighting. Clean the house Friday morning; prepare the Sabbath stew Friday afternoon. Church every Sunday. My monthly visit to the *mikvah*. The fasts of Esther, Gedalia, the Ninth of Av, and the Great Fast of Kippur. The Passover feast in the spring. Processions on the saints' days and on Corpus Christi. As our neighbors, one after another, produced their endless stream of babies, four or five times a year Bernardo and I would go to the circumcisions or naming parties and, for appearances' sake, the baptisms. With the new babies everybody always seemed so happy! I tried to smile, to laugh with the other women, but I had no infants at home so I had nothing to share with them. I prayed, of course, to Sarah, and even to Saint Anne, like the priests said we should, but my womb remained cold.

The Law of Moses and the Law of Jesus. It was how things were. The only processions we never went to were during Holy Week. What with priests in every pulpit preaching how the Jews killed Christ, and with Dominicans or Franciscans on every street corner shouting that conversos were no better than the Jews, it was safer to remain indoors. Whenever we went out the old-Christians jeered at us. It got so bad that most of us women rarely left our houses except for the daily marketing or the trips to the fountain, when we had to go in groups. Bernardo took to escorting baby Gonzalo and me to and from my mother's house. During Holy Week one year three men were murdered on the street that ran behind our house, bludgeoned to death by a mob. We knew one of the victims because every spring he bought a new pair of boots from Bernardo. Converso stores were looted, too; my father's was broken into twice, and most of his lace was stolen. Bernardo's workshop must have been too tiny to attract the mobs' notice, because he never had any trouble. Though he did form the habit of taking his tools home with him every night.

Even the simplest pleasures became risky. I remember how before things got bad, when the winter sun was high, my mother and her neighborhood friends used to bring their needlework out into the street. They would sit on their stools with their backs against the wall of our house to block the wind, where they would tat and sew and gossip to their hearts' content. I would sit to one side with my own stack of mending listening to their chatter. Now we worked indoors.

Then, early in 1463, after nearly thirteen years of marriage, my prayers were answered. I found myself pregnant once again. Early that summer, just after the Feast of Booths, baby Juan was born. There was no way I was going to allow my mother to steal Juan's childhood from me the way she had stolen his brother's. I had learned a few things and I knew how to defend myself now. Besides, my mother was getting old, and Bernardo and I had our own home so I didn't have to go to my parents' house every day. That way Mother had much less opportunity to smother Juan with her attention. And I couldn't get enough of Juan, he was so sweet. Smaller than his brother had been as a baby, quieter. His eyes did not seem to burn with his brother's curiosity. When I reached out to him he would nestle in my arms and coo with contentment. Bernardo seemed happy to have a second son as well.

By the Feast of the St. Martin I was pregnant with our third child.

Buena ventura, poco dura. Contentment, they say, is both a blessing and a curse. A curse because from one day to the next it can be snatched away and your life turned upside down. It was early in the winter, just after the Feast of the Nativity, when the frost bites at your nostrils and a haze of wood smoke hangs over the city. Bernardo finished his bread and cheese, his bowl of wheat gruel; he put on his hat, left the house as he always did without saying good-bye, and stepped into the street, where like a bolt of lightning a runaway horse knocked him flat. His head struck a stone, and he was dead before his blood had begun to puddle in the street. At first light I was a wife and mother; by mid-morning I was a widow with two orphaned sons and another child on the way.

The next three months were the darkest I had ever known. At least up until then. Compared to the storms that have swept over me since, the pain of those months seems like a brief, passing cloud. I spent the rest of that first day crying. My tears upset baby Juan so that he howled in chorus with my sobbing. My mother, who hadn't touched me in years, wrapped us both in her arms. She stroked my hair as I wept into her shoulder. Naturally she took complete charge of the funeral and the week of mourning that followed, issuing a stream of orders to me, my father, and her neighborhood friends who came to express their sympathy. The seven days of ritual mourning, she announced to everyone, would take place in her house, which was larger and better equipped to accommodate visitors than the two-room apartment I had shared with Bernardo. She had us cover the mirrors and pour out all the water standing in the pitchers in the house. She told us precisely how we were to tear our garments. We didn't cook during that week, of course; the neighbors took turns bringing us food. We ate cross-legged on the floor in the front room next to the place where Bernardo's body had rested before we took it to be buried.

We were never left alone with our grief. Though it was my husband, Bernardo, who had died, the visitors came not to see me but to express their sympathy to Mother at the loss of her son-in-law. I had no real friends of my own. I thought at first that Costanza might visit, or one of the other girls I had played with as a child, but they never appeared. I sat quietly in one corner of the room with baby Juan in my lap.

The person most deeply affected was Gonzalo. He seemed to resent the fact that the rest of us—me, in particular—were still alive while his beloved father was dead. We tried to comfort him, but none of us could break through the desolation that clouded his eyes. After the funeral, as we walked back to the house, when Father tried to ask him what he planned to do now, Gonzalo shrugged his shoulders and turned his face away. When Father repeated the question, adding that the cobbler shop now belonged to him, Gonzalo screamed at him, "Leave me alone! I can take care of myself." It was so startling that the rest of us stopped in our tracks and stared at him. "Leave me alone!" he shouted again, and stalked off, leaving us in the street.

That night, when Gonzalo didn't come home, my father went out to look for him. But he was nowhere to be seen. He searched the following days, too. Finally, on the seventh day of mourning, as we were finishing the hard-boiled eggs that one of mother's friends had brought to the house, Gonzalo reappeared. He stood stiff and formal, quite the young man, just inside the front door, brave and at the same time somehow vulnerable. I wanted to hug him. But his grandparents stole the moment by peppering him with questions about where he had been and what he had been doing while all of us had been worried sick about him. Rather than answer them, Gonzalo rattled off a little speech that he had obviously memorized and rehearsed.

"I've thought it over and I don't want to be a shoemaker. I would never be as good at it as Papa was. And I really don't like the work."

"But if you don't . . . What will you do . . . ?"

"Grandma, let me finish. I don't want to make shoes. I've decided. And I don't want to live at home anymore. I'm grown up now; I need to be on my own. My friend Ernesto has room for me in his house; that's where I've been staying this week. His uncle has a good business in Puertollano, buying and selling clothing, and he's promised to help get the two of us started. I should be able to earn enough to provide for myself, and if there is any extra, I will send it home to Mother."

My parents spluttered and badgered him, but Gonzalo wouldn't say anything more. After fifteen minutes he turned and left. He didn't say good-bye. I can see him in my mind as if it were yesterday and not twenty years ago. Proud and erect like the adult he wanted us to take him to be, but with a tremble in his lip that brought tears to my eyes then and still does. He was brave as a soldier who has never known war, as confident as a farmer who has never seen a locust or been crushed by a drought. A child-man, a fledged bird ready to leave the nest. And there was nothing we could do but let him go. I've never seen him again.

What was I supposed to do next? Was I to live the life of a widow, dress in black and sit quietly in the corners of my parents' house until I died? Was I to do nothing but take care of baby Juan until he, like Gonzalo, was old enough to go off on his own? And what about the new baby who was due in a few months? Without Bernardo's earnings, would there be enough money to feed us all?

My parents were asking the same questions. I gave up the apartment right away, and baby Juan and I moved back to my parents' house. Since Bernardo was dead I was once again my father's responsibility. Father was not rich. The lace that he bought in Almagro was not selling as well as it used to. I could hear my parents talking about it at night, although I couldn't always catch exactly what they were saying. I had no will of my own, and no energy to exert it if I had. Once again my parents treated me as if I were nothing but a child. They would decide what was best for me, and I would do what I was told.

CHAPTER 1

In early March, when the first white blossoms covered the almond trees, my father disappeared for ten days. When he returned to Ciudad Real he had in tow a man whom none of us had ever seen before.

"This is Fernán González," my father said. "He is going to be your new husband."

My mouth fell open in shock as my mother welcomed the man into our home. The smile on Mother's face told me that she knew all along where Father had gone and what he was doing. Baby Juan, who always picked up on my moods, began to cry. As my parents chattered away, I took a long look at the stranger. There wasn't much to raise my spirits: he was short, barrel-chested, and his straggly beard was already flecked with gray. He appeared to be ten or fifteen years older than Bernardo had been. He had nice teeth, though, regular and white. His face lit up when he smiled.

Fernán González. From the city of Guadalupe in Extremadura. During the next week he spent every day at our house talking with my parents, and sometimes with me, before withdrawing after the evening meal to the room he'd taken at an inn. The third day of his visit my parents took baby Juan into the kitchen and for the first time left me completely alone with Fernán. I had no idea what to say, so I sat with my hands tightly folded, hoping that my nervousness was not too obvious. Fernán must have been uncomfortable, too, because for the longest time he paced from one part of the room to another studying this and that: a milk pitcher; a stack of lace collars; a pillowcase, its embroidery half-finished. Finally he spoke.

"You'll like Guadalupe, Beatriz. It's in the mountains. The air is much cooler than here in Ciudad Real."

I still didn't know how to respond, so I just sat. The silence grew larger, filling the space between us.

"Beatriz, I want to marry you. Your father told me all about you. I know your husband died. I know you have two children, and that little Juan will come with us to Guadalupe."

"Do you know I'm going to have another child, Bernardo's child, in a few months?"

"I do, and that's fine. I'm a widower, too, I understand. None of that bothers me at all. I will treat your children as if they were my own. And I know that you will be a mother to my son, Manuel, just as I will be a father to your children."

So that was it! That was the reason he was looking for a wife. I felt my face begin to flush. He didn't want me for me; he wanted me to be his kid's nanny! That's the only reason a man like Fernán would marry a woman with two children and another on the way. Why hadn't I seen it? I'm not beautiful. I haven't got a dowry. He wants to hire me, to pay me with a ring and a house!

I wanted to run, to hide my angry face, to keep my disappointment from welling up in my eyes and embarrassing us both. There were so many things that I wanted to say, but the only word that escaped my lips was: "Manuel?"

That was all the encouragement Fernán needed to go on.

"He's a fine boy. Tall, good-looking. About the same age as your Gonzalo. He's been so lonely without his mother. I've tried, but he won't let me fill the empty space she left when she died. I know you'll like him, and he'll like you. A woman's touch. Someone who knows how to deal with children."

He smiled at me and reached out his hands. I mean, it's not like there was any question about whether I would accept him as a husband. My father had already decided that. But at that moment I couldn't show him my consent. I wasn't ready.

Fernán was trying so hard, I know that now. Trying to welcome me into his life, to be honest with me, to be kind. And I responded with cruelty. I let my romantic notions get in the way. You'd think I'd know better after thirteen years of marriage. But instead of showing him how grateful I was for his willingness to accept me, I just bit my lip and looked down at the floor.

As soon as Fernán left my father came back into the room.

"Juan?"

"Asleep in his grandmother's arms. She didn't want to wake him."

"Father, I don't want to do this. I can't leave Ciudad Real. What would I do in Guadalupe?" I think by then I was half sobbing. "And he has a son!"

"Listen to me, Beatriz. This man is perfect for you, for your children. You're a widow; he's a widower. Bernardo left you almost nothing, my business is failing, and Fernán has a prosperous career in Guadalupe. He's a man of letters, a scribe. I went to Guadalupe; I asked around. Fernán is a good man, with a reputation for fair dealing. Some people told me that his grandfather was a great rabbi. I don't know if that's true, but I do know that Fernán is true to the Law and he'll help you raise your children with the proper respect for our traditions."

I must have appeared unconvinced.

"He's a wealthy man, Beatriz. He'll take care of you and the children better than I ever could. You can't stay here with us forever."

"I don't see why . . . "

"You need a husband. Your children need a father. Your mother and I are getting older, and you know we are barely getting by. The lace provides barely enough to support your mother and me. Gonzalo has grown up and gone, so there's no money coming in there. And the extra mouths to feed . . . You know I'd rather . . . But I just don't see how we can do it."

"But Guadalupe is so far away. I'll never get to . . . "

"Don't be a goose. It's not as far as all that. You can come here to visit us, two or three times a year, whatever you and Fernán want. We'll come to Guadalupe, too, so you can show us how you are prospering in your new home."

"But I'm going to have Bernardo's baby!"

"He knows that, Beatriz, I told him from the start. It's all right; he has agreed to raise the child as if it were his own. He's an *ish tov*, Beatriz, a good man. Accept it and start your new life with a joyous heart. Be a good wife to him. And be a good mother to his son."

I'm not stupid. And I'm not ungrateful. My father was right. This was the best possible future for me. Also the only one. I nodded my assent.

That didn't mean that I was eager to leave Ciudad Real. Just the opposite. I'd agreed to marry Fernán, but if there was some way I could persuade him to move to Ciudad Real, to make our life there so I wouldn't have to leave the only place I had ever called home . . . Between feeling sorry for myself and wondering how I could get Fernán to change his mind, I didn't sleep all that night.

Our wedding wasn't much: my parents, baby Juan, Fernán and me. Father Juan Pablo—he was old, now, and hard of hearing—legitimized our union for the Church. The rabbi, who came quietly into our house after the sun had set, married us for real. We all ate together at my mother's house. The rabbi left, Mother took baby Juan, and then Fernán and I retired to my parents' second bedroom.

Almost without saying a word to each other we washed at the basin, undressed, and slipped between the sheets. Neither of us was ignorant of the mysteries of the marriage bed, but I felt strange, awkward. Maybe because it was because I was pregnant and starting to show. Maybe it was the ghosts of our dead spouses: Bernardo and I had passed our first night together in that bed. And hundreds more, until we had the apartment of our own. I had thought that all men were like Bernardo, but Fernán felt different, smelled different. And he was gentler, more patient with me. I'm certain that I felt strange to Fernán as well, but neither of us said anything about what was going on in our heads.

Afterward Fernán fell right to sleep, but I couldn't. Fernán didn't snore like Bernardo had. He didn't sprawl in the bed, or drape his arm across my breasts while he slept. It occurred to me that I didn't even know the name of Fernán's first wife.

I slipped out of bed, cleaned myself, and paced back and forth in the room. Quietly; I didn't want to wake him. I got back into bed, but I still couldn't sleep. I tried to imagine what Guadalupe looked like. Fernán had said there were mountains. And a monastery. And his big house. But my mind couldn't picture anyplace else. I really didn't want to leave Ciudad Real. Except for a few short walks beyond the city walls, that was all I knew.

In the morning Fernán told me his plan.

"It's time for us to go back to Guadalupe. I've already left Manuel on his own for nearly two weeks. That's too much, even with Mencia to make sure he gets fed and taken care of."

"Mencia?"

"The maid. She keeps the house going when I am away."

This was the first I had heard of a servant, and that triggered another wave of panic. Our family never had servants. Fernán lived in a different world from us.

How would I know how to act, what to say to his friends? What if Mencia saw through me, wouldn't respect me?

"The wagon will be ready the day after tomorrow," Fernán said.

"Two days from now! I . . . I can't get ready by then. Women need their things. I've got to decide which cook pots to take. And the linens! What about my Sabbath clothes? My spice box? And baby Juan's things and clothes for the new baby? How will it all fit?"

"Don't be foolish. The wagon master will help us load the cart. Besides, some of those things you won't even need. Do you think I don't have cook pots in Guadalupe? That there are no linens in my house?"

"But they are your wife's things . . . your other wife's things. I want my own."

Fernán gave it up. "All right, all right. It's a big wagon. You can bring whatever you like."

Fernán showed me a smile that was designed, no doubt, to set me at ease, even though it didn't. My mind was screaming: "How can you take me to a new city where I won't know anyone? Where I will be lonely." But my mouth stayed shut. Women don't say such things. We go where our husbands take us and we do what we are told.

Three days later we were on the road. As the wagon lurched from rut to pothole, baby Juan and I clutched swaths of linen to our mouths and noses to filter out the dust kicked up by the horses that made the King's Highway—Fernán told me—the busiest road in Castilla. I thought I was past my morning sickness by then, but the wagon brought it back. It was all I could do to keep from puking over the side. When I wasn't nauseated, I amused myself by trying to decide if the thumps in my belly came from the wagon jouncing on the road or were the first kicks of the new baby. Fernán didn't ride in the wagon with us. He was afraid of mules—as a scrivener he had never found a need to own one—and the animals could tell it. Fernán walked twenty paces in front of the wagon or behind, far enough away that neither of the two mules would be able to threaten him. Baby Juan was cutting a pair of new teeth, so he was fretful and that made the mules skittish. I held him in my arms and quieted him as best I could, nestling us deep into the pile of our household possessions to escape the icy March winds, but with each tremor of the wagon Juan cried louder. Fernán never noticed.

I don't think I uttered one complete sentence during the three days it took us to reach Toledo. I ached for Ciudad Real, and I dreaded what lay before me in Guadalupe. Yet thinking back on it now, that trip was an adventure. I was on the King's Highway, seeing new things, smelling new smells. The people we passed—soldiers with their steel helmets and halberds, monks with the cowls hiding everything but their noses, grand ladies in their carriages, wagons piled high with everything God had ever created—it was like one of Aunt Úrsula's stories.

We spent several nights in Toledo at an inn on the edge of the Jewish quarter. Fernán arranged for the innkeeper to bring Juan and me our meals in our room: they weren't much in taste or quantity, but at least they were foods that the Law did not forbid. Not that I was overly concerned: my pregnancy allowed me to eat just about anything, except for pork. But the innkeeper wasn't likely to serve that anyway, not given his clientele.

Fernán had been so eager to get back to Guadalupe, but now . . . "There's some business I have to attend to first," he told me when I pressed him. "For me, and for the monastery. We'll leave in a day or two, when I'm finished."

We stayed almost a week. Fernán left every morning early and didn't come back until dinnertime. I sat in our room with baby Juan. My pregnancy made me uncomfortable. And without work to do I was bored. The baby started to cough, so I took him downstairs to ask the innkeeper's wife for some broth for him. I've never met anyone who smelled so much of wood smoke as that woman did from standing at the hearth all day. As she pulled up a stool for me, she told me that her name was Sefronia. "My father liked books," she giggled.

"He's a pretty one, he is. Juan, you say? I have a Juan, too, one of eleven that my husband gave me. They're all out on their own now, the ones that lived. All except Marta. That's her over there clearing tables. Where did you say you were from? . . ."

Sefronia's chatter kept the boredom at bay, so I didn't mind so much being left alone.

One day Fernán took baby Juan and me out for a tour of the city.

Toledo must be the most beautiful city in the world. It's like I always imagined a fairy-tale city to be, or Jerusalem. The countryside around Ciudad Real is mostly flat, but Toledo is built on an enormous rock, surrounded on three sides by the Tajo River and on the fourth by a wall. The gate is guarded by a dozen soldiers, all wearing livery checkered with the castles of Castilla. The finest Christian houses are at the top of the hill, near the castle that people still call by its Moorish name, Alcázar. The Jews and most of the conversos live at the other end of town where the Tajo begins to flow out of the gorge. I had never seen so many tall buildings. They are heaped together, one on top of the other, so that there isn't an inch of open space anywhere in the city. Wherever I looked there were church steeples stabbing the sky. And there were more mosques and synagogues than I had ever seen before. The streets were crowded with Jews and conversos, Muslim laborers, and clergy from every Christian order in Castilla. In every plaza we saw beggars, knights with swords by their sides, squires in livery, water sellers, ladies in their fine silks . . . When the churches emptied, a little after noon, jugglers and minstrels entertained us in the street. Fernán bought Juan a cone of sugared citron for him to suck on.

Fernán said Toledo is the center of the world. Its nobles are the most powerful, its merchants the wealthiest, its doctors and musicians and philosophers the best in all of Spain. And its Jewish community is the largest in Castilla. The morería is even bigger than the Muslim district in Ciudad Real. The followers of Muhammad work the vegetable farms, make bricks, and build the churches and palaces that are going up all over town. Fernán said that was proof that the monarchs and nobles who employ the Jews and Muslims don't concern themselves very much with the fact that their subjects don't all follow the Law of Jesus Christ.

I was dazzled by all the colors, the fancy buildings, the variety of spices in the markets. As we walked along the streets, every house pumped out kitchen odors that made my mouth water. We stopped for lunch in one of the taverns that catered to traveling Jewish merchants. From an iron pot that was warming on one side of the enormous hearth, the serving girl ladled us each out a bowl of *adafina* made with eggplant and chickpeas and chunks of cod. It was tastier than any of the Sabbath stews my mother prepared back in Ciudad Real.

For the first time since Bernardo died I felt the warmth of happiness. Baby Juan—Fernán and I had taken turns carrying him—cooed at my delight.

Our wagon left the Tajo River at Puente del Arzobispo, creaked up the long climb to Puerto de San Vicente, where we passed the night, and the next morning crossed four ranges of low hills to Guadalupe. On the highest slopes I saw more pine trees in ten minutes than in my entire life in Ciudad Real. The sky seemed bluer than I remembered from home: crisper, scented with pine, not wheat dust and cow dung. It seemed like every few minutes we crossed some clear brook that bubbled down the hillsides, our wheels splashing us with drops that soon dried in the sun. Sheep puffed white in the meadows, and pigs, set out to forage by the owners of the large estates, rooted for last year's acorns in the woods.

As we neared Guadalupe my eyes were drawn to the crosses and stone kneelers that flanked the road every hundred yards or so.

"For the pilgrims," Fernán answered my unspoken question. "They come to make their vows before the statue of the Holy Virgin of Guadalupe, to leave their money and claim their miracles. By May we'll be seeing thousands of them."

At last the monastery came into view, soaring above the town of one- and two-story houses like a mountain! Towers and windows and masses of gray stone, as big as a cathedral. Maybe even bigger.

✠

Fernán's house was on the main street, just downhill from the monastery. Even before he unloaded the wagon, Fernán took me on a tour. My father had said that Fernán was comfortably well off, though far from rich. I had supposed that meant bigger rooms, a nicer kitchen, furniture that wasn't as chipped and scarred as what my parents had. But here was what I had imagined a nobleman's house would be like. Two stories tall. A downstairs great room opening onto the street, a sitting room and two more rooms, for working, I supposed. A paved central patio with its own well. The kitchen was splendid: a hearth wide enough for a small wagon; a wooden pot stand with holes for nine round-bottom water jugs; a rack of knives; a long polished oak work table; a cupboard with stacks of plates, bowls, mugs, and even what looked to be a dozen glass goblets. There was a box with more forks and spoons than I had ever seen before. In every room the windows were covered with panes of real glass. Upstairs, three bedrooms, each with its own fireplace; a long narrow room for the servant girl; and another windowless room outfitted with a table, several chairs, and a bookcase. The house had a stable, too—not that Fernán owned any mules or horses—and a slop yard.

Fernán's house was so splendidly equipped that the few pieces of furniture I had brought from Ciudad Real seemed ill at ease, like country cousins visiting the house of a rich relative. In the downstairs sitting room I counted five matching carved oak chairs, a long, low bench with silk cushions from Córdoba, a linen chest that doubled as a table, some tapestries on the walls to keep out the winter cold, and a large painting of Our Lady of Guadalupe in a walnut frame.

It was obvious that there were no babies in the house. No pails for soiled diapers, no toys strewn about, no cradle for rocking a child to sleep. Well, I'd take care of that soon enough.

The last things Fernán showed me were his desk and tools: a sheaf of goose quills; pots of vitriol and vials of tannic acid, distilled spirits and gum arabic for making ink; folders of white rag paper in various sizes that he said he bought in Talavera. As he was finishing, Mencia came in. The first thing she said was that Manuel was out with some friends and would be home by dinnertime. The second was how glad she was that Fernán was back home. Then she turned to me with a curtsy and a smile, and said that she was so pleased that her master had found a beautiful wife like me, and with such a darling baby. I had been dreading this moment, and I was so flustered I didn't know what to say. Should I use the familiar *tú* the way I had heard rich people did with their maids? Should I maintain a distance between us? Try to be friends? Tell her what I wanted done or let her show me what needed doing? I may have been an old widow woman, but I was so green about these things. Finally I stammered out a hello.

Mencia la Santandera was a roly-poly woman with glowing red cheeks. Her husband, Pedro Ortolano, farmed a small plot near Logrosán where he and his mother were raising Mencia's children. She was lacking three or four teeth, and two of the others were black as charcoal. Mencia was at least twenty years older than I was, but she never lorded it over me. She was so comfortable, so natural with me that I soon got over my nervousness. Distance between us was never a problem. She helped me; she suggested things. And she had the knack of making sure that I asked her advice before I committed myself to anything foolish. We didn't exactly become friends—that would have been unseemly—, but we soon came to enjoy each other's company.

I will never understand her treachery in testifying against me at my trial. But I don't want to think about that now. Angry tears won't help me a bit. What's done is done.

To my surprise, Fernán said that now that baby Juan and I had joined the household, one servant was not enough, and he asked me, with Mencia's help, of course, to engage two more, one to keep the house clean and one to help with the sewing and with my children; Mencia would help me supervise the others and would continue to look after Manuel. Within a day or two a parade of would-be maids appeared at our door. I couldn't distinguish among them, but after five minutes Mencia seemed to know which girls were lazy, or sluts, or dishonest, and which ones would be trustworthy and hardworking. We rejected five or six applicants before hiring Francisca Fernández, the wife of a farmer from Fresnedoso de Ibor. She and her husband, Bartolomé Martín, had no children, but both sets of their parents lived with them, and they were too old and weak to work. Francisca's idiot sister lived there, too. Seven mouths to feed, with only Francisca and Bartolomé to do the work. "They need the money," Mencia told me. "She's used to hard work, just look at her hands. And you'll never have to worry about her loyalty: if you throw her out, all of them will starve."

The second woman we hired was Juana Fernández, the town crier's wife. She was no relation to Francisca, despite their sharing a surname. "Maybe Juana's not quite so hardworking as Francisca," Mencia said, "but she knows everybody in Guadalupe, everything that's going on. You'll see how useful that will be to you, especially given . . . "

"Given what?"

"Given . . . given your husband's job at the priory, given his friends and his associates."

I didn't make out then what she meant, but now that I'm wiser about these things I'm sure that that's not what she was going to say. What she really meant was, "Given the fact that you are Jews." But those weren't words that a servant would ever speak aloud to her mistress. Then or now.

All three of our maids were local women, peasants, really, which means they were old-Christians, like the servants in the homes of the wealthy conversos in Ciudad Real. They weren't blind to our ways, the way we said our prayers and cleaned and cooked for the Sabbath, but they needed jobs and were discreet enough to keep their mouths shut about it. It was an open secret, tolerated but not talked about. It was not without danger, though. If one of the serving girls should be taken by an excess of religion, or develop some personal grudge against the family, it was easy for her to sell her employer out to the priests. It didn't happen very often. Snitches lost their jobs, and once their loyalty to their masters was questioned, they found it hard to find another who would employ them.

To tell the truth, Mencia managed the house, not me; but she had the courtesy to consult with me, or pretend to consult with me, about everything: what needed to be swept or scrubbed, mended or thrown out and replaced; how many turnips, carrots, and parsnips Francisca should buy at the market—the spring salad greens weren't ready for harvest yet, and the first ones would go straight to the priory anyway—; whether in the early spring drizzle the laundry was getting dry or whether the clotheslines should be brought into the stable. The mounds of sewing never grew any shorter. From the corner of the kitchen, our bedroom, the sitting room, their whisper of "Work to be done! Work to be done!" was a reminder that women's hands must never be idle. I didn't have to do it all myself, just the cross-stitchery and needlepoint. The servants were expected to take on most of the restitching of torn seams and the patching of work garments that had seen too much wear. Francisca had the gnarled fingers of a farm girl, as well as weak eyes: it could take her an hour to thread a needle, and her first attempts at sewing on a patch left one of my best aprons bunched up and lumpy. And since Mencia seemed always to be busy doing something else, the everyday mending fell to Juana Fernández. Juana didn't sleep at our house; she arrived each morning except Sunday after preparing breakfast for her own children and for her husband, the town crier, and after a few minutes of harrumphing about how badly she had slept and how her children were imps, sent by the Devil to try her patience, she picked up a stack of mending, settled herself at the corner of the hearth, and proceeded to tell us all the fresh news and old gossip she could remember about Guadalupe. On days when the sun warmed our patio enough for us to be able to sit outside on our wooden bench, she would take out her tatting pillow and bobbins to make lace. No matter how fast her fingers flew, even they could not keep up with the pace of her chatter. I half listened, but I found it difficult to follow the ins and outs of gossip about people I did not know. I didn't believe most of what she said anyway. Like they say, "*Quien comenta, inventa.*"

Twice that first month Fernán took me walking through the town. The brown-and-white-clad Jeronymite friars seemed to be everywhere, hurrying through the streets, buying pastries at the market stalls, slipping in and out of the great houses that lined the main street of the lower town. Many of the largest houses, Fernán pointed out, belonged to rich conversos who were growing even richer lending money to the friars. The monastery itself, as splendid as it was, seemed to be still under construction. The clink-clang of iron hammers striking stone rang like bells, nearly drowning out the shouts of the carpenters, glaziers, and blacksmiths who attended the stonecutters. I hadn't heard such noise in all my life! The masons were all gray with dust, like ghosts, and a thick gray fog hung in the air surrounding the monastery. The Guadalupe market was just like the markets at home, except that, beyond the cheese stalls, there were sheets of cork bark piled in high stacks. "For shoes," Fernán explained, "and stoppers for bottles."

The only thing that soured that first month for me was Fernán's son Manuel. He was a gawky, sallow-complexioned young man of thirteen or fourteen. By then he should have been apprenticed to some sort of trade, but Fernán said that he hadn't expressed any interest in one. As for his father's trade, that was out of the question. Manuel didn't have the firmness of hand or the attention to detail for scrivening. Fernán explained that he hadn't had the time to place his son somewhere. My new husband was so decisive in every other matter, I found this strange. I think he just didn't want to confront his son. Manuel took an active part in the minyan that gathered to pray on Friday evenings in our house, but aside from that and taking his meals

Beatriz Núñez

with us, he didn't do much of anything so far as I could tell. Fernán thought him frivolous and lazy; I found him sullen. For some reason he struck other people as sociable, funny, and a good friend. I seemed to be the only one who set Manuel off. When his father was present, Manuel was civil to me. When his father wasn't there, Manuel didn't speak to me at all, or answered my questions in a tone that I thought was insulting. Discipline was a joke. If I asked him—told him—to do something, he went immediately to his father who often as not countermanded my order. Fernán seemed to have a deaf ear for his son's petulance. When I complained, Fernán proclaimed that I had total authority over both the household and his son. But of the three of us, only Fernán believed that to be true.

Three weeks after I arrived in Guadalupe Manuel moved out. He and two of his friends, he announced to us at dinner, had found jobs in one of Guadalupe's many inns. They would get a small salary, their meals, and a place to sleep in the hayloft over the stable.

"Tell me about this inn," his father said. "Are they good people?" By this, of course, he meant do they follow the Law of Moses. Fernán knew every inn in Guadalupe, but I think he wanted to test Manuel; to see how perceptive he was, and how important his Jewishness was to him.

"Martín de la Sierra, who owns the place, is an old-Christian," Manuel admitted, "but most of the people who work there follow the Law of Moses. Sierra knows what he's about, and he will let us do what we have to do. He's a good businessman, and half the people who stay there are Jews or conversos. As long as we get our work done, he promises to give us half of each Saturday off."

Fernán's smile told me that he was familiar with the inn and its owner, and that he approved of Manuel's commitment.

"Sierra?" I asked.

"It's the big inn on the plaza in front of the priory," Fernán answered. "The best one in Guadalupe."

"What about the kitchen?" I asked Manuel. "How are you going to eat?"

"Don't worry: there are always two ollas on the fire, one for us and one for them. You can guess which one is bigger. And if we don't like the stew, there's always bread and cheese." Speaking to his father, Manuel sounded like a lawyer presenting a case. "Anyway, I'm not asking you. I'm telling. I'm fourteen now, grown up, and it's time for me to earn my own way in the world."

By noon the next day he was gone. Fernán and I could talk to one another again without having to worry about provoking an explosion in his son. The tension drained out of our house the way water drains from a pond when the dam cracks: at first a trickle, then a stream, then a surging flood that leaves the pond empty as a pauper's pocket. I could tell that Fernán was as relieved as I was, though all he ever said, that first night when the two of us were alone, was, "The boy is right; it was time." I began to relax and enjoy our new life together, more comfortable in my role as wife and manager of our house.

But then only a couple of weeks after Manuel's departure, two of the prior's bailiffs arrested Fernán. It was late Saturday afternoon, about an hour before the monastery's vesper bell rings out to signal the day's end. Fernán and I were dressed in our best clothes. He had spent the early afternoon with three of his friends in our upstairs sitting room, as he had every week since I had arrived. I had brought them a pitcher of wine and some spicy almond cookies halfway through the afternoon. The three men—Fernán never told me their names; they were always just "my friends"—left shortly after that. Baby Juan was napping in Francisca's lap in the servants' room. Fernán and I had just settled before the kitchen fire with the last bit of Sabbath wine when the pounding began at the door. Fernán opened it, and the two helmeted bailiffs, carrying pikes and wearing doublets that identified them as the monastery's men, pushed their way in.

"In the name of the Prior and by authority of the Bishop, we are here to arrest you."

Fernán turned white. I sprang out of my chair and backed against the wall, my chest pounding. I couldn't imagine what was happening. I wanted to say something, to shout at them that there must be some mistake, but my lips would not obey. My fingers clutched at the stone for support.

Fernán was not as tongue-tied as I. "What the devil is this? What do you think you're doing?" He said this as he tried, unsuccessfully, to shake loose from their tight grip on each of his arms. "Where are you taking me?"

"To the priory. They'll tell you all about it there."

Fernán turned his head to me as they pulled him toward the door. "It will be all right, Beatriz, don't worry. I should be right back. Hold dinner for me."

And with that the three of them were in the street. My Fernán was gone. The next thing I remember is Francisca pouring water on my face to revive me.

Those next few days I lived at our front door, expecting Fernán to walk in at any moment. The initial wave of panic deepened into an icy despair that froze my will. Baby Juan cried constantly for attention, but Francisca could soothe him now better than I could. What would I do? What if Fernán never came back? Juana tried to reassure me that he would return soon, that the minute she learned something she would let me know. But from the priory all she heard was silence.

"It's in God's hands," she would say.

I prayed for news. I fasted, despite the baby in my belly. I lit candles before the woodcut of Our Lady of Guadalupe. One day, in desperation, I got Juana Fernández to take me up to the priory, but when I asked the *portero* at the gate if he knew anything about my husband, he just turned me away.

The only thing that kept me alive for the next two months was the routine of caring for Juan and the household. I tried to lose myself in the sewing, the shopping, in shifting furniture around to better catch the light. But worry about Fernán kept intruding, like a nagging toothache that would not give me a moment's peace.

My only happy moments came when Francisca brought baby Juan to me, squealing with delight and bouncing with energy. In less than a blink of an eye he had grown from crawling to toddling to running, and his favorite game was to tear back and forth across the room from Francisca's outstretched hands to mine. When he tired, he would try to pull himself up onto Francisca's skirt to rest, but she usually brought him to me instead. Not that he could sit on my lap, of course: the baby in my belly had grown too big and active for that. But she would help me cradle him in one arm, with his head against my shoulder, his breath like a rose petal against my cheek, while I drowsed in his warmth.

I craved those moments: my other sleep was wracked with vivid dreams of Fernán. We still had no word at all about him, so my imagination painted horrible scenes of torture until I woke in a sweat. Even Juana, who presumed to know every time a donkey brayed or a leaf fell in Guadalupe, still could not—or would not—tell me anything about Fernán. My questions made the servants uncomfortable, so after a while I stopped asking. He had vanished, disappeared into the bowels of the earth.

Suddenly, one Thursday afternoon late in May, he came home. When he knocked—with no man around we kept the door barred—, Mencia went to see if it was one of the tradespeople who were always at us to buy their thread, or to inquire if something needed fixing. When she saw Fernán's face she gave

CHAPTER **1**

a startled "Ay!" of surprise. I pulled myself up from my chair—the baby was due any time now, so I found it increasingly hard to move about—and went to wrap my husband in my arms as best I could.

I could not believe my eyes. Fernán was dressed in the same clothes he had been wearing when he was arrested, but now they hung on him as if they had been made for a man twice his size. His hair and beard, which had been flecked with gray when he was taken, were now mostly the color of snow.

When I stopped crying, I peppered Fernán with questions. "Where were you? What happened? Are you all right?" But all he did was shake his head sadly from side to side. He was shivering, so I led him to the kitchen and settled him on a chair by the fire. I had Francisca bring him a blanket, and then I shooshed the servants out of the room. It seemed like an hour, but could not have been more than four or five minutes, when Fernán finally spoke, his voice so low that I had to strain to hear him.

"They called me a heretic. A Judaizer. They clapped me in a cell and told me to prepare myself to confess all my sins. And then nothing. Nothing at all. They locked me in a dark cell for I don't know how long. A week? Two weeks? From time to time they brought me a bowl of wheat gruel, or some turnips stewed with bacon. I tried not to eat the bacon, but, well, after a few days my hunger got the best of me."

"Shall I tell Mencia to get you something now? An egg? Some bread and fresh butter?"

"No, not just now." Fernán slumped in his chair. His breathing was labored. "Then came the questions. Over and over. Did I observe the Sabbath? Did our household cook with pork? Did I believe in my heart that Mary was a virgin, that Jesus alone was the true Savior, and all the rest of the stuff that the priests feed us in their Sunday sermons." His voice was barely a whisper now. "I lied to them. I lied to them as long as I could."

"What do you mean, you lied to them?"

"I told them that I was a good Christian, that I—that you, that none of us—even knew what Jewish customs were, not that we would ever dare to put such things into practice even if we did. But they didn't believe me. Eventually I had to tell them the truth."

He was silent for so long that I feared he had gone to sleep. But there was more.

"Then they pressed me for the details, over and over again."

I stood behind his chair, gently kneading his shoulders. There didn't seem to be any flesh at all between my fingers and his bones. "They set you free."

"Free. Oh yes, free." Fernán's voice had hardened. "Free to pay them a fine that is going to take me a year to raise. Free to go to church every Sunday and register with the priest. Free to go every single day if I want to. Free to cram myself with pork. Free to stay away from my friends. They made me swear all this, in church, before the prior and all the monks and the bishop's men. Everybody saw me."

I wanted to lean down and embrace him, but a sharp pain stopped me. "Oh, my God."

I had Fernán's attention now. "Are you all right?"

"God of all creation, help me." The contractions had begun, not slowly, as they had with baby Juan, but all at once, like a hammer blow. I screamed for Mencia to fetch the midwife who always attended to our people.

It was a hard labor, two endless days before baby Francisquito emerged. He was bigger than I would have thought possible, and feverish. We wrapped Francisco in the soft linen swaddling blanket that I had spent so many weeks embroidering, but he wouldn't stop shaking, and he wouldn't take my milk. A week later that same blanket became his shroud.

Francisquito was dead. Fernán came back from the priory changed. The crisp pine-scented air of Guadalupe was so different from Ciudad Real where the hot night wind tasted of sheep and winnowed wheat. In the midst of the simplest tasks I found myself daydreaming of my parents' house, of Bernardo, of our son Gonzalo who was just as gone from my life as his dead father. Except for baby Juan, I felt that all the bright colors in my world had faded to gray.

Fernán scurried about Guadalupe trying to reassure his old clients that they could rely on him the way they always had, that despite his arrest they could employ him with no risk to themselves. He put on a brave face, but his list of clients dwindled and his income soon shrunk by half. He seemed obsessed with the daily costs of maintaining our household. We bought less meat, ate more cabbage and turnips. We threw out nothing: no matter how worn a garment was, he insisted that we patch it, or reuse the cloth to fashion something else that we needed. We stopped buying candles, so, except for the kitchen fire, at night the house was dark. When Mencia la Santandera left us in November just before St. Martin's day we did not replace her. Mencia had to leave because they needed her at home, she said, but it could have been because she was afraid of working for a known heretic. Francisca wasn't clever enough to run the house, though she could manage the marketing, and Juana Fernández was too much of a gossip to be trusted completely, so I had to take over our household. I resented it at first, because all I wanted to do was play with Juan or to sit in the dark and mourn for poor dead Francisquito, but looking back on it now I see that it did me good by distracting me with detail and responsibility. And it did save us money.

Fray Lope de Villareal at the priory continued to give Fernán work and to pay him as he had before. In fact, the priory quickly became Fernán's most important client. When I asked Fernán how that could be, he said that Fray Lope was a good friend to our people.

"How could he be a friend? They arrested you. If they called you a heretic, wouldn't the prior . . . ?"

"You'd think so, but no. Fray Lope has a lot of support among the brothers. Some of those monks had grandparents who were just as Jewish as ours were. The Jeronymites are not like the Dominicans, you know, or the Franciscans. Anybody can profess with the Jeronymites. Let a man be Christian today, and who cares what God their ancestors believed in."

It still didn't make sense to me. The friars were our enemies: they taught that the Jews killed Jesus, and they had arrested Fernán and done God knows what to him there in the cellars of the monastery. What did he mean, "Let a man be Christian"? We were Christians, even though we still followed the old ways as well, the way our parents had taught us. That's the way we had always lived. That's the way I wanted to live.

I tried to put those thoughts into words, but Fernán would not listen.

"Hear what I am saying, Beatriz. Not all the friars hate us. Some of them know what the Sabbath is. They know how to pray to the God of Abraham. But they have enemies, too; not all the other friars accept them. Some of them are afraid of us, and some are afraid for themselves. They are divided into factions; they're at war with each other. The monastery will give me work but only if I give up the old ways and I am completely Christian. Beyond suspicion."

"But we can't."

"We can! I'm useful to them; I'm good at what I do. They'll pay me. But we have to be Christian in everything we do, everything that anyone ever sees us doing. Do you hear me?"

"But they arrested you!"

"That was a warning. To me, to all of us conversos. We have to keep away from the Jews, from anything that has the faintest odor of the old ways. If we don't, then . . . "

"Then what?"

"Don't ask me that. I don't know what. All I know is that it will be bad for us. Listen to me closely." Fernán's voice dropped as he took hold of my shoulders. His eyes were cold. "I forbid you to practice any of the old ways. Not in this house. Not ever again. Not ever! That's the past, and we have to live in the future."

I heard his words, but I had no idea at all what he meant. I only knew one way to be, the way my mother and my aunts and my father had taught me. The way I had taught Gonzalo, the way I would teach Juan, the way Fernán had taught Manuel. If I didn't live the way I was living, then I wouldn't be me. I tried to explain this to Fernán, but I couldn't make him understand. Fernán thought I could take off one life and put on another one as easily as I would change aprons. Finally I had to promise him I would do as he asked.

The next day was Friday. In the morning I bought some chard and a small piece of lamb, I soaked some chickpeas, cut an onion and some garlic, and set the adafina to stew over the fire the way I always did. When Fernán came home late in the afternoon he exploded at me.

"You can't do that. You promised me you wouldn't!"

"What are you talking about?"

Francisca was sitting in the corner with some mending; baby Juan was napping on a blanket on the floor by her chair. Juana was scurrying about in the front room. Fernán took me by the arm and pulled me out into the patio.

He spoke in a whisper, but his words were sharp as a knife. "The stew, Beatriz; the adafina. That's Jewish food. You can't let anybody see that you cook like that. What if the maids talk about it?"

"It's not Jewish food; it's just food. It's what we always eat for Saturday dinner. We have to eat!" I don't know if I was more puzzled or angry.

"Well, throw some bacon in it then, some salt pork, something to give it flavor. Something you can smell cooking from out in the street." Fernán glowered at me, and I glowered back at him, but I didn't say anything more.

We walked back into the kitchen together, and he stood there watching while I sliced up some pieces of salt pork that Francisca had bought for herself and stirred them into the olla.

That's the way it went. For a long time. I tried to do what he said, but it was impossible. I mean, I still had to keep myself clean: if I didn't wash my hands before and after eating, then my stomach got queasy. Our house had to be swept and Friday just seemed to be the right day to do it. As for the Sabbath, I had to rest once in a while, and the rhythm of Saturday was deep in my bones. I couldn't light candles anymore, or pray over them. But sometimes, when he was out, I lit them in our bedroom, although not at sunset, because that was the time he usually returned from his work.

What caused most of our hard feelings was the kitchen. I only knew one way of cooking, the way my mother had taught me. Her favorite recipes. The way she seasoned her food. The things we must never cook, never touch, never smell because they were unclean. Now Fernán wanted pork in everything. If I fried something—it didn't matter whether it was chopped cabbage, a piece of fish, or a slice of liver—I had to fry it in lard. The smell made me ill. A couple of times I had to run from the kitchen to the stable yard to empty my stomach in the wet straw. I tried to get Francisca to take over the cooking, but that was useless. She could shop, but she had a heavy hand with the salt and she overcooked everything until the meat was like leather, the fish dry and tasteless, the vegetables a flavorless gray-green mush. Fernán wouldn't eat them, and neither would I. So I gave it up and went back to cooking for my husband, making him what he wanted and for myself eating what I could. I told him I had a delicate stomach and that's why I preferred to fill myself with vegetables and fruits, when I could get them. I know he didn't believe me, but his silence on the matter meant that we had forged a kind of truce between us, at least with regard to the kitchen. That is not to say that I never ate pork stew. If we had a guest, or if I was hungry enough and there was nothing else available, as was often the case during the winter, well, I had to survive.

But it always hurt me. I'm not referring to the nausea that was my constant companion at mealtime. It hurt me in my soul. You angels know that. God watches everything, knows everything, and rewards and punishes us according to our deeds. I drank that truth with my mother's milk. Ten times a day I heard it from my mother's lips: "You have to wash your hands before eating. You have to clean the house on Friday. You cannot sew or spin on the Sabbath. God wants it that way. He set the rules, and we have to follow them. You want to go to heaven, don't you? You want your soul to be saved? Then do as I say; do as God says."

Why didn't I just go along with what my husband wanted like an obedient wife? Lord knows I wanted to, at least some part of me did. But I couldn't. It's not that I spent a lot of time worrying about what would happen to my soul when I was dead, like the priests tell us we must do. It's more like . . . like a feeling that I was doing wrong. I knew what I had to do to be a good person. It was all the things Mother and Aunt Úrsula and their friends had taught me. Whenever I broke one of those rules I felt like I was disobeying my parents, committing some sort of treachery against God, and against what I had been taught was right and good.

Twenty years have passed since Fernán came back to me from the priory. On the whole I suppose I have been happy. In time, as is the way of things, our house filled with children. Except for Francisquito, our other children were born healthy. The next to appear was Martín. By the time the midwife had swaddled him and left the room, Fernán and I were arguing about whether to have him circumcised. It didn't seem right to me not to do it; it put Martín's soul in danger, and my father would have gone into mourning. But Fernán won out, the way he always did, so he took the child to the priory to be baptized and we never sent for the mohel. Martín was a blue-eyed, ringleted baby who charmed everyone who saw him, and still does. And he is as sharp as the blade of a knife. He started to talk when he was only a year and a half old and hasn't stopped since. Always questions: Why is this? Where is that? His handwriting is nearly as good as his father's, and he seems marked to follow him in the scrivener trade.

After Martín came the girls: Beatriz and Catalina. Though they were born eighteen months apart, by the time Catalina was five they were so close to each other in size and appearance and character that people thought they were twins. They dote on their father, waiting by the door in the late afternoon for him to come home and grinning with glee when he takes them to Sunday mass. Fernán forbade me from teaching them the Old Law, so I never spoke of it. I bought them each toy brooms so they could follow along behind me when I cleaned. Fernán screamed at me for that, too.

"But they're having fun," I said; "and they have to learn for when they get married. Or do you want them to become nuns?"

I meant it as joke, but Fernán took it seriously. "If that's what they want to do, yes. But for now, all right; they can sweep all they want. Just not on Friday." Another thorn in my side.

Fernán and I never spoke of the girls' education again. I just do what I do and keep my mouth shut. I cook and clean and fear for my soul the way I always have, the way I was taught when I was their age. I never speak of the Law of Moses to them, as Fernán commanded, but they have learned my ways.

Fernán treated me well enough. Nobody got seriously sick. In the winters, when the icy winds rattled the windows, I liked curling up with the children in front of the hearth. Sometimes in the spring one of the maids and I would take the children for a walk through the barley fields that dot the valley below Guadalupe. The girls went wild for the flowers along the roadside! We would always pick a bouquet to take home with us. My favorites were the poppies, red as blood and light as a feather, even though they always wilted before we got them home. Sometimes the girls would play tag, or hopscotch, with the other children who lived near us, and I loved watching them from the stone bench outside our door. I enjoyed the church processions: the colors of the banners, the clouds of incense, the chanting, too, with the squeaky-voiced novices trying to stay in tune with the rumbling base notes of the older friars. It seems like every week they honored saint somebody-or-other. Fernán always made us go, even on those days when a gray sky and a bitter wind from the mountains made me wish that I was back indoors. And all those days when we didn't go out . . . well, I had the house to keep me busy.

There were bitter moments, too, days when I didn't want to get out of bed in the morning, nights when I couldn't sleep. Fernán and I didn't fight the way so many couples do—Juana Fernández never stopped gossiping about them: who threw a slop bucket at her husband, who punched his wife, which kids got paddled for letting the pigs escape into the forest. But Fernán and I had our moments. Our bitterest arguments were about visiting my family. I wanted to go back to Ciudad Real to see them. Every few months, when my missing them grew almost too much to bear, I'd beg Fernán to take me there for a week or two. But it was always: "Later. When I don't have so much work. When the spring rains stop." And we never did go, not even once.

And of course we never stopped arguing about my keeping the old ways. Every time one of our servant girls left and we hired another one, Fernán would tell me that I had to be extra careful to keep them from seeing anything that would lead them to suspect that we had once followed the Law of Moses. Every time he'd say that, I'd bite my tongue to keep from telling him that I still did, and that he should too if he valued his soul. Still, he was right about the danger, and I really tried to be discreet. But when someone works in your house, day after day . . . Over the years we had quite a lot of serving girls: Fernán García Calvo's two daughters, Inés and Catalina; and Juan González Serrano's two girls, Catalina and Mencia. All of them from Cañamero. All of them young, and peasants at heart; most of them pretty hardworking. They were pleasant enough but not really people I could share my thoughts with. And then there was Marina, who came to us when she was fifteen and lived with us for six years. Fernán couldn't keep his eyes off of her, and after a time the looks she gave him back burned like ice in my heart. She had a mouth on her, too, always sassing back when one of the other girls asked her to do something. I wanted to let her go, but Fernán wouldn't hear of it. Until somehow she got herself pregnant. Then he sent her back to her parents in disgrace.

I would have sworn that all those girls were loyal to us, but I know now that every single one of them told the inquisitors how I still followed the old ways. The questions that the friars keep hammering me with: I know that the details that feed their questions have to have come from the serving girls.

For the most part Fernán was happy, too, I think. His one big worry, aside from the fact that I wouldn't turn my back on the life that my parents had taught me, was his son Manuel. When Manuel ran off to Martín de la Sierra's inn he must have found the work harder than he imagined, for within six months he had quit and left Guadalupe, without even the decency to say good-bye or tell us where he was going. That just strengthened his father's belief that Manuel was a lazy, foolish, good-for-nothing. "*Pereza, pobreza*," he kept muttering. "Someday that boy will die of starvation." Later one of his friends brought Fernán word that Manuel was in Cádiz, working as a tailor by day and by night in one of the portside inns that catered to sailors and the men and women who worked the docks. "Whores and drunks and rough-necks," Fernán grumbled. "Better there than here, where we'd have to live in his shame." But I knew he didn't mean it. He loved his son, and I think he must have missed him just as much as I missed Gonzalo.

Then, two years later, Manuel came back to Guadalupe. He didn't come to see us or anything. Fernán ran into him in the street one day. At first, Fernán told me, he didn't recognize his son, who had grown two hands taller and sported a thick black beard. But then when Manuel called him by name, he rushed over to him and embraced him. The next afternoon, which was the eve of the Sabbath, Manuel joined us for dinner. He greeted me warmly enough, but I felt awkward around him, so I sat quietly, Martín squirming in my lap, one eye on Juan stacking wooden blocks in the corner as Manuel chattered to his father about his adventures in Andalucía and all the exotic people whom the ships brought to Cádiz: Turks, Arabs, Englishmen, and even Jews from Tangier and Oran. They had taught him dozens of prayers that he had never heard before, and he couldn't wait to share the melodies with his father's minyan.

"We don't do that anymore," Fernán told him.

Manuel could not believe his ears. "What do you mean, you don't do that anymore? You taught me how to pray. You've always prayed with your minyan. Don't they still come to our house?"

"Not anymore. I'm a Christian now." From the tone of his voice I could see that Fernán was embarrassed. As if he had let his son down and didn't want to admit it, didn't want to apologize. "I don't do those Jewish things anymore. You know I work for the friars, up at the priory, and I want to keep my job. They arrested me once—I suppose you've heard about that—and I never want to go through that again. I spent too long in the cells underneath that building to want to risk their putting me there again. Saturday is a work-day now: my Sabbath is Sunday."

Manuel's face had turned the color of ash. "But what about your soul?"

"My soul? The priests tell me that Jesus Christ is my Savior, and that's good enough for me. And if you've got any sense, you'll behave the same way. *Precavido es prevenido.*"

"What about Martín? He's been circumcised, hasn't he?"

"He was baptized. I told you, we're all Christian now. Only Christian."

It went on like that all evening. I knew that Fernán had to be lying, that in his heart he still believed in the Law of Moses. That he was too afraid to say so, too afraid that one of us might show people some sign that we were still Jews.

Manuel left, disgusted, a little before the priory bells tolled for midnight. Neither of us saw much of him after that.

It's funny how wrong both Fernán and I were to doubt that Manuel would ever amount to anything. Sierra gave him back his old job at the Mesón Blanco, and now Manuel took to the innkeeping business the way a bear takes to honey. He must have impressed Sierra with his ability to manage people and his head for making good decisions, because within a few years he was all but running the Mesón. When old man Sierra died he left the business to Manuel. Sullen little Manuel, the owner of the best business in Guadalupe!

Twenty years I've lived in Guadalupe. Fernán and me and the children. I never saw my parents again. Fernán said he wrote to them, but they never answered. I longed for a group of friends like my mother had. I wouldn't have needed many, one or two would have been enough; women I could sit with in the afternoon while we sewed, tell jokes to, unburden my soul. Women who cooked and cleaned and rested on the Sabbath and dressed the way I did. But Fernán never would have let me do that. "How about the women who fix the flowers for the church?" he said to me once when I told him that I was lonely. But I couldn't approach them; it just didn't seem right. Besides, I have never been able to make friends easily. I never know what to say. Even since I was little, when I am at the fountain or the market I hardly ever join in the chatter. What I like to do is listen. It makes me feel a part of things. But to open up to another woman and share my fears and dreams, to pull threads of comfort from the skein of our common lives . . . something inside me clamps my tongue. Costanza, the girl I used to play handclapping games with in Ciudad Real all those years ago, was not only my last real friend; if I'm honest, she was my only friend. I envied the other girls my age, the way they clumped together. I used to console myself with the thought that when I grew up just a little more I would come into my courage, and the world of people would reach out and embrace me.

That never happened. In Guadalupe my only friend was my husband, and the more he barked at me for following my parents' ways, the more distant we grew from each other. We ate together when he was home. We slept together. But we hardly ever talked, not about things that mattered. His life was his; and mine . . .

Mine was mostly the children, Beatriz and Catalina. Not so much Martín, he was his father's son. But the girls: I could play games with them, help them sew clothes for their dollies, teach them how to sweep toward the center of the room so the dirt wouldn't settle in the corners. Their favorite thing was to help in the kitchen. I had Fernán make them a little bench to stand on to reach the top of the table. They liked to race each other to see who could shell the most peas. And when we baked, they would help knead the dough with such enthusiasm that they covered themselves and everything else with flour. I always gave them their bath while our kitchen maid cleaned up the mess.

Two years ago—it seems like forever now!—two years ago my fear caught up with Fernán's. Two years ago the Inquisition set up in Ciudad Real. Queen

Isabel, our fairy-tale queen, had called up a dragon to devour us. At first we could not believe our ears. New-Christians who still followed the Old Law were arrested. The inquisitors tortured them to make them confess. Whole families burned at the stake. It threw all of us in Guadalupe into a panic. We were desperate for news, for names. Every day Fernán came home with details, though we didn't know if they were true or only rumors. People I had known in Ciudad Real—friends of my mother, business associates of my father—were swept away by the inquisitors. My childhood friend Costanza and her parents? Arrested, all of their possessions seized. We heard that they made them swear their allegiance to the Church in the plaza in front of Santo Domingo, where the great synagogue had been. Then Fernán had to tell me they had arrested my parents, that both of them had perished in the flames. I think I screamed. I know I fainted. Fernán had to pick me up and help me into bed. We didn't know what to say to the servants. That I'd screamed because I saw a rat? That I was feeling ill, so Fernán had put me to bed? Fernán was Christian, but he felt the loss of my parents as painfully as I did. All that week we didn't dare let the servants see we were mourning, so I didn't dress in black or tear my clothes. Fernán wouldn't have let me, anyway. We ate our regular meals, not eggs and fish, and we set our food on the table, not the floor. Only when I closed our bedroom door behind me could I allow myself to cry.

Fernán spent more time than ever in church, and he was even more demanding that I avoid anything that might hint at the Old Law. When he discovered that I was still lighting candles on Friday in the big upstairs room where nobody could see them, he hit me. It was the first time he had ever laid a hand on me, and it left a purple bruise on my cheek that I had to tell the servants came from my running into a door. On Saturdays he made me work all day, out in public, where I could be seen. If I sewed, it had to be on a bench in front of our house, facing the street, even if the wind was so cold that my fingers turned blue. We ate pork at every meal, not only Fernán, but the children and I as well. He made me stop bathing every week, stop washing my hands when we ate. We hung the woodcuts of Jesus and the Holy Family opposite the door, so that they could be seen from the street. Every day I put fresh flowers in front of our picture of the Virgin of Guadalupe.

The whole city was on edge, the friars as much as anyone. It was no secret that as many candles were lit Friday nights inside the priory as in the homes of the conversos. One night Fernán told me that back during the priorate of Fray Gonzalo de Madrid, years before I came to Guadalupe, some of the friars had even come to Fernán's minyan, and that right inside the monastery itself he had often discussed the Law with the brothers. Some of them, he said, wouldn't even eat pork! But now Fray Nuño de Arévalo was prior, and not only was he no friend of the Jews, he wanted the Jeronymites themselves to sweep every Judaizing practice out of the monastery before the inquisitors decided to come and do it for them. All of us, inside the priory and out, had to make sure our allegiance to the Law of Jesus was on public display.

Too late.

In January the inquisitors came to town. That first Sunday they made the whole city gather in the great plaza in front of the monastery. The prior read a proclamation, an edict, which told us to come to the monastery to confess our sins. He promised that even if we had done bad things, if we could show that we were now exclusively committed to the Law of Jesus, we would find the Church merciful and forgiving. But woe to anyone who did not come forward, who did not repent.

I was so frightened. I was certain that something terrible was going to happen to us. That night I asked Fernán what we should do.

"We have no choice. Both of us, we have to go to the friars and confess. I'll say that I used to follow a few of the old customs, but that since I was tried and given penance twenty years ago, I haven't Judaized, not even once. You have to tell them that you were taught the Law of Moses in your parents' house. They are dead now, anyway, so it doesn't matter if you identify them as Jews. Say that since you left Ciudad Real and came to Guadalupe you haven't practiced any of those things. And that you haven't taught anything like that to the children." We agreed that we would screw up our courage and do it before the week was out.

But we didn't move fast enough. The next morning the bailiffs arrested Fernán. They went to the Mesón Blanco and took Manuel, too. That same afternoon, I left Juan copying out some papers at his father's desk and Catalina and Beatriz playing in the patio with Mencia González, who by then was our only live-in servant, and I went up to the friary to confess. I told them all about my childhood in Ciudad Real. I even said that during my early years in Guadalupe I had kept up those Judaizing practices. I couldn't really deny it: over the years too many servants had seen the way I lived. But I was careful not to say anything that would make them think that Fernán and the children were guilty, too. I insisted that all the Judaizing was my doing; that since Fernán's arrest twenty years ago I had always hid that part of my life from my husband and my children. They were innocent of any wrongdoing. And I told them, too, that I had given up all those practices a few years back when I had accepted Jesus, and that since then I have lived only according to the Law of Jesus.

They held me for a month, a month of days filled with questions and nights sleepless with worry about my husband and my children. Then in a public auto-de-fé in the cemetery behind the monastery they made me swear to all I had confessed. Then they set me free.

From the monastery to our house was a matter of three minutes. As soon as I crossed the stoop, I called out for Juan and the girls. They came running into the front room and threw themselves at me. I hugged them tight, one after the other, even Juan. Mencia stood behind them, her eyes cast down.

"Has Fernán returned? Is he still in prison?" Something in the way she was standing made my heart sink.

"No, he's dead." Mencia said. "Hadn't you heard? With six others. They burned them in the cemetery at the auto-de-fé ten days ago. The priest said that they were giving the heretics a foretaste of the Hell that awaited their souls."

"Oh my God!" was all I could manage to say. The tears streamed down my face. Beatriz and Catalina were sobbing. Juan bit his lip to keep from breaking into tears. Martín had collapsed face-down on the floor. My soul was crumbling into pieces.

"I'm sorry, I'm so, so sorry," Mencia said.

That was in February. They arrested me again in April. The children tried to stop the bailiffs from seizing me, but Mencia held them back. I didn't even have a chance to say good-bye.

The inquisitors said I had lied to them about the sincerity of my conversion to the Law of Jesus. That's why they had brought me here again.

Now it is June, and here I sit, with only myself and my guardian angels to listen to my words.

Oh, my poor Juan, Martín. My darlings, Beatriz and Catalina. My long-lost son, Gonzalo. Where are you now? What will become of you?

Beatriz Núñez

Diego Arias tomo los manteles que estaban en la messa e pusolos por la cabeza e cuerpo como se ponen los rabies de los judios el taler quando quieren deçir oracion, e subiose en vn banco e començo a cantar vn responso. . . . E que asi acabados de deçir los dischos responses, que dixo: "¡O! ¡o! judios no sabeis el bien que teneis."

—AHN Inq. Leg. 1413, Exp. 7: 46v–47r

2

The Arias Dávila Clan

SPAIN, 1486

February 19, 1486. A street in Sevilla.

Bishop Juan Arias Dávila hurried along the muddy street, as fast as episcopal decorum would permit. Fifteen minutes ago he and the other Castilian prelates had been gathered in audience with the King to discuss what the Church was expected to contribute to the war against the Muslim kingdom of Granada. The bishops supported the monarchs wholeheartedly, but—they labored to insinuate without offending—perhaps not quite as richly as King Fernando and Queen Isabel seemed to expect. In mid-morning, when King Fernando paused to have mulled wine and trays of Sevilla's famous bitter oranges brought in for the bishops, one of Bishop Arias's servants approached the table and whispered to him that he was needed urgently back at his quarters. A messenger had just arrived from Segovia with news for Bishop Arias's ears only.

Protocol required that no one leave the table until the king dismissed them. When the orange peels had been cleared, the king turned the discussion to the disposition of moneys confiscated from heretics by the Holy Office of the Inquisition that had been authorized by the pope eight years before. While his colleagues voiced their concerns about being cut out of the divvy, Bishop Arias, for very personal reasons, remained silent. The king appeared immovable: a share of the confiscations would go to the Crown to help finance the holy war against the Muslim infidels in Granada, and the rest would remain with the Holy Office to defray its expenses. Finally King Fernando stood up. The bishops, struggling to mask their disappointment, filed out of the audience room. Bishop Arias did not linger to chew over the morning's debate with his colleagues. Instead he made straight for the inn where his Segovia delegation was quartered, a few hundred meters past the Cathedral, muttering to himself as he strode along the cobbled street.

Surely Fray Tomás could not have dared to start proceedings in Segovia in my absence. It would be a deliberate insult to the city's chief prelate. A blatant power play. It was true that the pope had confirmed the monarchs' nomination of the Dominican monk as the first Inquisitor General, raising him to a position of unprecedented power. And it was true that the bishops had acquiesced, with feigned enthusiasm, to Inquisition tribunals being established in their diocese. Several of them had fought it behind the scenes, of course, but they'd lost. What King Fernando and Queen Isabel wanted, they got. But for Torquemada to go ahead without consulting me, as if a bishop had no say in what went on in his own diocese!

Worse yet, Bishop Arias thought to himself as the soaring Gothic spires of Sevilla's Cathedral came into view—and this was the concern he could never speak aloud—what if I am Friar Tomás's target? What if Torquemada is going after me?

February 22, 1486. On the road near Ciudad Real.

Bishop Arias and the half-dozen lesser clerics who escorted him fought to keep their horses from slipping into the cart tracks that rutted Castilla's main highway from Andalucía to the northern plains. His trusted friend and advisor Father Antonio de Nieva rode by his side. Though the bishop was unarmed, Father Antonio and the others all had swords at their sides.

"At least the wind is at our backs." Father Antonio shook the water from his cape and wiped his eyes. There were two hours left before sunset.

"I recall an inn not more than a league up the road," the bishop said. "We can stop there. Maybe it will clear tomorrow."

After six weeks of incessant rain the road was a quagmire. They were lucky to have made it this far without incident. The Guadalquivir River and all its tributaries were in flood. In Sevilla the whole Triana district was under water and only accessible by boat. Hundreds of houses had collapsed, and everything stunk of mildew. He had heard Andrés Bernáldez, the queen's toady chronicler, who was always hovering at the back of every audience chamber with his notebooks and inkpots and quills, say at least seven times a day how "no living human being had ever been witness to so much flooding." Now, two days beyond the mountains that marked the boundary of Andalucía, the clerics rode without speaking across the rolling steppes of La Mancha, their shoulders hunched and their necks wrapped in broadcloth against the raw wind that buffeted them from the west.

Bishop Arias's mood was as bleak as the gray sky. He didn't know what was going on behind the closed doors of the inquisitors' audience chamber in Segovia, but he could imagine, and what he imagined made him angry. The investigation, no matter what its outcome, would weaken him, and it would distract him from the important business of his diocese: his program to build literacy among the rural clergy; the new choir stalls and the renovations to the cloister; the printing press; strengthening the diocesan castle in Turégano.

The bishop had no worries about his own orthodoxy: he was a Christian of unchallengeable integrity who had dedicated most of his life to serving the Church. His parents had Judaized, that was true. But they had both been dead now for more than twenty years. And he himself had never done anything even remotely Jewish. At least not since becoming bishop. His faith was unimpeachable. But neither did he have any illusions about the strength of the enemies who hated him as much for his liberal programs as for his Jewish ancestry.

They will come after me through my family.

April 19, 1486. Segovia, the afternoon audience, in the house of Gonzalo de Cáceres, commandeered by the Inquisition until a permanent audience chamber could be constructed.

The Jew Rabbi Simuel de Vides, a doctor in the service of the Duke of Alburquerque, took his seat at one end of the long oak table. Above his full gray beard his face was gaunt. There were deep circles under his eyes from not having slept since being told, two days ago, of this morning's appointment to testify. A simple cap of black velvet covered his head. Sewn to the left shoulder of his cloak was the yellow circle that identified him as a Jew. Rabbi Simuel had heard that the Inquisition had no jurisdiction over the beliefs of Jews, but still he struggled to keep his hands from trembling. The walls of the interrogation room were bare except for a small statue of the crucified Christ on the wall behind the black-and-white-robed Dominican monk sitting at the other end of the table. The cleric was a small man with pinched features, his closely cropped beard flecked with white. A second inquisitor, dressed in the black robe and mortarboard of a Master of Laws, sat on Rabbi Simuel's left in front of a sheaf of papers that seemed to be covered with writing. His fingers toyed with the ribbon that bound them. A third man, whose black habit identified him as a lay Dominican, occupied the chair to Rabbi Simuel's right. He slipped a sheet of blank paper from the stack in front of him on the table, dipped his quill into the yellow-glazed inkpot, and nodded to Fray Fernando de Santo Domingo that he was ready to record the old Jew's testimony.

Fray Fernando introduced himself and the lawyer, Master Cañas. Canon law required the presence of at least two inquisitors at all interrogations. The scribe, a silent recording device, did not merit an introduction.

In a barely audible voice, Fray Fernando ordered Rabbi Simuel to swear on the Jewish Bible that he would report truthfully everything he knew about the Judaizing activities of Diego Arias Dávila, the late Master of Accounts of the kingdom of Castilla, his second wife, Elvira González, their children, Pedro, Juan, and Ysabel, and their legion of nieces, nephews, and cousins.

"Diego Arias . . . " The rabbi began slowly to speak. "I remember— it was a long time ago—my father, Master Jusep, told me that one day when he was out walking with Diego Arias, the two of them found themselves a little distant from their companions. Diego Arias asked my father if he knew how to sing anything in Hebrew. He said he did, and Diego Arias asked him if he knew the *pizmón* '*Kol mebbaser*' that Jews sing. My father said that when he began to sing it, Diego Arias sang along with him and told my father that he didn't have the tune right, though he had started it off correctly. Then the two sang the hymn together."

Through the open window came a bumblebee, perhaps drawn to the monastery cloister by the early blooming narcissi in the small garden framed by the stone arches of the cloister. The bee lit on the table next to the inkpot, took four or five steps toward the scribe, and then stopped to groom its legs. No one moved to shoo it away. The room was chilly even though a shaft of sunlight dazzled the whitewashed stone wall behind the scribe. With his sleeve Rabbi Simuel wiped the sweat from his face.

"I often saw Diego Arias in the synagogue with his prayer shawl draped over his head like any Jew. He liked to sing, and his voice was better than any of ours. One Sabbath when I was at his house, I saw him climb up on a ladder with a linen *tallit* over his head like a rabbi and sing an evening song that Jews sing. He had a voice like an angel. Everyone was saying '*Guay!* what a melancholy voice he has!' ... You know, until I heard him singing in Hebrew I thought he was a dunce, a *hahedul*, but now I believe he was a clever man.

"Those conversos were always worrying about who might overhear them. I remember another time when we were all praying in Alonso González de la Hoz's house and Pedro Çalfati came in. Diego Arias told everyone to stop praying because a *meshumad*—that means a turncoat—had come in. And that wasn't the only time that happened. One time my brother-in-law Master Jerónimo de la Paz—you know he was a rabbi before he converted—, once he interrupted our minyan and Diego Arias screamed at him in fury: 'Who let you stick your nose in here?' Master Jerónimo answered, 'I only came in looking for a certain someone,' and Diego Arias hollered, 'Go on, get out!' Later I learned that Diego Arias fired the doorman for not being at his post when Master Jerónimo came in."

Rabbi Simuel droned on, recounting fragments of long ago events. Fray Fernando found his attention wandering. What could have stuck to the bee's legs that would induce it to stand so quietly for so long? Didn't it know how dangerous that was? If he lifted his hand to swat it away, how close could he get before the bee took fright and flew off?

The Jew spoke haltingly now, searching his memory with meager success for incidents that might indicate how Diego Arias had continued to Judaize after his conversion to Christianity. Fray Fernando had been a long time seated, and during the last few minutes of testimony he'd had to clench his teeth to stifle a yawn that was sure to embarrass everyone in the room. He signaled the guard to take the Jew out and then stood up and stretched. He walked to the open window and gazed at the gray clouds gathering over the Guadarrama Mountains. The temperature had dropped. He murmured a brief prayer that the rains that were washing away Andalucía were finally making their way to the high plains. If they didn't come soon, there would be no wheat this year. Reminded of his own thirst, he hefted the earthenware jug from the floor next to the window. He returned to his seat at the head of the table and summoned the guard to bring in the next witness. They had another hour left in the audience: maybe this one would say something useful.

✖

The Arias Dávila Clan

After a long day's work there were few things Fray Fernando de Santo Domingo enjoyed more than a brisk walk through the Clamores Gorge. The path was strewn with rocks, tricky walking if you didn't keep one eye to the ground. The steep slope rising to the city wall—built by the Romans, some people said—was studded with broad-leafed alders and choked with vines. Willows and black poplars bordered the river, little more than a stream when it was running full, and now, with the lack of rain, scarcely a trickle. Still, no matter how hotly the wind blew across the plains, here in the gorge the air was always humid, thick with a blend of blossoms and rotting vegetation. Fray Fernando could hear laughing from the two burly novices thirty paces behind him; he turned and put his finger to his lips to silence them. When he himself was a novice, he thought ruefully, he often came here by himself, to collect his thoughts and to listen to the birds that chattered in the thickets. But now . . . Inquisitors have enemies, and thus the bodyguards. Only two years ago the Inquisitor General of Aragón had been murdered in his own church! Across the river, the cemetery of the Jews was set into the groves of fragrant pines. Sometimes when he walked here he could hear them chanting the mournful prayer for the dead as they laid some newly departed member of the community into his rock-hewn grave.

Now Fray Fernando was coming to the two enormous plane trees that marked the point where the Eresma River joined the Clamores. The narrow triangle of rock crowned by the royal castle towered over his right shoulder. No wonder the Romans built here. Segovia has to have the best natural defenses of any city in the world, he thought to himself. And wealth: sheep and wheat from the high plains, lumber from the Guadarrama Mountains southeast of the city. Segovia pulsed with one of the busiest markets in all Castilla. The mansions of the merchant princes lined the best streets in town. Too bad so many of them were Jews or converts, like Arias and the González de la Hoz brothers and the Çalfatis.

Since Fray Fernando was last here someone had adzed off the side of a poplar log to make a bench and set it between the plane trees. The cleric sat and stretched out his legs, motioning to the two novices to keep their distance.

The Arias Dávilas! They had their fingers into everything. The old man Diego was dead, but his sons, and their cousins; you couldn't spend a maravedí in Segovia without half of it going into the pockets of one of them. Fray Fernando had lost track of how many people he and his colleague had interviewed over the last several months: neighbors and friends, family members, servants, business associates of old man Diego. Most of what they dredged up from their memories was trivial, but there were nuggets here and there. Fray Fernando reviewed what they had learned so far.

Not one witness had characterized Diego Arias Dávila as a nice man. Arrogant, yes. Ambitious, without question. Clever. Also willful, manipulative, corrupt, and greedy. Ill-tempered when sober, maudlin when drunk. And unusually proficient at acquiring and using power. The Jews and conversos who had testified had all respected him—fawned on him, some of them—though they didn't seem to like him very much. The old-Christian witnesses mostly despised the man.

No one could tell them about Arias's childhood, or about the early history of his family. Still, a few facts had emerged. The Arias family converted around 1411, the year that Friar Vicente Ferrer brought his conversionist campaign to the cities of Ávila and Segovia. As usual with conversions that long ago, no one had any insights about whether the Arias elders had been moved by religious conviction, fear, economic opportunism, or some combination of these factors. They couldn't even say whether the baptisms had been in Ávila or Segovia, or what their Hebrew names had been before they converted. Their Christian names, yes: Diego's father became Gonzalo Arias de Argüello. His mother? People remembered her name differently: Violante? Vellida? Velázquez maybe, or González.

After that it got clearer. Gonzalo Arias and whatever-her-name-was had three male children: Diego, Juan, and Francisco. When each of the boys turned five, their parents sent them off to learn their Hebrew letters. Several people had testified how Diego used to boast that when he was a child in the synagogue he would go up to the readers' platform to recite the blessings over the Torah. There was a daughter, too, named Çinha. Somehow she had remained Jewish while the rest of the family became Christian. At least technically. When Diego Arias built his mansion on the plaza in front of the Mercedarian church in Segovia, he moved Çinha in next door and cut a wall in the garden door between the properties so they could go back and forth without being seen. Just one more example of how Diego Arias had no respect for the law.

They had learned substantially more about the family of Diego's wife Elvira González. Her parents converted about the same time Diego's did. For one thing, everybody—Jews, conversos, Christians—seem to have liked her.

The Arias Dávila Clan

Her parents, like so many of the Jews converted by Vicente Ferrer, had picked out the most common possible names to mask the fact that they had ever been Jews: Catalina González and Ruy Díaz. Elvira had three sisters, one who converted and two who didn't. But when the girls were little, Elvira's mother didn't make distinctions. She initiated all four of them into Jewish home rituals. When Elvira's mother died, her father sent the girls to live with their cousin Jacob Melamed and his wife, who turned them into proper little Jewesses. When it came time to seek mates, Elvira and her sister Leonor married other new-Christians, while Ursol and Çinha married Jews and raised their children as Jews. In fact, Çinha's son Moshe seems to have been the most Jewish of all of them: he became a rabbi. Fray Fernando had interviewed him four times now. He had come in of his own volition to talk about his family, and so far he had been one of the most informative people they had talked to. They hadn't yet discussed why he had converted, or why he had chosen to call himself Jerónimo de la Paz. He was so eager to implicate his family members that Fray Fernando did not want to frighten him off by asking too many questions about his own motives and practices. Those questions would come, in time. But for now . . . Jerónimo always portrayed himself as a sincere Christian, but still . . .

That whole nest of families—Arias, González, González de la Hoz, all of them—no matter how often they went to church, they were all Jews. And he would prove it, too, just as Fray Tomás de Torquemada had instructed him. Jews. The dead ones and the live ones both. Especially Juan Arias Dávila, the bishop. He was the thorn in all their sides.

Fray Fernando swatted at the insects that with the deepening twilight were beginning to swarm around his head. He would sit another minute or two and then head up the Eresma Gorge to where the path branched off toward the city. The last rays of the setting sun made the castle windows high above him glow like the gilded tabernacle on the high altar. Except that this tabernacle on the cliff never held anything near as precious as the host, just the king and queen. He crossed himself at the heretical thought, one that he would never, ever speak aloud.

The king and queen, the Catholic Monarchs: they talk about purifying the kingdoms, they set up the Inquisition to purify the kingdoms, but they refuse to do the one thing that would make that possible: get rid of the Jews. Fray Fernando could feel his anger mounting as he toiled up the steep path. It just doesn't make sense. As long as there are synagogues on every

CHAPTER 2

corner—Segovia has five of them, three within earshot of the cathedral, and each one more pestilential than the other—, as long as Segovia's mosque is allowed to flourish, how does anyone expect the converts to turn themselves into Christians? The monarchs ordered the Jews and Muslims to live in neighborhoods separate from the converts, but everybody knows that is a joke. The conversos can still pray with their unbaptized cousins; they can still buy their bloodless meat, light their candles, and spend all day washing themselves. Fray Fernando told himself to calm down: everything in its time.

He slapped at a sharp sting on his cheek and saw that his hand was streaked with blood. He bent down, lifted up the hem of his habit, and wiped his hand clean. Time to return to the city, or he would be late for vespers, and that would not do. He picked up his pace and motioned to the novices to do the same.

April 21, 1486. Segovia, the morning audience.

Ysabel Rodríguez de San Martín sat on the edge of her chair, wisps of gray hair creeping out around the edges of her black cowl. She had come to this audience voluntarily . . . well, more or less voluntarily. Like most of the witnesses who lined up to testify, her sense of religious duty had been activated by the Edict of Grace that the cathedral deacon, in the bishop's absence, had read out a few weeks earlier from the west portal of the cathedral. The edict offered the Church's grace to anyone who freely confessed to heretical acts or freely denounced people they knew or suspected to have committed them, and it threatened dire consequences, both on earth and in the afterlife, to anyone who did not. The deacon made clear that the Inquisition had no jurisdiction over the beliefs or practices of Jews and Muslims, but it did require them to denounce the heretical activities of their Christian acquaintances. Any reluctance they might have to come forth was reinforced by the rumors of public burnings of heretics in Sevilla, Ciudad Real, and Guadalupe.

Ysabel's clenched knuckles and her quavering narration betrayed her nervousness. After the introductions, the oath, and fifteen minutes of her disjointed testimony, Fray Fernando cut off her rambling with a direct question.

"Tell me, did Diego Arias or his wife Elvira González observe the Jewish Sabbath?"

Ysabel's voice strengthened as she plowed on. "Yes. Everybody knows they did. Diego Arias, the Master of Accounts, always. His footman, Antón de Córdoba, told me that Arias used to pretend to be sick on Saturday so he

The Arias Dávila Clan

wouldn't have to go to work. Antón saw it himself; I can't tell you how many times he said so. Diego Arias didn't come out of his room until nightfall, he said. And he ate nothing but raisins and almonds until after sundown, when they always served him a roasted chicken. On Sundays he made his servants work in his vineyards or in his house.

"Elvira González's three nephews who were still Jews used to take turns bringing the Arias family adafina for their Saturday dinner, and the nephews took turns leading the family in prayer. Master Jerónimo de la Paz was one of them; he told me this himself, and he wouldn't lie. He was so zealous about his Catholic faith that I heard that he said to Fray Alonso Henríquez that if half his body were Catholic and the other half were heretic, then the Catholic half would denounce the other."

April 23, 1486. Segovia, the afternoon audience.

The Jew Jacob Castellano, an official of the wealthy Medina del Campo Jewish community, came into the audience chamber. Tall and broad-shouldered, he cut an imposing figure in his well-tailored black robe and his pleated pants. After the usual formalities, Fray Fernando gave him his prompt.

"Tell us, then, did Diego Arias pray Jewish prayers?"

Castellano showed no hesitation. "Of course he did. It's how he was raised."

"And you know that because . . . "

"I remember one time when I was about twelve, maybe a little older. Diego Arias Dávila came to Medina. He always used to stay with Francisco Ruiz and Gómez González, in their house in front of San Francisco Church. My master Meir ibn Farax—he's dead now—went to see him. I was there, too, along with don Yusef Abeata and don Zulema,—he later became a Christian; he's dead now, too. Anyway, we all gathered in an inside room in Ruiz's house. Since it was the Sabbath,—or it might have been some Jewish festival, I don't recall—Diego Arias took charge and ordered all the Christians who were there to leave the room. The servants, I mean; but the conversos, too, even though he was one himself. Arias looked around to see if there was some Christian who still needed to be thrown out. Then he noticed me. He could tell by my clothes that I was a Jew. He turned to the other Jews and asked them if I was a responsible kid, and they said I was. So he answered: 'Let him stay.' I recall that at that point a page came in and asked Arias if he wanted something to eat. Arias shouted at him to get out, and then he had the door of the room bolted. Arias climbed up on a bench near the bed and put a tablecloth over his head the way the Jewish chaplain puts on his big tallit before he prays. He began to sing a responsive prayer that we Jews recite on Saturday or on festival days when we go up to the reader's platform. He sang it just like we Jews do, and with as much style, and maybe even better. If my memory serves, it was the one that begins *Misurad colhay fasta cadis*. He chanted for about fifteen minutes, and after he had finished he climbed down from the bench. I heard him sigh: 'Ay, Jews, Jews. When you are at Sabbath prayers on Friday night and you are singing *Vay hod lo asamay*, you have put the cares of the world behind you, and there is nothing as good as that.'"

April 25, 1487. Segovia, the morning audience.

The witness was the former Jew Juan de Duratón, who lived in the village of Villafranca del Condado, near Segovia.

Fray Fernando's notes indicated that some months earlier Rabbi Yuçé Meme had testified how once an image seller had brought Arias the wooden statue of a saint and asked Arias how it looked to him. Arias answered Meme in Hebrew with a verse from Psalm 115: "It's very nice, *quemohén yhiyhu hacehem*, which means 'whoever makes idols will be just like them.'" That would be a good place to start.

"I've heard that Diego Arias had little respect for the saints or the Church. What do you know about that?"

"Well, Gonzalo del Aliseda—he used to squire for Diego Arias—I heard him say that one day Diego Arias's mule took fright at a statue of a saint that had been set by the roadside and Diego Arias had Aliseda tumble the statue into a gully."

"Had Arias been drinking?" Master Cañas asked. "They say that the Master of Accounts had a fondness for the grape, isn't that so?"

Duratón was loosening up now. "Let me tell you what one of the Zaragoza brothers said to me once. Early one Friday morning when he and Diego Arias were riding out to inspect some of Arias's property in Valdeprades, they ate some blood sausages for breakfast. When the sun came up Diego Arias began to chant the morning *beracha* in Hebrew, and Zaragoza asked him, 'My lord, what is this?' Zaragoza told me that Arias answered, 'Go on, you know there is no other Law but this one.' He said that Arias had drunk a lot of wine with the sausages, so he couldn't tell if it was the wine speaking or if Arias was out of his mind.

The Arias Dávila Clan

"Since the village of Valdeprades belonged to Diego Arias, Arias had ordered that the Valdeprades church be repaired. So when they got there Arias demanded to know what that church was called. When they told him it was Santa Catalina, he shouted: 'Get that woman out of there, Goddamn it! When they're tired of visiting the brothels they turn them into saints. Get her out of there, and get me a macho saint.' But evidently they didn't do it, because the statue of Santa Catalina went up over the door. So then later, in the winter, Arias rode out there to see how the work was going. There was a huge storm, with wind and hail. It was so strong that Arias thought the storm might kill him before he even reached the church. When he finally got there he asked people to tell him the name of the *santo* over the door, and they said to him, 'It's not a *santo*, it's a *santa*.' Then Diego Arias ordered them to take her out of there and set him up a macho saint, because on that old whore's account he had nearly died.

"Arias couldn't stand those images. Another time he saw a statue of a saint alongside the roadway, and he knocked it down and dragged it and beat it with his sword shouting, 'Go to the church, Goddamn it! Don't stand there assaulting men along the highway!'"

Fray Fernando struggled to maintain his habitual deadpan expression. "So we can assume that Arias did not speak well of the saints?"

"No, or of our Lord Jesus, either. I remember my father saying that one time one of Diego Arias's account clerks married his daughter to someone Arias didn't like and Arias went to the wedding with a thunderous face and struck terror into his poor clerk who quaked: 'Oh, my lord, for the love of Jesus Christ, please pardon me!' To which Diego Arias replied: 'For the love of God, maybe. Don't you think God will be upset if I don't invoke him instead of Jesus Christ who was the son of a whore.' It was a scandal. My father was there and heard him say it.

"Diego Arias hated priests. Well, not all priests, not his son Juan, the bishop, but priests in general. And he thought that Christian prayer was totally useless. I once heard Friar Alonso Henríquez—he used to be a Jew, too, before he joined the Mercedarians—say that when Gonzalo García de Llerena told Diego Arias that he intended to become a Mercedarian, Diego Arias told him to wise up. He said that even though he and his wife, Elvira, were going to be buried in the Mercedarian church in Segovia, he wasn't doing that because he expected any help in the afterlife from the friars or their prayers. He was doing it because the Mercedarian church was always crowded, so that even if people didn't know where his soul was, at least they would know where his body was. Arias said that if there really were someplace after this world for a person's soul, the friars' prayers wouldn't be of any value. What would matter would be the Jews' prayers, because right behind the Mercedarian church there is a synagogue."

This morning's audiences had run late. If they walked back to the Dominican monastery in whose refectory they generally took their lunch, the friars would have finished by the time they arrived. He instructed one of the bailiffs to bring them some bread and cheese and a bottle of that Cuéllar wine that they sold in the plaza at the end of the street. Fray Fernando had canceled this afternoon's session; he wanted to use the time to review with Master Cañas what they had learned about the Arias family over the past few months, to highlight the inconsistencies, to explore what lines of inquiry might now be most fruitful, to determine who else should be summoned to testify.

Once the plates were cleared and the last of the wine poured into their goblets, they reviewed their notes. Diego Arias had been dead for twenty-one years now, and people's recollections of him were blurred. The most telling anecdotes had clearly drifted into the realm of fable. Still, he and Master Cañas agreed that there was much of which they could be reasonably sure.

Diego Arias may have been a corrupt, power-hungry Judaizer, but he was always colorful. Diego Arias's rise from humble nobody to King Enrique IV's chief tax collector was nothing short of meteoric. As a young man, the story went, he earned his living as an itinerant spice dealer in the small villages around Segovia. Dismounting in the plaza, he would draw a crowd by singing Moorish ballads before unpacking his saddlebags to display his wares. He must have been very, very successful, because by the time he was thirty he had amassed sufficient money and prestige to purchase a seat on the Segovia City Council. Somewhere along the way he came to the notice of the powerful Marqués de Villena, one of young Crown Prince Enrique's key advisors. Villena put Diego in charge of collecting Enrique's rents and fees in the Segovia region. Arias skimmed enough, and invested his gleanings wisely enough, to become in short order a very rich man. And that combination of talent and wealth brought him to King Enrique's notice as well.

Fray Fernando and Master Cañas were certain of at least the main points of what they had been told. They also made note of the persistent rumor that there may have been a physical attraction between the handsome, honey-voiced tax farmer and the prince. Master Cañas put it bluntly: "I don't know whether they slept together, but King Enrique wasn't much for the ladies, was he? And Arias, he'd do damn near anything to get ahead, that's as clear as crystal."

Fray Fernando suppressed a smile. It's a good thing Master Cañas lets me ask all the questions in the audiences. With his mouth . . .

Whether the rumors of pederasty were true or not, unquestionably Arias had prospered in the prince's service as his personal secretary, the administrator of his properties, and the supervisor of his network of Jewish and converso tax collectors. He even supervised the prince's zoo. When the prince finally ascended to the throne in 1454 as King Enrique IV, he showered Arias with titles, benefices, and income-producing properties in more than a hundred Castilian towns. Arias controlled Segovia's weekly street market, the municipal slaughterhouse, and both the Christian and Jewish butcher shops. As Master of Accounts he was superbly positioned to wield power and to enrich himself, both of which he did.

The most annoying thing about the man was that he had no shame, no sense of propriety, let alone modesty. He built himself a tower house facing the Plaza de los Huertos, on the highest point in the city, right in the middle of the neighborhood where the nobles and rich Christian merchants had built their houses. His tower was higher than any of theirs, high as a church steeple, higher even than the dungeon tower in the royal castle at the west end of the city. The man just did not know his place.

After yesterday's audience he and Master Cañas had stepped into the Church of La Merced to say a brief prayer and deliver a message to the parish priest. There, right on the side of the main altar, was the burial chapel that Arias had built for himself and his family. It was a monument to Diego Arias's egotism. His first wife, Juana Rodríguez, had died young and childless. Did the inscription on her niche say anything nice about her, that she had been a faithful, loving, Christian wife? No. It was all about Diego's social status:

> Sepulcher of Juana Rodríguez, wife of Diego Arias de Ávila, Master of Accounts of the great high Prince, son of the great King Juan of Castilla, and of his Council, and secretary of our lord the King and councilman of this city.

Next to it was the tomb of Diego Arias's second wife, Elvira González, whom he married around 1430. Elvira was the mother of his three children and his constant companion until her death in 1463. But as far as this sepulcher was concerned, she too was a cipher:

> Here lies Lady Elvira González, wife of Diego Arias Dávila, Chief Master of Accounts and Chief Treasurer of our lord King Enrique IV, of his kingdoms, his properties, his princely domains, of the Chivalric orders of Santiago and Alcántara, and of his Council; Chief Recorder of Grants and Titles, Councilman of Toledo, Madrid, and Segovia; lord of Alcobendas, Villaflor, Casasola, San Agustín, Pedrezuela, and Villava.

"Don't mess with me!" the damn thing shouted. "I have the king's ear." Well, for all that, the worms had them both now.

April 26, 1487. The morning audience.

Master Cañas sat in his accustomed place at the side of the long table. He and Fray Fernando waited quietly for the bailiff to escort this morning's deponent into the audience chamber. Fray Fernando's thoughts wandered back to the previous afternoon.

Diego Arias was not the issue. He and Elvira González had been dead for some twenty years anyway. The Inquisition could dig up their bones and confiscate their property, which they undoubtedly would, but the man himself was beyond reach. No doubt burning in Hell. The issue, Fray Fernando reminded himself, was his son Juan Arias Dávila, the bishop. If they could find some way to prove that the bishop followed the Law of Moses, that he was a heretic wolf in cleric's clothing . . . And to do that, he and Master Cañas had agreed as they walked out of the church, for that Elvira González was the key. She had run the Arias household. She still had Jewish relatives all over the province of Segovia. And, most important, she was the bishop's mother, the teacher of his childhood.

Fray Fernando was well aware that Bishop Arias knew that they were attacking him through his family. The bishop had done all he could to quash the investigation. He had pushed his allies to intercede with Queen Isabel. He had petitioned Pope Innocent VIII to pull the investigation into the Curia, arguing that the papacy had to protect its exclusive jurisdiction over any matter involving one of the bishops. But somehow, Fray Fernando didn't know how, the Inquisition had prevailed. Torquemada himself had urged him to pursue with vigor any scrap of information that might implicate the bishop.

The Arias Dávila Clan

Fray Fernando had high hopes for this morning's witness. Master Jerón-imo de la Paz, the former rabbi who was Elvira's nephew, took his seat. He had been baptized in the early 1450s. This was his fifth voluntary deposition in a little over a year. He was what the Jews and Judaizing new-Christians called a *malsín*, an informer, a stool pigeon, and he had few friends now among the Jewish community. Affable, loquacious, and eager to tell them everything he knew about Segovia's conversos. He was also, Fray Fernando felt certain, a hypocrite par excellence. A double turncoat, defiling both his abominable Judaism and his Christianity. Fray Fernando marveled that no one had stuck a knife in his back long before this. If someone didn't kill Master Jerónimo first, the inquisitor was sure that his Judaizing activities would eventually lead him to the stake. For now, though, he was useful. The inquisitors were unlikely to find a witness who knew more about the Arias family and who was more willing to tell them every detail of what he knew. No threats for this one: only smiles. You catch more flies with honey . . .

"Master Jerónimo, how good to see you again."

"Your Grace."

"I take it you have recalled more details about your aunt Elvira's family and you are meeting your obligations to our Holy Mother Church by coming in to tell us what you know?" This was not a question but a statement of fact, as both Fray Fernando and Master Jerónimo were well aware.

As the morning wore on, Master Jerónimo rambled through stories that Fray Fernando had already heard dozens of times. The man was a cornucopia, but he just wouldn't focus! Perhaps if Fray Fernando steered the conversation toward the Arias's holiday observances. Young Juan must have taken part in those. The inquisitor glanced at the notes he had jotted down the previous night while reviewing the files. Several witnesses had reported bringing matza each year to Elvira's house at Passover. Fátima, a Muslim slave in the house-hold, had told them that when Elvira got older her brother-in-law Efraín de Vides used to send a dozen unleavened cakes each year at Passover for Elvira to eat, and how they used to break them up into crumbs for Elvira because by then she had lost most of her teeth. Other household servants had told them how Elvira sent leavened bread and lettuce to her Jewish relatives after Passover.

Fray Fernando was sure that this was a subject that Master Jerónimo, as Elvira's nephew, must know a great deal about.

"Master Jerónimo, tell us more about how your aunt Elvira celebrated the Jewish festivals. Passover, Purim, Yom Kippur. You used to celebrate with them, didn't you?"

"Yes I did, at least sometimes. The whole family did." A smile crept across Master Jerónimo's face as his mind traveled back over thirty years. "Everybody liked Passover the best. Diego Arias's wife used to invite us to her house to eat unleavened bread with her. All her relatives. When Diego Arias built his tower house on top of the hill by the market, he had them put in an enormous oven, right in the middle of the house. And when Elvira's Jewish relatives came to use it they would stay to eat lunch with her. Every woman brought her own dough to be baked, and each one gave Diego Arias's wife a few of the little unleavened cakes. Three or four different women used to go each time; most of them were Elvira's sisters and nieces. Who were they, you ask? Well, her sister Ursol, that's Efraín de Vides's wife; and of course my mother, Leticia; Ursol's daughter Luna, the one who married Mosén Zaragoza. That's all . . . no, and Esther, too. Prex's wife."

"Even though Elvira was a Christian, she let the Jews keep coming to her house?"

"Of course. They were family, and 'blood is thicker than the water of baptism,' as we say. Elvira didn't care if they were Jews. Just the opposite. When one of her nephews wanted to become Christian, she tried to talk him out of it, and then she had his parents lock him in his house so he couldn't go to the priests. She tried to talk me out of converting, too.

"There were always Jews at Elvira's house. On the Sabbath, on the holidays: Passover, Yom Kippur. They liked to play with Elvira's kids. Elvira kept the Great Fast as strictly as any Jewess could keep the Law of Moses.

"The children took part, too?"

"Ysabel, Pedro, and Juan, always. At least when they were little. When the boys got older . . . sometimes. Sometimes they were away. I don't recall exactly.

"Go on. You were saying about Elvira . . . "

Elvira, yes. My aunt Ursol and my mother Leticia used to consider their sister a good Jewess because they knew that she fasted the days that the Jews fast and she observed everything that followers of the Law of Moses observe. When I used to go to Elvira's house on some festival day, Elvira would ask me which holiday it was. I would tell her, and then she'd ask me what prayer the

Jews were saying on that festival, and I would recite it for her and she would listen. I know she really enjoyed listening to them because sometimes she would have me chant them twice.

"I don't mean to say that Elvira didn't know any Jewish prayers because that wasn't the case. Lots of people heard her praying. In fact, they used to gossip to me about it. Abraham Trancas told me that he had seen Elvira praying the Shema in the evening when they ring the bell for Ave María. That's how she knew it was time. And Catalina Sánchez—she used to run errands over to the Arias's house when she was a teenager,—she said that one time she saw Elvira standing with her face turned toward the wall reciting some words that Catalina could not understand. She said Elvira was bobbing her head up and down."

Master Jerónimo's own head bobbed up and down as he recalled this incident. Miming Elvira's actions? Returning unconsciously to the time when he was a Jewish rabbi and prayed in this fashion? This was going splendidly. Sometimes interrogating a willing witness was like chatting with an old friend.

"You saw these things, too, I presume?"

"Back when I was still a Jew? Yes, of course. One time, late at night, Elvira came to my father Isaac's house and my mother, Letiçia, came out to the doorway to whisper with her. Then the two of them left the house together. I ran after them, and I asked my mother where they were going at such a late hour? And she answered, 'Don't be so loud, don't say anything; we're going to the bathhouse where we make our *tibulá*.' They were in the mikvah for about an hour.

"I'll tell you something else. Elvira used to mourn for her dead relatives the way the Jews do. When Elvira's sister Ursol died, Lope González's wife Lucía went by her house and the door was open and she saw that there was somebody inside. She found Elvira sitting there with her head down and an old rag drawn around her face. Lucía told me she scolded Elvira and asked her what kind of person she was, a Jew or a Christian, to be sitting there contrary to our Christian law. Elvira answered that because it was her sister, her death hung heavy on her. That's why she was sitting that way. Then she begged Lucía not to say anything."

Master Jerónimo stopped to clear his throat. He seemed hoarse from so much talking. Master Cañas brought the jug from the floor by the window. He poured some water into a glass for Master Jerónimo. When Master Jerónimo could speak again, Fray Fernando picked up the thread.

"So Elvira was really close to her Jewish family, then, even after she accepted the Law of Christ?"

"Don't forget that she converted when she was just a child. Anyway, Jew or Christian, it didn't make any difference to her. Was she close to her Jewish relatives? You can't get much closer. And they were fond of her. Her cousins used to call her a really good *anuza*. I think they said that because Elvira tried to eat only kosher food, the way the Jews do. I know that she once asked a group of Jews if they had good meat to sell and if she could buy some. They asked her why didn't she buy her meat from some Christian butcher? Elvira made a sour face and said, 'No. I want good meat, not that other stuff.' She always had to have her adafina on Saturdays, too."

Fray Fernando cut him off. They had already heard so much about Elvira González's kosher-keeping habits that they didn't need any more of that. Time to try another tack.

"You told us that Elvira González was a charitable woman. You mean with Jews, I assume."

"Of course with Jews. She had a special place in her heart for poor girls whose parents couldn't scrape together a dowry. She gave Moshe Zaragoza seventy florins for his daughter's wedding. I hear the family bought part of the trousseau with that money. She also gave some cloth to a woman in Magaña for some Jewish girl to get married. She had me take it to them. I don't recall the girl's name. All together the cloth must have been worth a florin.

"Diego Arias's wife supported the synagogues pretty handsomely, too. She was always giving them things: a tallit for the cantor of the Segovia synagogue, a Torah cover for Madrid, a silver breastplate to hang on the Torah of I don't remember where. The Jews always need good oil for the synagogue lamps, and you know how expensive that is. You could count on Elvira González to provide it in Ávila, Turégano, or wherever. Here in Segovia she used to send oil every Friday night, sometimes by the barrel or the half barrel. She would even pay the bill when other people donated oil. But she always kept track of things. Simuel Meme told me that once she gave him twenty or thirty reales for oil and said to him, 'I'm giving this money to you because I know you'll do this for me, because when I give it to doña Luna she never follows through.'

"Let me tell you a story that I heard from Simoel Lumbroso, a Jewish friend of Master Semaya, King Enrique's physician, about something that happened when he was about fifteen years old. It was early one evening, just

The Arias Dávila Clan

before the beginning of Yom Kippur. Diego Arias's wife and their son don Juan Arias—he wasn't bishop yet; the appointment came a year after that—called Master Semaya to their house because they wanted to talk to him."

Fray Fernando's ears perked up at the mention of the bishop. Master Cañas coughed discreetly and leaned forward in his chair.

"So that very night Master Semaya, with Lumbroso and Semaya's squires walking in front of them with lighted torches, they all went to Diego Arias's house and found Arias's wife and don Juan Arias in an inside room with Elvira's brother don Efraín de Vides, Rabbi Simuel de Vides, and a lot of other Segovian Jews. After they had talked for a while they came out and the Jews all embraced Master Semaya and they all asked pardon of each other. Eventually everyone left, except Master Semaya, who was alone with Juan Arias and his mother. They talked for a bit more, some money changed hands, and then Juan Arias spoke these words loudly to Master Semaya: 'See that the clothing goes to whoever needs it most, and the rest of the money should go to the synagogue that they're working on now in Campo.' When he told me this, Lumbroso didn't recall whether they were building the Campo synagogue in Segovia or just repairing it."

Fray Fernando tried not to reveal his excitement. "Tell me: who gave the coins to Master Semaya, Juan Arias or his mother?"

"I can't say. Lumbroso never told me. He said that he only saw the coins in Master Semaya's hand, and he heard the clink of coins, but he didn't see which of the two gave them to Master Semaya. But it's clear that one of them must have."

"You're sure Lumbroso never told you which one it was?"

"I'm sorry. It was a long time ago."

Close, thought Fray Fernando, this time we are really close. It was late now, almost dark, and they had been at it for hours. Tomorrow he would take another deposition from another witness. There were still lots of fish in this stream.

Fray Fernando had not slept well in over a week. The large cell they had insisted he occupy in the Santa Cruz Monastery—as the lead inquisitor it was only his due—opened onto the cloister gallery. The ventilation was poor. He would have much preferred a room that looked out on the Guadarrama Mountains to the east. But the lack of air was not what was robbing him of sleep. That honor he owed to two quite separate irritants. The first was one voracious bedbug that he had been unable to catch and squash between his fingers the way he had thirty or forty others, a bedbug that had left his legs and back covered with red welts that itched mercilessly whenever his robe brushed against them. He had scratched until his legs were raw and crusted from the bites and the tracks of his fingernails. If the itching continued he would have to bathe, and he hated bathing. That was for Jews and Moors.

The other thing keeping him awake was the bishop. Over a hundred witnesses now, with enough information to send half of Segovia's former Jews straight to the fire. Evidence by the cartful of Diego Arias's and Elvira González's Judaizing habits. And those of their aunts and uncles, cousins and nephews. But nothing yet to implicate Bishop Juan Arias unequivocally. Confound the man! And his late brother, Pedro, too, and all the powerful squally Arias children with their tower houses and their greedy fingers, their important friends and their ready access to Queen Isabel's ear!

Bishop Juan was either very Christian or very careful. He was a prince of the Church, and he certainly behaved like one. Proud. Imperious. Wealthy, with the Church's money and his father's. So many people seemed to love him. Despite the fact that he changed things. That he rendered justice, even condemning people to death. The inquisitors had not yet found anyone who would denounce him, not even people who opposed his policies. He was the Catholic bishop, but even the Jews seemed to like him.

Even so, someday some witness would let slip some apparently trivial incident and Fray Fernando would pull the thread slowly, delicately, until he had the bishop right where Tomás de Torquemada wanted him. With proof that he was a damned Judaizer like so much of his family.

March 5, 1488. The afternoon audience.

Fray Fernando de Santo Domingo gritted his teeth and resisted the temptation to scratch his ankle one more time against the leg of the table. His skin itched, and his head was throbbing. The witness was Luna, Moshé Zaragoza's wife and Elvira González's niece. It seemed like she might pause for breath any moment now.

"I assume you know that Diego Arias, the father of the Bishop of Segovia, bought his Jewish sister a house right next to his, and she used to sneak through the garden to come visit him? She didn't cook much, so I used to bring her adafina to eat on Saturdays, and I . . . "

The Arias Dávila Clan

Fray Fernando interrupted her: "This adafina, you sent it to her, or to her son Juan Arias?"

Luna blanched at the question. "The adafina was for Elvira González. And for the Master of Accounts' sister, Çinha. Juan, never. Juan is the bishop!"

March 9, 1490. The Bishop's Palace in Segovia.

Bishop Juan Arias grimaced at the chaos of crates and trunks in his private suite on the third floor of the episcopal palace. Father Antonio de Nieva threw up his hands in frustration. Sweat poured from his ruddy face: he had been packing for several hours now. He was a head shorter than Bishop Juan but broader in the shoulders. After six hours of strenuous labor his arms were aching.

"These aren't nearly enough! I've had the sacristans turn out everything in the storerooms, but we need at least eight or nine more trunks."

"Can't you have some more boxes made?" Of the more than one hundred canons, presbyters, choristers, deacons, organists, sacristans, and secular priests attending on the cathedral, only Father Antonio was admitted to these rooms.

"There isn't time, Your Grace, not if you still plan to leave tomorrow."

Your Grace. Twenty years they had known each other, twenty years since the bishop had found in the young cleric a kindred spirit who shared his passion for educating the diocese's rural clergy, and he could still not get his friend to call him by his given name.

"I suppose you are right. We'll have to pare it down."

Bishop Juan walked over to the leaded window that overlooked the Street of the Jews that ran along the edge of the Clamores Gorge from the cathedral to the Mercedarian church. There was hardly anyone in the street, just three old men, their heads cowled, their yellow patches prominent on their shoulders, undoubtedly heading for the synagogue at the far end of the street. The tallest of the three looked like Jacob Castellano, the Jew from Medina whom he had known since he was a little boy. He couldn't make out the faces of the other two. But there was not one pastry seller, not one housewife on her way to market, not even a beggar. It was Friday afternoon, and the street should have been pulsing with Jews getting ready for the Sabbath. It must be the season, the bishop thought. With Holy Week approaching, the street preachers were stepping up their rhetoric, and it was prudent for Segovia's Jews to keep a low profile. Those Jews, that is, who still remained in the city.

"What should I take out? Do you want me to open the two trunks we have just sealed?"

Bishop Juan turned from the window. "No, leave them be. The embroidered surplices and pluvial capes will make good gifts, and the fifty bolts of Holland cloth, too." His eyes surveyed the clutter. "Empty that one over there." He pointed to a sturdy wooden box against the wall on which the boar hunt tapestry hung. "The *vihuelas* can go. I can always buy a lute for Cardinal Santino when I get to Rome. He'll expect something. The silver plate is more important for now."

Father Antonio removed the three vihuelas and set them on the cushions that covered the low bench facing the window. Carefully he placed the service of pitchers, enameled plates, and goblets into the box, wrapping each piece in soft cotton cloth. He closed the lid, turned each of the three keys in their locks, and handed the keys to the bishop.

"I'll have to get one of the sacristans to help me carry that one downstairs. And those." He pointed to the two iron strongboxes resting in the corner.

"That one holds the bullion. You can have the men carry it down, but don't let it out of your sight. The little one is empty, but I'll fill it tonight and take care of it myself."

Father Antonio de Nieva nodded to show that he understood the instructions. Curious as he was, he knew that if the bishop did not volunteer anything it was better not to ask questions. Maybe later, when they were on the road.

Bishop Juan turned to the window again.

After dark, that's when he would go. To the Mercedarian church, to his parents' burial niche on the Epistle side of the apse, where the bones of Diego Arias and Elvira González lay awaiting the resurrection of the flesh at the End of Days. Presuming that no one ordered them exhumed and burned in the meantime.

They would be safer in Rome.

⋇

November 7, 1763. Sevilla.

Your Grace,

Given the delicacy of your position in the Viceroy's court in Perú, Your Grace requested that I be discreet in my inquiries into the

The Arias Dávila Clan

origins of the ancestors of your daughter's proposed fiancé, Lieutenant Miguel Ángel Arias González de la Hoz. Specifically, you have importuned me to investigate the possibility of heresy and stain of Semitic blood rumored to be associated with the Arias and González de la Hoz families. I am honored by your trust, and I assure you that I have been, as I will always be, discreet. Since for many years I was Inquisitor of the Holy Office in Perú, I have had access to the documents necessary to the resolution of these questions, and I have spent the past eight months in Segovia, Toledo, and Sevilla diligently pursuing information related to those two families.

My report follows. Let me say at the outset, that you have no reason to worry about the insidious worm of heresy burrowing into the Christian respectability of your family. The Arias and González de la Hoz families have been irreproachably Catholic now for at least five generations.

However, I must regrettably inform you that the taint of Jewish ancestry is incontrovertible. The distant progenitors of your daughter's intended fiancé were Jews who were only brought to the true faith during the reign of King Juan II in the early 1400s.

The Christianization of these converso families took time and was not complete until the third generation, subsequent to which all members of the family have been solely, steadfastly Christian. My report, then, will treat separately the Judaizing parents, their children, and the most notable of their grandchildren.

Here is what I have learned of the children of King Enrique IV's Master of Accounts, Diego Arias, his wife, Elvira González, and the Segovian councilman Gómez González de la Hoz, all ancestors of Lieutenant Miguel Ángel Arias.

Diego Arias Dávila and Elvira González were brought to the baptismal font as children by San Vicente Ferrer of blessed memory. The Inquisition documents I have reviewed demonstrate unequivocally that both husband and wife, despite their external show of Catholicism, were practicing Jews up until the time of their deaths.

The marriage produced three children: Pedro, Ysabel, and Juan, whom I will discuss in turn. All three were educated in the

Church. Yet at the same time they were exposed at home to the Judaizing activities of their parents, uncles, aunts, and cousins. The surviving documents do not indicate whether the two boys were circumcised at birth, but it stands to reason that they were not. Diego Arias wanted his sons to succeed, and he knew that the paths to power in the service of king and church could be too easily blocked—if you will permit me—by a casual call of nature in the presence of witnesses.

Pedro Arias Dávila:
By the time their son Pedro was born in 1437, Diego Arias was already a trusted member of the administrative retinue of Crown Prince Enrique. Thus it was only natural that when Pedro was nine years old his father arranged for him to be admitted to royal service as a *doncel*, a page and apprentice soldier. This effectively separated Pedro Arias from his parents and thrust him into a wholly Christian environment. Evidently the combination of young Pedro's engaging character and his father's wealth and influence led to his rapid advancement. Even while Pedro was still a boy training to be a soldier, Enrique, first as prince and then as king, Enrique IV, showered him with titles and administrative posts. Pedro became a member of the King's Guard; Paymaster of the Royal Household; Holder for the King of the castles of Madrid and El Pardo; Master of Accounts of the bishoprics of Córdoba, Segovia, and a dozen other important towns; and a member of the Royal Council. Each position paid him a substantial income and piled prestige on both Pedro and his family. Despite the bureaucratic implications of these titles, Pedro's life was spent soldiering, a profession at which he excelled. When he was seventeen he led mounted knights into battle on the Granada frontier with such little regard for his personal safety that people nicknamed him Pedro el Valiente.

In the 1460s Pedro Arias found himself embroiled in the Castilian dynastic wars that were precipitated by the presumptive illegitimacy of Enrique's designated heir, the war that eventually put Queen Isabel la Católica on the throne. I have examined the several chronicles composed by King Enrique's and Queen Isabel's royal historians. They concur on two points: that King Enrique rewarded Pedro Arias for his loyal defense in the King's name of the city of Madrid by granting him the castle of Torrejón de Velasco; and that later King Enrique had Pedro Arias arrested, falsely accusing him of conspiring with the Marqués de Villena against him, subsequent to which Pedro indeed switched sides. He perished in 1476 fighting for Queen Isabel in the battle of Guadalajara.

Pedro had married María Ortiz, a member of the powerful Cota family. Despite the fact that they both had Jewish grandparents, I have been able to find no evidence that either Pedro or María was anything but a committed Christian. They were highly regarded for their support of Christian charitable organizations. The only thing that the people interrogated by the Holy Office with regard to his family said of Pedro was that he often spoke of his deceased parents as having gone to the holy Christian Paradise. I am led to conclude that Pedro Arias's Jewish origin did not imprint itself on his character or his behavior in any discernible way and in no way impinged upon his career.

From the marriage came nine children. Of the three girls, one died young, one married an old-Christian and moved to Ciudad Real, and one became a Franciscan nun. One of the boys became a priest. One was born an idiot and died young and childless. The other four married, in each case to an old-Christian. I have not found a single hint that any of them ever engaged in any heretical behavior.

Two of their boys distinguished themselves as soldiers. Juan Arias Dávila fought on behalf of Fernando and Isabel's grandson, King Carlos V, in the Comunidades War of 1520, and for his service was awarded the castle of Puñoenrostro in the Toledan village of Seseña, of which he and his descendants termed themselves counts. He died in 1538. His heirs, with considerable success, perpetrated a new genealogy for the family that held the counts of Puñoenrostro to be descended from old-Christian families in the northern province of Santander. My investigations convince me that the new genealogy was a fiction; nevertheless, it held, and is today widely accepted. Your Grace may feel secure in not calling it into question.

Pedrarias de Ávila was by far the most renowned of Pedro and María's children. Like his father, Pedro, he was trained in childhood as a doncel. Also like his father before him, in his youth he was granted several honorific titles and the income that accompanied them. He married Isabel de Bobadilla, and four of their nine children—three girls and a boy—joined monastic orders; I have not been able to discern any challenges to the purity of their bloodlines. As I am certain Your Grace is aware, Pedrarias acquired great fame as a soldier. In 1507 he helped quell riots in Segovia and took part in a royal expedition to Algiers, where he fought so bravely that King Fernando granted him a new coat of arms. In 1513 the king, anxious to extend Spanish dominions in the Americas, named him to head an expeditionary force to the Isthmus, where Pedrarias captured and beheaded the rebellious conquistador Núñez de Balboa and conquered the territory we now call Nicaragua. Pedrarias governed the new colony until his death in 1531. I understand that the city where he was buried has since been swallowed by the Momotombo Volcano.

Ysabel Arias Dávila y González:
As I mentioned, Diego Arias and Elvira González's daughter Ysabel married Gómez González de la Hoz. Unlike her brothers, Ysabel seems to have refused to put aside her parents' Jewish customs and beliefs. In this she was supported by her husband, Gómez, whose father, Gonzalo González de la Hoz, had regularly prayed as a Jew with Diego Arias. Despite his origins and his very public Judaizing, Gómez was considered a man of honor and granted access to every possible privilege. You will recall that this was several years before the Catholic Monarchs had the wisdom to establish the Holy Office to correct such excesses. Thus Gómez González was allowed to purchase a seat on Segovia's City Council. He amassed a great fortune by lending money at interest to Segovian nobles, churchmen, and even the Monarchs themselves. He adopted—I haven't been able to discern on what authority—a coat of arms featuring an hoz, the sickle intended to imply that his family were not Jewish merchants but came from landed agricultural stock. He also built a splendid townhouse on Segovia's most

The Arias Dávila Clan

prestigious commercial street, just inside the city gate. I've seen it, Your Grace. The house is covered with massive protruding stone points, and everyone in Segovia calls it the Casa de los Picos. The González de la Hoz family still owns it, and their sickle is carved on the escutcheon over the door.

The Holy Office dossiers that I have consulted say almost nothing about Pedro Arias, but they are a gold mine of information about Ysabel and her husband. There is no doubt whatsoever that they were Judaizers. Gómez González de la Hoz prayed regularly at Diego Arias's house, just as his father had before him. Ysabel maintained her home just as Jewishly as her grandparents had: they kept the Sabbath; they ate only Jewish food; they observed all the Jewish festivals. Ysabel even had some of her cousins, who had been trained as Jewish scholars, come to their home to guide them through the Sabbath prayers, or read them stories about the Jewish heroes of the Bible like Queen Esther. Ysabel and Gómez's Christianity was a façade: they supported Segovia's Jewish community in their hearts and with their purses. They contributed oil for the synagogues' lamps; they gave money to Jewish widows and orphans. Ysabel helped dress her Jewish cousins for their weddings; and when some member of her family was dying, she attended to their last needs and then buried them in the Jewish fashion.

Once it was clear that there would be an inquisition in Segovia, Ysabel undertook a flurry of very public Christian activities: attending mass, praying the rosary, and endowing the construction of religious buildings. Let me give you two examples from the dozens I copied out from the dossier that deals with her family. Her devious masquerading fooled a great number of people, as you will see. Here is what a Jewish jeweler named Abraham Meme said to the inquisitors: "One day I told my father that Ysabel Arias, the bishop's sister, was doing much harm to the Jews, because she was so Christianized. And my father told me that I was wrong in thinking that, because Ysabel Arias was a good Jew in her intentions and used to give him money for oil for the synagogue and alms for the poorest Jews." Some of Segovia's clergy were just as perplexed about her. Here is what a Franciscan friar said of Ysabel's behavior as her mother, Elvira González, lay dying: "I believe that at the time that Elvira González died, she confessed and took communion and received the sacraments of the Holy Mother Church; I believe that because her daughter Ysabel Arias was a very good Christian and they say she was present at her mother's death. And I believe that she would be diligent in having her mother receive the sacraments."

Gómez González de la Hoz had two brothers: Alonso, whose children appear to have been good Christians, and Baruch, who never converted and left no issue. Ysabel Arias and Gómez González de la Hoz had five children, and only their daughter Ysabel broke completely with her parents' Judaizing. Ysabel was married young to Juan de Luna, who must have been either an old-Christian or a completely Christianized converso, for after his death she became a nun in the Order of Santa Clara. The boys were another matter. For one thing, Ysabel and Gómez had the four of them circumcised when they were infants. They had to have known that this would impede the boys easily crossing the bridge from their Jewish past to a Christian future. In fact, that probably was their intent, for I found that all four of the boys continued to Judaize. Even the one who became a priest, Diego, continued to pray with his father's group. His brother Alonso married a Judaizing conversa and maintained a Jewish home. Another of the brothers, Juan, was observed praying just before his marriage with Jewish tefillin, whatever they are; no one has been able to tell me. Something like a rosary, I suppose.

The last of the brothers, Pedro, the one from whom your daughter's presumptive fiancé is descended, served like his father on the Segovia City Council. I found several references to his strange manner of prayer—kneeling on the ground, facing east, raising his hands over his head and then bowing to touch the ground—, but nothing that specifically accuses him of Judaizing. He was, however, known for his strident disapproval of the Inquisition. He claimed that it was motivated by greed and was unable to distinguish between Judaizers and sincerely Christianized conversos like himself. Your Grace will be happy to know, however, that I have not been able to find a single word about any alleged

The Arias Dávila Clan

Judaizing activity among Pedro's children, grandchildren, or any other direct forebear of Lieutenant Miguel Ángel Arias.

Juan Arias Dávila, the bishop:
Although Bishop Juan Arias Dávila was not an ancestor of your daughter's presumptive fiancé, he was the most illustrious of the vast Arias Dávila family, and as such will be of interest to Your Grace.

Both his choice of career and his meteoric rise are somewhat perplexing. To begin, why did Diego Arias work so hard to maneuver his son into the see? I can understand why he pushed his older son, Pedro, into the king's service, why he destined him to be a courtier and a soldier. In those days, as today, that was the road to political and economic power. Juan was brought up by a mother who was a diligent Jewess and a father who disdained Catholic theology. His childhood was spent in the company of his Jewish and Judaizing converso relatives. Why, then, did Juan become a priest? Presumably his father chose the profession for him. But he had to have known that the priesthood would require his son to distance himself from the family, and to reject everything that his father cherished.

I have learned almost nothing about Juan's relationship with his parents. His professional life is well documented. Diego Arias secured a place for him in the Colegio Mayor de San Bartolomé, the most prestigious college at the University of Salamanca. There Juan studied history and canon law. At some point he must have received the gift of faith, though I have found no reference to when or how he became aware of the error of his family's Judaizing and the transforming power of the hope of salvation through Christ. However it happened, at Salamanca Juan dedicated himself to the service of God and society. Still, neither his religious convictions, nor his excellent education, nor his superior native intelligence explains his rapid rise in the Church. That he must have owed to his father's influence. Even while Juan was still a student at Salamanca, Diego Arias got King Enrique to make him a royal chaplain and a member of the Royal Council. After his graduation, Juan was elevated swiftly through the ecclesiastical ranks: presbyter, apostolic notary, canon, dean of the cathedral and finally, bishop of Segovia.

It doesn't appear that the cathedral's trustees, who normally elect the new bishop, favored the appointment, for Arias senior convinced King Enrique to get Pope Pius II to appoint Juan to the post directly, despite the fact that in 1461 Juan Arias was only twenty-four, four years shy of the minimum age canon law requires for an appointment to a bishopric. The parties seemed to have reached a face-saving accommodation: the pope named Juan administrator of the cathedral and the diocese until the legal requirement could be met.

Once he had put on the miter, it is likely that Bishop Juan broke completely with his family. Before 1461 Juan seems to have been an active member of his parents' household, which means that he could not have avoided their Judaizing practices. The Sabbath prayers must have been as familiar to him as the Paternoster. After 1461 I have not found even one documented instance of any Judaizing activity. While there are two marginal notations in the Holy Office's Diego Arias file that suggest that accusations against Bishop Juan Arias were collected in a separate dossier, I have found no trace of such a file, nor even any credible evidence that it ever actually existed.

In fact, the documents point in quite the other direction: that Bishop Juan Arias Dávila was an exemplary Christian. Within two months of his appointment he had founded two chaplaincies to celebrate masses on behalf of his ancestors' souls, just as if they had died as Christians rather than as Jews. Despite his father's scorn for images and relics, the bishop ordered the cathedral's foundations to be scoured for some trace of the saint's bones over which it must have been built, and when the miraculously fragrant bones of San Frutos were discovered, the bishop initiated a cult to honor him. And he didn't stop there. He founded a hospice for the poor, invested in rebuilding the cathedral cloister, ordered new stalls carved for the cathedral choir, and began constructing a new bishop's palace. He bought books. He founded a grammar school. In 1472 he imported a printer from Heidelberg to launch the first presses in Castilla. He underwrote the expenses of Castilla's first printed book, the records of a synod that he himself had convoked to devise how to increase literacy among Segovia's clergy. Listen to how the bishop's fervor for education permeates every word:

The Arias Dávila Clan

Ignorance in other people is harmful and in clerics it is dangerous, because they, by example, must teach other people about science and doctrine and how they are to converse in the Lord's House. The clerics can't even read a word of Holy Scripture. . . . No later than four months from today they will begin to learn, and they will continue without interruption for the next four years . . . until they can read and write competently. . . . Every Sunday in mass after the offertory the priest or his agent shall explain to his parishioners in Spanish in a loud and clear voice the principal articles of our holy faith including the Ten Commandments, the Seven Sacraments, and the Seven Acts of Mercy.

Certainly you will agree that Bishop Arias had a better understanding of how to bring the message of Our Savior to the masses of parishioners than do many of our preachers today. I beg Your Grace to pardon my frankness and my prolixity; I fear I have been excessive. It is just that I find the man wholly admirable. As a clergyman he was not a direct progenitor of your prospective son-in-law; but if the intelligence and passion for Christian service of this branch of the Arias family has in some way survived in him, the young man has just reason to be proud.

Bishop Juan was not a warrior like his brother, but he was a potent actor on the political stage. In the 1460s, like his brother Pedro, he initially backed King Enrique IV in his war with his half siblings, Prince Alfonso and Princess Isabel. After his brother's brief unjust imprisonment, Bishop Juan switched his loyalty from the king to Prince Alfonso, and even helped facilitate the prince's entry into Segovia in 1467. As a result, King Enrique banished Juan from the city. Until the war ended, Bishop Arias took refuge in the diocesan castle of Turégano, from where he continued his activities as bishop and politician. When young Prince Alfonso died, Juan was key in having Segovia declare for Princess Isabel. In 1469 he helped negotiate the marriage between the teenage princes Fernando of Aragón and Isabel. Finally, when Enrique died at the end of 1471, Bishop Juan conducted the ceremony that declared Isabel queen of Castilla. In gratitude, Isabel named him to her Royal Council and made him her personal secretary.

The biggest burr under Juan's saddle was that as bishop he could not disassociate himself from the conflicts over what to do with Castilla's Jews and conversos. Most of the converts, like the Arias and the González de la Hoz families, were holding on perniciously to their heretical ways. The presence of so many unconverted Jews was an impediment to the conversos becoming wholly Christian. As a politician of long and distinguished service, Your Grace can well imagine the plots and counterplots, the veiled threats, the fierce attempts to influence the king and queen and the senior clergy to this position or that. Expel the Jews? Force their conversion? Kill them? Require the conversos to abandon their Jewish ways? Enforce that requirement? Eventually the correct and most holy Christian solutions were found: expel the Jews and create the Holy Office to ensure that the conversos were truly and completely Christian. But those decisions did not come easily, and Bishop Juan Arias was in the thick of the struggle.

It was convenient, at least for Bishop Arias's enemies, to call his Christian loyalty into question. The first test came in 1468 when people accused several Jews and conversos in the Guadalaja-ran city of Sepúlveda of ritually crucifying a Christian child during Holy Week. Bishop Juan was put in charge of the investigation. When fifteen of the alleged perpetrators were judged guilty, the Bishop had to order their executions. For this and other actions the Jews of Segovia largely came to consider him their enemy.

Juan's severest test came when the Inquisition tribunal was scheduled to be established in Segovia. Should he oppose the move as an encroachment on a bishop's judicial powers? Should he welcome the inquisitors and participate with enthusiasm? Should he stand silently by and let events take their course without him? His parents were well-known Judaizers. Even though they were both long dead—Elvira González in 1463 and Diego Arias in 1466—, was he personally at risk? Should he pack his bags and seek sanctuary in some friendly foreign land? The documents do not indicate how he deliberated about these matters, but they make clear his decision: he threw open the doors of welcome to the Inquisition.

Your Grace may be puzzled, as I was, with this decision, and you will not be surprised to hear that even his contemporaries had a hard time accounting for it. The Bishop's dilemma was reported to the Holy Office most poignantly by a Segovian monk who recounted his conversation with a former Arias family employee named Juan López. I quote from the file:

The Arias Dávila Clan

When they told us that the bishop had invited the Inquisition to come to this city, I spoke with the bishop and I said to him: "You, sir, have invited the Inquisition to come, but I swear to God that it will break on your father and mother and relatives. You know that I lived with them and I know this and that about them. And So-and-so and What's-his-name do, too. So you should take a hard look at what you have done."

Juan López was prescient, as the protracted inquiry into the Judaizing activities of Diego Arias and his relatives so clearly demonstrates. Over several years more than a hundred depositions were taken, and while several dozen members of the Arias and González de la Hoz families were shown to be Judaizers, none of the deponents laid a verbal finger on Bishop Juan Arias.

With each passing month the bishop seems to have grown more desperate. His attempts to get the Curia to have the Arias case transferred to Rome—attempts that drained both the bishop's political capital and his purse—failed completely. The Holy Office rejected every assault on its jurisdiction. Queen Isabel, too, resisted Pope Innocent's pressure and in the end prevailed.

Bishop Arias then seems to have made several attempts to suborn witnesses to testify for him, or at least not against him. I have uncovered two of these. A man named Isaac Zaragoza reported that the bishop had offered him 1,000 doubloons to keep quiet, and threatened him as well. The other, the bishop's majordomo, Fernando de Fontidueña, indicated that he had been given 30,000 maravedís for the same reason. Even now, more than two hundred years later, those are very considerable sums.

Finally, in June 1489, several members of the Arias family themselves were ordered to appear before the Holy Office. Instead, early the following month they sent their lawyers, who insisted that all the Arias clan were and had been faithful Christians. The lawyers then attacked the jurisdiction of the inquisitorial court because the statute of limitations since Diego Arias's death had expired and, more important, Juan Arias Dávila, as a bishop, could only be tried by the Curia in Rome.

Early in July of that year the Holy Office lodged formal charges of heresy against Diego, Elvira, and Elvira's mother,

CHAPTER 2

Catalina, all of them long since deceased. The bishop's lawyers redoubled their efforts to shift the venue, but it was increasingly clear to Juan that he had become a pawn in the struggle between Pope Innocent and Queen Isabel as to who would control the Holy Office.

After nearly a year of multiple ineffective attempts to have the impending trial quashed, Juan Arias exhumed his parents' bones—was it to keep them from being publicly burned? To hide any physical evidence of a Jewish-style burial?—and took them to Rome. There he haunted the back corridors of the Vatican, spending down his remaining funds in efforts to clear his name, until his death in 1497. His talent, his strength, and his connections notwithstanding, the Inquisition effectively destroyed him through his family.

Once more I beg Your Grace's forgiveness of my ineffectual attempts to curb the length of this letter. My desire to serve Your Grace remains undiminished, and I humbly await your further instructions.

I deeply hope and fervently pray that you and yours are in good health, and that my modest investigations will help you resolve what I know is a matter of concern to your good name.

Your humble and obedient servant, . . .

The Arias Dávila Clan

Halló solo al Doctor San Juan su padre y le preguntó qué había de hacer una persona para que salvase, y le había respondido que ser buena cristiana y creer lo que la Santa Madre Iglesia . . . y le había dicho por qué se lo preguntaba y le había respondido que no más de para sabello, y su padre le había dicho que no se metiese en honduras, y considerando que su padre que era letrado y toda la gente sabían más que su madre sola, desde entonces se había vuelto a ser buena cristiana.

—Gracia Boix, 137

3

The Doctor's Daughters

BAEZA, SPAIN, 1573

The six daughters in this story—Leonor, Elvira, Isabel, María, Bernardina, and Juana—really didn't know their old-Christian father very well. Dr. Galeno San Juan was a prosperous, well-respected member of the middle class of the Andalusian city of Baeza. He had a thriving practice ministering to ailing clergymen, government functionaries, and the wealthy wool merchants whose elegant palaces with each passing month were replacing the one-story houses on the streets running north from the cathedral. He had loved his wife, Luisa, dearly, even though he thought her a little strange, and with the years they had gradually grown apart. When she died of a cancer in '71, he was saddened but not crushed, unlike when his three sons were taken from him. Now it was his daughters who were the pride of his life, even though he was generally too busy to spend much time with them.

Dr. San Juan's reputation for medical knowledge, his gruff, no-nonsense way of speaking to his patients, and his luxuriant beard had made him one of Baeza's leading authorities on all things medical. It is true that in recent years he had had to share the medical laurels with Dr. Juan Huarte, a philosopher-physician who had been favored by King Felipe himself. Despite their vast difference in status, Dr. San Juan found Huarte pleasant enough, and they had worked together when the plague swept through Baeza in 1571. Still, whenever he heard Huarte speculating on the relationship between the soul and the body, Dr. San Juan closed his ears. Such talk was dangerous. Not to mention—he sometimes admitted to himself—beyond his understanding. Still, enough people in Baeza preferred his own style of practical doctoring that Huarte offered no serious threat to his reputation or his income. Proof was that the Carvajal and Benavides families, the rival noble clans who were vying for supremacy in Baeza, still sent for Dr. San Juan when one of their children became ill. Besides, the city was growing so fast that it could support half a dozen doctors. Even young and relatively inexperienced physicians, like his daughter Bernardina's husband, Dr. Juan Infante, could make a decent living in Baeza. When he took time to think about it, which was seldom, Dr. San Juan considered himself blessed by fortune.

Although the doctor's family roots were in the nearby city of Jaén, after his graduation from the university at Alcalá he had chosen to practice in Baeza, a rapidly developing Andalusian town that was riding the crest of rising wool prices. The cloth makers of Flanders and Holland, whose finely woven textiles were prized all over Europe, had an insatiable demand for Castilian wool. Baeza was strategically located atop a long ridge between the summer pastures in the mountains and the undulating plains where the sheep wintered in the stubble left by the wheat harvest. It was rich in oil, too, provided by the thousands of olive trees that marched along the ridge in neat rows. Baezans beamed with pride as the wool and oil flowed out and the money flowed in. In its wake came architects and masons, carpenters, tile makers, iron forgers, sculptors, and painters. A measure of the town's growing importance was its new university, authorized and funded in 1538 by no less a personage than Pope Paul III. Its rector, Juan de Ávila, a descendant of converted Jews, had turned the new university into one of the premier centers for training reform-minded clerics and experts in canon law. The renowned architect Andrés de Vandelvira's construction crew was putting the finishing touches on Baeza's brand-new Renaissance-style cathedral of Santa María, which incorporated elements from the earlier Gothic cathedral and an even earlier Islamic mosque. In fact, the paint was still wet on the ornate wrought iron grille that Maestro Bartolomé had built to screen the choir. The plaza in front of the cathedral sported a brand-new fountain. Even a casual visitor could tell that there was money in Baeza.

The San Juan house, now nearly twenty years old, was roomy and tall enough to catch the evening breezes that made the hot Baezan summer almost bearable. Although it was located in San Pablo Parish, the city's most prestigious, it was two long blocks removed from the Calle de San Pablo, which was the preserve of Baeza's aristocracy. The stone-arched entrance to Dr. San Juan's house, large enough to accommodate a carriage if the doctor had afforded himself one, was flanked with discreet fluted pilasters and topped with an equally modest Plateresque frieze. The house boasted no coat of arms, but its message was clear: modern, if conservative, respectability; modest wealth; solidity. He felt nothing but scorn for the flamboyant palaces that Baeza's nobles were building as showplaces. The doctor, like most conservative citizens of the city, thought the new façade of the Benavides palace a spectacular, if tasteless, example.

It was the demands of his profession, Dr. San Juan told himself, that had left him little time to enjoy his nine beloved children. As in most middle-class Spanish families, when the children were young his wife and the family servants took charge of their upbringing. The twin boys were handsome, popular children, and when they were tragically crushed by an overturned cart just after their seventh birthday, it seemed like the whole neighborhood went into mourning. After the accident Dr. San Juan pinned his hopes on his remaining son, Diego. He sent him to Baeza's finest Latin grammar school and then, as a graduation present, financed a trip to Italy so that Diego, like the sons of so many nobles and wealthy burghers, could finish his education by experiencing firsthand the wonders of the Italian Renaissance. Diego visited Florence, Sienna, Rome, and the Aragonese kingdom of Naples. But Ferrara had been his favorite city, he told everyone in Baeza who would tolerate his enthusiastic tales. Ferrara was a booming merchant city with new brick buildings going up on every street: just like Baeza, only bigger. Duke Alfonso II d'Este was a benevolent leader who in the interests of his city's prosperity encouraged productive people of every race and religion to conduct their business there. On the streets of Ferrara Diego had seen Africans with black skin and huge earrings and Turks with their rainbow of turbans. And there were Jews everywhere, even some who said they had been born in Spain. In Ferrara the cacophony of German, Hungarian, and Polish tickled Diego's ears with sounds even stranger than those coming from the mouths of Baeza's Arabic-speaking bricklayers. Before long, when Diego started to crow about Ferrara his Baeza friends yawned conspicuously and tried to change the subject. But his six sisters hung on his every word. Bernardina, her black eyes as big as saucers when her brother spoke, never tired of his stories and would sit for hours at his feet badgering him for details.

When Diego contracted the plague, not even his father could keep him from slipping over the edge of life. Just before what would have been his nineteenth birthday, Diego was buried in the side aisle of the Church of San Isidoro in a large grave niche that his father had purchased for the family. His sisters wept for days, especially Bernardina, who was certain her heart would break.

The doctor, inured by his profession to the fragility of human existence and buttressed by his Catholic faith that assured him that Diego had joined his brothers in a better world, was the first to regain his balance. He felt certain that the girls would brighten up with time. Fate had dealt him a devastating blow in taking his sons, but he still had six wonderful daughters. Leonor, Elvira, and Bernardina all had hardworking husbands. María's husband, Diego Moreno, had died a few years back, but she was still young and could marry again, if perhaps not quite so well as the first time. Isabel and Juana would marry, too. Before long, grandchildren would fill his house with laughter. His sons-in-law would prosper, and he could look forward to a peaceful, happy old age. His colleagues in Baeza thought that Dr. Galeno San Juan was a model of contentment, although they did not envy him the task of finding husbands for his three unmarried daughters.

No one anticipated the snake in the doctor's paradise.

Years earlier, when he was a young man in Jaén, the doctor's father, a man habitually strapped for funds, had chosen as his son's bride a daughter of the wealthy Gutiérrez family. Luisa Gutiérrez seemed modest enough. She was agreeably plump, and with her reddish brown hair and sparkling blue eyes she was passably good-looking. She appeared to be level-headed. As the eldest daughter in a large family, Luisa had learned from her mother the art of managing a complex household. And she came with a truly impressive dowry. It is no wonder, then, that the doctor's father had not expended much energy in investigating the Gutiérrez's family history.

If he had, he might have discovered that his daughter-in-law Luisa, Luisa's mother, and Luisa's three sisters were all fervent secret Jews.

Bernardina's husband's moment of truth.

The catastrophe began that Sunday morning early in January 1572, when the bishop of Jaén read out the Edict of Grace from the pulpit of Baeza's cathedral. Dr. Juan Infante, Bernardina de San Juan's husband, who usually drowsed through the bishop's homilies, caught himself up with a start. It was as if the bishop were talking directly to him. "You must come to the inquisitors and confess your lapses of faith. You must report what you know of your neighbors' sins. It is your Christian duty to bring this information to the Church. You are obligated to report every instance of suspicious belief, no matter how trivial it may seem to you. You must come forward, or the fires of Hell await you. The Inquisition prisons await you. Hold nothing back, and you may accept the mercy and grace that the Holy Mother Church extends to you. You must come forward now."

Juan could not put out of his head the vision of the unrepentant heretics whom he and Bernardina had seen burned alive at last year's auto-de-fé in Jaén. A half-dozen terrified men and women were bound tightly to a row of wooden stakes. Juan had recognized two or three of the faces, their eyes wild with fear as the faggots were heaped at their feet. He had stood silently, in shock, while the crowd around him jeered and catcalled at the poor wretches. Solemn monks had raised crucifixes to the lips of the condemned, offering them one last chance to recant their heresies and be mercifully garroted before the fires were lit, but all six had remained stubborn in their refusal. The monks backed away. The bailiffs thrust their torches into the dry wood. As the flames rose, the heretics screamed and twisted and the odor of their roasting flesh permeated the plaza. Although it was all he could do to keep from vomiting, Juan could not tear his eyes away from the spectacle. It was as if he were witnessing the fires of Hell.

And now, as the bishop enumerated the external signs of heresy, the sounds and smells of that awful day seethed in Juan's head. It was hot in the church. The smoke from the candles and the clouds of incense spewing from the altar boys' swinging censors thickened the air. Juan felt he might faint. Mercifully the reading of the edict was nearly over. The bishop began intoning the familiar Latin words that concluded the mass. Juan could barely utter the responses. When the bishop finally pronounced the "Ite missa est" that signaled the end of the ceremony, Juan broke for the front of the cathedral, elbowing his neighbors in his rush to the fresh air.

Outside, in the Plaza de Santa María, his eye was drawn to the broadsides affixed to the portals of the cathedral and the façade of the university across the plaza. They must have been pasted up during the mass. It was the Edict of Grace again, with its list of the customs that were the external signs of heresy. The large rectangle of paper drew him like a magnet. He craned his

The Doctor's Daughters

neck to read over the shoulders of the jostling crowd. With an unease that deepened and turned to dread, Juan silently mouthed the syllables of each article of heretical behavior. A knife twisted in his bowels. Point by damning point the list drew a picture intimately familiar to Juan, a picture of his wife, Bernardina, and her sisters. As if the compiler had been sitting in Juan's kitchen and bedroom. The edict laid their lives open.

Juan could not catch his breath. He staggered back from the posted edict and slumped on one of the stone benches that fronted Baeza's university. He couldn't go home just yet. He needed time to think. Bernardina had been his wife for eight years now, and even at twenty-four she was just as pretty as on the day the priest bound them in wedlock. He loved her, yes, but after the first giddy year, things between them had not been entirely easy. If only they had had children. If only Bernardina didn't spend so much time with her sisters. Lately she had been eating supper with María or another of her sisters two or three times a week. The excuse was always that ever since María's husband, Diego, had died María needed her sisters' support. Bernardina always prepared a hot meal for him before she left the house, but Juan missed the close times they had shared when they were first married.

Increasingly they were finding it hard to talk with each other, as one topic after another became taboo. The barrenness: was it her fault? His? Was it God's punishment for something one of them had done? And it seemed like any time he said anything even remotely critical of his wife's sisters, Bernardina nearly bit his head off. Or, even more frequently of late, pressed her lips together and froze him out with her silence. And since their bitter arguments of a year ago, any discussion of religion had become impossible.

As Juan sat on the bench with his head in his hands he realized that it was all coming disastrously together. The Jewish customs listed in the edict. Bernardina's preference for her sisters' company. The fact that the two of them rarely ate together anymore. And the wall that Bernardina put up any time he mentioned the Church or its teachings. How could he have been so blind?

Bernardina was in trouble. And that meant he was in trouble, too; the edict left no doubt about that. He was guilty for having allowed her behavior to go on under his nose for so long. He should have put a stop to it a long time ago. The enormity of his sin weighed heavily on his soul.

Four days later Dr. Juan Infante made an appointment to talk with the inquisitors.

�֎

The Palace of the Inquisition was only one short block west of the cathedral. A delicately sculpted window crowned its massive arched door. The ensemble seemed designed as a stone sermon about the power and the beauty of the one true faith. Inside, two long audience chambers flanked the central patio. The prisoners' cells were in the basement. The Palace's tightly locked stairways and thick stone walls muffled the sounds from the prison but could not keep the unmistakable odor of unwashed bodies from rising into the audience chambers. A bailiff ushered Juan from the street into one of these hearing rooms and closed the door behind him.

At the far end of the chamber's long oak table sat two Dominican friars and a tousled novice, whose ink-stained fingers and the stack of blank pages piled on the desk in front of him identified him as a scribe. Fray Pedro de Zúñiga, at the head of the table, was a clean-shaven monk of about forty; a small man, thin, delicately featured, with a thick pair of spectacles perched on his finely chiseled nose. His long fingers were immaculately clean, their nails freshly trimmed. Somehow his overall demeanor seemed welcoming, and his warm smile reassured Juan that he had done the right thing in coming to the Palace of the Inquisition to cleanse himself. Fray Pedro motioned for Juan to sit in the vacant chair at the other end of the table. Fray Pedro introduced himself and Fray Teófilo, an old Dominican with white hair that set off the deep lines in his face. Fray Pedro was clearly the one in charge. He swore Juan to tell the truth, accepted his mea culpa, and invited him to explain to them why he had requested the audience.

"It's because of my wife, Bernardina. She and I were getting along just fine, with hardly any friction between us. I mean, nothing more than the usual squabbles between husband and wife. She has been a good wife to me. Eight years we've been married. We have a house on Calle de la Yedra. It is true that we don't have any children yet, but we keep hoping that with God's grace . . . "

"Something caught your attention, didn't it?" This was the last audience of the afternoon session, and Fray Pedro's patience was wearing thin.

Juan swallowed hard and plunged ahead.

"When we were first married, Bernardina and I would talk about anything at all. And her sisters . . . she has five sisters: two of them are married. Well, three, but Maria's husband died some years ago. Anyway, her sisters always used to come to our house and we would all talk until late in the evening. We saw a lot of them; her family was very close. Well, one evening after dinner we were talking about faith, and I told them about the coming of the Antichrist. I learned about it in a Sunday sermon, and some of my friends were talking about it. I said to Bernardina—her unmarried sisters, Isabel, María, and Juana, were there that night, too; and I think Leonor, she's the oldest—I said to them that I wouldn't want to be alive when the Antichrist came, and I wouldn't want to trust my salvation to him. I couldn't believe the way the sisters all jumped on me. Bernardina said that for her part she did want to be alive when the Antichrist came, and one of them—I think it was Isabel—said that a person could suffer just about anything for the sake of God. After a while, when the sisters went home, I demanded that Bernardina tell me what she had meant by that. But she said she didn't want to talk about it.

"Then the next morning, while Bernardina and I were still in bed together, she told me she felt sorry for me. She said she doubted that I would be saved because I was living according to a law that humans had made and not the law of God. When I asked her what she meant by that, she said that she had been wrong to keep secrets from me. And the Antichrist that we had been talking about the night before, well, she and her sisters believed that he would be the Messiah.

"Then I got angry and I screamed at her. Bernardina started to cry. She said that she was not as lucky as her sister Elvira, because when Elvira told her husband, Francisco Zayas, about her religious views, she convinced him to believe the same things she did.

"I was scandalized. I told Bernardina she was crazy and that talking like that was sinful and dangerous. But she didn't seem to care. She said that all the women in her family were waiting for the Messiah who had promised to take them out of their troubles and suffering. He would carry them to a land where they would not be able to sin. That's what her mother, Lucía, had taught her and her sisters. Her mother said that their souls could only be saved in the Law of Moses.

"I told her she was wrong, that Jesus Christ was the Son of God who died for mankind. He was the only Messiah. But Bernardina wouldn't have it. She insisted that Jesus was nothing more than one of God's prophets, not his son.

"That was the first time I realized what was going on. I didn't know what to do. But I began to take careful note of how my wife and my sisters-in-law were living."

"Tell us more about that. Give us some examples." This came from Fray

Teófilo, the Dominican who sat on the side of the table with his back to the open window. Only by squinting could Juan make out the friar's silhouette.

"Examples?" Juan clenched his hands in his lap to keep them from trembling as he collected his thoughts. "Well, the first thing I noticed was that on Friday nights they didn't do any housework, even if there were things to do. Instead they went to each other's homes to visit. One Friday night when Bernardina happened not to go out, I asked her why she and her sisters didn't do any work on Friday nights. She said because it was the start of the Sabbath. That didn't make sense, so I asked her, well, if that was so, why did they work on Saturday? Didn't their law require her to observe Saturday? Then she started to cry, and she answered that they didn't dare do any more than that because they were afraid of being discovered."

Fray Pedro motioned with his hand for Dr. Juan Infante to be silent for a moment. He flashed the scribe a look that meant "Make sure you get this all written down perfectly." The woman's husband was dangerously close to incriminating himself. Either he knew his wife's practices were Jewish or he didn't. He couldn't have it both ways. This might bear following up. The scribe wrote furiously for a couple of moments and then glanced up at his superior.

Fray Pedro directed the doctor to continue. "What else can you tell us about your wife?"

Juan clasped his hands so tightly that the knuckles were white. All that writing had increased his nervousness. Had he made a mistake to ask for this interview? He shifted in his chair.

"Go on."

There was nothing for it. To hesitate now would make them think that he was guilty, too, that he had something to hide.

"I . . . I remember one time, I think it was last September, Bernardina asked me when the new moon was. A few days later I found that she had set out my dinner for me in my own room rather than the kitchen. One chair; one plate. I got so angry with her that I grabbed my cape and I marched out without eating. This was even before Bernardina and I had the conversation about how she and her sister followed the Law of Moses. Much later, after it all came out, she told me that the day I stamped out was the tenth day after the September new moon, and she had been fasting according to the Jewish law. That was the first time that she actually said that she was Jewish. You know, we had been married for eight years, since Bernardina was sixteen, and I don't think I noticed any of these things before . . . "

The Doctor's Daughters

The transcript of this interview went to the regional Inquisition headquarters in Jaén, where it was judged sufficient for the Chief Inquisitor to issue an arrest warrant against Bernardina.

At midnight on March 7, 1572, a squad of five men, hooded in black, made their way through Baeza's maze of streets. One carried a lit torch; another held a coil of rope. When they reached Dr. Juan Infante's door the leader of the squad rapped his fist sharply against the wood.

"Open for the Inquisition!"

He rapped again, more loudly this time, the sound of his hammering echoing in the empty street.

Dr. Juan Infante, wiping the sleep from his eyes, peered down from the second-story window at the hooded men. "Oh, my God, they've come! I have to open the door. They can't have come for me!" Juan ran down the stairs. Again the pounding, five sharp raps that sounded like harquebus fire. "God save me."

"Open for the Inquisition!"

The voice bristled with authority. It must have wakened everyone on the block. In addition to the fear that weakened Juan's legs, a wave of shame swept over him. *All the neighbors will know! We're ruined!*

Juan slid back the plank that barred the door on the inside. The door burst open, nearly knocking him from his feet as the five men poured into the house. The tallest one spoke.

"In the name of the Holy Office, we've come for Bernardina. Get her."

Bernardina was already at the head of the stairs in her white shift. She was barefoot, and her long black braid reached nearly to her waist. Before she could turn to run, the tallest of the men rushed up the stairs and seized her. Another quickly tied her hands behind her back. She was keening, "No, no, no." Juan hadn't blinked since the men swept in. Another of the men wrapped Bernardina in a black blanket—Juan hadn't noticed that he was carrying one—and half pushed and half carried her through the door. It slammed. Just like that, she was gone. Juan sank into a chair. *Oh, my God, what have I done? What will happen to her?*

What is going to happen to me?

Bernardina de San Juan's story.

Two days had passed. Bernardina sat on a straw pallet in the semidarkness with her back against the rough stone wall of her cell. Somewhere she could hear moaning. She did not know where the sound came from or whether it was a man or a woman. It was not cold in the room, but she was shivering, and she hugged her legs to her chest. Since her arrest she had not seen anyone but the dour clerics who had spoken to her in the audience chamber the first morning. Yesterday morning! Before her life had unraveled.

"Think about your sins." That is what the monk at the head of the table had instructed her. "Think about why you have been brought here. Tell us how you have offended the Holy Mother Church."

Bernardina wanted to say, "I don't know why I'm here. There must be some mistake." But she could not make her voice respond.

"We will ask you again," the monk had replied. The tone of his voice had been friendly, almost conversational. "You must cleanse your soul. We will ask you again, and you will tell us why you are here, or else it will go hard with you. Think how good it will feel after you have told us everything and you have released yourself from your burden of guilt."

They had led her back to her cell. That evening someone had brought her a cup of water and the end of a loaf of stale bread. She had nibbled on the bread and drunk half the water when her stomach betrayed her and she doubled over and spewed into a corner. After a while she had stretched out on the pallet and tried to sleep, but there was the smell of damp and vomit and the distant moaning and the scurrying of small feet somewhere much nearer. She pulled herself to her feet and paced back and forth for a while. Then she sunk down again, leaned her back against the rough stones of the wall, and tried to empty her mind so she could sleep.

"Or else it will go hard with you." It clung in her head like a snatch of melody that wouldn't go away. What sins could she confess? What could she say that would persuade the friars to let her go back to her husband? She could not tell them about how she kept the Sabbath with her sisters. That would condemn her for certain.

"Or else it will go hard with you." Bernardina could not wipe away the sight of those wretched people in Jaén tied to their stakes at the auto-de-fé, their muscles straining against their bonds as the first wisps of smoke touched their nostrils.

What could she say to the inquisitors? How much should she tell them? What did they already know?

The fifth day the bailiffs brought Bernardina back to the audience chamber.

The Doctor's Daughters

It was different from the first one. The only furniture here was a long planked walnut table and four chairs, devoid of carving. A Dominican monk, by his demeanor the one clearly in charge, sat at the far end of the table. On one side another Dominican, a scribe, sat before a stack of blank sheets of paper. The room's only decoration was a large carved crucifix on the wall over the far end of the table. The Jesus twisted in agony, rivulets of painted blood trickling from its hands, feet, and side. The crown looked like it was made of real thorns. There was no chair for her.

Bernardina had steeled herself for this, sworn to herself that she would tell the inquisitors nothing, convincing herself that if she could only remain strong they would have to set her free. She stood at one end of the long table while the monk who had spoken to her previously—at least she thought it was the same man—told her that they knew all about her Judaizing, all about her sisters, all about her mother, all about her husband. For the sake of her soul she must purge herself of sin, and the only way to do that was to confess everything she had done, every sin that she had committed against the Law of Christ.

"But I haven't done anything," Bernardina protested.

"We will ask you only one more time," the monk said. "Then it will go hard with you." And he gestured for the jailors to take her back to her cell.

The next few days seemed interminable. Bernardina's thoughts circled round and round searching for a way out of the trap. I will have to tell them. They already know what I've done, and if I don't tell them they will torture me, and then I'm sure to tell. What do I have to gain by keeping silent? If I tell them, they may kill me. But I have to tell them.

Bernardina paced back and forth in her cell—five steps, turn; five steps, turn. Maybe my mother was wrong and the Law of Jesus really is the only way for my soul to be saved. God, I don't want to burn in Hell for all eternity. I want to see my husband again. If I tell them what they want to hear, they will have to let me go.

But they won't. I'm sure of it. They know too much. And if I say anything at all, I'll have to tell them about my sisters. And my aunts. If I confess all of them will be arrested, too. The friars will torture them. Still, maybe they don't know everything; maybe they're trying to trick me into betraying my family. My tongue is my sisters' enemy. How can I keep from killing my sisters? God help me to be strong.

CHAPTER 3

She stopped pacing, suddenly, overcome by a new thought. Which God am I asking to help me? Is it Jesus or his Blessed Mother? Is it the God of the Church? Is it my mother's God, the God who created the heaven and the earth? If I am asking the wrong one for help, will that condemn my soul forever?

Bernardina slumped against the wall. Her head throbbed with weight of her dilemma and the effort to devise some plan that would relieve her torment.

I can try to be strong, but even if I am, that is not going to help me now. The inquisitors undoubtedly know everything; I know they do. Besides, I could never stand the pain of torture. For certain, one way or another I am going to have to tell them . . . Mother, forgive me.

The next morning Bernardina informed the jailor who brought her the bread and water that she wanted to speak with the inquisitors. Nine days had passed since her arrest.

Fray Pedro de Zúñiga directed Bernardina to sit down. There was a chair for her now, positioned so that she was no longer looking directly into the light. As usual, Fray Teófilo was sitting silently with his hands folded. The scribe dipped his quill into his inkpot.

"My child, tell us why you want to speak with us. Don't be afraid."

Bernardina took a deep breath. "I have sinned, just as you said. But it's mostly my mother's fault. She's the one who taught me. When I was fifteen years old my mother told me that my grandparents followed the Law of Moses and that they kept the Sabbath. She said they were waiting for the Messiah to come soon to free the Jews and everyone who lived according to the Law of Moses from their suffering. My mother told me that I could not be saved under the faith of Jesus Christ.

"She and my aunt Elvira and my aunt Catalina taught me all kinds of things about the Law of Moses. Like, how to keep the Sabbath from late Friday afternoon and how I should light my candles early that day. She told me not to eat salt pork, or fish without scales, or hare or rabbit. She said that God would send anyone who ate the meat of a pig or a rat straight down to Hell. She was my mother, so I did what she told me. I waited for the Messiah to come. I tried to tell my husband about this, but he stuck his fingers in his ears. We argued about these things all the time."

Fray Pedro smiled sympathetically, and then asked, as though to confirm what she had said: "You say that you fought about these things with your husband, Dr. Juan Infante? That he didn't want to believe you?"

"No; he hated for me to talk about those things. I think he was afraid of it. Juan is an old-Christian, like my father. Lots of times when we were alone together in bed I tried to tell him that the Law of Moses was the true one, and I asked him to follow it. He yelled at me and told me never to mention such a thing again and to put all that business out of my heart. I wanted so much . . ." Bernardina trailed off.

"Your brothers were Jews, though, weren't they?"

"My brother Diego—he is dead now—he brought me an amulet from Italy one time. There was a folded-up paper inside it with the names of the Messiah, Emanuel, and other names of God. It was in Hebrew, he said. I couldn't read it. When the Inquisition came here I ripped the paper up and threw it in the river so nobody would find it. I suppose my brother Diego was a Jew. The twins might have been, too. But they were awfully young when they were killed, so I really don't know.

"You say that your mother, Luisa Gutiérrez, she was the one who taught you all these things, isn't that right?" Today Fray Pedro was the only one asking the questions. His tone suggested that he thought everything she said was quite reasonable. Fray Teófilo, the open window at his back casting his face into deep shadow, was merely a silent presence. In the brief pauses between questions Bernardina could hear the scratching of the scribe's quill.

"Yes, I learned everything from her. And from my two aunts. When I first became a woman my mother taught me how to clean myself and how to pray according to the Jewish Law. We always recited the Psalms without saying 'glory to the Father, the Son, and the Holy Spirit.' She taught me the blessings over the table, too, the ones she had learned from my grandmother. She said that before I prayed I had to wash my hands and my mouth, and afterward I could not speak with anyone until I had finished praying.

"You did go to mass, though, isn't that right?"

"Of course. Sometimes my mother took us, and she'd say that I should never worship the host as God because it was only a piece of bread. She said that Jesus Christ was not the true Messiah and that Our Lady was not a virgin when she gave birth.

"And your father?"

"No; the times when my father went with us she never said any of those things.

"Mother used to tell us all kinds of things about Jews. She explained that there were twelve tribes in Israel, and that nine and a half tribes were locked up between two mountains and would not come out until the arrival of the Antichrist, who was their Messiah. She said that the conversos and everyone else who converts to Judaism make up the other two and a half tribes. My mother said the Antichrist will take us all to a rich land where the crops never fail and where we will not be able to sin."

Fray Pedro leaned forward, staring at her over the top of his spectacles for a long moment. It seemed to Bernardina that he was running out of things to ask her. Maybe she had told them everything they wanted to know and they would leave her alone now. She felt that he was accepting what she was saying. But Fray Teófilo broke the long silence with a last question that suggested that he was still skeptical.

"What about your father, Dr. Galeno San Juan? You claimed he is an old-Christian, but isn't he a Jew, too? Or at least a Judaizer? With all this going on in his household, his wife, his daughters, his sisters-in-law . . . ? He must have known. He must have condoned what you were doing."

"No, not our father. He is a good Christian in every way. He was hardly ever home, but when he was he used to talk to us about Jesus. Though I don't think he ever did that when my mother was there. You have to realize that my father doesn't notice very much. I don't think he's ever even heard of things like we were doing."

The barrage of questions went on for another hour or so. At the end of the session, the bailiff took her back to her cell. Another jailor brought Bernardina her lunch: bread, a cup of warm milk, and a plate of beans that had been boiled with salt pork. This was the first substantial food Bernardina had seen in over a week. The pork made her queasy, but she thought that she ought to eat it. Maybe Fray Pedro would take it as a sign that she was putting her Jewish ways behind her. She mopped up every bit of the bean juice with what was left of her bread and pushed herself back on her pallet to rest.

She felt better than she had since that horrible night when the hooded men came to her house. Maybe Fray Pedro was right. Maybe recognizing that what she had done was wrong, maybe bringing her Jewish practices out into the open, was a way to give herself a measure of peace. As long as she could convince the friars that she had put all those things behind her.

As the long night wore on, Bernardina began to think that everything her mother and her aunts had said about saving her soul in the Law of Moses was turning out to be wrong. Everything she had been taught to disdain, to shun, the friars were telling her that was the right way to live. She and her sisters had all been deceived into believing that the Jewish way was true. It was not their fault. That's what had led her to destruction. She would convince Fray Pedro of the sincerity of her resolve to be a good Christian. Then the inquisitors would have to set her free.

The next morning they brought Bernardina back to the audience room and again directed her to sit at the end of the table. Fray Pedro actually smiled at her. Fray Teófilo's face, as always, was stone.

"You feel better, don't you?"

She nodded yes.

"Now you know how good confession is for the soul. Pour out all your sins, and you will feel better, much better. You believe what I am telling you, don't you?"

Again she signaled her acceptance.

"Tell us more about your father and your husband. Remember now, you've sworn an oath. Don't hold anything back."

"I already told you, my father was an old-Christian. He didn't know anything about this."

"And your husband, Dr. Juan Infante?"

"Juan, too. He is a good man, a good husband. We fight sometimes, but he loves me a lot. He knows about me and my sisters, of course, but he is a Christian. He doesn't do any of the things we do. Never."

Bernardina had a sudden thought. Juan was always so critical of the women's Jewish practices. His harping on it was often what started the two of them fighting. The inquisitors would be bound to interview him. Maybe they already had. What could he have told them about her?

Fray Pedro interrupted her musings with another question. "You said it was mainly your mother and your aunts who taught you the rites of the Law of Moses. Did they teach you anything else that you haven't confessed yet?"

This was the question that Bernardina had dreaded the most, the invitation to tell the inquisitors every detail of her life. She knew that everything that happened behind the tribunal doors was supposed to be kept secret, but word trickled out and was passed in hushed tones from one person to the next. Bernardina had been awake the whole night thinking about this

CHAPTER 3

question. She had no way of knowing how much specific information the inquisitors knew about her. She had no way of knowing who had denounced her. If she told a story that was significantly different from what others had said, they would torture her until they were satisfied that she had told the truth. The only way to protect herself, she had convinced herself, was to tell everything, to hold nothing back. And, if what the friars were telling her was true, it was also the only way that her soul could be saved. In the hours before dawn she had made her mental list.

Taking a deep breath, Bernardina plunged in.

"Well, one thing that my aunt Catalina told us was that when someone died we had to pour out all the water standing in the house because the dead person's soul would stay around to bathe in any water that it found. And when a person was dying we had to turn their face toward the east so they wouldn't suffer so much. And the shroud had to be made only of linen. We should have done that for the twins, but my mother was afraid my father wouldn't let her, so we didn't. We didn't do it for my brother Diego either, though we put a few scraps of linen into his coffin. It made my mother sad, and she used to cry about it sometimes when my father wasn't home."

"Go on."

"Here is another thing I remember. When the Council of Trent was about to end, my mother fasted for forty days and would not eat anything until after the stars had come out. She wouldn't speak to us during the day, and she said lots of prayers so that the Council would make all Christians follow the Law of Moses and praise God and not Jesus Christ because the Christians were all misguided. I used to fast, too."

"Used to fast?"

"With my mother until she died. And then later, by myself."

For the next hour Bernardina poured out a litany of the Judaizing practices of the women in her family. Eventually she slowed down. She knew there was more, but she felt dizzy, short of breath. She could no longer remember what she had said or whether she had begun to repeat herself.

"And for how long did you do these things?"

"I believed in the Jewish Law up until the night they brought me here."

The cliff's edge.

Bernardina's arrest in March swept through the family like an evil wind. Bernardina's sisters trembled to think who would be next. The Inquisition was on to them, but how much the inquisitors knew, and whether it knew about all of them or only about Bernardina, was a mystery. How many of their neighbors, their friends, and their servants had already been called in to testify? By twos and threes the sisters whispered together, their eyes darting this way and that to make certain no one was watching, their ears alert to any telltale sound.

When they were alone, each of the girls searched her memory: Who had seen her lighting her candles on Friday evenings? Who had noticed that she almost never worked on Saturday? Who, sitting next to her at mass, was aware that she did not speak aloud any of the responses that mentioned God's son?

They worried, too, about their father, Dr. Galeno San Juan. So upright, so respectable, so old-Christian. His daughters had all tried to keep their Judaizing secret from him, and he had never given them any overt sign that he was aware of what was going on. Could it be true that he never noticed? And if he did know, would his years of keeping quiet lay a large enough burden of guilt on him that he would remain silent under these new conditions? Or would his testimony be their downfall?

They couldn't ask him. Not now. It would be admitting to him that they had been living a double life, that for all those years they had been unfaithful to what he had taught them. Besides, since Bernardina's arrest they had scarcely seen him. He had busied himself in his work, leaving the house at dawn, returning only late at night, shutting himself in his office, turning his eyes away whenever he saw them. Was he afraid? Had he already talked to the friars about them?

And what about Bernardina's husband, Dr. Juan Infante? They all knew how he felt about their Judaizing activities. Would he be the one to open the door to their ruin?

The Holy Office had Bernardina, but she was strong, maybe the strongest of any of them. Still, the inquisitors had their ways. It was an open secret. The rack that pulls your joints apart. The water torture that makes you feel like you are drowning. The hanging torture that dislocates your joints. Would Bernardina be able to hold out, to resist telling the interrogators how the San Juan women spent their Sabbaths? Or how they ran their kitchens?

Each of the five women, half maddened by fear, kept circling back to the same question: what shall I do? Should I stay here in Baeza or flee? If I run, where could I go? I have no money, I don't have any idea how to go about reaching a safe haven. People talk about Istanbul, wherever that is, or Ferrara, where Diego had seen Jews walking peacefully in the streets. How could I get there? What language do people speak in those places? Would I be able to eat their food? Would any of my sisters come with me? Would the Spanish border guards let us out? Would the inquisitors chase after us? Can I talk about these things with my sisters, or would that just add to our conspiracy of guilt?

God help me, what should I do?

The Holy Office seized Bernardina in March 1572. It arrested Leonor, Elvira, and Isabel in May. María and Juana were taken in June. The girls were put into separate cells where they could not communicate with each other or with anyone else. Elvira was the first of Bernardina's sisters to be summoned to the audience chamber.

Elvira de San Juan's story.

Fray Pedro de Zúñiga asked Elvira to tell them what sins had led to her arrest. Elvira knew this question was coming and had prepared herself to deflect the inquisitors' attention to her brother Diego, who was safely, untouchably deceased.

She sat up straight in her chair, her elbows resting on the table, her hands folded. She looked squarely at Fray Pedro, her brown eyes—she hoped—projecting candor, willingness to cooperate.

"I don't really know why I'm here. But I suspect it is because my brother brought me an amulet from Italy that had the names Adonay, Shaday, and Paletín written on it. My sister Bernardina had one, too, but after a while we thought they must be evil so we destroyed them. That's the only reason I can think of."

Fray Pedro, glowering, informed her that she should think about her sins and that in the next audience they expected her to make a full and honest confession. The bailiffs led her back to her cell. At her second interview she continued to deny any wrongdoing. Again she was escorted down the dank corridor to her cell. Elvira expected to be called back in a day or two, but that was not to be. Instead the days grew into weeks and then into long empty months during which she swung between bouts of depression and boredom and fits of frantic apprehension. She replayed in her mind every detail that she could remember from her former life with her sisters: every holiday meal, every argument, every happy occasion. She dreamed about her aunts, too.

She could smell the stews simmering in their iron pots in the banked embers, waiting to be unsealed and ladled out when the women gathered on Saturday. She could hear the prayers they chanted over the candles they lit before sundown on Friday afternoon when their men were not around. Elvira wondered if her sisters had remained firm under the inquisitors' pressure. Bernardina would resist, she was certain of that. Leonor was strong, and would surely live up to the oath they had sworn to each other never to talk about what went on in their homes. But Isabel . . . "Veleta" was what they called her among themselves, because like a weather vane she always pointed whichever way the wind was blowing. No spine at all. Isabel was bound to give them all up.

Gradually Elvira convinced herself that further resistance was probably futile and that by now one or another of her sisters had surely detailed the girls' Judaizing activities to the friars. In July Elvira asked to talk with the inquisitors again. In the audience chamber she told the two friars how when she was thirteen or fourteen her mother had instructed her in the Law of Moses, and how she and her sisters had supported each other's Judaizing customs.

When the inquisitors asked whether she had taught these things to her husband, Francisco, Elvira vehemently denied the charge.

"Don't forget that you are bound by oath to tell us nothing but the truth, Elvira. We have heard witnesses who said that you did teach him."

"Let me explain. I never tried to teach the Law of Moses to Francisco. Never. But I didn't tell my sisters that. I wanted them to think that . . . that I was more committed to the Law of Moses than they were."

The inquisitors could not decide whether to believe their informants or her denial. So, as the law permitted in such quandaries, they ordered that she ratify her statements under duress. Four bailiffs carried her to the torture chamber and, as Fray Pedro watched, stripped off her outer shirt and began to tie her arms behind her in preparation for the *garrucha*, the hanging torture. The threat was sufficient to open the floodgates.

"Stop, please stop. Stop! I was not telling the truth about lying to my sisters. I beg you, stop. I swear I'll tell you the truth now."

Fray Pedro motioned the men to wait. The witnessing scribe took up his pen as the bonds were loosened.

"What's true is this: I did teach the Law of Moses to my husband, Francisco de Zayas. He didn't want to believe at first. He told me I was evil, stupid; that my soul would be damned. But after a while he began to think that

I was right, and he asked me to show him how to follow that Law. It took me a long time to convince him. But then, like me, he kept lots of the Jewish fasts. We recited the Psalms together without adding 'Glory to the Father.' When I saw that now he truly believed in the Law of Moses, I told him that my mother and my sisters also followed the Law, so he could talk freely with them. But he was afraid to, and he told me not to reveal him to them either. That's so that if the others were arrested they would not be able to testify against him."

The inquisitors had heard enough. No need to torture her now. They returned Elvira to her cell to meditate further on her sins. They would recommend a sentence to the Suprema, the Inquisition's highest council. Elvira would learn her fate at the next public auto-de-fé.

Leonor de San Juan's story.

Leonor, widow of the spice dealer Juan Gómez, was the third sister to be called to the audience chamber. At forty she was the oldest of the San Juan girls. Tall, somewhat stoop-shouldered, and with graying hair that she preferred to think of as a sign of wisdom, she believed herself to be the smartest and the strongest of the sisters. Because her late husband, Juan, had possessed a legalistic mind and liked to comment at the dinner table about who in Baeza had been arrested and what sorts of defense the accused party was mounting, she thought she knew a bit about the law. If her sister Isabel la Veleta could just for once manage to keep her mouth shut, then Leonor believed she had a chance.

At the first audience, in early June, ten days after her arrest, Leonor played the ignorance card and denied everything. At the second, in September, the inquisitors summarized for her the testimony of twenty-eight witnesses to her Judaizing, without disclosing their identities, as the rulebook dictated. Leonor thought she might know who the denouncers were, and she decided to try to impugn their objectivity. Canon law allowed her to discredit hostile witnesses as long as her explanations of why they were her enemies were compelling and were corroborated by at least one credible witness.

"Catalina López is my enemy," she began, "because once I beat her for breaking one of my best plates when she was washing our dishes." Catalina had served for three years as a scullery maid in the Gómez household. "My neighbor Teresa Alvar, who was in my kitchen at the time, is my witness.

"The miller Pedro Mojado is my enemy," Leonor went on. "I bought three sacks of fine white flour from him and paid him good money, but when I got home one of the three sacks was wormy. I demanded my money back, and he refused and called me an old whore. My witnesses are the brothers Manuelito and Pascual Pastor, who were serving their apprenticeship with Pedro Mojado at that time.

"Fat Manuela de los Pozos is my enemy because one day in the market she made eyes at my husband, Juan. I threw a cabbage at her and she jumped on me and scratched me before people could pull her away. Everyone was laughing at her. My witnesses are Martín Berruete, the knife sharpener, and Clara Hinojosa, who sells onions in the market."

Leonor did not know whether these three people, or any of the other twenty-five whom she named and attempted to discredit, had been the ones who denounced her. But better a long list than a short one. If she guessed right and the Inquisition lawyers believed her, that enemy's testimony would be thrown out. As long as Leonor did not lie, and had witnesses to what she claimed, the tactic was safe enough. And if all the accusations were disallowed, she persuaded herself, the Holy Office would have to release her.

But to her surprise, and then to her despair, there was no official response to her attempt to disqualify her enemies. No one answered her inquiries. In fact, no one but the jailor who brought food to her cell spoke to her at all.

For the next sixteen months Leonor sat in her stone box wondering what would become of her. She tried to call up in her mind the image of her daughter Leticia, who had taken her first wobbly steps just one week before Leonor was arrested. Leticia would be talking a blue streak by now. She thought that one of her other sisters, or her aunts, must be taking care of the girl, but she couldn't be certain. If all the family women had been arrested, then the child's grandfather, Dr. San Juan, might have taken the girl in. Or someone from the family of her late husband. Or maybe one of their neighbors. After all these months, would Leticia even recognize her mother? At first, when these thoughts began to blacken her spirit, Leonor struggled to contain her tears. But she no longer fought it: now when she thought of her daughter she just sat in one corner of the cell and sobbed.

Finally, in early February 1574, Leonor was called back to the audience chamber where the accusations of still more witnesses were summarized for her. Many of them touched on her deceased mother Luisa Gutiérrez's role in instructing her daughters in crypto-Judaism. Leonor felt trapped. It was time to give them something.

"I have no reason to defend my mother," she began. "In fact, I'm pretty certain that she did not die as a Christian."

"What makes you think that?"

All of a sudden Leonor felt herself overcome by the immensity of what she had started to do. The resolve drained out of her voice. "I . . . I never saw her working on Saturday, and sometimes she fasted, and . . . I don't remember anything else." Leonor trailed off. She should have prepared herself better for this interview. She knew that one day it had to be coming. At first she had rehearsed it in her mind. But after all these months the words had slipped away. Her mind was blank. Slumped at one end of the long oak table, she felt like she was drowning. She couldn't think of anything to say that would not implicate herself or someone she loved dearly. What had happened to her clever wit and her gift for words?

Again the bailiffs returned her to the cell that had become her home. A terrible lethargy overcame her. She had resisted for so long, and now there did not seem to be any point in it. All her defenses had crumbled. She wept to think that she could not protect anyone, not even the memory of her mother.

Ten days later, on February 25, 1574, Leonor asked for another audience and told the inquisitors how her mother and her aunts had instructed her in the Law of Moses. She enumerated all the Judaizing customs that she and her sisters had tried to follow as scrupulously as they could without their father finding out, and how she had kept some of the Jewish fasts even while she was in prison.

When they asked her why she had not confessed al this earlier, she replied with tears streaming down her face, "I really thought that you might set me free. And I have a daughter whom I wanted to keep from being called the daughter of a Jew. If you want me to confess all this publicly in the auto-de-fé I will. Only have pity on me."

Isabel de San Juan's story.

Isabel, the girl her sisters called behind her back "Weather Vane," had just turned thirty at the time of her arrest. She was the fourth to be summoned to the audience chamber. Tall like her sisters, and light haired, she had an engaging smile that rarely left her face, even though she never seemed to look straight at the person she was talking with. When she took her seat at the oak table, Fray Pedro de Zúñiga noted that she seemed confused, unfocused, as if her mind were somewhere else.

Fray Pedro commanded her to confess her wrongdoings, but Isabel said nothing because she could not think of anything to say.

"Tell us, why do you think you have been arrested?"

Isabel shrugged her shoulders, as if to say that she had no idea at all.

They sent her back to her cell.

But a few days later, at her second hearing, when they told Isabel of some of the charges against her, she had a better idea of what the inquisitors wanted: names and details. Since they obviously knew everything already, she would ingratiate herself with them by holding nothing back.

Like her sister Elvira, Isabel first asserted that she must have been imprisoned because of the amulet with the Hebrew writing that her brother Diego had brought her from Italy. "It was paper, with dozens of names written on it. I memorized some of them: *Agios atanatos, uti misis, dominatoribus, adradon eloyn or adonay, Agolite Voritan.* There were many more. I don't know exactly what they mean, but I think they were names of gods in the Law of Moses. I used to pray them when one of my brothers got sick, so they would get better. I would say those names along with some other prayers that my sisters and my mother taught me. I used to fast for them to get better, too. My mother was a stickler for fasting. She said it was necessary for the salvation of our souls."

"And where is this amulet now?"

"I don't have it. When Bernardina and Elvira were arrested I destroyed the amulet because I thought it might be something Lutheran, what with being foreign and all."

"What about the other charges against you? Shall we go over them one by one?"

"Everything you told me that those people said about me is true. My mother taught me the Law of Moses when I was fourteen or fifteen, and I believed in it until my sister Bernardina was arrested. But ever since then I have been a faithful Catholic. My mother taught the Old Law to all us girls. To my three brothers, too, though they are all dead now. My aunt Elvira Gutiérrez instructed us, too. And my sister Elvira told me that she had taught the law to her husband, Francisco de Zayas.

"Before she died, my mother always used to tell me and my sisters that if we were ever arrested by the Inquisition we should not confess any of these things, because even if we confessed voluntarily they would have us tortured to death."

Isabel went on like this for hours, in session after session, detailing the practices of her mother and her aunts and her sisters and insisting that she was now a true Christian. She recited the Our Father for them, and the Credo and the Hail Mary. When at last she ran out of things to say and stopped requesting more audiences, they let her molder in her cell.

Where she sat. And wept for the life they had taken from her. She prayed her Christian prayers, too, when she thought of it: loudly, hoping to be over-heard and believed. And she pondered eternity and what she must do to save her soul.

In January 1574, after more than a year had gone by, Isabel begged to be given another audience. Fray Pedro de Zúñiga reviewed her file and then had her brought from her cell. Given the weight of the paper in her dossier, they were dubious that the girl had any Judaizing customs left to declare. But Isabel surprised them.

"I asked for this audience because I wanted to tell you the truth. I still believe in the Law of Moses. That's the faith that I drank with my mother's milk."

No preamble; no rambling asides; none of the mewling requests for mercy that padded her written record. The inquisitors were stunned. This was something they did not hear every day. Isabel was freely confessing that she had lied and was still a heretic. This was very likely a one-way ticket to the stake.

"When you inspired me to go back to the faith of Our Lord Jesus Christ," Isabel went on, "I thought that I might lose my soul. I was very confused. I struggled with it so much that one night in my cell I even tried to kill myself. To tell you the truth, I still have doubts. I'm telling you this because I don't want to deceive anyone. My heart is not firmly set. But I am determined to die for my faith. I admit that earlier I said that I had gone back to our Holy Catholic Faith so that you wouldn't burn me. What's true is that I wanted to return. I did everything I could think of to help myself come back to the Holy Faith and believe in it firmly."

The scribe was scribbling as fast as he could. He wanted to make certain not to miss one word of what this suicidal girl was telling them. Fray Pedro and Fray Teófilo wore the implacable expressions that they had been trained to present to witnesses, but inside their hearts were pounding. Isabel sat with her hands folded. She stared straight ahead, without blinking, without looking into the eyes of either of the inquisitors whose attention was riveted on her words. She looked almost as if she were in a trance, or as if she had rehearsed this speech many times in her cell and now wanted to unburden herself of it before her resolve cracked.

"I mean it. I really wanted to be Catholic. But what my mother taught me was pulling me so strongly that it drew me back to the Law of Moses. I was so confused that I despaired. Then there was that part where my mother said I shouldn't believe that God came into the consecrated host. I thought to myself: how could the power and majesty of God come into a piece of bread and enter the body of a sinner? After all, when Moses called on God because he wanted to see him, the world nearly fell apart and the bush began to burn. When I tried to believe in Our Lord Jesus Christ, all these things came into my heart and twisted me this way and that. If God doesn't shine his light on me, I'll never figure it out. Can't you help me? Aren't there some prayers that will make me truly convert?"

At that moment all the inquisitors could think to tell her was to be strong, to keep trying, and to have faith, because Jesus would never abandon her.

Three days later Isabel asked to be brought to the audience room yet again because she had something important to tell the inquisitors. This time there was no delay in granting her request.

"I have thought it through and now I am determined to live and die in the Law of Jesus Christ the way my father has taught me. May I be sent straight to Hell without God's mercy if I make any other decision and if my heart turns around again. I know that I must die for the way I have shifted my faith, saying one day 'yes' and the next day 'no.' But I have to die in the faith of Jesus Christ. I have to do this, because my father is such a good Christian.

"The Law of Moses cannot be the true Law. I know that, because I used to deny myself food and recite the prayers of the Law of Moses so that I could marry a cousin of mine, but those prayers did me no good whatsoever. Then I learned from some women that I was doing it wrong, that going to church nine times to see the Virgin would get you what you wanted.

"Another thing: my mother used to say that all of the descendants of the people of Israel would be saved. I thought about that, and it seemed silly, because according to that you could worship idols and live immodestly and do whatever you wanted. And if you did all that, how could you be saved?

Besides, in prison I've been keeping lots of Jewish fasts so that God would free me from here. But it didn't work and I'm still here. All of that: that's why I resolved to be a Christian.

"I beg you now to give me some wise person to be my confessor and give me some book so I can learn all about the Christian faith."

Without prompting, Isabel rose to her feet to be returned to her cell. Once she had gone, the scribe put down his quill, capped his inkpot, and left the room, closing the door behind him. He had lots to say about the confessions he had heard over the last three days, but scribes were not allowed to initiate conversations. When he had gone, the two inquisitors, each absorbed in his own thoughts, sat without moving.

"That poor girl." Fray Pedro shook his head in disbelief. "She has no idea who she is, or what she wants, or where her lack of faith is taking her."

"How could her father have never figured out . . . ?" Fray Teófilo seemed to have directed his question to a fly stain on the wall above his colleague's head. "I mean, right under his nose, in his own house . . . "

"Maybe it is like they all say, that he was never home. He is a doctor. Or maybe his wife prevented him from getting close to his daughters. More likely he just didn't want to know, didn't want to admit what he was seeing."

Fray Pedro de Zúñiga stood and walked to the window. It had begun to rain. He took a deep breath. "We have to find her the right confessor. Maybe . . . Fray Martín de la Huerta? He seems to have a way with reaching the young."

"Young?" Fray Teófilo said. "She is thirty years old! If she doesn't know her own mind by now . . . "

"Not young in years, young in . . . naïve." Fray Pedro reflected on what they had heard. "The way she took both what her father told her and what her mother told her at face value, without ever questioning. Then at last when she finally saw the contradictions, the chasm opening up between her two parents, she fell right into it and she can't get out. Without God's grace, without our help as God's ministers . . . "

"I'll grant you that. But don't forget, she is a sinner. She has violated her faith, abandoned Our Savior to go back to her Old Law." Was Fray Teófilo taking the hard Church line or playing Devil's advocate? "The rules are clear. You can't just sweep her behavior away."

"So what should we recommend to the Supreme Council?" Fray Pedro asked. "What do you think the Suprema will do?"

The Doctor's Daughters

María de San Juan's story.

When they arrested twenty-nine-year-old María de San Juan in early June she was not surprised. With her sisters disappearing one by one into the Inquisition prison, she suspected that they would come for her soon. Though for a brief moment she had entertained thoughts of fleeing, she knew that it was not really an option. They would just come and find her, and besides, where could she go? No, the best thing to do when the questioning began, she decided, was to cooperate fully. Despite the primitive conditions of her cell, she prepared herself each morning for the eventual call: she drew her fingers like a comb through her long black hair; she smoothed the wrinkles from her skirt and blouse; and twice a day when they brought food to her cell, she even managed to splash a little water from the tin cup onto her face.

She told herself over and over that she would hold nothing back, that she would answer the inquisitors' questions as frankly and with as much calm cheer as she could manage. Finally, on the tenth day after her arrest, the bailiffs delivered her to the audience chamber.

Fray Pedro opened the interrogation, as was now his custom with the San Juan sisters, by inviting them to talk about their mother.

"My grandparents and my mother were new-Christians from Jewish stock." María smiled at Fray Pedro as she spoke, hoping it would mask her nervousness. "When I was around thirteen, my mother asked me who I worshiped and believed in. 'What do you mean?' I asked her. 'I believe in God and his Blessed Mother.' Then she told me that was wrong, that I had to believe only in God who created the heaven and the earth, and not in anybody else. Afterward she explained to me all the customs of the Law of Moses that we had to keep at home, and I did those things faithfully for two years.

"Then one Holy Thursday I went to see the processions, and when I saw the statue of Christ and of the Mother of God, whom I used to be very devoted to, and I saw how everyone was weeping and worshiping Christ, I got very envious and started to cry. My heart ached to love Jesus and Mary the way I had before. I was really upset, and as soon as I got home I asked my father what people had to do to be saved. He told me that they had to be good Christians and believe what the Holy Roman Church taught them. He told me to recite the Apostles' Creed and to believe everything it said. Then he asked me why I was questioning him about those things. I told him 'I just wanted to know,' and he said that I should not worry myself about such deep matters.

"Well, he was my father. And he was very well educated, and he and everybody else seemed to know a lot more about being saved than my mother did. So from then on I went back to being a good Christian."

"Then since that Holy Thursday you have lived and believed only as a Christian?" Fray Pedro tone let her know he was skeptical.

"Well, not exactly. I wanted to—that part is true—but my mother wouldn't leave me alone. First she told me that I should never marry an old-Christian unless she gave me her permission. But I didn't pay much attention to that because whom I married was for my father to decide, not her. Later my father arranged for me to marry Diego Moreno, and he was an old-Christian. My mother couldn't do anything to prevent it."

"Let me be sure we have this right. After you married Moreno, you didn't Judaize ever again?"

"No, I didn't. At least not at my own home, anyway. Only at my mother's house while she was alive, which was another seven or eight years after I was married. She had taught me how to fast like a Jew, so when I went to her house on some special day I told her that I was fasting the way she had showed me, and that I had come to her house because I couldn't fast at home. But I always snuck a meal before I went there. I used to tell my mother that I was doing everything the way she told me. But I only told her that so that she would leave me alone."

This did not square precisely with what the other sisters had told the interrogators, so Fray Pedro tried to pin María down. "So: when you were at your mother's house, and your other sisters were there, too, you all Judaized together?"

"No, it wasn't like that. I *suspect* that my mother taught my sisters about the Law of Moses the way she had instructed me, but I never saw it with my own eyes. And my mother told me never to share our secret with anyone, not even with my sisters."

"So which were you, a Jew or a Christian?"

"A Christian. Well, both, I guess, at least back then. For the next two years I continued to Judaize with my mother. But since that time, for the last thirteen years or so, I have been a good Christian."

"Your sisters, too?"

María didn't answer immediately. She clenched and unclenched her hands as the loyalty and love she felt toward her sisters struggled with her desire to speak frankly in answer to the inquisitors' questions.

The Doctor's Daughters

Fray Teófilo repeated Fray Pedro's question. "What about your sisters then?"

"I'm sorry. I . . . I don't remember. I really don't know."

"And your three brothers?"

"My brothers, yes. Diego, anyway. When the twins were killed they were still too young to know what they believed. When my brother Diego died he still believed as the Jews believe. But it wasn't like that with me at all. I just pretended to Judaize so that my mother and my sisters would give me some peace."

Fray Pedro seized on the point: "No, no; wait a moment. You say that you didn't know whether your sisters were Judaizers or not, but a little while ago you told us that they pressured you to Judaize with them . . . ?"

"Maybe they were just pretending, the way I was."

Fray Teófilo's normally implacable face was twisted into a scowl. "Tell us, María, why didn't you confess all these things when the Edict of Grace was read in the church? Why did you wait so long? Isn't it true that you were still believing as the Jews believe?"

"No, it wasn't like that at all." María's words tumbled out in a rush, sped by the panic that she felt rising in her breast. "It was because my mother told me that you would kill me if I ever confessed that we were Judaizing. But then, when I was arrested, and they held me that first night in the familiar's house, his wife told me that it didn't matter what heresies I had committed, because if I confessed, you would have mercy on me. That's why I am telling you all this now."

"All right." Fray Pedro de Zúñiga cut her off. "That is all for today. We will continue in the morning."

When she had gone, the two monks reviewed what they had heard. These San Juan girls would never cease surprising them. This one, María, seemed to have been the family shuttlecock, batted back and forth between her father and her mother: Jew, Christian; Christian, Jew. But her testimony was shot through with inconsistencies. She did not appear to be very bright; she projected a simplicity, a transparency. But could her religious life have really been that black and white, wholly Christian one day, enthusiastically Judaizing the next? And what about her relationship with her sisters? She claimed not to know whether they Judaized or not, but then she insisted that to keep them from hounding her she had to pretend to follow the Law of Moses herself the way they did. María said that she only surmised that her mother had indoctrinated her sisters the way she tried to indoctrinate her, but then she spoke as if her sisters and her mother were in league with each other against her. Under the circumstances, their next investigative tool was clear.

Bailiffs brought María back into the audience room. This time there was no chair for her. She stood at the foot of the long table with a bailiff at each elbow.

Fray Pedro de Zúñiga gave her the news. "There are some matters that you need to clear up for us, so we have ordered one session of torture for you."

María turned white, and her knees began to quaver. The bailiffs held her tightly so that she could not fall.

"No, don't do that. You don't have to do that. I'll tell you what you want to know. You're right; I didn't tell the entire truth yesterday, I admit it. It was not exactly the way I said. But you don't have to worry, I'll tell you everything this time."

Fray Pedro's face showed no sign of emotion, but inside he was smiling. Often the threat of torture was more effective than the act itself. And if after hearing what she had to say they were still unconvinced she was being frank with them . . .

"I know I said I saw things clearly, but that's not true. I really didn't. I was always confused. My mother taught me one thing, and the Church taught me another. My father, too. I always favored the Christian Law, even though sometimes I kept the Jewish fasts, and when I was with my sisters it's true I did see them fasting. And it hasn't been thirteen years that I've been a Christian; it's only been four. For the last four years I have never observed a Jewish custom, not even one. The reason is because I've not been living with my sisters. I haven't even seen them or dealt with them in four years. You can look: you won't find anybody who says that I have. It's just that I was in doubt for so long.

"But I always wanted to follow the Christian Law the most."

Fray Pedro indicated that they had heard enough. María was sent back to her cell to wait to learn her sentence.

Juana de San Juan's story.

Like her sister María, Juana de San Juan was arrested in June 1573. She was twenty years old. Her story was consistent with those of her older sisters:

indoctrinated at thirteen by her mother, sworn to secrecy, and years of Juda-izing along with her mother, her sisters, and her aunt Elvira Gutiérrez. She told the inquisitors that it was when her sisters were arrested that she began to doubt whether the Law of Moses was valid.

"What convinced me was realizing that the Jews are so badly treated and despised because Our Lord ordered it so on account of their false beliefs. That is why I resolved to believe that the Law of Christ was the best."

The Doctor.

Dr. Galcno de San Juan was summoned twice to the Palace of the Inquisition, but the interviews were perfunctory, and after that they let him alone. It seemed clear that he had been truly blind to his wife's and daughters' behavior. But the damage was done. As Dr. San Juan's daughters disappeared one by one, so did his clients. The Carvajal and Benavides clans, who were the pinnacle of Baezan society, would no longer tolerate him anywhere near their doors. And when they shunned him, so did every other respectable citizen of Baeza. As he gradually came to realize how thoroughly his wife and his six daughters had deceived him, the bitterness swelled in his heart. In June 1573, when Juana, his last daughter, was arrested, Dr. San Juan sold his house and furniture for a fraction of their worth, packed his medical instruments into three large trunks, and set off for Madrid to rebuild whatever he could of his shattered life.

... guardaron los sabados, y dejaron de comer tocino, y todo lo que la dicha portuguesa les enseño, lo cual hicieron en guarda y observancia de la ley de Moysen. Y les duro esta creencia por el tiempo de los 30 años, hasta que habia un mes, que por un milagro que habia hecho Nuestra Señora de Esperanza, en el Monasterio de Santa Cruz la Real, le dijo ... doña Costanza su hermana que ya no habia que esperar mas, y asi con eso se determinaron de no guardar la ley de Moysen y decir su culpa en este Santo Oficio. Aunque el temor de la honra les ha detenido algunos dias.

—AHN Inq. Leg. 1953, Exp. 29: 18

4

The Rojas and Torres Women

GRANADA, 1591

Early in November 1591, six women of the interrelated Rojas and Torres families made their way to the audience chamber of the Inquisition in Granada to confess their past observance of the Law of Moses and to beg the Holy Office for mercy. Although the Inquisition had been active in Granada since 1526, it had concerned itself principally with Protestants, randy priests, bigamists, heterodox mystics, flagrant practitioners of the rites of Islam, and the occasional witch or exorcist. It did not turn its full attention to the province's large community of former Jews until the mid-1580s. Granada's clergymen read out Edicts of Grace inviting self-incrimination and neighborly denunciation of Judaizing heretics. Informers lined up to report alleged Jewish behaviors. A legion of Inquisition staff members culled through the mounting files to determine which cases were strong enough to prosecute.

The six women volunteered their testimony; but it must have been clear to them that if they had not taken the initiative, sooner or later they would have been brought to the attention of the Holy Office.

Three sisters: Catalina, Leonor, and Juana de Rojas. Leonor's daughter, Costanza Vázquez. And the three sisters' nieces: Catalina de la Torre and Inés de Torres.

The Rojas and Torres women were members of a close-knit family with the habit of relying on each other. They came to the Inquisition office in two groups. Although each of the six women was interviewed separately while the others waited outside the audience chamber, the stories they told were much the same, with just enough variation that their testimonies rang of truth and not of collusion on a script. It is almost as if the women had all crowded into the audience chamber together and were speaking in chorus.

That is how we will listen to them here.

Catalina: Your Worships want to know where and when I began to do those things? It was about thirty years ago. Maybe a little more. I must have been ten or eleven. I am the eldest daughter in the Rojas family, you see, so it was my job to help Mother take care of my sisters, Leonor and Juana. We have a brother, too: Blas. He is a lot older than I am, and he had already married and moved out when I was little, so I don't remember him ever doing anything around our house. Sweeping the kitchen, keeping the water jugs filled . . . that was mostly up to me.

Leonor: You take the credit now, but when it came to cleaning and mending and bringing in wood for the fire and running the errands, you know perfectly well that I did just as much as you did. And Juana helped, too, even when she was little. Don't tell people you took care of me; you're only one year older than I am. The way I remember it was that you were always getting into trouble and I had to cover for you with Mother and Father. Remember the time that you dressed up in Mother's best skirt, and you stepped on the hem and ripped it? You were so flustered that you were all thumbs, and I had to sew it up for you before Mother got back from her errands.

Catalina: Of course I do. But I also remember that you were the one who broke the milk pitcher and I had to . . . Yes, Your Worship, I understand. You want me to tell about those things we used to do. But it won't make sense if you don't understand about our family, the way it was.

I'm sorry. I shouldn't have said that. I know that Your Worship is the judge of what's important. All right.

Let me get back to telling you about our family.

We weren't ever rich, but we were comfortable. Father worked for the Cancillería de Granada with the transfers of title and tax receipts, the patents of nobility, the certificates of purity of blood: things like that. We had a nice house just a few blocks from the Plaza de Bibarrambla. There was a bedroom for the three of us girls and another for our parents. The room where our brother, Blas, used to sleep Father turned into an office once he moved out. Downstairs off the courtyard, next to the stable, there were two small rooms for our servants. There was a kitchen with a fireplace that took up one whole side of the room, another a room where we used to sit and work in the summer when it was too hot to sew or spin in the kitchen because it had windows on both sides and could catch the breeze that comes down from the mountains . . . I know, I know. You want to hear about those things we did. I'm getting to that. But you have to understand . . .

Leonor: What she is trying to say is that you have to know about our servants.

Catalina: Leonor, let me tell this. You'll get your turn.
    Your Worship, as I said, we were a modest household, just my parents and the three of us girls. I mean after our brother, Blas, had gone off on his own. We had two servants to look after us. Gil was even younger than Leonor and me, about Juana's age. He came from someplace up toward the mountains. Near La Zubia, I think he said it was. Not a town, just a clump of houses. That's what he told us, anyway. He slept out in the stable.

Juana: He was cute, too. Remember that long sandy hair that he used to tie in the back?

Leonor: What I remember is that you couldn't look at him without turning beet red. That's when you were eleven or twelve.

Catalina: Leonor! Please . . . ! All right, all right.
    Gil's main job was taking care of my father's horse. Currying, combing his mane, sweeping out the stables. Things like that. He also ran errands for the family, and sometimes we got to go with him. Always at least two of us. It was about the only time Papa would let us out of the house.

Leonor: And if Papa had been aware of the way Juana felt about Gil, he wouldn't have allowed that either. It's a good thing that he never paid much attention to what was going on in the house. Most of the time he was either away at work or shut up with his papers at home.

Juana: I think we used to make too much racket for him. It was the only thing that made him raise his voice: "Quiet down, I'm trying to work in here!" Well, what did he expect, since we were cooped up in the house all the time. The three of us didn't really have many friends outside of the family, just each other.

Leonor: She's right: even after we got married, I think we were closer to each other than we were to our husbands.

Catalina: Yes, yes. You're right. But I was trying to get to the important part, about Guiomar. She was our other servant. She came into our household after Blas moved out and got married. I don't know where my parents found her, but we loved her from the first time we saw her. She was Portuguese, so her Spanish had a funny sound to it, but she knew a lot of stories and she kept us all entertained.

Leonor: Guiomar cooked, cleaned the house, washed our clothes, and pretty much looked after us when Mother was busy. In fact, I think we saw more of her than we ever did of Mother. Mother spent a lot of time out visiting with her sisters and with her friends.

Juana: And then Mother died. Guiomar stayed on and took care of us. Father . . . well, after Mother's death, Papa left Guiomar pretty much in charge of everything.

Catalina: I think Guiomar must have been a widow. A lot of the Portuguese housemaids were.

Leonor: What on earth made you say that? Guiomar never said that. We don't know for sure. We never came right out and asked her.

Catalina: Well, she didn't have any children of her own. We were her children.

Leonor: That's true enough. Our Portuguese mama, that's what we used to call her, especially after our mother died. She had long gray hair, braided in a pigtail. And she always wore that apron embroidered with chains of flowers in red thread. You'd ask her a question, and she'd smile at you with her eyes like she was saying: "Of course I know the answer to that. I'm so glad you asked me." She made us feel important.

Juana: What I remember is that Guiomar always smelled of cinnamon. And she was all plump and bosomy. We adored it when she would hug us or sit us on her lap and tell us stories about knights and fairies and her village in Portugal.

Leonor: I don't know where she got all those tales; she didn't know how to read. But she certainly had a head full of stories.

Catalina: She didn't have to know how to read to tell us about the world. Guiomar taught us everything about keeping a house: marketing, cooking, washing, everything.

Leonor: She'd always laugh and say, "Pay attention, just in case you marry wonderful men who don't have quite enough money to hire somebody like me to do things for you."

Juana: She taught us everything. She taught me how to chain stitch.

Catalina: She taught us religion, too. Well, our parents taught us some things, and of course we did go with them to mass and to listen to the Sunday sermons. Gil went with us, too. And sometimes Guiomar, but not very often.

Juana: Somebody had to tend to the kitchen while we were at church, that's what she used to say.

Catalina: No, Your Worship. Guiomar didn't catechize us. I mean, she didn't set us down and lecture us, make us memorize things. It wasn't like that at all.

Leonor: What happened was that eventually Catalina and I got to the age where we began to dream about boys and whom we would get to marry. Of

The Rojas and Torres Women

course we didn't want to leave the selection entirely to chance. Our father would arrange our marriages; we knew that. I mean, who wants to have three old maid daughters hanging around the house? But to us he was ancient, and a man, so he couldn't possibly understand the way we felt or what our hopes were. Catalina and I used to save any coins that came our way and send them to the Church of San Francisco de Paula to pay for masses so that God would make our father choose handsome, rich, enchanting young men for us to marry. Then one time we asked Guiomar to take the money to the church for us.

Catalina: *We* didn't ask her: *you* asked her. I was too embarrassed.

Leonor: Well, Guiomar just smiled that smile of hers and told us that there was a better way than that to make sure we got the right husbands. She said that it was only a few days until the Great Fast of September when God pardons all sins and that if Catalina and I fasted that day we would soon be married. She told us that we had to fast all day, from sundown the night before until sundown the day of the fast.

Catalina: It was exciting! All we had to do was fast that one day and not let anyone know what we were doing, and then our dream husbands would be ours.

Leonor: No, that wasn't all: there was a special prayer we had to say, too, the day we fasted and every time we prayed after that. Not to Jesus, to Moses. He was in the Bible, Guiomar told us. And we heard the priests talk about him, too, so that was all right. Before she would teach it to us she made us swear never to tell anyone about it, not even our parents. We didn't have to pray it out loud, she said. We could whisper, or even just say it in our heads.

Catalina: Naturally we swore not to tell. Who can resist a secret? So we fasted just the way Guiomar told us, and said the prayer.

No, Your Worship: I don't remember what it was. I haven't prayed it in years. Anyway, it must have worked, because inside of a year both of us were married.

Leonor: My husband, may he rest in peace, was named Alfonso Vázquez. He might not have been the handsomest man in Granada, or the richest. But he was kind, and he treated me and my daughter, Costanza, well, and he earned a good income wholesaling tooled leather. Seven years we lived together before he died. He got sick—let me see—about sixteen years ago. In 1575.

Costanza Vázquez: Mother is right. I was only six when Papa died, but I remember him very clearly. I loved him a lot. When my husband, Gonzalo de Santo Simián, and I have children, I hope that Gonzalo can spend as much time with our children as my father did with me. I don't think it's going to happen, though. Gonzalo is a doctor, not a Chancery clerk, so once his practice grows I know he will be at the beck and call of his patients. We've been married for four years, and we don't have any children yet. But we're hoping. Maybe if he were home more often . . .

Leonor: Costanza, be patient: God will provide. They don't want to hear about these things. You heard them: they want to know what else Guiomar taught us.

Costanza Vázquez: I'm sorry; I just thought . . .

Catalina: As I said, it's not like Guiomar sat us down and gave us lessons. She didn't tell us everything all at once. It just seemed like every week there was some other thing she said we had to do . . .

Leonor: . . . or be careful not to do. Like no pork.

Juana: I learned that, too: no salt pork, no bacon, no sausage.

Catalina: Guiomar told us that salt pork had been cursed by God.

Juana: And that it was dirty.

Leonor: She also said we weren't supposed to eat any fish that didn't have scales. And we couldn't eat rabbits. Or partridges. Or any meat that hadn't been slaughtered by having its throat cut. Guiomar did most of the shopping, even when Mother was alive, and she never paid attention to where Guiomar bought the meat or what kind of fish it was. So it wasn't too hard for us to stick to Guiomar's rules.

The Rojas and Torres Women

Catalina: And if sometimes Papa said that the stew was too bland, that it needed more salt pork, then Guiomar would cook it that way for a while. She just wouldn't eat it. Then when Mother died . . .

Leonor: When Mother died Guiomar ran the house pretty much however she wanted.

Juana: And we all got to help her. You know—I never told you this—, I think we had even more fun back when we had to keep all those Guiomar things a secret. After Mother died . . . well, it just got to be the normal way we did things.

Catalina: Your Worships want to know about Saturdays? Well, Saturday was a special day for Guiomar. She called it the Sabbath and told us that it was the most important part of the Law of Moses. She taught us how to honor it by not doing any work, or at least as little as we could manage. Sometimes Papa asked us to do something for him, like heat him a cup of hot milk, so of course we had to do that. But beyond that . . . Guiomar told us to carry our spinning or our needlework around with us, but we weren't supposed to actually work on it unless somebody was watching us.

Leonor: The Law of Moses: that's what she called all those things. She said his law was stronger than the law we learned in church.

Juana: Guiomar was a fiend for fasting. Oh, I'm not supposed to say fiend, am I? I don't mean that she . . .
    Yes, Your Worship. Thank you. I will go on.
    What I meant was that Guiomar made sure we fasted when we were supposed to. Not only the Great Fast of September but sometimes on Monday and Thursday, too. She had us tell our parents that we didn't feel well, or that we had eaten so much the night before that we just weren't hungry.

Leonor: But her big thing was that when we prayed we had to pray to one God alone, not to a Holy Family of Gods.

Juana: Not a Holy Family; a *whole* family. That's what Guiomar used to call it.

Leonor: Anyway, so that's how we mostly prayed, except every Sunday when we went to church. Then we prayed what everybody else prayed.

Catalina: Your Worships ask whether all this happened when we were living at home with our father, after our mother died? Of course it did. Because later when we got married it was a lot harder for us to do what Guiomar had taught us. One problem then was that we didn't always know when the fasts were. When we were living at home Guiomar would tell us. But when we got married there was nobody. I mean, we had each other, but none of us knew any more than the other. It's not like we knew any other people who did these things. Once in a while we could go back to our father's house to ask Guiomar—she kept on taking care of him for a few years after Juana left. Juana was the last to get married. Guiomar was really old by then, and she died . . . it must have been about nine years ago.

Juana: But before that we couldn't go to see her very often: our husbands didn't like it.

Leonor: Our husbands?! We couldn't ask them, Your Worships. Good Lord, no! About those Guiomar things? They'd have been horrified. All three of them.

Catalina: What happened was this: one day a neighbor of mine, Marina del Mercado—everybody called her La Tuerta, the cross-eyed lady—, she noticed that on Saturdays I didn't seem to be working. Well, one day she struck up a conversation with me, and after a while she told me that she followed the Law of Moses, too. She knew a lot more about it than I did. She would tell me when the fasts were, and I would tell my sisters. She taught me a couple of other prayers, too. When did I meet her? Let me think. Maybe . . . when was it?

Leonor: Sixteen or seventeen years ago?

Juana: Tell them what Cross-Eyed told you about Moses.

Catalina: Marina said that God had opened up twelve paths across the Red

The Rojas and Torres Women

Sea for Moses so that each of the twelve tribes could cross. And she said that Moses could help me a lot, and that I should think of him when I was praying to God, because only Moses could save my soul.

My late husband, Jerónimo de Nájera—may he rest in peace—he was a secretary in the Chancery where my father had worked. He died about ten years ago and I never remarried. The problem with Jerónimo was . . . well, I think he was worried that people wouldn't think he was a good Christian. He took me to mass at least once a week, and he went to confession all the time. He always used to say that he came from a long line of Christians on both sides of his family. We had crucifixes and woodcuts of the Holy Family in every room of our house. We didn't have any servants, so I was the one who cooked for him. He wanted his meat and vegetables prepared the way his mother used to make them, with lots of salt pork or sausage for flavor. Jerónimo and I ate supper together, naturally, so I had to eat what he was having, even though it bothered me to be eating pork. When Jerónimo wasn't there, I almost never ate pork. And I worked as little as I could on the Sabbath. And I fasted when I could, sometimes just a half day, even though Guiomar told us that the only fasts that counted with God were when you didn't eat or drink for twenty-four hours straight.

Inés de Torres: It was just the way Aunt Catalina says. Guiomar said we earned more merit if we fasted for a full day.

Which one am I? Inés de Torres, Your Worships. Blas de Torres is my father, and Catalina, Leonor, and Juana are my aunts.

Juana: I had the same problem when I married Juan Baptista. He's a lawyer for the Chancery. His ancestors were old-Christian on both sides, my father made sure of that, so I can't let him see any of the things Guiomar taught us to do. He hits me sometimes if he catches me. I do as much as I can, but I have to be careful around him.

Leonor: It was the same with my husband, Alfonso Vázquez. He was an old-Christian, too, so I always had to watch myself. Then after he died, well . . . in some ways it was easier. We had only one daughter—that's Costanza who's sitting over there—, and I could share things with her. In fact, I . . .

All right, Your Worship. I hear you. You want us to take things in order.

CHAPTER 4

You want to know when each of us began to follow the practices of the Law of Moses?

Costanza Vázquez: With me it was when I got old enough to help my mother, Leonor, keep house and cook. Then about seven or eight years ago she told me that we were following the Law of Moses, and we had to keep it secret. I think maybe I was twelve. It was something we could talk about together. Sharing our secret . . . it made us feel close.

Juana: I was younger than that when I learned, maybe nine or ten. Guiomar told me that if I wanted to serve God the way my two sisters were doing, then she would tell me the secret. But first I had to swear to her never to tell anybody else, not even our own mother. She was still alive then. I promised Guiomar that I wouldn't, and then she told me about believing in only one God, and what I wasn't supposed to eat, and about the Sabbath and the Great Fast. That was around sixteen years ago. Later she showed me how to wash myself every month. I tried to do most of what she told me to do. But I didn't do everything, because that was too hard.

Catalina de Torres: What about me? I'm Catalina, Catalina de Torres. I didn't say anything before because I didn't have anything to say. My aunts and my sister, Inés, have said it all.

One day back before I was married—I think that was about fifteen years ago—I was visiting my three aunts when I saw them whispering about something with each other. Naturally, since I was curious and at that age had no sense of modesty at all, I walked right up and asked them what they were whispering about. One of them, I think it was Aunt Catalina, snipped at me: "Go on, you stupid girl! What do you want to know about anyway?" Well, I'm not stupid. And they weren't going to put me off so easily. So I asked them again: "What is so important that you have to keep it all to yourselves?" Then they told me that if I'd promise to keep their secret they would tell me something important for my soul, and that terrible things would happen if anybody ever found out. Naturally that made me even more curious! So I promised them I'd never reveal anything to anyone, and then they told me about there being only one God, and all about fasting and what I was supposed to eat, and things like that. What everybody else has said.

The Rojas and Torres Women

When I was twenty I married Antonio de Torres—he was an attorney for the Chancery—and from then on I stopped doing everything my aunts had told me except what I could do by myself in secret. Then Antonio died; we had been married only three years. After that I never started doing all those fasts and things again. Well, just some of them.

Inés de Torres: With me it was just like with my sister Catalina. Blas was my father, too. Since I am three years younger than she is, I did what she did and what our aunts told me to do. I was just a little girl. It never occurred to me to question them.

Costanza Vázquez: With me it was exactly like with my cousin Catalina de Torres, though I was older than she was when I found out. One day I happened to see my mother, Leonor, and her sisters with their heads together. I asked them what they were whispering about, and they told me to keep my voice down. My aunts looked around to make sure nobody was watching us or listening, and then my mother told me that for my soul to be saved I had to do all the things that she and my aunts have already told you. That's it.

Leonor: What do you mean, how long were we all practicing Jews? That wasn't the way it was at all. We weren't Jews. Your Worships have missed the point.

I'm sorry. I . . . I know that Your Worships know much more about these things than we do. But it's just that none of us ever thought of ourselves as Jews. Our Portuguese mother told us that doing all those things was the best way for us to serve God. That there was only one God, the God who created all things, and that's what the priests told us, too. She said that God created everything, even Jesus and his Mother. The only difference was that Guiomar insisted that the God we were to believe in was one God alone, not three. We were all very young, and that made good sense to us. I mean, why wouldn't we follow God's law?

Catalina: We certainly weren't Jews though. I never thought there was any conflict between what we were doing and the Holy Catholic faith. There was no reason for us not to follow them both.

Yes, yes, as you say; now I know better.

When did I realize that all those Law of Moses things were wrong? Let me . . .

Juana: I'll tell you when it was for me. It was a couple of years after Guiomar explained the Law of Moses to me. Bit by bit I came to realize that what we were doing was against the Law of Jesus Christ. I loved Jesus, like the priests told me to, but I still believed that Guiomar's way was the best way for my soul to be saved, just like Guiomar had taught us. So I kept on doing those things. Not every one of them, but some. Even after I got married.

Costanza Vázquez: Me, too. Somewhere along the way—I can't tell you exactly when—I began to see that what I was doing was not what the Church was telling me. I knew that what we were doing was part of the Law of Moses—Guiomar had told us that—, so I always suspected it was wrong. But I didn't really know they were Jewish things. Not at first. Even so, I kept doing them until I got married four years ago. Then I stopped.

Catalina: With me it was like my niece Costanza says. Except that even while I was doing all those things, my heart never stopped believing in Jesus Christ. I always went to mass on festival days and I worshiped the Holy Sacrament when it was consecrated. It's like I was blind during all those years. That's why I never told any of this to my confessor. Instead, I prayed all the time for God's light to shine on me and teach me how I was in error. I always had this thorn in my heart.

Inés de Torres: That's the way I felt, too. I followed the Law of Moses, and I truly did believe that that was the only way for my soul to be saved, but somehow I knew that the Law of Jesus was the right one. So about a year ago when I realized that my mother and my aunts had stopped doing those things, I stopped doing them, too. I went back to the faith of Jesus Christ. Those Moses things were like a big cancer in my heart that broke out on my body, too. It made me sick.

Leonor: With me it took a miracle. You know about what happened to that lady about a month ago in the Monastery of Santa Cruz la Real? The blind woman? The one who when she prayed to the image of Our Lady of Good Hope all of a sudden she could see again? That was a sign for me, clear as a bell, about how everything I had been doing all those years was wrong and sinful and that my only salvation was through the Law of Jesus Christ. My

The Rojas and Torres Women

sister Catalina said to me: "There's no reason for us to wait any longer! We need to stop doing those Jewish things and tell the priests of the Holy Office that we have stopped sinning and have gone back to the Law of Jesus."

No, what Your Worship says is true. I admit it: I didn't come to the Holy Office immediately. I waited a few days. You must know that coming here is a big step, and I was afraid that people would find out that I had been here and that it would affect my honor. And besides, my niece Inés was about to give birth and I wanted to be with her. But mostly I was afraid of the punishment you might give me.

Inés de Torres: I wanted to come. But I was pregnant, and then I gave birth to Alfonsito, and then I got sick, and . . . well, it took me a long time. I'm sorry. I know that was wrong.

Juana: I know I've sinned by following the Law of Moses. But inside me I never ever left the Law or the faith of Jesus Christ. Never.

Catalina: You have to believe me. With all my heart I truly ask forgiveness for my sins. I beg you to give me the penance that I deserve, and to have mercy on me. All I want—all any of us want—is to live and die in the faith of Jesus Christ.

Y lo que convenia hera que esta se casase con Hector de Fonsseca . . . porque
aunque estava casado con una Xptiana vieja al uso y conforme a la yglessia catolica,
y que assi no hera balido el dicho matrimonio, alegando una authoridad de
Esdras donde dice que mando Dios a los hijos de Ysrael que dexassen las mugeres
con quien se avian casado estando captivos, y se casassen con las del pueblo de
Israelitico. . . . [Dijo] Hector de Fonsseca . . . que se irian todos a una juderia donde
con libertad guardassen la Ley de Moissen, porque vivia condenada con estar
casada con Xptiana vieja, y que si hiciesen, que le sacaria de un ynfierno.

—AGN Inq., Vol. 158, Exp. 1: 58v

5

The Miners Fonseca

MEXICO, 1596

There were three Fonseca miners, all of them dead now.

Old Tomás was a gruff, uncouth bear of a man with enormous appetites, quick to anger, unforgiving of his enemies. I called him Great-Uncle Tomás, and he treated me like his nephew. My mother was never clear to me about exactly how we were related. Since then I have learned a great deal about the three Fonseca miners, and though I would have it otherwise, I have come to this conclusion: we really weren't part of the same family at all. We just happened to share the name Fonseca, along with ten other unrelated Fonsecas whom I've come to know in my travels.

Old Tomás worked a silver mine in Tlalpujahua, out in Michoacán. I've never been there, but they say the pine-covered mountains are beautiful. And that when the butterflies come back in November the hills look to be covered with gold. That's on the outside. Inside, those hills are laced with silver, though the trick is to find it, and then to dig it out, and to keep from being killed or cheated in the process. Great-Uncle Tomás's clothing always gave off the smell of wood smoke, or maybe tobacco. He died when I was ten, so I have only a child's recollections.

The second Fonseca miner was Héctor—Cousin Héctor to me—as unpleasant a man who ever dug for silver. To tell the truth, I have very few fond memories of him. How his wife, Juana López, put up with him I'll never know. His idea of being a husband was to beat her with his belt whenever he felt she had done something wrong, or when he had been drinking, which was more often than not. Juana used to say that the only good thing about Héctor was that he hardly ever came home. Everybody knew that he was screwing half the whores in Taxco, and in mining towns that's a lot of women. One time, after he had been away for nearly two months, he came home with his face and arms covered with running sores. That was the last straw. His wife threw him out and told him not to come back until he was completely cured. Some quack slathered him with poultices and wrapped him in a canvas sheet to make him sweat out the poison. I don't think his wife, Juana, ever slept with him again. When the Inquisition released Héctor, after his first trial, Juana tried to divorce him, alleging that the shame of it would destroy her and their children. Cousin Héctor's lawyer argued how with that as precedent the spouse of anyone who ever wore a sambenito could break the holy sacrament of marriage, and Juana's petition was denied. They never got back together, though. Years later Cousin Héctor died in the Indian Hospital in Mexico City. They say his whole body was a stinking, oozing mass. The Holy Office had sent him there, fearful that he might contaminate their precious prison cells.

Then there was Young Tomás, who was Old Tomás's nephew. My sisters and I called him "uncle," even though, again, there were no blood ties between us. This uncle Tomás owned a couple of small mines near Taxco. His full name was Tomás de Fonseca Castellanos, but most people called him the Taxco Fonseca. He was a shopkeeper, an importer, and in later years an investor in the silver mines. His store in Taxco was one of the biggest and richest in the whole region. Uncle Tomás used to say that mining was like throwing dice. It was possible to make a fortune in silver, and some people did, but most miners died poor. Clothing, on the other hand, was a sure thing: everybody needed it, and when it wore out they had to replace it. It produced a steady income: slow but sure. Young Uncle Tomás owned some mining shares, like most of the merchants in Taxco, but the only time he ever lifted a shovel was to pass it across the counter to a customer. Young Uncle Tomás was a good friend of Luis de Carvajal: but then, who wasn't in those days? At least among the Portuguese community. Luis used to stay with Uncle Tomás when he had business in Taxco, and the two of them would spend the whole night talking about Moses and fasting and God knows what. Uncle Tomás knew a lot of bible stories—*The Mirror of Consolation* was his favorite book—and he liked to tell them to us kids. But he wasn't obsessed with religion the way the Carvajal family was. The Inquisition got my uncle Tomás, too, four years after Luis went up in smoke.

My whole childhood was colored by what had happened to the three Fonseca miners. Their trials and their executions stigmatized even their distant relatives. My mother had also been born in Taxco, and she knew all three of the Fonseca men. None of their money ever fell into her pockets, though. She was the poor relation, the widow struggling to raise her two children, too Christian and too rude in her ways to be welcome in their company. We had a house—my father had left her that—but not much else. People brought Mother their clothing to wash or mend, and some kind souls gave her charity. She wouldn't take anything from the Portuguese merchants though: she told us never to have anything to do with them because they were a plague and in league with the Devil, and she didn't want the Holy Office sniffing around our house. She raised us to be good Christians, making sure that we knew all the prayers and never missed a Sunday mass. Despite our modest circumstances, somehow Mother managed to get me into a school where I learned my letters. I was a proper young man by the time the three of us moved to Mexico City.

But this story isn't about me, it's about my great-uncle, my uncle, and my cousin, the three Fonseca miners, and the disgrace they brought on the family. My mother told me to put them out of my mind, but I couldn't. In fact, they have become an obsession with me. They were all accused of practicing the dead Law of Moses. They were all penanced by the Inquisition. Their sambenitos hung in the Church of Santo Domingo in Mexico City for everyone to see. Their fame, their infamy, ruined things for the other Fonsecas in Taxco. No matter that we were all good Christians. No matter that we knew almost nothing about the Old Law, or that we had never practiced any of its heinous customs.

Is it difficult to understand, then, that as a teenager I was so fascinated by what my uncles and my cousin had done? I quizzed everyone who had known them. I sought out every Portuguese trader coming to Mexico City from the mines to ask if they could they tell me anything about them. I didn't let my mother know what I was doing, of course. She would have been scandalized. But detail by detail I began to piece their stories together.

The Miners Fonseca

The more I learned, the more I condemned them in my mind. At first I believed that if the Fonseca miners had only accepted Jesus Christ as their Lord and Savior when they were my age, if they had stayed away from the Carvajals and Manuel de Lucena and that crowd who seduced them into believing in the Old Law, if they really cared about what would become of their eternal souls, then none of this would have happened to them. Or to me either. At twelve or thirteen it was all about me.

When I was fifteen I realized that, fair or not, the stigma of the three Fonseca miners would shadow me wherever I went in New Spain. That summer I kissed my mother good-bye—who knows if forever?—and took passage in the silver fleet returning to Spain. I made my way from Cádiz to Sevilla and Madrid. In each city I managed to find one or two people who knew something about the Fonseca miners.

By then, despite the risk that the inquisitors might catch wind of me, I had feigned a few Jewish customs myself: I dressed up for the Sabbath, and could even mumble a few Jewish prayers. Initially my purpose was to gain the confidence of people who had been part of the Fonsecas' and Carvajals' circle of friends so they would talk to me about my disgraced relatives. But before long I began to feel myself torn between my mother's Catholicism and my new colleagues' whispered enthusiasm for the Law of Moses. I couldn't tell whether my faith was being shaken or awakened; or for that matter, where it would settle. It was like the toy I had played with as a child, a ball on a string that I had to catch in a wooden cup. Left side the Old Law, right side the New Law, my soul bouncing wildly as I tried to catch it in the cup of Grace. Forgive me the metaphor.

I often wondered if the three Fonseca miners had ever wrestled with similar doubts.

Everyone who knew something about them told me that to learn more I would have to look outside of Spain, beyond the long reach of the Holy Office. In Bayonne and Rouen, Antwerp and Amsterdam, Liorno and Venice and Ferrara, and the dominions of the Great Turk. That's where the Portuguese merchants with something on their consciences tended to go when they came back from the New World. People in those places could talk freely about the three Fonseca miners.

I became a trader and a traveler. I have a good head for numbers, and I know the arts of persuasion, so I had little trouble finding backers who, for a share of the profits, would lend me money for the spices and Flemish cloth, the jewels and oriental carpets that became my stock-in-trade. My itinerary was shaped by opportunity and by my obsession with gathering up the scattered memories of my family.

Old Tomás de Fonseca from Tlalpujahua

The man we called Great-Uncle Tomás—like all of our family, truth be told—came from the rough border country between Spain and Portugal. Were we Spanish? Yes. Were we Portuguese? Yes. Were we Jews? Christians? Yes. Yes again. We were border people, even those like me who were born in the New World.

I've not been able to learn anything about Great-Uncle Tomás's grandparents, though I suppose that like most people of the Nation they fled Spain in the 1490s—or maybe earlier, who knows?—to avoid having to convert. Then in Portugal sometime later they turned Christian. Great-Uncle Tomás's grandparents settled in Freixo de Espada à Cinta, in the mountains near Braganza. Why Freixo? Who can say? People tell me it was a thriving little market town where a man could make a decent living selling dry goods slipped from Spain through the Duero River canyons past the cash-blinded eyes of the Portuguese customs officials. Freixo was chock full of Spaniards, enough of them to be able to gather a minyan on Friday night and then fill the parish church for the Sunday mass. They were all good Christians, naturally, but you could buy kosher meat in Freixo's butcher shop, and at the spring fair potters came from far and wide to sell new dishes for Passover. The Inquisition was burning Judaizers by the dozen in Spain, but in those days Portugal left the new-Christians pretty much alone.

Tomás's father, Gabriel, was born in Freixo. At home he and his parents prayed to Adonai; in church they knelt before images of Jesus. Gabriel grew up in the family business. He married another Spanish refugee, Felipa de Fonseca. I don't know how his life would have been different if Felipa hadn't died giving birth to Tomás. But as it was, Gabriel turned restless and sour tempered. He found fault with the neighbor women who were helping him raise his son, and he picked fights with their husbands. People began to avoid going into his shop. So early in summer 1526, by then nearly friendless and with his business going downhill, he loaded up his wagon and took his son, Tomás, back to Spain.

Gabriel made straight for Extremadura, a region of cattle ranches and cork forests lying close enough to the border for new-Christians to slip back to Portugal when mob violence or the Inquisition put their lives in danger. He rented a small house in Jarandilla, the market town for the Vera Valley. At some point—I don't know whether it was in Portugal or in Jarandilla— Gabriel took up with a new-Christian woman named Blanca Rodríguez. I say "took up with," because even though Gabriel called her his wife, the gossips said that she already had a husband and that Gabriel had spirited her away to keep him from abusing her. She was pregnant when they left. Whether the child was her husband's or Gabriel's there is no way of saying. Evil tongues, of course, assumed it was Gabriel's. However it was, Blanca stayed with Gabriel in Jarandilla, came with him to Mexico, and lived with him until she died, many years later. Their second son, Julián Castellanos, was born in Jarandilla, and three more children—Isabel, Lope, and Guiomar, all of whom took the name Fonseca—were *criollos*, which is what they call Spaniards like me who are born in Mexico. Guiomar is married, and Julián died back in '95 in the Hospital de San Hipólito in Mexico City. I don't know about the others.

Great-Uncle Tomás must have been happy in Jarandilla, because when we were kids he used to tell us stories about how he and his father, and some-times baby Julián, used to travel up and down the Vera selling tin ware from a wagon. In Tomás's mind the Vera was the most beautiful place in the world: rich farms that even in winter were sheltered from the west winds by the snow-covered peaks of the Gredos mountains. Pine forests on the slopes. Crystal brooks where sometimes he and his friends would fish for trout. He told us that Jarandilla was so much like Paradise that our Emperor Charles gave up his throne and retired to a little monastery there to nurse his gout and pass the warm afternoons fishing. Or so they say. I've never been there, and the emperor died long before I was born, and long after Great-Uncle Tomás came to Mexico.

Tomás's father loved Jarandilla even though he was always looking over his shoulder. For one thing, there was the business of Blanca's former hus-band. If the rumors are true, which I've come to believe was the case, then she was guilty of bigamy and Gabriel of fornication, matters that the Church seldom took lightly. In those days on the Spanish side of the border conversos had to avoid drawing attention to their religious views, let alone their lin-eage. Gabriel and his Portuguese friends never missed a Sunday mass. They all carried big rosaries and crossed themselves every time they passed a church door. The only school in Jarandilla was run by priests, so naturally Gabriel sent Tomás there to learn his letters and how to be a good Christian. Gabriel didn't see any contradiction between teaching his son to be a Christian and at the same time observing the Sabbath at home or banning pork from his kitchen. One life was public, the other private. He wasn't much concerned about the final destination of his soul.

Jarandilla may have been Paradise, but too many people knew him there. Besides, a deep restlessness had settled in his blood, and he dreamed constantly of what life might be if he just moved on. The story goes that when Emperor Charles decided that the New World colonies could be turned into productive sources of revenue for the crown, Gabriel was one of the first volunteers. He and his children sailed to Veracruz from Cádiz with the summer fleet in 1534 or 1535. To hear people talk today, half of Extremadura crossed the ocean with them. Restless second sons who would never receive an inheritance. Tainted young women hopeful of making a better match in the New World than the Old. Adventurers who preferred the risks of travel to the mind-numbing certainties of small town farming. Con men and cutpurses fleeing Spanish prisons. Missionary friars determined to save Indian souls. And grandees determined to put those same souls to work. Not to mention a host of new-Christians who thought their true beliefs might be less noticeable in the vastness of the New World than in the priest-choked streets of mother Spain. False hopes, of course, but that came later.

Gabriel settled his family in Mexico City where, what with buying this and selling that, he soon had built up enough capital to open a small shop just off Calle Tacuba, the city's main business street. By then his son Julián was old enough to be put to work in the shop. He was a tall handsome lad, if not overly bright, with a winning smile that was a magnet for customers. His other son, Great-Uncle Tomás, was not nearly so sunny of character, but he had a good brain, and Gabriel figured him to take over the business side of things one day. So he sent him off to Dr. Blas de Bustamante's Dominican grammar school to sharpen his writing and mathematical skills. Gabriel dreamed of the family living a comfortable life together in Mexico City. But he didn't take account of the fact that Tomás would turn out to be so headstrong. Or that Julián's fleeting bouts of ambition would dissipate like the morning dew.

There were three ways to make a fortune in New Spain in those days: you could harvest your money off the land as sugar, cacao, corn, or cattle. You could dig your money out of the ground as gold or silver. Or you could sell things to the planters and the miners. The biggest landholders were the conquistadors or their heirs, whom the emperor had rewarded for their service with vast land grants that included the Indian populations who did the work. If you weren't among the first Spaniards at the table, then you had to buy land, which put ranching, sugaring, or making liquor out of the reach of the majority of the newcomers. Most of our people—you can see how I've come to think of myself—, who have no long tradition of landholding, did what they had done in Spain and Portugal. They made things with their hands, or else they bought and sold things that other people had made. They built up their network of business contacts and they dreamed of one day rising from street peddler to shopkeeper to wholesaler and banker. Only a few—the clever, the risk-takers, and the lucky—ever made it to the top. Mining, on the other hand, was the poor adventurer's lottery. All you needed was a pick and shovel, a couple of mules, a good eye for rock, and the kiss of luck. Few miners struck it rich, but enough did to fan into flame the dreams of half the young men in New Spain.

Gabriel caught the mining fever early. In fact, after only four years in the New World, he left his "wife" Blanca and their son Julián to take care of the shop and took Tomás to a small silver stake in Ayoteco, not far from Cortés's estates near Cuautla. The man who sold the mine to him swore that it had great potential, and that he would have worked it himself if the rheumatism hadn't got to him. He showed Gabriel a few chunks of rock laced with silver that, he said, he had found a dozen yards into the small tunnel he had already dug into the mountainside. That was enough proof for a shopkeeper. They shook hands, Gabriel forked over his meager savings, and just like that, he and Great-Uncle Tomás were miners. How hard could it be?

Great-Uncle Tomás used to say that the blisters on their hands burst on the second day and that before two weeks had passed their calluses were as hard as horses' hoofs. The mine shaft was always choked with dust, so their coughing made conversation impossible. The tunnel wasn't wide enough to swing a pick, so they had to use an iron pry bar and a hammer to loosen the lumps of ore. They did find silver: a few grains here, a tiny lump or two there, a telltale thread of greenish black that yielded grudgingly to the hammer blows. Twelve years they worked that claim, eking out just enough to buy a few beans and corn and maybe a haunch of goat once or twice a month. By living low they managed to stay out of debt and keep themselves supplied with tools, as well as an occasional excursion into Ayoteco or Cuautla for a pitcher of wine and some female companionship. They rarely went back to

Mexico City: it was as if Blanca and Julián didn't exist. For a while Great-Uncle Tomás kept company with an Indian woman who washed clothes for the miners in Ayoteco. Before long he had a son with her. The boy's name was Teodosio and the Indian woman's . . . who knows? No one I have talked to has any idea what happened to either of them.

One sure thing is that Great-Uncle Tomás was never one for accepting responsibility. Whether eventually he grew tired of working for his father, whether the Indian woman became too demanding, or whether the thought of having to deal with a child terrified him, one night Tomás gathered up his gear and headed north to Pachuca, where people told him vast mountains of silver had just been discovered. I don't think he even said good-bye to his father. That must have been around 1550. Tomás was nearly thirty.

For every exhausted miner who scratched at the earth in Ayoteco, there were twenty eager young men combing the mountains around Pachuca. It seems that almost every week some lucky prospector sauntered into one of the stamping mills in Pachuca with a sack of ore so heavy in silver it would take your breath away. At least that's what Great-Uncle Tomás used to say, his eyes sparkling with the memory of the riches he had seen. Seen, but never found. His own mine shafts produced silver, but in dribs and drabs, not torrents of wealth. Enough to keep him going, enough to keep him hoping, enough to build a decent little house and put food on the table. Enough to buy a black slave and hire a few free Indians to take over the backbreaking work of chiseling out the rock and loading it into canvas bags for his mules to haul down to the smelting mills in Pachuca. But never enough for him to make the leap from miner to magnate.

Unlike Ayoteco, which was so small that if a mule farted at one end of town you could smell it at the other, Pachuca was big. There were hundreds, maybe thousands, of miners working in the rugged mountains that rimmed the town to the north. Some of them had struck it rich enough to delegate the day-to-day mining operations to their employees while they built splendid mansions in the center of Pachuca. The roads from Mexico City and Puebla pulsed with carts bringing mining supplies and luxury goods to the new city. Everywhere were stores, livery stables, taverns, and brothels. Churches, too, and a sturdy jail, and a garrison for the king's soldiers.

What Great-Uncle Tomás liked best about Pachuca was the companionship of its Portuguese merchants. They brought him news of mutual friends in Mexico City and Puebla. They welcomed Tomás and the handful of other

Portuguese miners to the Friday evening gatherings where they would talk about the Old Law and, often as not, make fun of their image-worshiping old-Christian neighbors. I don't remember Great-Uncle Tomás telling us much about these things when we were children. Most of what I know comes from my cousins and from other people who spent those years in the mining communities. In cities like Pachuca, where you were never out of sight of a church, the Portuguese had to walk carefully. They heard mass every Sunday, prayed their rosaries, went to confession, kept the Church fasts, and guarded their tongues. Out in the hills none of this mattered so much. The miners tended to be religious men, in their way, but on the whole they were a rough, superstitious lot. They called on their personal saints to bring them luck; they begged the Virgin to protect them from the dangers of mining, and, with the next breath, they shouted curses at those same holy figures in language that in the city would likely have sent them straight to jail. Mining was largely solitary work, at least insofar as whites were concerned. Out in the diggings, the miners who followed the Law of Moses were pretty much on their own. They had little sense of time passing, just endless days of hard work. The Sabbaths, the festivals, the fasts . . . even if the Portuguese miners knew when they were, there was little they could do to observe them. They ate whatever there was, with little concern for the dietary laws they had learned as children. Their religious life shrank to a prayer before going to bed or when they first got up in the morning. Maybe in their hearts they were Jews, but in their daily lives they were miners. If their black and Indian laborers noticed any of their religious peculiarities, they kept their mouths shut.

Tomás's life quickly settled into a routine. Five days of pick and shovel, pry bar and hammer, choking dust and aching muscles. On Friday mornings Tomás scraped together the week's diggings, had his slave and his Indians load them on his three mules, and made his way down to Pachuca, where he sold his ore to one of Pachuca's stamping mills. Friday night and Saturday morning he prayed and talked and ate with his Portuguese friends. Sometimes after prayers he visited a tavern or a brothel. Early Saturday afternoon, after making certain to be seen crossing himself in front of the church, he trudged back up the steep slopes to the mines.

After eight years of this, one day the taverns in Pachuca began to buzz with news of fabulous silver strikes near Tlalpujahua on the border of the Purépecha country of Michoacán. Maybe Great-Uncle Tomás's luck would change there.

CHAPTER 5

It turns out that it didn't; not appreciably anyway. Tomás found enough silver in Tlalpujahua to eke out a decent, if precarious, living, but it was never enough to build a fancy house, let alone to finance his own *ingenio* to extract the silver from the chunks of ore. During the times when his mines went dry, he took his mules down to the Mixteca and bought cacao and sugar to sell to the miners. Still, all in all, he didn't move on. Tlalpujahua seems to have been his last dream. Something about the place calmed his wanderlust. Maybe the green-forested hills reminded him of his childhood in Spain in the Vera. Maybe it was that he was getting older: he was thirty-eight when he first went to Tlalpujahua. Maybe it was the fact that in Tlalpujahua he finally found a woman to settle down with. Not to marry—Great-Uncle Tomás wasn't the marrying kind—, but to live with as if she were his wife. Cohabitation ran against Church law, but that was mainly city stuff. Miners are miners, and the risk in towns like Tlalpujahua wasn't great.

The woman's name was Ana Jiménez. The people I've talked to, who knew her in her old age, said that she was a short, plump woman with a heart of gold. Unlike Great-Uncle Tomás, who preferred his own company and never developed the knack of acquiring close friends, Ana knew everybody in Tlalpujahua. Tomás scraped together enough to build her a small house in town, and he would come down from his mine to spend the weekend with her. Ana's neighbors loved and respected her. She and Tomás didn't have much, but what they had, she freely shared. Children's clothes for families too poor to buy or make them. Hot soup for the sick. A coin or two for an orphan's dowry. She was devout, too. You could always find her with the *beatas*, Tlalpujahua's gaggle of churchy women, praying the rosary late in the afternoon. She brought fresh flowers every Sunday to the Franciscan church. Tomás could keep his Jewish fasts with his Portuguese friends if he wanted to but not in their house. Ana Jiménez was a devout Catholic from head to toe. As would be—she was adamant about this—their children. I don't think Great-Uncle Tomás cared one way or the other. There were five children in five years: Beatriz, Lope, Teodoro, Ana, and Gabriel, the youngest, who was born around 1575. As far as I've been able to determine, the children all still live in Tlalpujahua, married and with kids of their own.

For thirty-two years Great-Uncle Tomás dug silver from the hills around Tlalpujahua. His most productive mine was in a gully about an hour west of the village, and it was there that he put up his shack. The arroyo carried enough water to run the small crushing mill that Tomás constructed on a flat a little below the mine. But he was always in trouble with his neighbors, especially the Ramírez brothers, Cristóbal and Antonio, whose mine was upstream from Great-Uncle Tomás's. When they cut off his water, he sued them, and they wrangled for years until finally the Alcalde de Minas ordered the brothers to release enough water to power Great-Uncle Tomás's mill. With soldiers standing guard, Tomás's Indians hacked out a new ditch to carry the flow. Then Antonio Palacios, farther down the hill, sued Tomás for the same reason, and they were all back in court again.

Great-Uncle Tomás lived in Tlalpujahua until he was seventy, when the Inquisition picked him up. During the first years after the silver strike there wasn't much to the town, just scrap-wood shacks near the entrances to the mine shafts that dotted the hills. There were a few taverns of course, with tables where you could gamble your day's gleanings on a hand of cards or flush them away with pitchers of cheap wine or cactus liquor. There were a handful of rudimentary churches, too—the Cofradía, the Virgen del Carmen, and a couple of others—, but nothing substantial.

Mexico City was a long way from Tlalpujahua, so Great-Uncle Tomás didn't make the journey very often. Maybe once or twice a year. His longest stay in the city, I think, was with his father, Gabriel, during the old man's last illness, around 1568. The woman who should have been there to comfort Gabriel was long since in her grave. Tomás's half brother, Julián Castellanos, lived only a couple of doors from Gabriel. By this time Julián had run his father's original store into the ground. People say that he lacked drive, that the dreams he brought with him to the New World had died early. He peddled stuff in the streets for a while, but he no longer had the knack of selling, so his suppliers stopped advancing him merchandise. He took jobs as a clerk, a coach driver, a guard, but nothing seemed to last more than a week or two. What little he earned he spent on drink. Finally he settled for work as a common laborer, a *bracero*, eking out a living with his pick and shovel in competition with the Indians and blacks. When he was in really dire straits, his father kept him from starving. You'd have thought Julián would at least help shoulder the burden of caring for his father in his last illness; but he didn't, so the weight fell on Great-Uncle Tomás.

I think that must have been the source of the friction between Julián and Old Tomás. Cain and Abel stuff. Tomás was independent. Not rich, but independent. He took risks, he worked hard, he made a life for himself. So why hadn't Julián? If their father had money, shouldn't it have gone to both sons, not just to Julián? When Gabriel finally died and the priests had gone home, the brothers got to look at the old man's will. There wasn't much, but what there was Gabriel had divided 70–30, not 50–50, with Julián getting the lion's share. Tomás was incensed; he had never believed that Julián was Gabriel's true son anyway. Julián wasn't happy either. He thought that as the most in need he should have gotten it all. The two brothers never spoke to each other again.

And the years went by. On Tomás's infrequent visits to Mexico City he lodged with Manuel de Lucena or the Carvajal family, swapping Bible stories and talking about the coming Messiah. He knew most of the Portuguese business community, borrowing money from some, lending to others, sharing the meals that the Lucena and Carvajal women cooked for them on Friday evenings. People tell me that despite the rough edges that made it hard to like him, he was respected for his knowledge of the Bible.

In July 1590 a commissioner of the Holy Office arrested Great-Uncle Tomás in Tlalpujahua as a Judaizer and ordered him returned to Mexico City. Old Tomás, never a man to mince words and as choleric at seventy as he had been at twenty, turned purple and began to scream at the commissioner and the bailiffs.

"Get your hands off me! You think I'm a Muslim? Hell, I don't know the first damn thing about the rites of Muhammad. Or of Moses either. Or of Martin Luther. What do you think you're doing? I don't know anything about those things, and I don't deal with anybody who does! My whole family are old-Christians. Every last sainted one of them!"

Everybody within harquebus shot of Tomás's house must have heard him, he raised such a ruckus. It didn't do him any good though, because in short order he found himself in the Inquisition prison in Mexico City.

The first thing the inquisitors tell you when you are arrested is never to talk about your case with anybody, under any circumstances, under pain of punishment in this world and the next. But as I've said, Great-Uncle Tomás's tongue was as independent as he was, so I've been able to find out a good deal of what happened to him in prison.

For a start, no matter what they accused him of, he put up the same two defenses. First, he denied absolutely everything. And second, he insisted that

The Miners Fonseca

the accusations against him were out-and-out lies, fabricated by his enemies and spread by malicious gossips. Naturally, his enemy number one was his brother—or half brother—Julián de Castellanos.

If the inquisitors accused him of associating with New Spain's Portuguese community, Tomás replied that he hated and distrusted the Portuguese, who were all a scurvy-ridden rabble, unlike the noble and well-behaved sons of Castilla like himself. If they accused him of quoting the Book of Esdras to deny that the Messiah had come, he said that he didn't read much of anything, not since he'd been a kid in school, so how could he quote some book? If they accused him of disrespecting holy images—this came from his one-time cellmate Thomas Day, an English merchant who had been accused of Lutheranism—, he argued that he had told Day that there was a difference between idols and holy images, and that the English did right in condemning the former, but they were wrong in not having statues of Jesus and Mary and the saints. If the friars accused him of disparaging miracles, then he countered with one that had happened in his own family, to Julián de Castellanos's daughter some forty years previous. One day the girl was sick to the point of death with a swollen stomach, so her parents had taken her by canoe to the sanctuary of Our Lady of Guadalupe. As they neared the sanctuary she had spewed out all her sickness from her mouth and nose—and the other end too—, and everybody said Our Lady had worked a miracle.

Did Tomás keep the Sabbath? they asked him. Ah, well, Old Tomás said, that required a little more explanation. It was true that in Mexico City he had often eaten supper with the Carvajals. And some of those meals could have been on Friday night. And, to tell the truth, Luis and his brother Baltazar—the one who later, in Europe called himself Jacob Lumbroso—had indeed spoken to him of the Law that God gave to Moses, and he acknowledged that he had been remiss in not reporting this to the Holy Office. As a matter of fact, the two brothers' preaching had nearly convinced him to believe in that Law, and because of them he had observed twenty or thirty Sabbaths, and had prayed the Psalms with them without adding the "Gloria Patri" at the end. But he swore on his mother's milk and the Blessed Virgin and Jesus and all the saints that his Judaizing hadn't lasted very long. Because soon after that, while he was on the road back to Tlalpujahua, he read Saint Anastasio's Psalm, and he quickly came to see that the Carvajal brothers, both of them mere children, had pulled the wool over an old man's eyes. And from that moment on he had been unwaveringly Christian.

CHAPTER 5

Well, none of this convinced the inquisitors, who saw Great-Uncle Tomás's testimony as shot through with contradictions. He was a reader who did not read. A man with no interest in theology who could cite the Bible and the literature of Christian contemplatives. A reformed Judaizer who maintained his friendship with Lucena and the Carvajals. The inquisitors felt compelled to sort it all out, to get Great-Uncle Tomás to detail for them the evolution of his religious convictions, to express his contrition and accept his penance like a man. So they niggled at him, holding him in prison and questioning him intermittently for the next six years.

Nothing came of it though, except that what with his age and the poor food and the damp conditions Great-Uncle Tomás began to take sick. So sick that he thought he might die, and—always the clever man—, he turned that into another defense. "Since I have one foot in the grave," he told them, "and have turned all my thoughts to the salvation of my eternal soul, what possible motive could I have to lie to you?"

That didn't convince them either. In 1596 he marched with the penitents in that year's auto-de-fé where he confessed his sins, was ordered to wear the sambenito, and was then released with a hefty fine and an obligation to attend church regularly. Jacob Lumbroso told me that after the auto Tomás went straight to Francisca de Carvajal's house and danced for joy with her and her daughters Mariana and Leonor.

It was a brief moment of joy. Great-Uncle Tomás was too old, or sick, or depressed to make the long journey back to Tlalpujahua, so he wrote out a document assigning the administration of his mine to his son Lope. But by then there wasn't much to administer, as the Inquisition commissioner found out when he went to seize Great-Uncle Tomás's remaining possessions. The wooden braces in his mine had all rotted away so that cave-ins had closed the shaft. The ramshackle house out by the mine hadn't fared much better. What the dry rot hadn't crumbled, his neighbors had stolen to patch up their own shacks. His mining tools and his mules had been sold to pay his expenses in jail. The only thing he had left was his good name, and after the auto-de-fé that was in shambles, too. I don't believe he ever again saw Ana or his children, except for Lope, who came occasionally to Mexico City on business.

All Great-Uncle Tomás had left was his freedom; but that didn't last long, because two years later he was arrested again. Same charges. Same witnesses. More questions. I've not been able to find out what happened in prison during the three years before the 1601 auto-de-fé, but I imagine that

Tomás's defense was not as spirited as it had been before. After all, by then he had passed his eightieth birthday. This time the Holy Office condemned him to spend the rest of his life, such as it was, in jail.

In early February 1602 Great-Uncle Tomás was carried on a litter to the Convalescent Hospital in Mexico City, and from there, ten days later, to the Church of San Hipólito, where he was buried in consecrated ground. A token, at least, of the Holy Office's acceptance of Great-Uncle Tomás's unwavering insistence that he was at heart a true Christian.

Héctor de Fonseca, from Taxco

Cousin Héctor was thirty years younger than my great-uncle Tomás. I only met Héctor once, when I was still a child, but he made a strong impression on me. He was short and solid, hairy like all the Fonseca men. A bushy gray beard sprouted from both cheeks so that his round face looked like the moon peeping out from between clouds. When he let me climb in his lap, I thought he was a tree.

When Cousin Héctor spoke, I could tell that his first language was Portuguese. Not surprising, I later realized, given that all the Mexican Fonsecas had Portuguese branches on their family trees. Most of their ancestors fled from Spain to Portugal at the time of the great expulsion, though many eventually returned to Spain in search of work, or to escape the law, or to put distance between themselves and the newly fired-up Portuguese Inquisition. And from Spain they sailed to the New World, answering the siren's call of the silver mountains. Cousin Héctor's parents, Felipa de Fonseca and Antonio Fernández de Almeida, were both from Viseo, a ducal city filled with Fonsecas, a third of whose women must have been named Felipa. This is by way of saying that Héctor's mother, Felipa, and Great-Uncle Tomás's mother, Felipa, were two different people, conceivably not even related. None of which mattered a whit in Mexico. We called Héctor our cousin, and that was that.

Some people have told me that Héctor's father had killed someone in Viseo, and that was what prompted the family to move back to Spain. Verín, where they settled, is a good-size town on a major road just across the border from Portugal, so there were lots of business opportunities there. His father opened a dry-goods store. In Verín they speak a dialect of Portuguese that the family found easy to understand. And in Spain, of course, the Portuguese authorities couldn't touch them. I spent a week in Verín telling people that I was trying to locate potential heirs to an estate in Mexico, but I couldn't find anyone who remembered the family.

The Fonseca-Almeidas had two daughters who died when they were infants and four sons, all of whom eventually came to New Spain. The eldest, Jorge de Almeida, was a forceful, controlling man; sure of himself, convinced that anyone who didn't go along with his ideas was either an enemy or a fool. His dark complexion was marred by a childhood bout of the pox and a scar on his cheek that he refused to discuss with anyone. People have told me that even as a boy he was always telling the younger children what to do, whom they could make friends with. Héctor used to complain that Jorge acted more like a father than a brother; when they were young, Jorge was two heads taller than Héctor and nearly double his weight, so there wasn't much that Héctor could do about Jorge's pushing him around. Despite his size, Jorge preferred working with his head rather than his hands. Those people he couldn't intimidate, he could outsmart. Or ingratiate, a negotiating tactic that he mastered in the course of his travels. Or buy off, once he had made his fortune. Given his skills, that didn't take him long. His creed seems to have been: go where the money is, then take it. Taxco, where the hills were laced with silver, was perfect for him. Within a few years he had bought a hacienda with a big house where he and his Mexican wife, Leonor de Carvajal—yes, those Carvajals—entertained not only the Portuguese community but also half the dignitaries in New Spain.

Miguel Hernández, the third bother, lived for a few years at Jorge's hacienda not doing much of anything. Whether he got restless or Jorge eventually threw him out is a mystery; but he left Mexico sometime in the mid-1580s. Héctor's youngest brother, Francisco Hernández, left Mexico about the same time. Neither Miguel nor Francisco seems to have married, or had children, or made any money to speak of. Maybe they went to Perú or back to Spain. Or maybe they died. I've not met anyone who knows what happened to either of them after they left New Spain.

But I'm getting ahead of myself.

Like most of the Fonseca men, Cousin Héctor could read and write— Portuguese, Castilian, Latin—by the time he reached his teens. He knew Scripture, too. He showed enough promise that when he was fourteen his parents were able to secure him a job as a page in the household of the marqués de Villareal. I don't know what happened in the palace, but after only a year the marqués sent him home again. Was Héctor too rough-mannered for life at court? Did somebody overhear him praying the way he'd been taught at home? Whatever triggered his dismissal, Cousin Héctor spent the next few years helping his father and his brother Jorge in their store in Verín. Then, suddenly, his parents picked up and moved with their four boys to Saelices, a small town in La Mancha de Cuenca. Why they moved there I have no idea. Was there some family connection in La Mancha? Some notion that a dusty road town in the middle of nowhere might be safer for the Fonsecas than a big city? Whatever it was, their hopes obviously didn't work out, because only a few months later the family was on its way to Mexico.

Cousin Héctor was twenty-one years old when he clambered ashore in Veracruz in 1569. By then he was sick of his brother and fed up with marching to his parents' orders. As far as he was concerned, they and Jorge could look for work in Mexico City if they wanted to, but not him. Héctor was off to the fabled silver mines in Zacatecas where, he felt certain, in a year or two he would make his fortune. Of course it didn't work out that way; it hardly ever does. Héctor found that the richest veins in Zacatecas had long since been staked out. So while the dusty silver-spattered hills surrounding the major claims offered him a chance to learn the mining trade, instant wealth eluded him. And Cousin Héctor was impatient.

When after six months he heard of rich new strikes in Mazapil, far to the north in territory being explored and developed by Captain Luis de Carvajal, he headed that way in the company of some of his Zacatecas friends. The "Six Mighty Miners" they called themselves. Twice along the road north Chichimeca Indians attacked their band, and twice they drove them off after suffering only minor wounds. When the six men finally reached Mazapil, they found that the new city was not much more than a scattering of adobe huts, one ingenio for pulverizing the silver ore, two diked flats for curing the ore with mercury, an assay office for registering and taxing the refined silver, the usual handful of taverns, and a half-built church. The tavern kitchens served mainly goat and nopal cactus leaves. Mazapil's water was brackish and the wine expensive. The only women were Chichimecas. Aside from watching Captain Carvajal and his troops ride through the settlement a couple of times, the place was dull, dull, dull. After nosing around for six weeks or so and not finding one speck of silver, Cousin Héctor and his friends repacked their mules and set out for the civilized south. I heard this in Mexico City years later from the last surviving member of the Mighty Miners.

They took the southern road toward Michoacán, and, after several weeks, as they neared the silver diggings of Tlalpujahua, something tickled the back of Héctor's memory. It was possible he had a cousin in those mines, a Tomás de Fonseca, older even than Héctor's father. Maybe Cousin Tomás could help him and his friends do some prospecting there.

Tlalpujahua was not as big as Zacatecas, but it was substantially larger than Mazapil. While his companions lazed in the plaza or plunked down their silver reales in the taverns, Héctor went looking for his relative. After an hour of asking in the taverns, the market stalls, the parish church, and at the ingenio, he was directed to Tomás's stake on a dry, oaky slope a league and a half out of town. Both the mine entrance and the door to the shack that stood next to it were bolted tight. A tall, sun-blackened man working a shaft farther down the slope told Héctor that Tomás had gone to Mexico City to take care of his ailing father, and nobody knew when he would be back. The boys hung around Tlalpujahua for a few weeks prospecting—unsuccessfully— and waiting for Tomás. But they soon ran out of patience and again headed south, this time to the well-established mining community of Taxco. By that time Héctor's brother Jorge de Almeida was established there. Whether that was an attraction or a disincentive, I cannot say.

In the course of that long journey to Taxco from the northern mining towns, Cousin Héctor had absorbed a good deal about the business. He had become skilled with a pick and shovel. He had begun to know rocks, to read the flecks and mineral threads, the textures and smells and taste of the stone. The way hunters find game by reading hoofprints, bent twigs, and torn grasses, he had learned to read the telltale signs of iron, copper, and silver. But he also had begun to intuit which mineral veins ran true and straight into the mountain and which were only surface glimmers, hinting of riches they had no ability to deliver. The best prospectors—according to the disgruntled failures nursing their mugs of maguey brandy in the taverns—had a spiritual connection with the mountains. In hushed tones they would tell Héctor how God, or the Devil, or the spirits of the earth, would plant a hunch in the miner's mind, a hunch that grew into a certainty that this was the place his foul luck would finally change.

Late one afternoon, emerging from his dust-choked hole after sweating there for twelve hours with his pry bar and shovel, Cousin Héctor had a revelation. There are miners, and then there are people in the mining business, like his brother Jorge de Almeida. Both had to know rocks. But the businessman had to learn to read people, too. He needed skill in trading: buying and selling shares of mine shafts, offloading mines that he suspected had already yielded their best or exchanging them for diggings that hinted at greater potential. He could buy up other miners' ore, leaving them free to continue digging while the businessman trucked it to the city to be melted into bars. Marketing the silver ingots was not an issue: the King bought it all, by law, and shipped most of it back to Spain to gild his churches, pay his soldiers, and make the Genoese bankers rich. Not to mention the British and Barbary pirates who siphoned off a third of the treasure before it ever reached the shores of Iberia. None of which was the miners' concern.

The first step in becoming a mining businessman was to find the capital to begin trading.

The hills surrounding Taxco had been dug for years, but there were still promising spots for aspiring new arrivals to try their luck. Cousin Héctor found silver after only two months of digging. With his first profits he bought a black slave and hired three free Indians to work that mine while he went looking for another vein. Within a month he had found a vein of copper pyrite from which the ingenio extracted iron, copper, and sulfur. He sold a half interest in those two mines and bought five shares of Pedro de Prado's Margarita mine, just before Prado struck the lode of silver that made him rich. Over the next few years, exploring and digging, selling and buying, Cousin Héctor came to own six mines outright—three of pyrite and three of silver— and to own shares in another half dozen or so. He was not a silver magnate who could afford a palatial house near the plaza, but he acquired enough to live quite comfortably in the home he had built near the entrance to his most productive silver mine in Camistla, not far from the center of Taxco.

Except for brief business trips to Mexico City, Héctor remained in Taxco for the next twenty-seven years. He made his last trip to Mexico City as a guest of the Holy Office.

The inquisitors charged Héctor with behaving and believing like a Jew. And from the dribbles of information the surviving members of his generation have shared with me, I suspect that they were mostly right.

There's not much doubt about where Cousin Héctor learned the rudiments of his Judaizing: at his home in Spain, as a child. He always claimed that he descended from an old-Christian Portuguese family, boasting that his grandfather, Héctor Fernández de Abreu, had been a knight of the Order of Santiago. And that, he used to say, was in the days when knights were fighting men, not like today, when most of them are courtiers who buy their titles or have connections. Likewise, he insisted that his father, Antonio Fernández de Almeida, had been *alcaide* of Almeida's castle, in charge of its security and administration. If those things were indeed true, then it is possible that his boast of being an old-Christian—at least on his father's side—may have been true as well.

Yet he and his brothers seem to have arrived in the New World with a good deal of knowledge about Jewish practice. And sympathy for it, too. Maybe that came from his mother, from the Fonseca side of the family. Even in Mexico everybody knew that Viseo, where the Fonsecas hailed from, was full of conversos. So his boasts about the knight and the alcaide didn't convince anyone. Cousin Héctor stuck to his story, but his acquaintances smirked behind his back.

The Holy Office didn't believe it either, given the reams of testimony that they had assembled against him. Eventually Héctor admitted to his Judaism. He had to. There were so many witnesses that the inquisitors had him dead to rights. But he never wavered in his claims of being an old-Christian. The Judaizing, he told them, began later, in Mexico, where evil companions had played on his weakness and gullibility. Besides, he always insisted, his Judaizing was only intermittent; he was always a true Christian at heart.

Héctor claimed that his first conversion came on one of his business trips to Mexico City when he was about thirty-five years old. He was staying at Luis Díaz's house, and a man named Luis Rodríguez Platero, one of Díaz's Judaizing friends, approached him. Héctor was flattered that Rodríguez and Master Morales, a doctor, who were the center of the Diaz group, accepted him so warmly into their company. Anyway, one night Luis Rodríguez drew Cousin Héctor aside, saying that he felt compelled to tell him something that was crucial for the salvation of his soul but that he would only reveal it if Héctor swore never to repeat a word of the conversation. Héctor agreed. Luis told Héctor to look up at the stars and tell him if the sky had changed in any significant way. Héctor said no, it's the same as it always is, and Luis replied that if creation has not changed, then the Creator must never have changed either. God gave the Law to Moses. God told him it would last forever. So how could it be, as the Christians say, that the Law of Moses has come to an end? Héctor agreed that he made a good point. Then Luis took out a book and read to him about the Law of Moses. How only that law could save him. How the Messiah had not yet come, so Jesus could not be the Messiah. How he must respect the Sabbath and the other festivals. As they were talking Dr. Morales came in, and Luis Rodríguez winked at him and said: "This Héctor Fonseca is a very good man." It was clear to Héctor what he meant.

Well, as Cousin Héctor related years later to one of his cellmates (from whom I heard the story), that conversation left him roiling in confusion. Could his new friends be right? Could the priests be wrong? Héctor said he went straightaway to the cathedral where he sank to his knees in front of an image of Our Lady of Pardon to beg Jesus to advise him which was the true path to salvation. And there, with tears streaming down his face, he recanted what he had done and swore his eternal adherence to the Law of our Lord and Savior.

The tears didn't last. Héctor said later that in spite of his good intentions Rodríguez's and Morales's arguments soon persuaded him to leave the Law of Jesus once and for all. For the next few weeks he and Díaz and his friends met frequently to talk of Scripture and the Old Law and what they had to do to ready their souls for salvation.

But on the road back to Taxco, as he rode up through the forested hills that enclosed the Valley of Mexico, Héctor's resolve began to weaken, and by the time he reached Malinalco it had vanished. He knew an Augustinian cleric in the monastery there, Fray Pedro Júarez de Escobar, the same man who is now bishop of Guadalajara, and he sought him out to make a full confession of his doubts. But once Héctor was on his knees, he was frightened by the consequences of confession, so he ended up confessing only the usual salad of miners' sins, without ever mentioning his flirtation with heresy. Or so he later said.

For the next two and a half years Cousin Héctor did not leave Taxco even once. I think he was afraid to go back to Mexico City where those Jews—Díaz and Morales and the rest—would undermine his commitment to living exclusively by the Law of Christ. Within a few months of returning to Taxco he married a local girl, Juana López de la Torre, the daughter of one of the officials in the extracting mill. A hardworking old-Christian, saint-for-every-purpose sort of girl, who crossed herself a hundred times a day and never ate an unlarded meal in her life. Whether Héctor wanted a bedmate, a helpmate, or a buttress for his quavering Christianity, who can say?

He held his doubts in tight check for well over a year, clenching his teeth as his wife's Christian obsessions grew more annoying. Héctor had long since rued the day that he had married an old-Christian. In fact, every few weeks, when Juana's pieties accumulated to the point that they broke his poor camel's back, he would go out into the hills and howl at the moon, repenting of his sins and swearing to live as a good Jew if only God would free him from this hell of a Christian marriage. After a few months her Jesus-talk drove him from her bed to the spare room and from there to the bed of a woman named Zarza, a widow he had met one day when he went into her late husband's store to buy a length of rope for one of his mines. Héctor told Juana that he was sleeping out at the mines to make sure that his slave and employees were not stealing his ore. But his friends knew to look for him at the widow's house. After a year their son was born: Francisco Núñez, which was the name of Zarza's husband who had died before being able to sire him. When he grew up Francisco went into the China trade; I believe he lives now in Macao or Manila or someplace like that. In addition to Francisco, Cousin Héctor fathered two daughters with the widow, María and Antonia de la Zarza. The four of them were never really a family, though Héctor felt some affection for them and from time to time gave money for their support. Because the children were bastards, Héctor worried that the two girls might never be able to marry decently. And Zarza insisted that her daughters were Christians and must be married to pure-blooded practicing Christians. That complicated things, too, because Héctor's few close friends in Taxco were Judaizing new-Christians. In fact, when one of them, Felipe Freire, presented himself as a suitor for María, young Tomás de Fonseca, the third Fonseca miner whom I'll tell you about later, intervened and broke it up. After all, the girls didn't even know what a Jew was. Up until then they had been shielded from the religious practices of the Fonsecas. In Young Tomás's eyes there was too much risk that one day Catholic María would inadvertently, or deliberately, reveal the family's Judaizing to the Inquisition. Freire swore that he would get even with both Young Tomás and Héctor.

After this, Héctor was so worried about his daughters' futures that he made a gesture toward responsibility by having a document drawn up that in the event of his death 1,500 pesos from his estate would pass to the two girls as their dowry. As for his wife, Juana, whether she even knew about her husband's bastard children, or about the will, who could say? Her iciness toward her husband came from within: it didn't need any external provocation.

Cousin Héctor told both the widow and his wife that he was a Christian, and he swore that he was trying to fulfill the obligations that the Church imposed. But they both must have sensed that there was heresy in his heart.

The Miners Fonseca

Héctor must have known that eventually something or someone would force him to openly confront the issues of choice. But as long as he stayed put and didn't go back to Mexico City, he believed that he was safe.

Which of us ever knows where the rabbit will jump? Or when. By this time Cousin Héctor had a dozen men working for him. One day, as he approached his Camistla mine, he heard one of his men, Francisco Jorge, called "El Tuerto" because of his crossed eyes, reciting a prayer that sounded suspiciously like the ones that Luis Díaz had taught Héctor in Mexico City. When the servant realized that he had been overheard, he fell on his knees and begged Cousin Héctor not to reveal his secret.

Startled, Héctor broke into a cold sweat. Decision time was now. Expose himself by admitting that he recognized the prayers? Reassure El Tuerto that Héctor, too, had been a Judaizer? Denounce the man to the Inquisition, which would inevitably cause the inquisitors to look into his own life as well? Overlook the whole business and trust to El Tuerto's ability to keep his mouth shut? What he couldn't do was stand there much longer gaping at his employee.

"I never want to hear those prayers spoken aloud again. Do you understand me?"

He put as much sternness into his voice as he could muster. "Never again. This never happened."

But El Tuerto wouldn't let it be. "If you know what I was saying, then you must be a Jew like me."

"No, no; not at all," Cousin Héctor protested, realizing his mistake. "Somebody taught me those prayers when he was trying to convert me. I'm not a Jew; I'm a Christian. I've always been a Christian. In fact, I was thinking of reporting that person to the Holy Office."

"No, you mustn't do that. It's not right. And you have to look to your soul." By then his servant was sniveling and wrapping his arms around Cousin Héctor's feet so that he couldn't move. "You have to see that in accepting the Law of Christ you have been blind to the truth. Look to your soul's salvation, that's the only thing that matters in this world!"

Well, what with this and that, with cross-eyed Francisco Jorge's tears and the turmoil that Héctor carried inside himself, he found himself once again on the horns of his dilemma. Where did his salvation lie: with Moses or with Jesus?

If—as it appears to me—Cousin Héctor had lived for the previous two years with the Zarza woman in a state of complacency—or perhaps denial—, giving his full attention to his mining business and thinking of religion as little as possible, this encounter with cross-eyed Francisco Jorge set him to brooding. The months of choosing not to choose were behind him. In Taxco he began to attend church regularly. Yet during his visits to Mexico City, now occurring almost monthly, he began to spend more and more time with his Portuguese friends and their Judaizing colleagues: Ruy Díaz Nieto, who had come to New Spain from Italy; Antonio Méndez, the rich store keeper; Sebastián Rodríguez, who imported fine goods from China; the dueling master Marco Antonio; Manuel de Lucena, the magnate with mansions in both Pachuca and Mexico City; and especially the Carvajals.

It was destined. Héctor's brother Jorge de Almeida had married Leonor de Carvajal, Luis's sister. Young Luis de Carvajal was the nephew of Old Luis de Carvajal, the captain and governor whom Cousin Héctor had seen years before leading his troop through Mazapil. Young Luis, as everyone in New Spain is well aware after his scandalous execution in the Great Auto-de-fé of 1596, was the chief dogmatizer of Mexico's Judaizing community. Cousin Héctor knew them all: Morales and Lucena; the Díaz men, Francisco, Luis, and wealthy Antonio, who were no relation to one another; the Álvarez and the Rodríguez clans; Justa Méndez, said to be the prettiest girl in New Spain. Héctor visited them in their houses. He dined and fasted with them. He prayed with them and reveled in their discussions of the Law of Moses.

I won't say much here about Luis de Carvajal, the hub of the wheel, since everybody knows about him. How he traveled all over New Spain preaching to the core of Jewish heretics. How he nosed out any new-Christian who wasn't firmly churched and drew him back into the Jewish fold. His knowledge of the Bible, his gifts of persuasion, his unflagging energy, his relentless zeal. Luis was like the resin that seeps from the pine trees on the mountain slopes, sweetly perfumed and as compelling as burnished amber. But get some on your hands or in your hair, and you'll spend from now until the Devil speaks true trying to scrape it off.

Luis de Carvajal and his brother Baltazar were traveling merchants, selling wine, cloth, and ready-made clothing to the mining camps. For Luis's missionary life, his job was ideal. He was the postman for Mexico's Judaizers, delivering messages between distant friends and relatives. The Jewish customs he learned from new immigrants to Mexico City he soon spread across the colony. He taught people prayers. He let them know when the Jewish festivals would occur. He knew whose daughter was reaching marriageable age and where a suitable husband might be found. The vast spaces between Mexican towns were his inspiration and his pulpit. On the roads he could sing, write his poems, and forge bonds of intimacy with his traveling companions.

One of whom was often Cousin Héctor. As they rode their mules side by side on the Taxco road, their favorite topic of conversation was the Law of Moses. I think Carvajal must have liked Héctor because his knowledge of Scripture was almost has good as Luis's own, so they could discuss things almost as equals. Héctor's Latin was as good as Luis's, too, maybe even better, and over the years he had memorized long sections from Scripture, as had Luis. Their quote and counterquote, their philosophical thrust and parry, must have been something to hear! The prophecies of Daniel and Isaiah. The wisdom of Solomon. The lessons of the patriarchs, the battle kings and martyrs.

Even so, their conversations were about more than taking pleasure in the holy writings. They were both well aware that while Luis's faith was rock firm, Héctor was still searching, still sorting things out. And that let Luis exercise his role as teacher. Their conversations about the Book of Ezra, which Luis later used as the basis of more than one sermon, acquired a certain fame. Héctor asked Luis if the fourth chapter of Ezra, the one that condemns the Jews for their sinful ways, meant that God had abandoned the Jews and switched his support to the Christians. Luis told Héctor that he was misinterpreting the verses. God was not abandoning the Jews; he was speaking to them as a loving father hoping to correct the sinful behavior of his disobedient children. God's love of the Jews was eternal and unchangeable, which is why Héctor and the rest of their Judaizing community must remain firm in their faith.

By then Héctor's brother Jorge de Almeida had purchased from Hernán Cortés's sons the Cantarranas Hacienda not far from Taxco. With its three ingenios, quarters for slaves and servants, its own church, and an enormous manor house, it was like a small city. There was plenty of room for Carvajal and other new-Christian merchants to stay over. Luis's visits were always an occasion, an invitation to Taxco's Judaizing community to come together to share a meal, listen to Luis read from the Bible and preach, and bask in the warmth of each other's friendship. Héctor came whenever he could, as did Héctor's brother Miguel Hernández, before he left Mexico, and Young Tomás de Fonseca, before he and Héctor had their falling out. Héctor's employee El Tuerto and Almeida's men Francisco Daza and Juan Rodríguez de Silva were often there. Manuel de Lucena, who knew almost as much Judaism as Luis de Carvajal and loved debating with him before an audience, often showed up. And that's only a few of the regulars.

When he was visiting Mexico City in those years Cousin Héctor usually stayed with the Carvajals, who always had an extra bed or two prepared for guests. On the road, one-on-one with Luis, Héctor was never shy about speaking his mind. But in the noisy gatherings in the Carvajal household he tended to hold back, floating in the current of debate without putting his own oar into the water. From shyness? Not likely. My guess is that he was being cautious. There were so many people coming and going in the Carvajal household, and so much unmasked Judaizing taking place within its walls, that if anyone, just one person, informed the Holy Office, it seems likely that the whole group would be marched off to prison. Maybe that's why Cousin Héctor kept quiet. They could accuse him of being there, but no one could ever say they had heard him speak as a Jew or had seen him observing Jewish customs. Some of the Carvajal women, like Leonor, Jorge de Almeida's wife, sometimes wondered in private whether Héctor was a Jew at all, even though Luis reassured them he was. Wasn't it proof enough, he told them, that Héctor kept attending their gatherings, and that he listened to them pray and discuss the Law without ever raising any objections? Manuel de Lucena agreed with Luis: everybody knew that the Carvajal family Judaized, so why would Héctor even risk coming to Luis's house if he were not a Jew? And if Héctor were a confirmed Christian, why would Luis take the risk of inviting him? Besides, it wasn't true that Héctor never participated: Luis's sister Mariana told him she had heard Héctor singing hymns with the group when they gathered for the Great Fast.

Mariana. If it hadn't been for Mariana, the Carvajals and their relatives and friends might have lived in harmony indefinitely. But that was not to be. Mariana was bewitching, as much for the fervor of her commitment to the Law of Moses as for her beauty. By the time she was twelve she knew almost as much of the Bible as Luis, and in their family gatherings she would recite long passages. Prayers, too, in Spanish, Portuguese, and Latin. Her head was filled with religious fantasies. She told her mother that she wanted to become a nun, and when her mother informed her that there were no nuns in the Law of Moses, she became so upset that she had to be restrained. Next she wanted to denounce herself to the Inquisition so that she could die a martyr for her faith. The Carvajal family was scandalized: that would doom them all. They held endless discussions about how to keep her muzzled.

Though people used to say that Justa Méndez was the most beautiful girl in New Spain, at least among Mexico's community of Judaizers, she couldn't compete with young Mariana. In 1587 Mariana was small and slim, yet shapely enough at fifteen that she seemed more a woman than a child. The sparkle in her brown eyes picked up the flecks of light in her hair. She had delicate features, and she moved with a graceful ease that hinted of dance and mystery. Men were fascinated by her agile mind, but it was her smile that turned their knees to water and troubled their dreams.

The first to succumb was Jorge de Almeida, Héctor's brother and the husband of Mariana's sister Leonor. Every time he saw Mariana at one of the Carvajal gatherings, he found himself losing his wits. Mariana was oblivious to the attention, but Jorge's obvious discomfiture made Luis, his brother Baltazar, and some of the other men exchange worried glances. Then one morning in spring 1587 Jorge de Almeida, dressed in his best clothes, presented himself at the Carvajal home in Mexico City with a bizarre proposition: he wanted to marry Mariana!

Marriage to Jorge de Almeida?! Mariana's mother, doña Francisca, couldn't believe her ears. Luis and Baltazar could barely contain themselves. The effrontery! The impropriety! Almeida was Mariana's brother-in-law. He was happily married, so everyone believed, to Mariana's sister Leonor. There were laws against bigamy and against plural marriage. The Inquisition was vigilant. The proposition was dangerous, scandalous, heretical by any law. How could Almeida even dare to propose such an abomination? Besides, doña Francisca had already promised Mariana to Jorge de León, a young cloth merchant who was doña Francisca's first cousin. As her mother and brothers delivered this tirade, Almeida stood his ground. Mariana sat silently in the corner with who knows what thoughts raging in her head.

Almeida was not to be dissuaded. Once the Carvajals had calmed down, he laid out his case, pacing back and forth as he spoke. First of all, though it was true that Francisca's cousin Jorge de León was a new-Christian and casually observed one or two Jewish customs, he was nowhere near as committed to Judaizing as the Carvajal family deserved in a son-in-law. The fact that the Lisbon Inquisition had released Jorge de León without imposing any penance on him proved that he was no real Jew. Think of the grandchildren, Almeida told them: they would almost certainly be raised as Christians, even over Francisca's and Mariana's objections. They should also bear in mind that Almeida was far wealthier than León could ever hope to be. And as for the business about Almeida already being wed to Mariana's sister, it should not be a problem. As a good Jew he was only proposing to follow the precedent set by the Patriarch Jacob, who married both Rachel and her sister Leah.

Well, money talks, and it's true there was a biblical precedent of a sort. Doña Francisca said that she needed to think about it, that Almeida should come back the next day for her answer. Jorge must have spent a sleepless night, by turns dreaming of Mariana, worrying that he had overstepped the bounds of convention, and terrified of having to tell his wife, Leonor, of his plans to marry her sister. By first light he was ready to return to the Carvajal house, but he prudently waited until mid-morning, when he thought they might be more receptive. He knocked. Doña Francisca let him in. Luis and Baltazar were out somewhere attending to business. Doña Francisca led him into her private sitting room.

Without preliminaries she plunged right in. She had rethought the promised match with her cousin Jorge de León, and she now agreed with Almeida that León wasn't sufficiently Jewish. Yes, Almeida could wed Mariana, but not right away, and only if two conditions were met. First, the proposed union would not be announced until Almeida had taken the whole Carvajal family back to Europe, to the Low Countries, Turkey, or one of the Italian states, where they would be free to practice their Judaism openly. And second, only if plural marriage was still acceptable to that Jewish community.

Jorge Almeida was the sort of man who rarely worried about the soundness of his decisions. But when he heard doña Francisca's answer, he found himself having second thoughts. He could agree to her conditions; but did he truly want to go through with them? He wanted Mariana right now, not in some vague, distant future. Still, he thought, "later" was better than "not at all." He didn't really want to leave Mexico: he had made a fortune there. He had powerful friends in the government and the Church, so he felt reasonably secure in his Taxco hacienda. But then freedom in Europe wouldn't be so bad either. And Mariana was surely worth it. He began pondering which of his properties he should convert to cash and how long that would take. He had the resources to pay everyone's travel to Europe, but how much of the vast, extended Carvajal family would want to go? And where should he take them? France? Italy? Turkey? He could probably arrange things so that the Inquisition would not try to stop them. So much to plan, so many details.

Then he caught himself short. How would he explain all this to his wife, Leonor? Maybe he should slow things down for a while to let matters sort themselves out.

That afternoon doña Francisca told Luis and several other family members what she and Jorge de Almeida had agreed to. Shock? It was if she had proposed they break the Yom Kippur fast with roast pork! Everyone was angry: with her, with Jorge de Almeida, and even with Mariana (who only barely had a grasp of what was going on). Antonio Díaz de Cáceres, Catalina Carvajal's husband, reminded them that Judaism had abandoned plural marriage centuries ago. Luis and his brother Baltazar, the best talkers in the family, argued that there was no way they could ever agree to Almeida marrying his own sister-in-law. Besides, a promise was a promise: doña Francisca had to honor her word to Jorge de León. And then the clincher: going ahead with this obscene proposal was bound to split the family apart.

Which it did. León's family found out about the agreement even before doña Francisca had a chance to talk with them. You can imagine their reaction: it was wrong, scandalous, illegal; a blatant violation of the spirit of the Law of Moses. Worse, it constituted an insult to the entire León clan, regardless of the fact that they were Francisca's cousins. They swore vengeance, mayhem, even murder.

Luis, who was the unofficial leader of the Carvajal family, even though it was his mother's prerogative to determine questions of marriage, proposed an alternative plan. If it was inappropriate for Mariana to marry Jorge de Almeida because of what it would do to Leonor, maybe Mariana could wed Jorge's brother Héctor de Fonseca! The family's mouths fell open in disbelief, but Luis pushed on. All right, so by Catholic law Héctor was already married; but his wife was an old-Christian, by all signs a religious fanatic. Since Héctor was a Jew, Luis argued, technically that marriage did not count.

The idea was preposterous. Doña Francisca was convinced her son had lost his mind. She began to pummel him with objections, all of which Luis countered with authority. Didn't it say in chapter 10 of the Book of Ezra that the men of Israel should cast off the wives that they had taken when they were captives and instead marry Israelite women? Maybe Héctor had already cast off his wife—he wasn't living with Juana López anyway. Jorge de León and the business about a promise being a promise conveniently disappeared from the discussion. Though Luis's brothers continued to gape, the upshot was that doña Francisca reluctantly endorsed Luis's alternative plan.

That afternoon Luis told the unsuspecting Héctor of both his proposal and the biblical authority that sanctioned it. After the initial shock, Héctor seized on the idea as if it were a rope tossed to a drowning man. Luis was providing a way for him to walk away from his marriage to that old-Christian fanatic. Mariana was beautiful, modest, young, and just the wife to bring him fully back into the Jewish fold. He didn't even blink at the condition that Luis imposed: Héctor and Mariana could marry now, secretly, but they could not begin to live together as man and wife until they reached a European Jewry where they could practice their faith openly. Luis set the betrothal for the next morning, and there, in the Carvajal home, doña Francisca swore before God that Mariana would be Héctor's wife and no one else's. With that the pact was sealed. Hector's brothers were not invited.

When Jorge de Almeida learned of Mariana's betrothal to Héctor, he was beside himself with rage. This was treachery! Luis de Carvajal had stuck one knife in his back, and his brother Héctor had shoved in another. Almeida swore he would challenge Héctor to a duel. But he never did. I think he was afraid or maybe embarrassed to confront either Luis or Héctor directly.

A week went by, and then a month. In Mexico City the passions of most of the participants in the frenetic marriage negotiations began to cool. The León clan toned down their threats of violence and consoled themselves with the thought that someday, somehow, they would avenge themselves of this insult. They also resolved never to speak to Jorge de Almeida or the Carvajals again. Cousin Héctor's rashness in accepting this second marriage began to gnaw at him. He felt remorse that he had undercut the dreams of his own brother. He feared the Christian law and the Inquisition. So for a time he tried to patch up his relationship with Juana López, his old-Christian wife back in Taxco, who, thank God, had not yet heard any gossip about her husband's role in the marriage muddle in Mexico City. He went to church and left some part of his burden with his confessor. Doña Francisca, who seems to me to have been a woman whose mind was made up by the last person she talked with, put the whole business behind her. The wedding had been promised, but no one took any steps to make it a reality.

And Mariana? Despite her earlier incomprehension of what was being proposed for her, eventually it all sank in, and that drove her starkly insane. She took to screaming out a mixture of blasphemies, obscenities, and religious texts, or to babbling unintelligibly. She said she wanted to become a nun. She would not eat; she would throw herself suddenly to the floor; she pulled out most of her chestnut hair; she rebuffed any attempt to help her keep herself clean. For a while doña Francisca struggled to cope with her, but Mariana treated her more like an enemy than a mother. Finally the family paid a trusted acquaintance, Mariana de Peralta, to keep Mariana safe, out of sight, and presumably out of mind. There Mariana remained for the next three years. She spent most of them chained to her bed, ranting and mistreating her body, or motionless as a stone in fits of black melancholy. And then, suddenly, on the Feast of the Immaculate Conception in 1599, Mariana came back to the world, declaring that she had been blind all the years that she had Judaized with her family but that now that Our Lady had rescued her from her madness, she would live forever more as a faithful Christian. A promise that turned out to be as fragile as a primrose.

I've come to believe that for Cousin Héctor the few years preceding the marriage episode that he spent in intermittent company of the Carvajals and their circle of friends were the happiest in his life. At their large festival gatherings Héctor rarely spoke out, though in private conversations with the most learned of the group—Luis, Manuel de Lucena, Luis's sister Isabel—he opened up. He felt that they liked him and respected him for his knowledge. These people were his friends, the closest friends since long ago when the Six Mighty Miners had set out to the northern diggings.

But Héctor's quasi-marriage to Mariana had raised so much tension among the extended Carvajal-Almeida-León clan that companionable religious debate had become impossible. Everybody was on edge. One Friday evening the remaining members of the group, those who were not allied with Almeida or León, were all gathered at Luis's house when Antonio Díaz de Cáceres said something that seemed to impugn Cousin Héctor's honesty in buying and selling mining shares. Héctor, always quick to anger, called him a loud-mouthed ass. Díaz answered that better an ass than a thin-skinned cheat who couldn't even tell whether he'd been insulted or not. "I'll show you an insult!" screamed Héctor, drawing his knife. Doña Francisca tried get between them, but Héctor shoved her out of the way. Francisca's daughters were irate at Cousin Héctor's lack of respect for their mother. Antonio Díaz, now also knife in hand, rushed at Héctor, who, if he hadn't ducked in time, would have been skewered. The women began to throw things at him: silverware, chairs, hearthstones, whatever they could lay their hands on. Héctor rushed out of the house in full retreat. He swore never again to set foot in the Carvajal home, or to speak to anyone in Luis's family. In addition, it was widely rumored that Luis and Baltazar promised money and freedom to one of Antonio Díaz's black slaves to ambush Cousin Héctor and kill him. But, like Jorge de Almeida's threat to kill Cousin Héctor in a duel, nothing came of it. As for Héctor taking Mariana to Europe where they would live as man and wife, that dream had popped like a soap bubble.

Luis kept visiting Taxco, of course, but now he could not stay with Héctor. So instead he accepted lodging in the home of Héctor's nephew Young Tomás de Fonseca Castellanos, the third Fonseca miner, and that led to a split between Héctor and Young Tomás as well.

There were days when Cousin Héctor felt that he did not have a friend left in the world. He kept to Taxco, throwing himself into his business ventures and even wielding a pick and shovel in his mines alongside his slaves and servants, something that he hadn't done in years. He lived alone now. Some evenings he found solace in Taxco's brothels. On Saturdays he sometimes played with his children at the Zarza woman's home since he didn't want to be seen with them in the streets. On Sundays he went to church. He journeyed to Mexico City only when business made it absolutely necessary. It was not a happy life, but it passed the time.

In 1589, as everyone in Mexico knows, the Inquisition scooped up Luis de Carvajal and half his family as suspected Judaizers. The Portuguese community quaked: Luis was connected to everyone. He knew who dressed up for the Sabbath, who kept the Great September Fast, whose stomach turned at the odor of frying pork. If Luis cracked under pressure, all their lives would be in danger. More than one man converted his goods to cash and bought passage for Spain, hoping to slip from there to one of Europe's safe havens. I have talked with some of those Mexicans on the streets of Antwerp and Salonica and in the cafés of Ferrara. Most of them have vivid memories of the Carvajals, and some of them have told me stories of the three Fonseca miners as well.

While many of the Carvajal circle fled for Europe, Cousin Héctor anchored himself in Taxco, making sure that his church attendance and his devotion to the rosary did not go unnoticed. It was only in February 1590, when Luis publicly abjured his Judaizing and was sentenced to a couple of years' confinement as a Latin teacher in the convent school of Santiago de Tlatelolco, that Héctor and the rest of Mexico's Judaizers breathed a collective, if short-lived, sigh of relief. If they had been a little more prudent . . . But then, who was prudent in those days? Héctor's mine was producing more silver than it ever had, prompting him to petition the Alcalde de Minas for an extra allotment of mercury to amalgamate with the metal in the crushed ore. If Luis was safe, then why should Héctor run?

Five years went by before Carvajal's second arrest, and during those five years a sort of reconciliation was achieved among the warring parties. Héctor again began to visit the Carvajals, first in Tlatelolco and later in Mexico City. For a few months doña Francisca and her daughters relocated to Taxco, and although they didn't stay with Cousin Héctor, at least they began speaking to each other. Jorge de Almeida seemed to have mellowed as well, and for a while he hosted the Carvajals and the Fonsecas—both Héctor and young Tomás, although those two still tried to avoid speaking with each other—out at his Cantarranas Hacienda. In these gatherings when Cousin Héctor wasn't complaining about his old-Christian wife, he sometimes read them prayers, psalms, and poems that he had copied in tiny script into a small notebook. His favorite was one that began "Omnipotent Lord God, God of our fathers Abraham, Isaac, and Jacob . . . " It was obvious that Carvajal had once again persuaded Cousin Héctor to rededicate himself to the Law of Moses.

If in the calm and presumed safety of Taxco the others were happy, Héctor's brother Jorge de Almeida continued to brood. He convinced himself that the Carvajals and their friends were marked men, and the inquisitors would soon be knocking at his door. So he decided to return to Spain while he still could. His idea was to use his money and influence to negotiate a pardon for Luis and the other Carvajals who had been convicted of Judaizing. With a pardon they wouldn't have to wear the sambenito, and, in addition, they could apply for permission to leave New Spain. I've been told that in the back of Almeida's mind was the hope that if he could bring the Carvajals back to Europe, then he might still manage to get Mariana into his bed. Be that as it may, before long Almeida was back in Madrid, pulling strings and stuffing pockets to secure the pardon. While he was at it, he secured for himself a lucrative permit to import slaves into New Spain. In 1594, having spent most of the capital he had brought from Mexico, the commutations were granted. But it was too late.

While Almeida was negotiating in Spain, the Mexican Holy Office was methodically building its case against the Carvajal family and dozens of other Portuguese new-Christians in the Mexican territories, including

Cousin Héctor. They interviewed new witnesses, collated testimonies, and had genealogical evidence sent from Spain. Many of their targets had money: mines, haciendas, slaves, or stores with inventories of imported goods. The people I've talked with in Europe are convinced that money was what motivated the purge. But the Carvajals themselves weren't rich, and it seems to me that it was just as much religious zeal that drove the inquisitors' investigations as it was greed.

In February 1595 the Holy Office clapped Luis back in prison. In quick succession they arrested his mother, Francisca, and his sisters, Catalina, Leonor, and Isabel. Leonor's husband, Jorge de Almeida, was indicted, too, in absentia, and his Cantarranas estate seized and sold at auction. More members of the Carvajal clan were arrested later: Mariana, her sanity recovered and now mostly Christian; Catalina's husband, Antonio Díaz de Cáceres, and their daughter, Leonor de Cáceres; Justa Méndez; and Manuel de Lucena. The Fonseca miners were swept up, too. The bailiffs came for Héctor in March 1596.

Cellmates and corridor gossip. As I said, the Inquisition routinely swears all prisoners to secrecy, but people are people, sound carries, and in the patios and the sumps where the prisoners empty their slop buckets there is opportunity to greet old friends from the outside world. And once they've been released—free of prison, of Mexico, and best of all, of the Iberian world—people seem more than willing to share their memories. To brag about how they survived their suffering. To recount stories of vanished colleagues and family members. So it was not too difficult for me during my wanderings to learn a good deal about what happened to Cousin Héctor and the other Fonsecas in the Prisión Secreta behind Mexico City's Dominican monastery where accused heretics are kept until their trials are concluded.

The greatest founts of information were Luis de Carvajal's two brothers, who by then had exchanged the name Carvajal for Lumbroso. Baltazar, who now calls himself Jacob Lumbroso, I first talked with at the medical faculty in Venice and then later in Florence where he has become one of the most sought-after physicians in the city. I didn't meet Luis's second brother until years later when I had some business in the Turkish city of Salonica. I asked, as I always did, if any of the local Jews had ties with New Spain, and I was immediately directed to the noted Rabbi David Lumbroso, who was said to know more about Mexico than anyone else in the sultanate. My suspicions were confirmed when the rabbi told me that he was Miguelico Carvajal, Luis's younger brother. He knew the Fonsecas well, all of them, and remembered my cousin Héctor most of all.

I found it hard to believe the Lumbrosos' depiction of the freedom that most of those not-so-secret Jews were allowed within the Secret Prison. Though they slept two or three to a cell and were forbidden to speak to one another about their cases, in reality the prisoners seem to have mingled quite freely in the patios and other public areas. There were so many of our people in the prison in those days—Cousin Héctor, Antonio Díaz Márquez, Ruy Díaz Nieto, Duarte Rodríguez, Captain Estéban de Lemos; I can't tell you how many others. They would pass the word about when it was appropriate to fast. And if they didn't make too much of a fuss about it, they could even celebrate some of the Jewish festivals. Both Lumbrosos told me how they were able to build a little hut in one corner of the patio and celebrate the Feast of Booths together by pretending it was a party for one of the jailor's saint's day. I heard that story in Amsterdam, too.

Cousin Héctor was strong-willed about most things, but he seemed to have no backbone when it came to jail. The Lumbrosos, like most of the people I talked with, were disgusted by Cousin Héctor's behavior in prison. More than once Héctor broke down in the audience chamber and whimpered that he was a Christian, that in his heart he had always been a Christian. He would seize the crucifix from the audience table and then, falling on his knees, kiss it and bathe it with tears. When the friars confronted him with what they considered irrefutable proof of all the Jewish activities in which he had taken part, Héctor claimed that the so-called proofs were lies circulated by his mortal enemies. Justa Méndez, because Héctor had undercut her proposed marriage to a secret Jew up in Querétaro. Antonio Díaz de Cáceres, because Díaz was a cantankerous person and a dishonest businessman in league with the Carvajals. The Carvajal women, because once at Jorge de Almeida's house Héctor had propositioned Isabel de Carvajal. He shouldn't have, but he did. Afterward, the Carvajal women couldn't avoid him because he was Leonor's brother-in-law, but they never stopped hating him. And Jorge de Almeida and all his allies because of the muddle of Mariana's proposed wedding. The two aged Lumbrosos confirmed that for years they had harbored no kind thoughts for Cousin Héctor but that once they were safe in Europe they had put him out of mind. Ancient history. It was only under my questioning that they recalled what they had heard about how the inquisitors had brushed aside Héctor's attempts to discredit the accusations.

"Even if all these people are your enemies," the inquisitors persisted, "isn't it true that for a long time you considered yourself to be a Jew? That you took to heart the theological arguments of the Carvajal brothers, Lucena, and the rest?"

"Yes," Héctor had to admit. "But I swear to God that that was the Devil's work. I never really understood their arguments. May I go straight to Hell if that is not the truth." Then, just a few days after pleading incomprehension, Héctor told them just the opposite. Of course he had understood their arguments. He had really and truly believed in the Law of Moses and had only played at being Christian for appearance's sake.

When they asked Héctor why he had never brought his Judaizing activities to the attention of his confessor, he said that it was because he was afraid. Afraid for his life. Afraid to sully the honor of his Christian wife and the children that he had fathered with the Zarza woman. He had planned to confess everything one day, he told them, but only after the two girls were married.

And was he a Christian now? Yes, of course. Really he always had been. He had only flirted with Judaism. From time to time. To accommodate his friends. To feel accepted as a member of a community. In moments of weakness. The Devil's work.

They held Cousin Héctor for a long time, questioning him sporadically, and then letting him sit for weeks, sometimes for months, to stew in his cell.

Héctor didn't do well in prison. The cold chilled him to the bone. The damp rotted his feet. And the pox, which he probably picked up years previous with the prostitutes of Taxco, began to show itself in running ulcers on his nose, his cheeks, and his groin. For two weeks in late summer 1597 the inquisitors transferred him to the Hospital de las Bubas to have his pox treated; but it didn't do much good. When they returned him to his cell, the pox only grew worse. In October 1599 they sent him back to the hospital, with the same lack of results. Then it was back to his cell again for another two years until finally—the wheels of justice having ground both slowly and inexorably—he was paraded before the city in the auto-de-fé of 1601, along with a host of others, including Ana and Mariana de Carvajal, the rest of the imprisoned Carvajal family having been burned at the stake back in December 1596. One by one, the penitents stood before the Grand

Inquisitor, their yellow candles in their hands, to hear their sentences read. Ana de Carvajal: two years imprisonment. Mariana de Carvajal: to be strangled and then burned. Héctor de Fonseca: one hundred lashes and perpetual incarceration.

In Cousin Héctor's case perpetuity was short: within a year he was back on the street, although by then he was a broken man. He lived long enough to petition the inquisitors to be allowed to return to Spain. The petition was granted, but it came late. I've not been able to discover precisely where in Mexico City Cousin Héctor's bones found their final resting place.

Young Tomás de Fonseca, from Taxco

My uncle Tomás de Fonseca Castellanos, the third Fonseca miner, was known universally as Young Tomás de Fonseca, or sometimes "Tomás from Taxco," to distinguish him from his own uncle Tomás who worked mainly in Tlalpujahua. The name Young Tomás fit him, of course, since he was the youngest of the three Fonseca miners. But unlike Great-Uncle Tomás or Cousin Héctor, he was really a shopkeeper at heart, not a miner.

Uncle Tomás grew up in Portugal, in Viseo. His father, Álvaro de Fonseca, had died before Tomás was old enough to remember him. His mother, Isabel, raised him as a Christian, even though she wouldn't allow pork in the house and always made him change his clothes on Friday afternoon. But one Friday evening, when he was eleven or twelve, he asked his mother to tell him about his father, and the whole story came spilling out. Isabel and Álvaro were first cousins, but since they never got a Church dispensation to marry, they never had. In fact, they had never even lived together openly because they were afraid that someone would charge them with incest. What's more, they had never bothered to have Tomás baptized, what with his being illegitimate and his mother believing in the Law of Moses. Isabel was so afraid of being found out that when Álvaro died she left Viseo for Almeida. There she met Tomás Méndez and married him, even though he was a true practicing Christian who wouldn't hear of her keeping any of the old Jewish customs.

Uncle Tomás used to say that the only thing his mother and his stepfather ever fought about was his religious upbringing. His stepfather insisted that Tomás attend church and follow all the Christian precepts. His mother told him to conform on the surface to what his stepfather wanted, but she insisted that he commit his heart to the Law of Moses, obey its laws, and wait for the Messiah to come and save his soul. She also warned him never to tell any of that to his stepfather, who would beat him if he found out. His stepfather wasn't around much, but when he was, Tomás and his mother didn't dare observe any Jewish customs; the best they could do was to keep the Sabbath in their hearts.

Tomás's stepfather wanted the boy out of the house, so over Isabel's objections he sent Tomás to Lisbon, where he boarded with his stepfather's sister and clerked in her husband's store. But Tomás didn't like them, didn't like the work, and cared even less for the stifling atmosphere of Portugal. Uncle Tomás had heard tales about how his grandfather, Gabriel de Castellanos, had run off to Mexico when he was a boy to seek his fortune, so he got it in his head to follow him—without his mother's or his stepfather's permission, of course. On the Lisbon docks Tomás found that he didn't have the cash for passage to New Spain, but a slaver said he'd let him work his way to Cape Verde, and from there he could easily find a ship to take him to Veracruz. At age fifteen that sounded like a great adventure.

I suppose it must have been, even though slave ships are not known for their comfort, their odor, the quality of their food, or the kindness of their captains and mates. No matter. In the four months it took Tomás to reach Veracruz his muscles hardened, his vocabulary broadened, and he became convinced that from then on he could put up with anything the world cared to throw at him.

In Mexico City it did not take Tomás long to locate his grandfather Gabriel de Castellanos. Everybody knew Gabriel: how he had come to New Spain back in the late 1530s with the first wave of settlers; how he had set up one of the first grammar schools for the children of the conquistadors; how later he had served in the administration that transformed the Aztec capital of Tenochtitlán into the Spanish city of Mexico. And how he had used his connections and savings to go into business, successfully enough so that now he owned a chain of small shops. He specialized in mining supplies, stylish clothing that he imported from Spain and the Orient, African spices, and, most lucratively, alcohol. Tomás found his grandfather in the spice shop that he called his headquarters. The teenager and the old man embraced and exchanged family news. Before the afternoon was over Gabriel had arranged for Uncle Tomás to board with Guiomar de Fonseca, one of Gabriel's nieces, and had found him a job. His hardware shop needed someone to keep the books and help manage the inventory. If Tomás proved capable, in a month or two Gabriel would set him up in a store of his own.

The Miners Fonseca

True to his word, Gabriel installed him in a wine shop a couple of blocks off Calle Tacuba to the east of the Zócalo. It was not the best neighborhood, but then the store didn't stock the higher-quality wines. Tomás dispatched drinks by the glass to mule drivers, pushcart peddlers, and the countless pick-and-shovel and bricks-and-mortar men who were building the Spanish city, and by the barrel to the proprietors of the cheaper sort of taverns. The first year Young Tomás found the business fascinating. By the middle of the second year he was bored, and at the end of that year, almost to the day, he returned the business to his grandfather, bade his city friends good-bye, and headed up the road to Tlalpujahua to ask his uncle Old Tomás to teach him how to be a miner.

Six years he stayed with Old Tomás. Young Tomás learned how to read the rocks, how to shore up a mine shaft with timber so that the mountain wouldn't come crashing in, how to channel water to rinse the slurry from the crushed rock, how to manage his uncle's workmen, how to get his fair share of the mercury needed to separate the silver from the pulverized ore, and how to buy and sell mining shares. The most important insight came not from his uncle but from his own keen wit and powers of observation. Miners worked like slaves, buoyed by a hope, rarely realized, of striking the lode that would make them rich. On the other hand, merchants, especially in the larger towns, almost always prospered. The day Tomás put these vague thoughts into a plan was the day he said good-bye to Old Tomás and Tlalpujahua and packed up for Taxco, a town he judged large enough and rich enough for him to do well for himself. And there he lived for the next twenty years, building up his business, acquiring customers and enemies, and getting to know and earn the trust of his cousins Héctor de Fonseca and Jorge de Almeida. He also found the time to sire three bastard children—Francisco, María, and Álvaro—though he never actually lived with any of their mothers. Then in June 1589 the Inquisition arrested him and accused him of Judaizing.

From the time he had left home until he moved to Taxco, Uncle Tomás hadn't given much thought to his religion. No one has suggested to me that during those years Uncle Tomás observed any of the Judaizing customs he had learned as a child. Instead, he went to church when it was required, he confessed himself before Holy Week as Church law dictated, he watched the processions of holy images through the streets, he crossed himself when he passed a church—acts that he could be sure people would notice. No crises of conscience, at least not any that spilled out into public knowledge. As for Judaizing, not a sign. Well, maybe one: not only did Tomás refrain from eating meat on Fridays and during Lent, but he tried not to eat it at any other time either. Whether this was because the heavy food didn't agree with him, as he always claimed, or whether he carried on his mother's aversion to pork, who can say?

But Young Tomás's aversion to pork wasn't the issue. The real problem was that he was a cousin of Jorge de Almeida, whom everybody knew to be a hard-line Judaizer. The two of them were seen in each other's company often enough in Taxco that the inquisitors just naturally assumed that Young Tomás shared his cousin's religious convictions. They diligently interviewed Uncle Tomás's servants, neighbors, and friends and drew up a list of particulars that confirmed their preconceived conclusion. They didn't count on Tomás's determination to defend himself. From what I've been able to piece together, their list of charges against him went something like this:

You don't keep Christian images in your house.

You show up late to mass.

People say you never go to confession, or cross yourself, or take off your hat when you pass a church door.

When you say Grace you leave out "Glory be to the Father, the Son, and the Holy Spirit."

You don't eat pork.

You don't come out of your house to watch the Corpus Christi processions.

You observe the Sabbath of the Jews.

Uncle Tomás denied almost everything, of course, claiming that the accusations were all lies spread by his enemies. The charges he couldn't deny, he tried to render harmless by explaining their extenuating circumstances.

"I did observe the Sabbath. That's true, but it's because Francisco de Cáceres showed me a little book with the Ten Commandments in it, and one of them was 'Sabata sanctifica,' so it seemed natural and right for me to honor the Sabbath on Saturday. But in church I learned that Jesus had changed the Sabbath to Sunday, so I honored that, too, by going to mass and doing the other things that the church required.

"Not eat bacon? Wrong. For eight years I took my meals in Gaspar del Encino's house in Taxco, and his wife, Felipa de Fonseca, who was my cousin, cooked every single dish with pork. Just ask Gaspar. Though it's true that once or twice, when I was sick, my doctor told me to stay away from pork, so for a while I did. Maybe you're referring to those times.

"No images in my store? That's true, but the reason is that the storeroom just above it is filthy, and every time I move something up there the dust sifts down. I didn't want to soil them. But every other room in my house has statues and woodcuts of the saints and the Holy Family. All you have to do is go inside.

"Not attend the Corpus Christi processions? Not true. I went every year, and if I ever had to miss one, I went to mass twice that day. Just ask the people who marched next to me in the procession. You can ask them about how often I cross myself, too. As far as mass is concerned, you can ask any priest in Taxco. They'll tell you that I never missed a Sunday or a holiday. And I didn't come in late, either.

"Who says that I didn't educate my household? I made sure my black slaves and the Indians and the serving boys never skipped going to mass. The ones who slept in my house, I listened every night to make sure that they recited the four prayers, and watched that they crossed themselves properly. They have to show respect to all the images in my house, too, and if they don't, I beat them. They'll tell you.

"As for not saying the 'Gloria patri' at the end of my prayers, that's a lie. Maybe it's because I have a low voice, and I don't shout out my prayers so that any idiot in the street can hear them. Also, you know, I'm a businessman, a storekeeper, and if a client comes in before I finish reciting one of the prayers, then I have to break off in the middle and finish the prayer after my customer has left. But sometimes I pray with my friends, and any of them can tell you that I always say the 'Gloria patri' when I can. Grace after meals, too: sometimes 'Thanks be to God,' and sometimes 'Christ be praised.'

"I don't know why you believe all those lies. Obviously the people spreading them are my enemies. Everybody in Taxco knows who they are: Felipe Freire, Mateo Ruiz, Diego Rodríguez, Baltazar de Tejeda. Freire hates me because he knows I broke up his proposed marriage with one of Héctor de Fonseca's bastard daughters when I explained to Héctor how Freire was a lazy good-for-nothing who only had money because he was stealing it from Héctor. I can't tell you how evil Freire is. He said his wife was sleeping with my mulatto mule driver, Francisco, which was true, and Freire was so jealous that he tried to kill him. But he also accused me publicly of having sex with his wife, and that wasn't true at all. Just take a look at her. Who would want to?

"As for Mateo Ruiz, when he gets drunk, he gets violent. And jealous, too. He tried to kill Jorge de Almeida's servant Pedro, and I had to stop him. He hasn't spoken to me since, and everyone in Taxco knows how much he hates me.

"I forgot Francisco de Cáceres. He hates me because I refused to testify on his behalf in a lawsuit he had with Pedro de la Piedra."

Evidently all that was enough to discredit every accusation the inquisitors had, because they absolved Uncle Tomás and sent him home again without so much as a fine. If Young Tomás had been smart he would have left New Spain then and there. But he obviously thought that he was safe, that nothing more could happen to him. Still, two years later, in June 1591, he found himself back in the Secret Prison in Mexico City, again charged with Judaizing. So what happened? What by now you must suspect: the Carvajals.

By the end of the 1580s Young Tomás had grown to be one of the most important merchants in Taxco. His store stocked everything a person could want. He and a couple of his colleagues in Mexico City chartered whole ships to import goods from Europe. He bought goods from China, too, carting them up from Acapulco. You could find mule trains carrying his merchandise on every road from the coasts to Taxco.

As Tomás's fortunes grew, he built himself a substantial house near the center of Taxco, a house big enough for him, his two black slaves, the Indian women who cooked and cleaned for him, his mulatta housemaids and sometimes bedmates, and his serving boys. There were a few extra beds for hosting friends, from time to time his children, and several times each month the traveling shippers who supplied his store. The merchants who didn't lodge at Jorge de Almeida's hacienda of Cantarranas stayed with Young Tomás in the center of town. Most of them followed the Law of Moses. Among them were Manuel de Lucena, Sebastián de la Peña, Francisco and Sebastián Rodríguez, and the Carvajals. David Lumbroso told me all this in Florence. They didn't pray with Uncle Tomás, Lumbroso said. They weren't at all sure whether he was a Christian or a Judaizer—, but that didn't keep them from currying friendships with him. It was just good business.

As Luis de Carvajal later told his inquisitors, he and Young Tomás sometimes found themselves together on the road to Taxco. One afternoon, around sunset, Carvajal pulled a small book out of his saddlebag and began to pray from it. Uncle Tomás recognized the prayer as one he had heard as a child, and he panicked. "Put it away," he begged Luis. "My God, this is a public highway. If anyone sees you reading that stuff, or overhears you . . . "

Luis did what Uncle Tomás asked, but of course by then their shared knowledge of Judaizing hung in the air, so Luis felt confident in going further. Before long Tomás's shoulders were shaking with sobs as childhood memories overwhelmed him. They talked no more that day; but the next day and the one following, Carvajal began to persuade him—with his usual litany of biblical quotations—how Tomás was living in error, and how he could only be saved if he returned to the Law of Moses. As he probed Uncle Tomás's spirit, Luis began to realize the depth of his companion's misgivings about Christianity. The Holy Trinity made no sense to Tomás. He couldn't see how the man-God Jesus could possibly be the Messiah promised by the Law of Moses. Tomás used to tell Luis that he saw himself like the prophet Saul, so distant from God in his daily life and so alienated from serving Him. Yet when he found himself in the company of a true believer, he felt like a member of God's holy community.

It was fertile ground, and Luis plowed it with vigor. Before long Luis's fervor, his command of theological arguments and biblical authority, and the charismatic certainty with which he laid open and then resolved each of my uncle's doubts, turned Young Tomás into an enthusiastic Judaizer. At least that's what the people who knew Uncle Tomás in those days have told me. They also told me that Tomás's second round of troubles with the Inquisition began not with Luis de Carvajal but with one of Tomás's mulatta servants, María González.

This María and her husband, Francisco Pérez, both of them branded slaves, belonged to Felipa de Fonseca and Gaspar de Enciso, the couple Tomás had taken his meals with during his first years in Taxco. When Tomás built his big house, Felipa sent the slave couple to staff it for him. Since the mulattos ran Tomás's house and his kitchen, naturally they were witness to his newfound Judaism. María heated his bath for him on Friday afternoon. She laid out a clean shirt for him. She cut and twisted the wicks for the lamps that he lit Friday evening in his room where they couldn't be seen from the street. When he ordered leg of lamb, he had María dig out the vein and trim off the fat before she cooked it. Pork vanished from his house, and his neighbors sometimes wrinkled up their noses at the smell of olive oil sizzling in the fry pans in his kitchen.

The slave couple was basically lazy. They did what they were told, but they never went one step further than Uncle Tomás's express orders. If he directed Francisco to chop wood, he would chop it. But he wouldn't stack it, or bring it into the house. If he told María to sweep the floor, she would—, but as for carrying the sweepings out to the yard, not unless he spelled it out in detail. To say he didn't get along with them is to put it mildly. As far as Tomás was concerned, the two of them were insolent, slovenly, and dishonest.

When the inquisitors in Mexico City read him the new charges that had been leveled against him, Tomás knew in an instant that their source was the mulatto couple. Rather than defend himself orally, he asked the inquisitors for paper so that he could write out a proper defense. He must have made several copies, because when I started my investigations in Mexico, the year before I decided that life would be safer for me in Europe, one of Tomás's former cellmates showed me one that he had smuggled out of prison. Here is some of what it said:

> The witnesses against me have to be Francisco the mulatto and his wife, María, who for a long time have been my mortal enemies. This is because one day I seized the leather trunk that held all of María's clothes and sent it back to her owner, Felipa de Fonseca, saying that I could no longer stand to have that insufferable woman around me and it was time to let somebody else put up with her. Felipa wrote back saying that I should send María to the Devil and throw her out of my house. That's why they have raised this false testimony against me.
>
> Besides being mulattos, Francisco and his wife, Maria, are vile, base persons, gossipmongers who set all the miners in Taxco against me. She even provoked fights in which I wounded a couple of people. At that time I begged Felipa de Fonseca for the love of God to remove these two evil beasts from my house. She wrote back that I should kill them, and she would make sure that I went free. She told Tomás Cardoso that: you can ask him.
>
> Not only that, Francisco is a thief, a murderer, a gambler, a liar, and a malicious hate monger. Not one word of truth has ever come out of his mouth. And he robs people on the highways, like the time he stole three pesos and a blanket from Soto's mulatta and then raped her. Or the time he stole the bread that some of Soto's Indians were taking up to the mines. He's a pimp, too, renting out women to Indians and black slaves, and to one of my sons whom he seduced into these dishonest behaviors, introducing him to vile, infamous rogues who involved him in brawling.
>
> As for María, she used to punch her husband while insulting him by

The Miners Fonseca

calling him a cuckolded dog. But he wasn't insulted at all. He approved, replying that she was only a whore who strutted around in the clothes her lovers gave her. And once, on their way to Mexico City, they stole a horse from Juan de Aguilar that was worth more than sixty pesos.

That's the sort of people they are, capable of any evil deed. Everybody in the mines knows this. They're famous. In fact everybody says they should have been hung a long time ago.

Young Tomás's enemies list didn't stop with the mulatto couple though. His register went on and on, not only people he had denounced in his first trial, but a whole new set. There was Tomás de Cardoso, because he had gotten one of Uncle Tomás's daughters pregnant. Manuel de Lucena, Manuel Gómez, Sebastián and Manuel Rodríguez, and Lucena's wife, because at one time or another Uncle Tomás had traded insults with all of them. Doña Francisca de Carvajal and all her brood were enemies because they said he owed them money and he claimed he didn't, and they called him a thief, and . . .

This time Uncle Tomás fared less well. After the first trial, it seems his neighbors had kept close watch on his activities. And the Carvajals and their allies had long memories and big mouths. The upshot was that several people not on his enemies list had seen him order his cook to trim the vein and all the excess fat from his roast. They swore they had never seen him eat pork products. And that he routinely put on clean clothes for the Sabbath. The charges were serious but not damning. After nearly a year in prison, the Inquisition fined uncle Tomás 300 gold pesos—to cover the cost of his incarceration—, and made him abjure his Judaizing in a public auto-de-fé. Then they set him free.

Uncle Tomás returned to Taxco with a new resolve. If his tormentors were so insistent that he was a Jew at heart, then he would be one. The Law of Moses was in his blood, in his heritage. The Old Law obsessed his community of Portuguese friends, even the ones he often numbered among his enemies. They were always at him to worship with them. Well, then, he would.

On Fridays he changed the bedclothes and lit candles in the evening the way he had been taught. He banished all pork from his house. When his new cook roasted a leg of mutton—he had finally rid himself of the mulatto couple—he had her remove the vein and trim off the fat. He fasted once or twice a week. When he went to mass with his Portuguese friends, which he still had to do for appearances' sake, he used to mutter to them that Jesus was nothing but a Samaritan fisherman, the son of a carpenter, and certainly not the promised Messiah; that Christians were idiots for worshiping a piece of bread that they said was the body of Jesus; that the Holy Office was only after people's money. And that the pope had no power to take souls out of Purgatory, because only God could do that.

Jorge de Almeida had gone to Europe, leaving his brother Héctor and Young Tomás to manage his affairs. The merchants who used to lodge out at Cantarranas now all slept at Tomás's house. There were so many of them that often there weren't enough beds to go around. The Carvajals and their Judaizing friends were frequent visitors. Uncle Tomás would share with Sebastián de la Peña, while on the other side of the room Luis de Carvajal and Sebastián Rodríguez huddled together under their blankets, and the four of them talked until dawn. Luis's brother Baltazar Carvajal frequently visited, too—he told me that when I talked with him in Rome—, as did Manuel de Lucena. The other Fonsecas, Héctor and Old Tomás, sometimes joined their conversations about the Law of Moses. Marco Antonio, whose mule trains brought salt from the coast up to Taxco, used to make fun of the priests and the way their cassocks made them look like women. With every conversation, Uncle Tomás learned more about the Law of Moses and felt closer to his friends. Close enough, in fact, that he could join in their efforts to convince other strayed members of the Portuguese community, like Tomás Cardoso and Duarte Rodríguez, to come into the Judaizing fold.

Now Uncle Tomás began to time his visits to Mexico City to coincide with the Jewish festivals, which he always celebrated in the company of the Carvajals. On Passover there might be as many as a dozen guests. Since they would all dress in their finest clothes and since Mexico City's streets tended to be a stew of garbage, offal, and sticky mud, Uncle Tomás and Manuel de Lucena took it on themselves to bring the women like Catalina Enríquez and Justa Méndez to the gathering on the backs of their horses. At the Carvajal home they would all crowd into the one large room that didn't have windows to the street. Luis would read portions of the Book of Exodus to them, translating as he went from the Latin Bible, which was the only one he dared keep in the house. Usually they ate Lenten foods so that the kitchen girls and the neighbors would not notice anything amiss. But there were always cakes of unleavened bread, or at least tortillas, which they washed down with great quantities of wine. I'm told that toward the end of the evening, Uncle Tomás, with tears streaming down his face, used to blubber that this was the happiest

The Miners Fonseca

he had been since his childhood in Portugal. Luis would lead them in hymns like "With joy let's sing the praises of Lord God the King," to which everyone answered, "Whoever confides in Him will never lack for his support." Sometimes Luis would read them poems he had written and Uncle Tomás would weep some more.

Though he always celebrated Passover in Mexico City, he tended to observe the Great Fast of Yom Kippur in Taxco, often in the company of his city friends. At sunset they began to discuss the Law, and for the next twenty-four hours they prayed and sang and talked about the salvation of their souls. When the stars finally came back to the night sky, they broke their fast with fish, eggs, chickpeas, and fruit, dishes that Luis de Carvajal told them were obligatory on that occasion.

Uncle Tomás thought he was safe—I guess they all did—, but on June 13, 1595, Inquisition bailiffs arrested him in his home in Taxco and carted him back to jail in Mexico City.

He denied everything, or at least almost everything. Remove the vein from lamb? He didn't even know where the vein was. Not eat pork? Well, bacon made him sick, but he ate everything else. Rest on the Sabbath? Don't be absurd. Saturdays were smelting days, when all the miners came into town with their ore. It was the busiest day of the week in his store, so he couldn't be absent for a single minute. And so forth, with all the disclaimers he had used previously.

But there was so much evidence. Tomás couldn't avoid confirming that at various points in his life he had indeed followed the dead Law of Moses. When he was a child, living with his mother. With his grandfather Gabriel when he first came to Mexico City. When the Carvajal brothers and Manuel de Lucena had persuaded him, for a while, to join them in their Judaizing. But after his second trial, when he had abjured all his previous sins at the auto-de-fé, he insisted that he had not kept one single Judaizing custom.

"With no doubts at all about the choice you had made?" they asked him. Well, of course he had doubts. But he prayed to Jesus to help him resist them. Sometimes his soul would wrestle for an hour or two, or even a whole day, about whether the Law of Jesus or the Law of Moses was the one he ought to follow. He had heard so many conflicting claims about the two laws that he could never completely decide. The inquisitors kept coming back to Uncle Tomás's insistence that he was at heart a true Christian. "If that is so," they asked him, "why did you never tell any of this to your confessor?" Sometimes he said that he wished he had confessed, because then they wouldn't have arrested him again. Other times he said that he was always afraid. Afraid for his honor; afraid for his children. Afraid the Holy Office would take away all his property. Afraid of torture. One time he protested that he had confessed to a Fray Antonio de Ribas, but that unfortunately the friar was dead and couldn't verify his claim.

The inquisitors seemed especially bothered by the fact that Uncle Tomás said that he had never been baptized and had never done anything about it, even though he claimed that his mother had told him to send to Rome for a papal dispensation that would permit him to be baptized now. "If you weren't baptized," they kept hammering, "how could you have had the gall to receive the sacraments, being as you were in a state of mortal sin?"

"I never gave it much thought."

"And you never confessed any of this?"

"I'm confessing it now."

"Why now, if you never confessed it before?"

"For the good of my soul, so I will be saved."

None of this did him any good. His cellmates reported to the friars how Uncle Tomás refused to eat meat, insisting instead that the jailors bring him fresh fruit and boxes of conserves, all of which he washed down with as much wine as he could persuade his friends to send to the prison. They found a tiny book of devotions written in Uncle Tomás's hand sewn into his shirtsleeve. It was liberally sprinkled with references to Adonai, without a single mention of Jesus or the Virgin Mary. I think Tomás's excuse must have seemed lame even to him: "When I mention God, that automatically includes Jesus and his Holy Mother. Besides, until I am baptized, I am not formally a Christian, so it would be inappropriate for me to pray to them."

The inquisitors struggled to understand; but by then Uncle Tomás was so fluffy-headed that he contradicted himself in every second sentence. No, he wasn't a Jew, but he had undoubtedly said some things that made his friends think he was, though he couldn't remember any details about what, or when, or who might have heard him. He hadn't Judaized in years, but he remembered every word of the Judaizing prayers that his mother had taught him in Portugal, especially the ones that begin "Blessed is our God, Adonai, God of our fathers Abraham, Isaac, and Jacob, who lives and reigns over all the world."

※

Votes were taken. The death sentence was approved for the Great Auto-de-fé of 1596. But then at the last minute—Tomás had already been draped with the sambenito of the condemned and his hands tied—the sentence was suspended, and he was returned to his cell. Evidently the inquisitors thought that with this scare Uncle Tomás would reveal more names and more details about the Carvajals and their friends. And it worked. Every few months during the next four years they brought Uncle Tomás back to the audience chamber, where he spelled out more particulars of the Mexican community of Judaizers.

Finally their patience, and Uncle Tomás's store of knowledge, were both exhausted. At the auto-de-fé of October 20, 1600, Uncle Tomás was burned at the stake.

Rome

I am writing this in Rome, seated at an outside table of a small tavern in Trastevere where I like to take my breakfast. I can hear the boatmen on the Tiber calling out to one another. In the morning, when the summer heat is just beginning to swell, the walls of the Castel Sant'Angelo shade the tavern's tables. By afternoon the place is insufferable to all but the most steadfast drunkards. It is the year of our Lord—their Lord—1640, and I am an old man.

I have enjoyed living in Trastevere, perhaps because so many Portuguese and Spaniards have made it their home. Some of us are Jews; others are Church-lovers. But we're all free to make our friends where we see fit. Pope Urban is our neighbor, but we don't talk to him much.

Up until last year our Jewish community lived here more or less peacefully, taking pride in our doctors and poets, our philosophers and merchants. On the whole we have prospered, despite having to wear the yellow badge when we go out in public. And paying exorbitant taxes. Pope Urban VIII, like his predecessors, seems to love money more than he hates Jews, so he has allowed us to flourish. But we're always on the knife's edge. Any little incident can turn the Christian populace against us.

Which is what happened last May. When the Jew Fullo Seratino's second son was born, Seratino jokingly remarked that he'd have his son baptized if the pope would consent to be godfather. The clergy were outraged at the Jew's lack of respect. Pope Urban had the child seized and forcibly baptized, and many of Rome's Jews rioted in protest. But only briefly, because the Papal

Guard quashed them. Since then there has been no peace for us. Rapes. Beatings in the street. And always the demeaning insults.

So it is time for me to move on again, to somewhere where Jews are protected and respected. There aren't many good choices, I'm afraid. I reach into my purse for one of Pope Urban's new coins, the one with his head on one side and the newly finished Basilica of St. Peter on the other.

Pope Urban: I make for Amsterdam, a city where the pontiff's head is worth no more than any other man's.

St. Peter's: I purchase a berth on a boat to Salonica, where the crescent moon trumps the cross.

I already know both cities; I have friends in each. Tomorrow I'll start getting my things together. Or maybe the day after. That should be soon enough.

Dijo que . . . el nacio en Africa en Alcazarquivir . . . de padres moros aunque la
madre era hebrea y guardaba la ley de Moysen y este la guardo hasta la edad de seis
años, . . . y este se fue con su padre y desde aquella edad hasta que tuvo doce años
guardo la secta de Mahoma, y en aquella edad le toco Dios, y andaba procurando
modos como venirse a España para volverse cristiano.

—AHN Inq. Leg. 156, Exp. 4: 53v

6

Francisco Gutiérrez:
A Man of Three Faiths
TOLEDO, 1614

January 8, 1614. In the audience chamber of the Inquisition.

At his own request, Juan Bautista Ramírez was brought from his cell to testify with regard to his knowledge of Francisco Gutiérrez, the fruit seller. After
having been duly sworn, he said:

I state for the record that my name is Juan Bautista Ramírez. I am a resident of Madrid, and I am of Hebrew descent. I am about twenty-eight years
old. I was born in Africa, in Fez, where I studied the Holy Scripture intend-
ing to become a rabbi to the Jews, for there are many of them in that part of
Africa. Six years ago I crossed over to Spain with the intention of becoming a Catholic Christian and of being baptized, though until that time I had
professed Judaism and had lived according to the Law of Moses. I came to
Sevilla, where I was baptized in the cathedral in the presence of my godfather,
Hernán Ramírez de Molina, a resident of Sevilla. I have already admitted
in a previous audience that after my baptism I continued to observe certain
Jewish practices.

I personally know many Jews in Africa and here in Spain. I am well
acquainted with Francisco Gutiérrez, the one-handed fruit and fish vendor,
who sells fresh fish in the Plaza of Antón Martín and who lives in his own

rooms near the plaza. He is a tall, thin, dark-haired man, about thirty years old. He doesn't have much of a beard. He is married to María Romana, an old-Christian, who also sells fish and fruit in the Plaza of Antón Martín.

Francisco Gutiérrez is a Jew, even though he says that he is a Moor. I knew his parents, Moroccan Moors, both of them, though his mother was born a Jew. We were good friends in Alcázarquivir. After the two of us came to Spain I often heard him say that he wanted to journey to Italy, to the duchy of Venice, because he had an uncle there. The problem was that he didn't know how to get to Italy, but he told me that if I went with him he would pay all our expenses. I said I would, that I'd be pleased to go with him. So I accompanied him from Sevilla to Madrid.

During the eight months we spent together in Madrid, many times Francisco Gutiérrez and I discussed the ceremonies of the Law of Moses. He said he didn't believe in the Law of Jesus Christ. He didn't believe in confession either, and he claimed he only went because his wife, María Romana, compelled him to. He said he had no use for holy images, and he couldn't wait to emigrate to someplace where he wouldn't have to work and could spend all day studying the Law of Moses. Sometimes he and I used to read psalms together in Hebrew, or he would recite to me bits of Scripture that he knew by heart.

I realized Francisco Gutiérrez was here in the Inquisition prison in Toledo when I saw him as we were each being escorted to the toilet. He whispered to me, "Why are you here?" But that wasn't the time or the place to explain things to him. So I found a scrap of paper, about the size of my palm, and with the point of a burnt stick I wrote to him saying that I was here because someone had denounced me to the Holy Office. I also wrote that I was sorry that I had denounced him. I wrapped the paper around a stone and tossed it through the bars of the window of his cell. Eventually he let me know that I was in prison because he had denounced me the way I had informed on him.

February 17, 1614. Francisco Enríquez was brought into the audience chamber.

After having been duly sworn, he said:

I state for the record that my name is Francisco Enríquez; I am a resident of Madrid. I live on the Calle de Estrella, in front of San Bernardo Church. I am of Hebrew descent, and I was baptized about seven years ago.

I have known Francisco Gutiérrez for a long time. He told me that he was a Jew and said that he came to Madrid to teach Hebrew to the Trinitarian fathers. He seemed preoccupied by the question of the salvation of his soul. He used to ask me whether the Law of Moses was the right law. I told him it was not, because Christ's coming had put an end to that Law, and since then you can only be saved in the Law of Jesus Christ. But Gutiérrez wouldn't let the matter go. He said that a rabbi who had come to Madrid from Africa three or four years ago had muddled his thinking on these matters. The rabbi warned him not to reject his mother's teachings by believing as the Christians do, and reassured him that he was solid in his faith. But Gutiérrez told me that since he was an uneducated man and only knew what people told him, this rabbi's words had made him waiver. So I explained to him that the rabbi had misunderstood that verse from the first chapter of Solomon's Proverbs and had applied it badly, because other places in Scripture it says that if your mother or father tries to persuade you to worship in ways that go against God and his Law, then you are forbidden to follow them. What that rabbi meant was that you should only follow your parents' teaching if it is correct. So then Francisco Gutiérrez wanted to face up to his sin and tell me the name of the rabbi who had led him into such an error. He said the rabbi was Juan Bautista Ramírez, who is of the Hebrew nation.

I asked Francisco Gutiérrez whether he had observed any Jewish ceremonies with Juan Bautista Ramírez. He did not answer, but he gave thanks to God that he had run into me, because I had enlightened him and taught him the true way to save his soul. He begged me to take him to a priest right away, so I took him to the Trinitarians to make his confession to Fray Manuel de Espinosa, who assigned him some minor penance.

I can tell you one thing: Francisco Gutiérrez has a really hot temper. One night about nine o'clock I went to visit his wife, María Romana, who was sick. Gutiérrez wasn't at home when I got there. When he finally came in his wife tore into him about coming home so late. It was dark in the room, and Gutiérrez tripped over something and fell and split the ruffled collar that he was wearing, and he broke into a torrent of blasphemy. I don't recall the exact words, something about denying his God, and I wouldn't want to repeat them anyway. I was so shocked. "What are you trying to do," I asked him, "bring the Inquisition to take you away and burn you?" He didn't answer me; he just stalked out. I don't think he came back to the house at all that night. His sister-in-law and her husband were there, too, and they heard the whole thing.

Francisco Gutiérrez: A Man of Three Faiths

March 10, 1614. In the audience chamber of the Inquisition in Toledo.

At his own request, Juan Bautista Ramírez was brought again from prison to testify with regard to the case of Francisco Gutiérrez. After having been duly sworn, he said:

To tell the truth, I never actually saw Francisco Gutiérrez perform any ceremonies of the Law of Moses. Watching him, you'd think he was a Christian. One time the two of us were walking in Madrid and we came to that cross that stands in front of the Trinitarian monastery. Gutiérrez took off his hat, and I asked him why he worshiped a piece of wood like that. He just set his lips and didn't say anything at all. Another time I heard him swearing by the cross, and I asked him why he did such a thing, seeing that he didn't believe in it any more than I did. He told me it was out of respect, but I didn't believe him. That's because often when we were alone together in the countryside and nobody else could hear us, he complained that in Spain he had to protect himself by making sure that people saw him doing Christian things. He confessed to me that he was Jew and that he wanted to go to Italy so that he could live freely as a Jew. If he could only find a way to go there, he surely would.

As I stated in my earlier deposition, because I had been cheated by some merchants in Madrid, I went to the city of Pisa to see if I could find the people who had taken my property. Well, eventually I returned to Spain. One day, about five years ago, I ran into Francisco Gutiérrez, and he asked me about what I had seen in Italy. He wanted to know what I thought of the Christianity they practiced there, and if I had met any Jews in Italy. I told him about meeting some rabbis in Pisa, and about the time I had spent with them there, all of which I have already detailed to the Holy Office. I told him that when I converted to Christianity it was because I truly wanted to be a Christian, since I had come to believe that the Law of Our Lord Jesus Christ was the true Law. But I said that talking with those rabbis had convinced me of exactly the opposite. Then Gutiérrez said to me that since I had obviously learned so much about the Law of Moses, and he was not as learned as I, that my becoming a Jew again had persuaded him to believe in that Law.

March 11, 1614. Warrant for the arrest of Francisco Gutiérrez (a printed form with the names written in).

We order you, Melchor Dano Laboleto, Chief Warden of the Holy Inquisition of Toledo, to arrest Francisco Gutiérrez, the fruit and fish seller, a resident of Madrid, who lives in his own house near the Plaza of Antón Martín and who is married to María Romana, who sells fruit and fish in the Plaza of Antón Martín and in the Plaza Mayor.

Seize him wherever you may find him, even if it is in a church, monastery, or any other place that may be holy, fortified, or exempted by privilege. When you have arrested him, search his body and his clothes to make certain that he is not hiding any arms, money, gold and silver, jewels, or papers. Confiscate all such items, his movable and immovable possessions, wherever you may find them, and surrender them for safe keeping to the Receiver of this Holy Office. From these funds reserve twenty ducats for any expenses that you may incur in the line of duty, such as food and lodging of yourself and your prisoner. If you do not find cash, sell the least valuable items at public auction under supervision of the Commissioner of this Holy Office until you have realized said sum. Turn all other moneys over to Felipe González, Provisioner of the Prisons of this Holy Office, that he may use them to provide food for the prisoner. Convey the clothing and underwear necessary for his personal use to the Chief Warden of the Prisons of this Holy Office. Before you put him in his cell, search his body again in the customary fashion.

[On the back of the arrest warrant is a handwritten note attesting that the orders have been carried out but that Francisco Gutiérrez "has no possessions whatsoever because he is so poor that he owns only the clothes on his back."]

March 18, 1614.

Francisco Gutiérrez, arrested one week previous, was brought from his cell, at his own request, to give an account of himself to the inquisitors. After having been duly sworn, he said:

I state for the record that my name is Francisco Gutiérrez. I am twenty-five years old, and I live in the Calle del Gobernador, next to the Fuente del Piojo.

I was born in Africa in Alcázarquivir, five leagues inland from Larache. My parents were Moors. My father's name is Ahamed Asi, and my mother is called Yamena the Moor. I don't know anything about my grandparents, although I know they were all African. Though my father is a Muslim, my mother, despite what people called her, was a Hebrew who followed the Law of Moses. Since I lived with my mother until I was six years old, naturally I did, too. When I turned six, my mother informed me that my father was a Moor. So I went with him, and from then until I was twelve I followed the

Sect of Muhammad. When I was twelve, I was touched by the hand of God, so I tried to figure out how I could cross over to Spain to become Christian. Here's how I did it.

By then my father had placed me with another Moor to be his servant. This man wanted to take me with him to Mecca, but when we got near the city of Oran I slipped away with the intention of crossing over to Spain and being baptized. I traveled to Oran with some other Moors who had merchandise that they hoped to sell in Spain, but the authorities wouldn't let them into the city because they thought that we were spies. So I left them and went to Tlemcen, and from there to the city of Melilla, because I had heard that they would let you enter that city if you told them you were coming there in order to turn Christian. That's exactly what I did, and five days later they gave me passage to Málaga.

Well, during those five days in Melilla I met a Jew named Abraham. Then about ten months ago I ran into him here in Madrid. Now he calls himself Juan Bautista Ramírez, and he has converted to our Holy Faith. I couldn't understand it, so I asked him, if he considered himself a Jew, why had he wanted to come to Spain to become Christian? Why didn't he just stay in Africa where he could follow his Jewish Law? He didn't give me any answer. He only said that he had come to Málaga three years earlier where they had baptized him. Right after that he moved to Madrid, where he has lived ever since.

One day he and I were going along some street together, and we passed a cross, so naturally I took off my hat, and Juan Bautista asked me why I was taking off my hat to honor a piece of wood? I told him that it wasn't just wood, it was a cross, a replica of the one where God was crucified. "Don't you know," he said to me, "that the Scripture says '*Shema beni musar avicha, v-al titosh torat imeja*,' which means 'Hear, my son, the instruction of thy father, and forsake not the teaching of thy mother'?"

"Yes, I know that," I answered. But still I was very troubled not to know whether the Law of the Christians was the right law or not. I was very confused. At mass, when the priest was raising the host to be consecrated, I asked God to teach me which was the right law.

Soon after that—it was about two years ago—I went to visit Juan Bautista one day in the civil jail where he was being held for robbery. They had tortured him and branded him on one of his arms as a thief and sentenced him to exile from Madrid. When I saw him, I made the sign of the cross in front of his face with my two fingers and he said to me in Arabic, '*Faja mercuz*,' which in Castilian means that 'the cross is in the toilet.'

That left me more confused than ever, so I went to see a man named don Francisco—he wears a student's habit and is a descendant of Jews, though from what I've seen of him he is a Christian—and I told him everything that had happened between me and Juan Bautista. I asked him to enlighten me, and to tell me if the Laws of Moses were still valid. He said that after Christ's death more than three thousand laws had been invalidated. I reminded him about the verse from Proverbs that Juan Bautista had recited to me and asked him how he would interpret that business about "Hear, my son, the instruction of thy father, and forsake not the teaching of thy mother." Don Francisco said that the punishment referred to in the next part of that verse is God's punishment. What it means is that we should not leave the Law of the Church, who is our mother.

He also told me that I had better go to confession so that I wouldn't be excommunicated; so I went to the Trinitarian church where Fray Manuel de Espinosa heard my confession. The friar also told me to go confess all this to a commissioner of the Holy Office, which I did. The commissioner was a chaplain named Padre Agustín, and he wrote down what I told him: how I had been in a state of doubt for ten months, even though during that time I had never abandoned the beliefs of our Holy Catholic Faith. That's the Law I want to live under, so that I can be a model to all the new converts. That is all I have to say about that.

I want you to know that I am a good Christian, even though I have never been confirmed. I go to mass almost every day except sometimes during the holy days when I am busy selling fruit or fish. Whenever I have a little spare change I donate it to the Church. Last year during Lent I went to confession at the Church of the Discalced Augustinians, where I confessed to the prior. He wouldn't let me take communion, though, because I had not been absolved of the doubts I had had about which one was the true faith.

I can recite the Our Father, the Apostles' Creed, the Hail Mary, and the Salve Regina. I know the Ten Commandments and the Twelve Articles of the Faith. I don't own any heretical books; in fact I don't own any books at all, although I have read some psalms from a Book of Hours in Hebrew at the stall of a bookseller named Antonio Gómez Rodríguez near the Santa Cruz Cemetery. They didn't have the Gloria Patri in them, but I always began my reading by saying, "Glory be to the Father." Surely there is nothing wrong with my doing that. The book was printed in Venice, with the permission of the pope, and people told me that it was all right to pray the Psalms that way. Besides, I don't know my letters in Castilian, although I can read and write perfectly well in Hebrew and Arabic.

[*Undated note in margin*: Get this Hebrew Book of Hours from Antonio the bookseller.]

[*April 16, 1614*. Antonio Gómez Rodríguez surrendered a parchment book of sixteen illuminated pages, bound in black boards and written in Hebrew letters.]

[*Undated note in margin*: This book is not in the file.]

I want to make it clear that I didn't read those Psalms as part of any ceremony of the Law of Moses. I did observe some of those ceremonies when I was living with my mother, who was a Jew, but only until I was six years old. After I converted and after I was baptized, I never practiced any custom of the Law of Moses or the Sect of Muhammad.

I have a wife. Her name is María Romana, and she is a member of the old-Christian Romana family from Pinto. Other than that, I don't know anything about her family, except that one of her uncles is a monastic provincial and another one, Miguel García Capón, lives in Vallecas. María and I have been married for eight years, and we do not have any children. There was some unpleasantness right after we got married when I was arrested by the Holy Office because some other fruit sellers had told them that although I had been married with the blessings of the Church, I was not a Christian. Inquisitor Flores had me arrested, and I was held for a time in the home of somebody-or-other Navarro. They asked me if I had been baptized, and I said yes, I had been baptized in Málaga in the Church of the Holy Martyrs, so they sent off to that city for a copy of my baptismal certificate.

Sometimes my wife and I get along, and sometimes we don't. When I get mad at her I'm likely to say things that I really don't mean. Like about ten or eleven months ago—I can't remember exactly when—I was walking along the Calle de las Eras and my wife, María Romana, was a couple of steps behind me, nagging me about my being interested in some other woman whom she was jealous of. I got so angry that I turned around and screamed at her, "I'm sorry I ever got baptized!" I didn't mean it, of course, but lots of people heard me say it. The same thing happened again about a month ago. I came home late, maybe ten or eleven o'clock, and it so happens that I had lost some money gambling. My wife began scolding me, saying that I had no business going out, and I blew up and shouted, "A curse on God!" A man named don Francisco something-or-other, who also descends from Jews, was there and heard me say it. I stormed out of the house and spent the rest of the night somewhere else. Another time when she was nagging me I yelled, "By God, woman, I'm either going to have to leave you or kill you!" My brother-in-law, Diego de Palacios, heard me say it. More than once, too.

About a year and a half ago I was walking along the Calle de Cantarranas in Madrid when I bumped into Juan Bautista Ramírez who was having a conversation with some tonsured Franciscan monk whose name I don't know. Juan Bautista asked me what I was doing on the Calle de Cantarranas, and I said that I was looking for some work, anything to earn myself a few reales. "Why do you want to work so hard?" he asked me. "Why not just go back to our homeland?" I didn't answer him the way I should have because I was afraid of him: he was wearing a sword, and I thought he might kill me. Instead, I told him: "God willing, I hope to go back there sometime and to bring a little money back with me." That's what I said with my mouth, to please Juan Bautista, but those words weren't in my heart. I never wanted to go back to the land of the Berbers. I wanted to keep following the Law of Jesus Christ, which is what brought me here in the first place.

For a long time Juan Bautista and I were close friends. In fact we used to sell bolts of linen cloth together on the street here in Madrid. That's before I got into the fruit and fish business. He was so much a Jew, though, that one day I asked him if he had really been baptized, and he said he had. After a while the two of us went to Florence, and from there to Pisa, or maybe it was Livorno, I don't remember exactly. We got there on a Friday night, and we asked where we could find the rabbi of the Law of Moses. We told him in Hebrew that we had come to his city to live on account of some trouble back in Spain. We went to the synagogue the next day, which was Saturday, the day that the Jews teach their Law from a *siddur*, which is what we here in Spain call a Bible. While we were there the captain of the boat that had brought us to Italy came in, and he said, "Juan, what are you doing here?" Juan Bautista told him, "I'm not called Juan anymore; I'm Abraham."

Juan Bautista made a donation of fifty ducats to the synagogue. That really impressed people, because most people give eight or ten reales at the most. The upshot of all this was that within six months he got married to a Portuguese Jewish woman with whom he had been living. He even preached the sermon at his own wedding, telling people all about the Jews who were being held captive in the land of the Berbers. He preached so well that people became calling him "Abraham the Sage"!

He and I parted company there, and after a while Juan Bautista came back to Spain where he found a job as a court bailiff in Morón. He must have left his Portuguese wife in Italy, because in Morón he met a young woman, a cousin of his, and promised to marry her. He left her pregnant, telling her that he was off to Rome to ask for a papal dispensation so that he could marry her, what with her being his cousin and all. He said he would go back to Morón to marry her, but I'm not aware that he ever did.

May 17, 1614.

Juan Guerra de Villalobos was brought from prison, and after having been duly sworn, he said:

I state for the record that my name is Juan Guerra de Villalobos. I am twenty-two years old and a native of the village Salvatierra de Tormes. I am in prison because they accuse me of being a con man and a caster of spells. In an audience two weeks ago I did indeed confess to using some little lead statues to tell the future and to cast spells. I also confessed to reading books that instructed me how to cast spells and to find treasures, and to pretending to exorcise evil spirits from certain people. At your request, today I am testifying about what I have learned from one of my cellmates, Francisco Gutiérrez.

Although we are not allowed to communicate with other prisoners, Francisco Gutiérrez used to kneel on the floor and peer through the cat hole in the door of our cell to try to see if he knew any other prisoners who might be passing along the corridor. Several times I overheard Francisco Gutiérrez talking with Juan Bautista, although since they spoke in Arabic I could not understand them. But later Francisco Gutiérrez told me that what Juan Bautista had said was that he was sorry that what he had told the inquisitors had led to Gutiérrez's arrest. Gutiérrez answered that he was happy to come before the tribunal so that he could put his errors behind him. He also told Juan Bautista that since they had acted in those things together, that they should not be afraid to confess the truth, and they should plead for mercy with tears in their eyes.

A couple of times he and Juan Bautista even exchanged written notes. One time a scrap of paper wrapped around a stone came sailing through the bars of our cell's window. It was about half the size of your hand, and it was written in Spanish, so Francisco Gutiérrez didn't know it was from Juan Bautista until I read it to him. The note repeated what Bautista and Gutiérrez had talked about through the cat hole and promised that if Bautista ever got out of here he would write to the inquisitors to tell them that Gutiérrez was a man of God. Gutiérrez asked me to write a reply. Since we didn't have any ink, I used a charred stick to write. We told Bautista that we had received his note and asked him if he had already ratified what he told the inquisitors about Gutiérrez wanting to go back to Africa, and about his not believing in the holiness of images, and about his only going to confession because his wife made him go. This was because Francisco Gutiérrez was afraid that pretty soon he was going to be questioned under torture, and he wanted to find out if Bautista was the one who had denounced him for these things, because he wanted to get it right.

I have to say that Francisco Gutiérrez can be pretty violent at times. I have heard him threaten to break a pitcher over the warden's head. And one day he threw a bowl full of stew at our other cellmate, Juan Guerra de Villalobos. It's a good thing he didn't hit him, because it was a heavy bowl.

During the time that we were together I noticed that Gutiérrez washed himself a lot, his legs and thighs and arms and throat and face and hair. First thing in the morning and last thing at night. I asked him if he wasn't afraid to be doing that, and he said that he didn't know there was anything wrong with washing, that he just did it to keep his body clean. Afterward he would dry himself with his sheet. He would sing, too, but since it was in Arabic I didn't understand what he was singing. It might have been some psalms, and he may have been singing them in Hebrew; I can't be sure.

Since I don't know much about the ceremonies of the Jews and the Moors, I asked Francisco Gutiérrez a lot of questions. He said that back in Africa, when they didn't have enough water for washing, they would rub their hands with dust before praying. Or else they would lay their hands against a wall or a clean stone and then bring their hands to their faces and their chests three times. He told me that over there they have rosaries, too, and that they know that there is a God, because their Qur'an says so. He used to say that the Muslim Law is not as good as that of the Jews, because the Messiah the Muslims were waiting for would come to earth only as the

Francisco Gutiérrez: A Man of Three Faiths

spirit of God. I laughed at him and told him that if they didn't believe in the Holy Trinity and the Virgin Birth and everything else that the Holy Mother Church believes, then they were all living in error, and what it said in their Qur'an was only to make them even more blind. And Francisco Gutiérrez agreed that what I said I was right.

I asked him how they prayed over in that land, and he told me they directed their prayers to Allah the King, and that their prayers repeated the word *Allah* over and over. The Jewish prayers were much the same, except they called God *Adonai*.

Gutiérrez was always worrying about how the Holy Office would treat him. Sometimes he seemed thankful to have been arrested, saying that God was giving him the chance to pay for his sins. He also used to worry that every time he had given a deposition to the tribunal he had told them something different. The one thing he kept coming back to was that he had lied to the inquisitors about the reason he had told Juan Bautista that he was eager to go with him to Italy to become a Jew again. He told them that it was because he was afraid to say no to Juan Bautista. The real truth was that he had never been afraid of Bautista.

Gutiérrez hardly ever told the same story twice. He was always complaining that he didn't know why he was in this prison; but then he also told me that he had been arrested more than twenty times previously for similar matters. Another time he said that he was only here because for eighteen months he had lived with doubts about the truth of the teachings of our Holy Catholic Faith and had confessed that to some Trinitarian friars who had scolded him about it. Since that time he had not made confession. "In that case," I told him, "you have been separated from the faith, and you need to put things right."

May 21, 1614.

María Romana, the wife of Francisco Gutiérrez, was brought in to testify about her husband's alleged Judaizing. After having been duly sworn, she said:

I state for the record that my name is María Romana. I sell fish in Madrid in the Plaza Mayor and the Plaza of Antón Martín. I live in my own rooms in the Calle del Gobernador, next to the Hospital of Antón Martín. My family comes from Pinto, and we are all old-Christians.

With regard to my husband, Francisco Gutiérrez, I know of nothing that he has done or said that goes contrary to our Holy Catholic Faith. We have a good marriage, although my husband has a hot temper and sometimes he curses and shouts at me. He never really means anything by it, and if he says something that he shouldn't, he goes to the Virgen de Atocha Church to make it right. Both my sister, Isabel Romana, and her husband, Diego Palacios, who weaves linen cloth, can testify to this. They live in the Calle de las Huertas right near the Discalced Trinitarians.

Francisco Gutiérrez's petition to the Notary of Property (undated).

Brother Pedro, please do me the favor of turning over to the bearer of this petition my personal effects that you are keeping in your charge, which are as follows: a pair of trousers and short blouse adorned with embroidered red and green roses with a black button and a collar with twelve gold decorations, all of which are wrapped up in a hand towel. I've asked him to sell them because I am sick in bed, and greatly in need. From the proceeds he will pay you the two hundred reales that you lent me.

Signed [phonetically in Arabic script] Francisco Gutiérrez.

Sentencing document.

The prisoner shows signs of contrition and repentance, begging Our Lord God to pardon his sins and begging us to show mercy in assigning him his penance, professing that from now on he intends to live and die in our Holy Catholic Faith. With a pure heart and unfeigned faith he has confessed the entire truth, not holding back information about any person, living or dead.

We absolve him of his excommunication and condemn him to be incarcerated for three years in a place of our choosing. For the first six months of this incarceration he shall go daily to a monastery of our choosing to be instructed in our Holy Faith. He must wear the sambenito whenever he goes out in public. He, his children, and his grandchildren are rendered ineligible to wear jewels or bright colors, ride horses, carry arms, or hold any public offices, titles, or honors.

Undated, unsigned petition.

Francisco Gutiérrez is in extreme need, and because of the loss of his hand there is no way he can help himself. He is married to an old-Christian who refuses to live with him or take responsibility for his needs. He humbly petitions the Inquisition to review his case and show mercy to him by commuting his prison sentence into some other sort of penance.

On the back of this petition is a note from the warden.

Because during the seven months he has been in prison Francisco Gutiérrez has regularly attended mass and has shown himself in every way to be a good Christian, his petition shall be granted.

January 14, 1616. Deposition of Eugenio Fernández, familiar of the Holy Office.

Yesterday, when I was visiting the Inquisition prison, I saw a prisoner named Francisquillo spitting and saying that he'd be God damned if there was a not a great deal of honor in what he had done; and if the king should give him a blow, then he'd give him one right back. The man's wife was there, crying, and he said to her, "Hush up, don't worry. Just let them try to make me go back to church! I swear to God that I am going to go someplace where there are no Christians. I've sworn to God since the day I was born, and I always will. This sambenito of mine doesn't offend God in any way." All this time his wife was sobbing and sighing, "Oh, what will become of me!" This provoked Francisquillo to respond, "Shut up! Don't let this bother you. Wherever I end up, you'll end up there, too."

Y estando un dia juntos y a solas . . . pregunto . . . el dicho su padre que que diria y
creeria si alguien le dijese que no guardase la dicha ley de Jesucristo Nuestro Señor,
y que no habia Trinidad sino un solo dios. . . . Aqueste confesante le respondio que
. . . le tuviere por un grande hereje. Y el dicho su padre le dijo a esto "¿Y si yo te lo
dijese y persuadiese, que dirias?"

—AGN Inq. Vol. 344, Exp. 1: 220

7

Jerónimo Salgado

MEXICO, 1624

"So, tell me about this man Salgado."

The inquisitor don Juan Gutiérrez Flores leaned forward. A steaming
cup of bitter chocolate sat on the table next to the neatly stacked papers of
the Salgado file.

"He's a small man with a big nose. Sunken eyes. A dark black mustache
and beard. On the whole, ugly."

"Pedro, you know that's not what I mean." Pedro de Vega, one of the
Mexican Inquisition's *letrados*, had been Gutiérrez Flores's close friend since
long before either of them occupied their current positions. "You have met
with him. What sort of man is he? How does he think? Would you like a
cup? It's fresh from Nicaragua." Vega was not startled by his friend's abrupt
change of subject. It was part of Gutiérrez Flores's standard repertoire, honed
during years of difficult interrogations. Designed to keep a prisoner off balance and crack his resolve. Now it was mere force of habit, one of the ways
that the Inquisition puts its stamp on a man.

Gutiérrez Flores clapped his hands twice, and an Indian girl appeared.
Her black hair, its two long braids tied together with a snip of blue ribbon,
framed a dark, chiseled face, pitted with scars from the pox. The fringe on

her plain white *huipil* picked up the blue of the ribbon. Her feet were bare and calloused.

"Justina, chocolate for our guest." Gutiérrez Flores spoke each word loudly with exaggerated precision, his index finger signaling the number one before pointing first at his own cup and then at the black-robed cleric who sat facing him across the pine table that served as the inquisitor's desk. "One of our commissioners brought Justina with him from Michoacán before he died. Justina is loyal, but she's a bit slow and hard of hearing. And she still doesn't know much Spanish. But then, I've never learned her Purépecha tongue either. She's not likely to repeat anything she hears in this room."

Justina glided in silently with a tray. She placed a green terracotta cup in front of Pedro de Vega and filled it with steaming froth from an unglazed pitcher. Gutiérrez could not remember drinking anything like it as a child in Spain. There was something about the taste of black cacao beans and the contrasting flavors of the pepper, vanilla, and chili that always made him crave more. In the morning Justina heated the watered chocolate paste until it was steaming and pungent and then whipped it with a flanged stick that she rolled between her palms until it was frothy; in the afternoon she served it cold. Either way, if you could afford the cacao beans, this drink was one of the true pleasures of living in New Spain. Don Juan accepted a refill and then waved his servant out of the room. She had yet to speak a single word. Now it was just the two of them, the chocolate, and a large stack of papers.

"You are Jéronimo de Salgado's *letrado*." Vega nodded his assent. "So as his defense advisor you must have a good take on what sort of man he is. Tell me about him. In your own words. You don't have to repeat what's in his dossier. I've skimmed that, and I know that my colleagues have recommended a two-year prison sentence." Gutiérrez Flores extracted an embroidered handkerchief from somewhere under his robe and wiped a thread of chocolate from his lips, leaving a brown smudge on the cloth. The corners of his mouth turned down in disapproval at the stain. He folded the handkerchief and laid it down, aligning it squarely with the table's edge.

"That's what troubles me," Gutierrez said, "the sentence. Somehow it doesn't seem right. If this man Salgado is a Jew, maybe even a dogmatizer, then it is far too lenient. But if he is a Christian, and all his endless talk has just been his way of shoring up the bases of his faith, then maybe . . . Anyway, that's why I asked you to come in, to help me sort this out. You know the man. Consider this an informal review. Off the record." The two men sipped for a moment while Vega collected his thoughts.

"Salgado was afraid of being caught, I presume," Gutiérrez prompted.

"It's more like he was prudent," Vega said. "But I haven't ever observed any of that obsessive secrecy that indicates a sense of guilt. With his friends he feels free to say anything at all. With them he's always been completely open. It was only if there was a chance they could be overheard by strangers that he shut the conversation down. He's very well educated, you know, for a shopkeeper. Even though he's largely self-taught. I don't know how he's managed to read so much. Where he finds the books, or the time. Maybe he reads in the saddle, or on shipboard. He certainly has had the opportunity, with all that travel."

"But he really is a Jew, isn't he? At heart?"

"I . . . I'm not certain." Vega drained the last of his cup. "He *was* a Jew, certainly, for a while. But I don't have the sense that he was very committed to it deep down. It's true he celebrated some of the Jewish festivals with his Portuguese friends. And he kept up some of the practices his father taught him when he was in his twenties. But . . . "

"But you're not sure?"

Vega was resolved not to let himself be rushed. His hands fiddled with his chocolate cup as he took a few moments to frame his answer. "This is what I can't figure out: Salgado's heart doesn't seem to have been it. In believing, I mean. Any kind of belief. He seems to live only in the here and now. What's missing is any hint that Salgado is concerned for the disposition of his soul."

Don Juan Gutiérrez Flores raised his eyebrows in surprise. "But isn't that what drives most of these doubters, these heretics? Whether the dead Law of Moses or the Law of Our Lord Jesus Christ is the path to their salvation?"

"Of course. But in Salgado's case . . . Frankly, I think what he liked most was talking about it. Not about salvation, but about the two Laws. To show off how much he had read. To impress his friends with his command of Scripture. Both the Old and the New. Any excuse would do to spend a few hours debating religious subjects. He was all the time thinking, questioning. Probing his friends," Vega said. He took another sip of chocolate. "And probably himself, too."

"Probing without commitment? Without belief?" Gutiérrez seemed skeptical.

Jerónimo Salgado

"It could be. Maybe that's the key to it. Without belief. He never seems to have said as much; at least not openly, not where he could be overheard. But all those questions, all that reading. Point and counterpoint. It's as if . . . as if the debating were a game to him. Not the means to an end but the end, in and of itself. He talked with so many different people. But if you ask me, I think that all along he was mostly debating with himself."

"In search of his faith?"

"Maybe. But maybe just for the pleasure of it."

"I suppose . . . I suppose that's possible. Unusual, certainly." Don Juan Gutiérrez Flores shook his head slowly in puzzlement. "Tell me . . . tell me about Salgado's childhood. Where did he come from? Who were his people?"

Pedro de Vega leaned back in his chair. He realized that he had been sitting on the edge of his seat, his chest almost touching the table. This was a much easier question, the sort of thing he dealt with every day. Less speculative. Facts, not conjectures.

"He was born in 1590, which made him thirty-four when they arrested him in Nicaragua as a Judaizer. He's Portuguese, that goes without saying, like so many of these people. From Viñáez, near Braganza. His mother was an Oliveira, and his grandmother, a Váez. Common enough names. Probably they were all Spanish Jews who fled to Portugal. Lots of uncles and cousins. After the 1580 merger of the two kingdoms, about half of his relatives seem to have gone back to Castilla, with some of them settling in the Galician border. And from there . . . from there to here and to everywhere else. Perú. Panamá. I wouldn't be surprised if they all spent some time in France. It's hard to say."

"Any prior Inquisition history in his family?"

"Salgado claims not. And no one has been able to turn up anything."

"Did his relatives turn completely Christian, or were they Judaizers who just weren't caught?"

"Not caught, that's my guess. There's no question at all that Salgado's father was a Judaizing heretic. His mother? Maybe yes, maybe no. Either way, his parents took care to isolate Jerónimo from everything Jewish when he was a child. It's as if they wanted a clean break from the past for their children. They might have been Jews, but their young Jerónimo would be Christian. Presumably his brothers and sisters, too, at least what I've learned of them. They sent Jerónimo to be schooled with a priest in Viñáez. He seems to have been a good student because by the time he was ten he could both read and speak Latin. He must have had a quick mind even then, most impressive. But as for being Jewish . . . "

Vega reached toward the stack of papers on the table. "May I?"

Don Juan Gutiérrez Flores indicated his permission, and Pedro de Vega, already familiar with most of the documents, quickly found what he was looking for.

"Listen to what Salgado said; this was in August 1624, right after they began interrogating him after they brought him up to Mexico. He makes it clear that his parents, or his father at least, were playing a double game. Here it is." Vega lifted up one of the folios.

> 'My parents brought me up in the Holy Catholic Faith, and in fact I did not know that any other Law even existed. I left home when I was eleven and went to Palencia and Jaén and all over Andalucía.'

"He was probably apprenticed to one of his relatives during those years, learning the merchant trade. That's the usual pattern. Now, here is the key passage:

> 'In 1613 my father came to Jaén from Portugal. And one day when we were alone together in our room in the Callejuela Inn, I think it was in September or October of that year, my father asked me if I was a good Christian. And whom did I believe in. I answered that I was trying to lead my life like a good Christian who followed the Law of Our Lord Jesus Christ. Then my father asked me what I would say if somebody told me not to follow the Law of Our Lord because there was no Trinity, only one single God. "If somebody told me that," I replied, "I would consider him a great heretic." "And if I were the one who persuaded you that it was so . . . ?" my father continued. "I wouldn't believe it," I said. But he insisted, saying that the Trinity did not exist, that there was only one God, a single being without Christ or the Holy Spirit; that the Messiah had not yet come. And that if I wanted my soul to be saved, then that is what I had to believe.'

"There's no reason to think that Salgado was not telling the truth," Vega went on. "The emotions he hints at—shock, horror—seem entirely credible to me. All that time he thought his father was a good Christian, and then this. A little later his father tried again, explaining to him how to observe the dead Law of Moses: the Sabbath, the fasts, prayers directed to the God of Creation. The usual things. But evidently his father saw that Jerónimo was not convinced by what he was telling him, because the very next day his

Jerónimo Salgado

father brought in a dogmatizer, a graybeard named Álvaro Méndez, who had spent the last few years over the border in San Juan de Luz, in France."

Vega answered the question implied in Gutiérrez Flores's raised eyebrows. "Of course. We notified the Holy Office back in Castilla and in France, but so far they haven't been able to locate this Méndez fellow."

"Méndez was his rabbi, then."

"Exactly. And that very same afternoon Méndez began Salgado's lessons. Remember, by then Jerónimo Salgado was no longer a child; he was twenty-three, fully formed. He had been traveling with his relatives for years over the length and breadth of Spain. He may have still believed that his father was a true Christian, but there is no way that he could have been ignorant of Judaism, not with all the Portuguese connections that the family had. Given how bright Salgado obviously is, and how well educated, he has to have known whom he was dealing with."

"I see that. But if that's true, then why did his father think it so necessary to bring in a dogmatizer to teach him the basics of Judaizing? That doesn't make sense."

Pedro de Vega smiled for the first time since he had entered the room. He felt confident now, on familiar turf. He laid his hand on the mound of papers that constituted the Salgado file. "You're absolutely right. And that's not the only thing in this case that doesn't make sense. But even so, it all seems to have happened the way Salgado confessed it. His father told him straight out that he was a Jew. Méndez gave him the full curriculum. The God of the Judaizers had only one nature, not three. His name was Adonai, God of Abraham, Isaac, Jacob, Israel. And all the rest. Jesus was a rabbi who had not come to change the Law but only to fulfill it. And as to Jesus being the promised Messiah, that was nothing but tales that sprang up after his death. Méndez taught him how to celebrate the Jewish festivals, made him memorize the dietary laws, a bundle of prayers including the one called the Shema, a song about the birth of Abraham. The usual."

"So from then on Salgado was a confirmed Judaizer?"

Again Vega hesitated. "Well yes, and no."

"What do you mean?" Gutiérrez was growing impatient now. He had the feeling that his friend Vega was toying with him, dragging things out for dramatic effect. Something few people dared to do to one of Mexico's chief inquisitors.

CHAPTER 7

"You remember how I said that Salgado's heart never quite seemed to be in it? I think the man was ambivalent right from the first. Listen to how he tells it." Vega extracted another folio from the sheaf of papers. "This could be a strategy to set up a later plea for mercy, but Salgado doesn't strike me as a long-range planner. He lives in the moment, not the future. Here it is:

> 'I never learned all the prayers because, besides being so long, they had a lot of Hebrew words in them that I couldn't understand. And Álvaro Méndez recited them at such a breakneck pace that I couldn't memorize them. He wouldn't write them down, he said; that was too dangerous because someone might see them.'

"Then Salgado confesses that he knew that what they were doing was wrong and that he was afraid of being found out. Here's what he says:

> 'He, that is, Méndez, he told me I had to give the external appearance of being Christian, to go to mass often and confess and take communion; but at the same time I had to keep the Jewish fasts and eat only the prescribed foods, and so forth.'"

"Salgado was afraid, or Méndez was afraid?"

"Méndez, certainly. Salgado, perhaps. Either way, I suppose he took the caution to heart."

"All right, then; let me make sure I understand this. From the time Méndez instructed him, Salgado began to observe all the Jewish customs?"

"Only more or less. Sporadically. Again, here is how Salgado puts it: 'After that, though I believed Sabbaths were Jewish festival days, I did not observe them because I had too much to do in my business, and I had to be in the store.'"

"That does speak to his intent, though, doesn't it?" Vega detected in Gutiérrez Flores a note of pleasure at a point well scored.

"Yes," Vega answered slowly, conceding the point. "But not to the sincerity of that intent, or its strength, or its duration."

"You're talking like a lawyer again. Come on, Pedro. You're not defending Salgado here; you're helping an old friend try to understand what was going on in this man's mind."

Gutiérrez Flores clapped his hands, and again Justina glided in. "Justina, bring us a light lunch, please. We'll work straight through." He turned back to

Jerónimo Salgado

Pedro de Vega. "I have other obligations in midafternoon; I think we should be finished easily by then. The *muchacha* will bring us something to quiet our stomachs enough to hear ourselves talk. Now, where were we? The witness depositions: so did people see Salgado Judaizing or not?"

"Some did. But most of the people who thought Salgado was a Jew based their conclusions on what they heard him say, not what they saw him do. His friend Francisco de Maldonado thought Salgado's criticism of the Church meant that he had to be Jewish, and stated as much in one of their discussions. Salgado instructed him to argue from the Christian position while he'd present a Jewish one, challenging Maldonado to best him in debate. Then there's Diego Fuentes, another of Salgado's friends. We gave him penance here under the name Fuentes, and then he went to Lima and changed his name to Juan Flores de Espinacedo. In his deposition in Perú he said that Salgado liked to debate with him, too. Juan Bautista de Riberola, the same. It's all circumstantial stuff, mostly shirking his Christian responsibilities. Not going regularly to mass? Obviously he must be a Jew. Eating meat during Lent? The same. That sort of thing. Not to mention the fact that so many of Salgado's friends were known Judaizers. In fact the way some of these witnesses jump to conclusions, it makes you wonder if any of them have a logical bone in their bodies. You get the feeling that they weren't judging according to what they saw; they were using what they saw to confirm judgments they had already made."

Vega picked up a handful of papers. "Take Martín Fernández de Victoria, for example: he saw Salgado staying out until three in the morning in Nicaragua with his friend Diego de Gómez Salazar, something—I'm quoting here—'that no sane person would do.' Therefore Salgado has to be a Jew. Other witnesses seem a little more reasoned. That same Diego Gómez de Salazar from Nicaragua—by the way, he also claims to have run into Salgado in Rouen—stated categorically . . . " Vega thumbed through several folios of the dossier before he found the passage he was looking for. "'I've never seen Jerónimo Salgado fast nor observe any other Jewish ceremonies, and that's all I have to say.'"

"So he wasn't observant, then. Or probably wasn't."

"'Probably wasn't observant' is a good way of putting it. But other times his actions suggest that he might have been. At least two witnesses, for example, claim to have been part of a large group, including Salgado, which fasted on Yom Kippur. But, frankly, there is not as much of that sort of thing as I had expected. Except . . ."

"Except . . . ?"

"Except for the time Salgado supposedly spent in France. First of all, lots of people claim to have seen him there. A couple of the Lima Judaizers swore they saw Salgado attending a synagogue in Bordeaux in 1613. And Diego Gómez de Salazar claimed that Salgado had observed several Jewish fasts with him and his family in Rouen. Salgado denied all that, of course, claiming never to have been to France, and not even to know what a synagogue is, but that just doesn't ring true. But then, the alleged Bordeaux and Rouen episodes may have been a witness falsification. There's a serious problem with the dates, because the witnesses claim Salgado was in Bordeaux around 1615, when we know for a fact that he was already in New Spain by then."

The study door swung open, and Justina appeared with a lacquered tray bearing cheese, strips of dried beef, thin green slices of freshly peeled nopal cactus, and chunks of what looked like yesterday's bread. She placed the tray on the table and went out again.

"I've tried to teach her to buy fresh bread every morning and throw the old bread out, but she just won't learn. She'll buy those flat corn cakes five times a day, but I can't abide them. I'm a Spaniard, damn it! Jesus said, 'Give us each day our daily bread.' Bread, not tortillas. Daily bread."

With anyone else Vega would have smiled.

Justina came back with two plates and two glasses. A silver beaker of spiced wine replaced the chocolate pitcher. Gutiérrez Flores laced a piece of the bread with nopal strips and a slice of cheese and popped it into his mouth. He searched for his handkerchief. Not finding it, he wiped his lips on his sleeve before picking up the thread of the conversation. Vega gnawed on a strip of dried, spiced meat, flavorful but too salty for his taste. He drained his glass of wine, poured himself another, and then nibbled a piece of cheese. For a while the two friends sat in companionable silence.

"What do you think brought Salgado here to Mexico?" Gutiérrez Flores's question brought their lunch to an end.

"He came to the New World in 1613," Pedro de Vega said. "Just why he came is unclear. To make money, I suppose, like most of these people. Not to save souls, not even his own. He sailed with Vanegas, who put him ashore in Portobelo, in Nicaragua. He must have brought some money with him, because he set up a business right away, moving shop goods to Cartagena and Realejo. He came to Mexico City four years later. And then for a time he went back and forth to Honduras, taking silk cloth south and bringing back sacks of cacao beans. It could be that he imported this morning's chocolate."

Vega meant it to be a joke, but Gutiérrez didn't show even the trace of acknowledgment. His sense of humor hasn't improved much over the years, Vega thought. Juan Gutiérrez Flores was a good friend, and Vega had always admired his sharp mind. But even when they were younger they never went to the taverns together, never to the performances in the theaters or the convent patios. Gutiérrez Flores had never found the student life amusing in any way. Whether it was that he didn't understand his colleagues' jokes or just found them trivial or boring, he never laughed at them and rarely even smiled. The other students found him sour. Before long, Vega, who shared Gutiérrez Flores's intellect and love of logical argument, was his only friend. Even then they had rarely exchanged confidences the way intimate friends do. One time another student had remarked that Gutiérrez Flores was all focus and no fun. The characterization still rang true, even after more than two decades.

The inquisitor was still looking expectantly at don Pedro. "Salgado owned a store for a while there in Granada, selling silk," Vega went on. "He had a good location, too, right under the arcades of the plaza."

"I take it he did very well for himself, then."

"I suppose you could say so. Yes. Well-off without being rich. A couple of things jump off the inventory that the Inquisition commissioner made of the goods they seized from Salgado in Nicaragua. They found no cash to speak of, so they had to sell off everything he owned just to pay for his travel back to Mexico City. He bought a lot of different things for his store: cloth, mostly, but only in dribs and drabs. For selling to individuals, not the quantities he'd need to be able to sell to other stores. Some of his stock he bought from importers—Chinese silk and damask, for example, or Flemish fine weave, both of linen and silk—but a lot of it was manufactured here in New Spain. Pretty basic stuff: black Mexican taffeta; woven blankets; blouses covered with baubles. On the other hand, his personal effects were meager and in poor condition: torn black stockings; some tattered bed linens; a beat-up shotgun; a sword without a sheath; one old chair with a cushion half-eaten by mice. As for housewares, only a couple of torn tablecloths. He obviously didn't cook or have someone to cook for him: no pots, pans, canisters, spices. Nothing to suggest the touch of a woman's hand. When I talked with him I got the same impression: he was content to live badly. In squalor, really. And celibate. His head was somewhere else."

"This was all in Nicaragua, in Granada?"

"Nicaragua was his home base. When he came north he stayed with friends here in Mexico City or in Puebla. Judaizers mostly, we presume, some of them penanced years ago and put back on the street with their sambenitos."

"You're saying that there's a strong case for guilt by association?"

"It's very hard to say. It's pretty clear that after his father and Álvaro Méndez indoctrinated him in 1613, Salgado began to Judaize, though in a halfhearted way. Always more talk than practice. That seems to have lasted until three or four years ago when he evidently suffered a crisis of conscience. Whether it was the books he was reading, or all those debates about Scripture, or some road-to-Damascus incident is hard to tell. Wait just a moment."

The lawyer pulled the mound of papers to his side of the table and began flipping through them. "Here it is. Here's how he describes the crisis that turned him around. This is from one of his early audiences with us here in Mexico City. He says: 'Though I still followed the Law of Moses, I longed to find some learned Catholic person with whom I could discuss my doubts and concerns; though since I didn't want to run the risk of being found out, I put off actually doing it. What really inspired my conversion, though, was that at that time I was reading Fray Luis de Granada's *Introduction to the Symbols of Faith*, and it resolved all my misgivings. Since that time I have been wholly Christian.'"

"And you believe that?" Gutiérrez's tone was flat, but Vega could sense that it rested on a bed of skepticism.

"Yes, I believe it. Well, up to a point. But you have to consider his statement in the context of all those debates with his colleagues and acquaintances. Remember what I said about Salgado's intellectual detachment?"

Vega looked up to make certain that Gutiérrez Flores was following him, but the inquisitor's face showed nothing.

"Let's break for a bit. Have some cheese." Gutiérrez Flores pointed at the tray. Two slices of cheese and a chunk of thick bread crust remained. The nopal was long since gone, but there was enough wine left in the beaker for Gutiérrez Flores to refill their glasses. The inquisitor stood up and excused

Jerónimo Salgado

himself. "I'll be back in a moment. Then I think you'd better tell me about these debates you keep alluding to. They do seem to have been the heart of this matter, don't they?"

Gutiérrez Flores closed the door behind him as he stepped out of the room. Pedro de Vega could hear the sound of urine ringing into a tin chamber pot. Vega stood up and stretched. He walked several times to the window and back to the long table. His joints ached, whether from sitting or from holding himself so tightly as he answered his friend's questions he could not determine. His head had begun to ache as well. It was going to be a long day, and if they talked much longer he would have to excuse himself as well. Maybe he should wait until Justina emptied and cleaned the pot. No, it would be more prudent to relieve himself now.

Gutiérrez Flores came back into the room. "Do you mind?" Vega asked, indicating the door through which his friend had just come.

"By all means."

When Vega returned, Gutiérrez Flores was still standing at the window. He pointed at the plaza. "There's a man selling songbirds. Look, there must be twenty cages of them stacked up in that pile. Some sort of thrushes, I suppose, or finches. I wonder how he catches them, and how can he keep track of so many?"

Vega looked where the inquisitor was pointing. "Maybe he uses a net. Maybe people bring them to him to sell. He doesn't seem to have any customers, though. No one's paying any attention to him."

"The way of the world, I'm afraid." Gutiérrez Flores settled himself in his chair. "You were going to tell me about those religious debates that Salgado loved so much. Though from what I've read in the file, they seem more like discussions than debates. Not a matter of winners and losers. Tell me, am I missing something here?"

Don Pedro de Vega picked up the Salgado file. How best to convey to Gutiérrez Flores what a complex fellow this man Salgado was? A good example, a telling incident, that's what he needed. Where was the damned thing?

Gutiérrez resettled himself in his chair. "What are you looking for?"

"As I said, there must be a dozen of these discussions recorded in the witness testimony. Maybe two dozen. Not rehashing the same incident either. Different conversations, with a variety of people. And in great detail. They show you how the minds of these people work. Ah, here it is." Vega drew out a folio from the stack of papers. "This is a conversation with Lucas de Valdés Daza, Justa Méndez's nephew. It was before our time, but I'm sure you've heard of her. Justa Méndez? The prettiest Jew in New Spain? Sentenced as a Judaizer in the Great Auto-de-Fé back in '96?"

"Oh yes, doña Justa: beloved of many, and as foul a heretic who ever walked these streets. Thick as thieves with the Carvajal clan. People still talk about her. This Valdés Daza was her nephew?"

"Yes, and proud of his lineage. Most of the Dazas seem to have been all right, though. Good Christians."

"Master Benito Daza, the Inquisition notary: the same family?"

"The same. Lucas is his mother's brother. No hint of scandal there. Lucas de Valdés Daza, though . . . He is a glass grinder by trade; sells eyeglasses here in Mexico City and in Nicaragua in a store in Granada near the Alcaicería. He does some silversmithing, too. I wouldn't be surprised if he and Salgado traveled back and forth from Mexico together."

"Plenty of time to talk with each other, then. And opportunity."

"Both. Lucas de Valdés seems to have suspected that his friend was a Jew. He testified that he never saw him observing any Jewish customs, but he heard him talk disrespectfully about the Church, and inferred from that. He made a deposition last June in Nicaragua to the Inquisition commissioner in Granada. Here's how Valdés put it; forgive me, it's a bit long:

> 'Salgado used to gossip about priests and holy objects with words pregnant with double meanings. When he talked about the precepts of the Church he used bad language that sounded to me Jewish. He loved to talk about the mysteries of faith, especially in relation to the Old Testament, which he obviously knew well, admired, and spoke of with authority and respect. One night he took me and Diego de Fuentes to his house ["He doesn't say whether this was in Mexico or in Granada," Vega interjected] and after he read to us from some books of canon law and some other books dealing with Christian conscience, Salgado criticized them both. He claimed that they just said what the pope wanted them to say, not what Christ had said at all. He said they were just ropes that the Church used to bind men to its commands.
>
> Another time Salgado came out of mass saying that Father Cabrera had not preached the truth in his sermon because in the Holy Scriptures there wasn't a single mention of the Trinity. Salgado insisted that the divine voice had always said *I am that I am*, and *I alone am God*. He kept up this kind of talk until nearly dawn. Naturally Fuentes and I were scandalized.'"

Jerónimo Salgado

"So why do you call those conversations debates?" Gutiérrez Flores interrupted. "They seem like the inventories of accusations that I hear every day."

"Of course, you're right. But Salgado himself called them debates. In the evening he'd say to his friends, 'We're alone with nothing else to do: let's debate some matters of faith. One of us can take the Jewish position, another can take the Christian one.' Mostly people just went along with it: good friends, a private setting, hours of conversation . . . Then every once in a while Salgado would say something so outrageous that everyone was scandalized. At least that's according to Valdés Daza."

Gutiérrez Flores cut in again. "Maybe they were scandalized, and maybe Valdés Daza was only trying to make the point in his deposition that he was a solid Christian. If Valdés Daza was easily horrified, he would have walked out."

"Maybe. Anyway, he didn't do that. Instead, he claimed that he tried a counterargument, just like in a debate. Listen:

> 'When I heard Salgado say that the Trinity didn't make sense, because how could three separate beings coexist in a single person, I answered him with the example of the sun, that had in itself the essence of the sun, the light of the sun, and the heat of the sun. That's how you have to understand the ineffable mystery of the Trinity, as three essences in one substance, each with its separate characteristics but all sharing in a single indivisible nature. That's the way that the Trinity has to be understood. The Father is not older than the Son or the Holy Spirit. None of the three is stronger than the others because substantially they are all one in the same.'

"Point to Valdés Daza. But Salgado hit it right back, like in one of the French king's tennis games. 'I know perfectly well what the Church teaches. But that flies in the face of reason.'

"According to Valdés Daza, Diego de Fuentes was there, too, and he tried to convince Salgado with another comparison. Fuentes folded his two hands together and said that they were different but part of the same body, and you couldn't say that one was older or better than the other. Salgado replied that that was just as foolish as when Father Cabrera said in his sermon that the three stones that Jacob placed at the foot of the ladder to heaven in his dreams had merged to become a single stone. Salgado insisted that because there was no scriptural evidence for any of that nonsense, it couldn't be true.

Valdés Daza admitted that if he hadn't been armed by his Christian faith he would easily have believed Salgado's arguments."

For the first time Vega could hear enthusiasm in Gutiérrez Flores's voice. "What you're telling me, then, is that Salgado was trying to refute beliefs grounded in faith with text-based arguments supported by reason?"

"In this example, yes, very much so."

"In your view that is the key to the man, then? That for Salgado his faith has never been strong enough to overcome his rationality?" Gutiérrez Flores struck Vega as fully engaged now, fascinated by the theological concerns. This is what the man was cut out for, the give-and-take of intellect. Not the endless quibbling about who said what to whom, and who was listening, the interminable trivia that made up most of what the two of them dealt with daily in the course of their jobs.

"That is one of the keys," Vega said. "But another is Salgado's skepticism, profound skepticism. It seems to have infused almost everything he said. He always seems to begin with the conviction that if he hasn't seen something with his own eyes, or if he hasn't read it in some irrefutably true text—and for him there are precious few of those—then there is no reason to believe it. Rather, there is a compelling reason to disbelieve it.

"You can sense this in Salgado's criticism of everything having to do with the Church. The depositions mention it over and over. Lucas de Valdés Daza was so shocked that he began to keep a written list of the things that Salgado said. They mostly come down to the fact that Salgado didn't believe that our Christian teachings were in any way legitimate. He scoffed at the miracle of transubstantiation. He refused to accept the validity of the sacraments, even the mass. 'The Bible doesn't report that the apostles ever said mass,' he'd argue. 'That's just another invention to keep us all flocking to church.' For him Jesus was not the Son of God, except in the sense that we all are. He liked to say that there were lots of people named Jesus, but none of them was the Messiah. And that the Jews didn't kill Jesus, the Gentiles did. Then, to prove it, he'd cite chapter and verse from memory. When Valdés Daza warned him that Judgment Day was coming soon and that it would be announced by signs and wonders in the sun, the moon, and the stars, Salgado just laughed. 'Who told you that?' Valdés said he'd read it in the four Gospels. 'Well, it's not in the Old Testament,' Salgado replied, 'so it can't be true.' Salgado didn't think much of the saints either. He used to tell people that saints were not made in heaven but down here, on earth, by the Church."

Jerónimo Salgado

Gutiérrez shook his head. "Didn't he ever have anything nice to say about us?"

"Not so far as I can tell. It's not in the record, anyway. And the few times I talked with him his criticism of the Church was a constant theme. The Church is illegitimate; it's wrong in its theology; and it's as greedy as a miser. Our holy images don't work miracles, he'd say; they just put the statues in the churches to keep the priests and monks from dying of hunger. He said the only reason the Church prohibited marriage between cousins was so that they could make money from selling dispensations. And as for the clergy . . . "

"No respect for the Church is unforgivable. The clergy are another matter. I've been in this job long enough to have seen plenty of clergy who are not worthy of the Church's grace. Most of the clerics I know are good people, but . . . "

"We both know that. But Salgado never makes those kinds of distinctions. For churchmen of any sort he has no respect at all, not even for people like me who were trying to help him. And he has even less for the people who defend priests when they sin like the human beings they are. Let me give you an example. Lots of people knew about this incident, because it shows up in a half dozen of the depositions. There was this Franciscan monk in Granada, not the holiest of men. In fact everybody knew he was a fornicator. It's just that nobody would say so. When the rumors began, nobody in Granada would even say his name. Except Jerónimo Salgado, of course. When one of Salgado's neighbors, a man named Sánchez, overheard him criticizing the Franciscan, he screamed that Salgado was an abomination to speak that disrespectfully of a cleric. Salgado screamed right back at him. I'm quoting now: 'Not *a* cleric, *this* cleric: Fray Antonio Río. First he had one of his parishioners beaten and then he fucked him and rubbed ground chili peppers on his ass. I swear to God, anyone who denies that that happened is a goddamn heretic.' The witness said that two men rushed at each other, and if he hadn't wrapped his arms around Sánchez they would have come to blows."

"He must not have had anything nice to say about the Inquisition either." As if to ward off the implied criticism, don Juan Gutiérrez Flores brushed a few dribblings of cheese from his cassock where they had settled in the crease above his stomach.

"Not at all." Pedro de Vega picked up another folio of Lucas de Valdés Daza's testimony. "I'm quoting here: 'Salgado said that the Inquisition never goes after poor people, only the rich, because that way the Holy Office can seize all their property.' Actually, several witnesses swore they heard him say things like that at different times, in various contexts."

"No wonder Valdés Daza thought he was a Jew."

"That's not the half of it. Whenever anybody says anything negative about the Jews, Salgado always rushes to their defense. Valdés said that they were talking one day and he said something about the Jews crucifying Jesus, and Salgado jumped all over him, claiming it wasn't the Jews who crucified him, it was the Gentiles. Valdés told him he was crazy, that everybody knew it was the Jews. But Salgado began to cite texts, all out of his head, of course, and finally Valdés realized that there was no way to argue with the man.

"Then another time—Valdés Daza couldn't remember who it was they were talking with—this other person claimed that you could always spot Jews because they were ugly. Salgado wasn't about to let that one pass." The lawyer picked up a folio and began to read. "'From among all the things in the world God chose one to be the best, and among lineages of men the best were the Jews, because God had chosen them. So it is an absurdity to say that Jews have long noses and are ugly, because the truth is exactly the opposite; they are the handsomest people in the world.'"

"More foul than handsome, it seems to me," the inquisitor said. "So, then: from everything Valdés Daza reports, it's pretty obvious that Salgado was a Jew."

"Well, yes, but remember all this was Salgado's talk, not his actions. Valdés claimed he never saw Salgado actually observe any Jewish customs."

"Now you're talking like a defense lawyer again. I presume that was the basis of your argument, of the advice you gave Salgado?"

"There wasn't much else I could offer him," Vega admitted. "Still, I think most of the evidence against him is not exactly conclusive. Or if it is, the sin is blasphemy, not Judaizing. The heart of it is skepticism. Disbelief."

"Disbelief in . . . ?"

"In just about everything. Everything that isn't in the Old Testament, at least. Listen to what Valdés Daza says about Salgado's lack of belief that Our Lord Jesus Christ is the Messiah. One time—this was in here in Mexico, not Nicaragua—, Valdés asked Salgado what he thought about the Antichrist, and Salgado answered that there was no such being. He said that Scripture never mentions the Antichrist, only the Messiah. And what's more, it doesn't say that the Messiah would be poor. Or that God himself would come down to earth. Or that he would be sacrificing his own son. Salgado challenged

Jerónimo Salgado

Valdés to tell him where all that was written, because it certainly isn't in the Old Testament. And he laughed when Valdés told him that John the Baptist had said it."

"Does Valdés Daza have more to say?"

"No; that's all we know about Salgado's conversations with him. You could always call Valdés Daza back to see if he remembers anything else. Maybe under threat of torture he'd recall some more. On the other hand, up until now Valdés has been a willing witness, almost eager. He's provided lots of information about the Judaizers in Nicaragua and Honduras. Here in New Spain, too. There's no reason to suspect that he's holding back."

Hold on a moment." Gutiérrez Flores clapped his hands, and a moment later Justina glided in. "Another pitcher of wine," he mimed, "and something sweet to finish off lunch."

The room had grown hot, and Gutiérrez Flores opened the shutters to let in fresh air. Or at least, as fresh as it could be, given the dung- and garbage-strewn unpaved streets of Mexico City. Justina appeared with a pitcher, some sliced prickly pears, and a bar of almond nougat.

"From Valencia; imported. Nobody makes *turrón* like the Valencianos."

When the last crumbs of turrón were gone, Gutiérrez poured them each another glass of wine.

"I can see that you've given this business a lot of thought. Salgado puzzles you, too, doesn't he?"

"He does. He knows so much. But his knowledge certainly hasn't led him to the truth. It seems to take him in the other direction. One might almost think it was the Devil's work."

The inquisitor crossed himself. "Either that, or an excess of intellect untempered by faith. I've seen that before. Without the guiding hand of belief on the tiller, no ship can sail a true course."

"His lack of faith is indisputable. But it doesn't explain where he got so many crazy ideas. The record is full of them. Every conversation: if it touched on religion, Salgado would fire off some *disparate*, some wild opinion. Don Pedro de Vega picked up another folio. "Listen to what he said to Diego de Fuentes."

"Fuentes?" Gutiérrez searched his memory.

"The man who tried to escape capture by changing his name to Juan Flores de Espinacedo. That man was certainly a Jew. Dyed in the wool. In fact . . . "

"Yes, Fuentes; Flores de Espinacedo. I remember him. Also from Nicaragua. A real chameleon."

"That's the man," Vega confirmed. "Anyway, once, when the two of them were in Granada, Salgado told Fuentes how he admired Islam because Muhammad's religion was based on Judaism and Christianity, and that was a good thing."

"I wonder where he picked that up."

"Probably from his reading, though I have no idea from where. It's hard to believe how much Salgado has read. Everything he could get his hands on. The Old Testament of course, especially the historical books and the Psalms. He knows the Old Testament in and out and considers its laws authoritative and unchangeable. Even by Christ, as he said more than once to his friends. The miracles of the Old Testament he accepts; it is only the Gospels that provoke him. His favorite story, at least according to the people who remember hearing him tell it, has to do with how the Bible came to be. If you will allow me."

The lawyer took up another of the folios. "'There was a king who had put together the best legal library in the world. For the Hebrew Law he chose seventy-two wise old Hebrews and locked them up, each in his own room, with orders to write down the Law as they remembered it, each without consulting any of the others. And when they had finished there wasn't a single letter of difference among them.'"

"An old story, and most likely true, I expect. God works in wondrous ways."

"Yes; but Salgado also maintained that it was Joshua who wrote the Five Books, not Moses, because he had a book of saints' lives that said so." Vega put down the paper.

"You said he read everything. Like what sorts of things?"

"Biographies of saints. Alemán's *Life of Saint Anthony of Padua*. He seems to have memorized the entire *Flos sanctorum*. And he was always quoting Luis de Granada's *Introduction to the Symbols of Faith*. Fonseca's *Essay on God's Love*. Tasso's *Jerusalem Set Free*. Lope de Vega's *Shepherds of Bethlehem*. Suciro's translation of Tacitus. He had copies of most of these in his library when they arrested him in Granada. The man must have spent a fortune on books."

"I assume that someone has gone through them page by page, to see what's underlined, what kinds of marginal notes he has written in. That sort of thing gives away what a man is thinking."

The question caught Vega by surprise. Usually the interrogators were

Jerónimo Salgado

so thorough. But he couldn't recall seeing any reference to anyone having scrutinized Salgado's library page by page. He felt embarrassed that he hadn't noticed it before this.

"I'm afraid I don't know. I haven't seen the books, just the commissioner's report that they were seized when the rest of Salgado's goods were sequestered, that they were inventoried, and that they are still being held in Granada pending some formal request that they be shipped to Mexico. What with the Holy Office's spiraling costs, and the directives it keeps issuing to be frugal . . . "

"All right. I'll order they be brought here for somebody to take a look at."

"What's clear to me, though, even without any marginal notes, is that Salgado's familiarity with those texts is extraordinary. He often quotes long passages from memory. And he almost always finds fault with them. He told his friends that Nieva was wrong in defending Sunday as God's day of rest when there was so much evidence that Saturday was the true Sabbath. He scoffs at Alemán's insistence that our holy images can work miracles. He never seems to worry that somebody might accuse him of meddling where he has no business, that these matters are best left to trained theologians. Just the opposite, in fact." Vega rummaged in the stack of papers. "Here it is. 'All a person needs is to understand the language well like a good grammarian, so he can admire the able wit with which God has endowed the writer. So what if he brings in stories from Holy Scripture, providing he talks about their literal meaning and doesn't veer off into spiritual matters the way theologians do. So what if a book quotes the Psalms, as long as they've been ably translated into good verse.'

"It's curious that most of his friends didn't criticize him for this. In fact, they loved it! One of Salgado's Mexico City friends said in his deposition—Vega was reading again—'When Jerónimo Salgado was away in Cartagena we all missed him and were anxious for him to return because he was such a well-educated man. And when Salgado did return, his friends praised everything that he told them.'"

"He sounds to me like both a heretic and a dogmatizer. You've developed a pretty good case against him. Maybe you should give up your letrado position and come over to the prosecution as a *fiscal*."

None of that called for a response, so Vega didn't give one. Gutiérrez forged on.

"Concede for a moment that Salgado is a heretic. But what kind of heretic? A Jew? You seem to be saying that in some ways he was, and in some ways he wasn't. A Lutheran? All that Bible reading, all that claiming to be able to decide for himself what the truth is, instead of accepting with faith and obedience the truth that the Church has always stood for? As if he were a professor of theology."

"A Lutheran, no." Vega was certain of that. "In fact, I'd be surprised if he had even ever met one. There aren't many of them left, thank God; not here in Mexico anyway. Though with Salgado's attitude toward priests, and love of Scripture . . . You know, if some Lutheran had engaged him, if he had a community of Protestant friends to debate with, I think he might have gone in that direction."

Vega paused for a moment to reflect. "Maybe he wouldn't have, though. The Lutherans, for all their misguided heresies, are men of faith. My understanding is that they believe passionately, even though what they believe is in error. Salgado isn't like that at all. For him, faith is not superior to reason, or even coequal with reason. There is a story he was fond of reciting to his friends. Vega picked up yet another folio. Here is Lucas de Valdés Daza's recollection of it, though he's not the only witness to mention it. Let me read it to you. According to Valdés, Salgado says:

> 'After a while lies turn into common opinion, and after a long while people hold them to be true fact. There was a French chronicler who wrote that their king Francis had captured our Emperor Charles V in a battle. And when another historian told him he had it backward, that Charles was the victor and Francis was the prisoner, he told him to keep quiet, explaining that he could write this now because people thought he had witnessed it; and after 200 years most people will believe it, even though they still argue about it. But 400 years after that everybody will accept my apocryphal version of events as the truth.'"

"He was wrong, though," Gutiérrez Flores objected. "Because everybody knows that it was Charles who took Francis prisoner."

"Everybody knows," Vega agreed. "But can we be sure that's the way it was? Is truth decided by popular opinion? If that were so, fornication would not be a sin. And the Church, as arbiter of the truth, would be superfluous."

Gutiérrez Flores fidgeted in his chair. Clearly he found this line of argument uncomfortable. "I understand your point. Salgado's point. So where are you going with this?"

"Remember that Salgado is a man of reason, not of faith. A man of erudition, at least for a layman, erudition that overpowers and delights his debating partners, his audience. Salgado isn't the sort of man to board himself up in a room with his texts and his thoughts. He is no Saint Jerome. Salgado's erudition seems to have satisfied him mainly in performance. Like a seven-year-old showing off: 'Look: see how clever I am!'"

"All right. I can see that."

"But as to what sort of heretic he is . . . Everything we have been talking about happened during the seven years or so when Salgado considered himself a Jew. Or, at least, when he leaned toward Judaism. But during the last four years he's seems to have held himself to be a Christian."

"A Catholic who decides the truth for himself?"

"I didn't say he was a good Catholic. More like . . . an odd Catholic, just the way he was an odd sort of Jew. No matter what, he never seems to acknowledge the primacy of faith. Salgado always gives the privileged place to reason. Remember how he said that it was Fray Luis de Granada's *Introduction to the Symbols of Faith* that brought him back to Christ? We've all read it. Think about it. All those detailed descriptions of the wonders of creation that lead one inexorably, logically, to a knowledge of God. God the creator, naturally. Architecture that confirms the existence of its Architect. You can read a long way in the *Symbols* without finding the name 'Jesus.'"

"That's true. Still," objected Gutiérrez Flores, "it is clear that when Luis de Granada talks about God, he means the Trinitarian God, including Jesus."

"That may be so, but I have the feeling that Salgado wouldn't interpret it that way. He denied the Trinity often enough when he was a Jew; it's hard to believe that he would embrace that concept on faith when he converted to Christianity. No; reason is his thing. He said so explicitly on more than one occasion. Like the time one of his friends berated him, insisting that to be authentic Salgado's Christianity had to be based on faith. Salgado wouldn't buy it. His counterargument was that faith is never perfect and that imperfect faith always leads to logical inconsistencies, doubts, and that the way to overcome that is by refuting the contradictions, using the power of the intellect. He didn't use those exact words, but it is pretty clear that's what he meant."

"You're positive?"

"Absolutely. And that's not the only case. The best example by far is Salgado's defense against what he calls the false accusations of his enemies. Written in his own hand. He submitted it voluntarily. It's almost a map of how the man's mind works." Vega went to the end of the stack of folios, extracted three, and began to read. "Listen to this: it's a long passage, but it really defines the man. At least in my view.

'The witnesses are lying. But it doesn't matter. I've already freely confessed sins much more serious than the ones they're accusing me of.'

"A simple enough argument, but it takes all those accusations off the table.

'If it weren't for the oath that I have taken to declare the whole truth, I could lie about it. But I'd rather lighten the workload of you holy and most illustrious gentlemen.'

"Ironic? Sarcastic? Or is he just being polite?

'I've already confessed that I abandoned the Catholic faith for the dead Law of Moses. And since that is so, whether I've committed many or few sins has no bearing on my guilt. Likewise, it is irrelevant how much or how little time I persisted in that error. There is no reason to believe that I am holding anything back. I've told you about my parents. I've told you about the people who might well have paid me not to disclose their Judaizing habits. What can they say that I myself have not already discredited?

I've already told you that when I was sick here in Mexico City I stayed with Benito Torres, and that his son Luis, the priest, in our long conversations together, resolved all my doubts.'

"Note that he doesn't say that Torres inspired him to have faith, or persuaded him to love Jesus, only that Torres clarified his thinking.

'He gave me a copy of the *Symbols of Faith* by Fray Luis de Granada, the Cicero of Spain.'

"He could have praised Luis de Granada a hundred different ways; but by calling him Cicero he emphasizes Fray Luis's rhetorical power in the service of logical argument.

'Reading that book several times, particularly the dialog about God as Master Teacher, I emerged from my blindness and returned to our Holy Catholic Faith. And since then I have done or said nothing contrary to Catholicism.

I know that Lucas de Valdés Daza has accused me of saying many heretical things. But how is it possible to believe that I or anyone would speak so freely in front of a man who said that one of his brothers was a familiar of the Holy Office and another was a priest? Why should I speak with him if that involved so much risk to me? Even if I were the sort of man who went about the world trying to distance people from the Evangelical Law in favor of the dead Law of Moses, why would I talk about it with such a man?'"

Vega put down the sheaf of papers. "Then he goes on to accuse Valdés Daza of being a cheat, a fornicator, a traitor to his friends, and a depraved liar. But all that's beside the point here. Jerónimo Salgado may be a simple store-keeper and traveling merchant, but he presents his case like a lawyer. He may be a layman, albeit a well-read one, but he debates like a theologian."

"You sound like you admire the man. You wouldn't be . . . "

"No, no. God forbid." Vega sensed that he had ventured onto dangerous ground. Their being old friends didn't change the fact that Gutiérrez Flores was one of Mexico's chief inquisitors. "This Salgado is a heretic. I refute everything he stands for, everything he believes. Or doesn't believe. But don't forget, I *am* a lawyer. I have to admire clarity of argument, even when the argument leads one into error."

"Because . . . ," Gutiérrez Flores seemed reluctant to let this go.

"Because logic, in the abstract, is beautiful. It is the foundation stone of rational thought. In conjunction with Christian faith and belief in the saving power of the Law of Jesus, it is what distinguishes us from lesser beings. Salgado errs not in the development of his arguments but in his premises. He believes that reason trumps faith, when in reality they are in harmony, with any conflict always resolved in the direction of faith."

Without saying another word, Gutiérrez Flores got up from the table, stretched, and walked over to the window. He looked out on the Plaza de Santo Domingo, at this hour of the day cluttered with food stalls, children selling tin religious trinkets from trays, and middle-rank officials bringing documents to be printed in the small shops that lined the plaza's arcades. Several upper-class women, wrapped so completely in their embroidered shawls that only their eyes could be seen, made their way toward Santo Domingo Church accompanied by their Indian servants.

It was clear that the conversation was over. Pedro de Vega neatened up the folios of Jerónimo Salgado's dossier that in his enthusiasm he had strewn across one end of the inquisitor's table.

"It's getting late," Gutiérrez Flores said. "And that's a lot for today. You have given me a great deal to think about, my friend. Thank God I am under no pressure from the Supreme Council to hurry my recommendations. I appreciate your coming. And for keeping this conversation strictly secret. At least for now . . . I think in Salgado's case I need to read the whole file. Maybe when I've examined the books in his library. When I've finished, perhaps it would be useful for us to talk again."

Jerónimo Salgado

8

Diego Pérez de Alburquerque

ON THE HIGH SEAS, 1629

The ocean is flat today, flat and greasy, with a sheen that mirrors the leaden clouds. Light gray, dark gray, with flecks of crystal that glimmer like the silver ore that boasting miners pull out of their rucksacks in the taverns of Zacatecas. The sails droop. Nothing separates the gray sky from the gray sea. The horizon is as hazy as the line between lies and truth.

It is Friday, and the sky and the sea look the way they did on Tuesday. The ship leaves no wake. The crewmen grumble from task to task. I crossed this ocean as a wide-eyed teenager a dozen years ago. I never thought I would be going back to Spain this way. If I returned at all, it would be as a merchant weighted down with enough silver to build myself a fine house in Madrid or, better yet, Bordeaux. To live like a gentleman, like one of the dukes of Alburquerque.

Three times a week the quartermaster opens the hatch and orders me and the ship's other prisoner to haul ourselves up onto the deck dragging the chains that were welded to our leg irons in Veracruz. Tuesday and Friday for an hour of fresh air and exercise and hygiene. Except that the air is fetid, exercise is clumping from one mid-ship rail to the other, and hygiene is dousing with a bucket of seawater. Sunday we hear mass with the crew and the ship's company of marines. The chaplain does not offer us the communion wafer. A quick *Ite, missa est*, and the quartermaster shoves us back into the hold.

The other prisoner is Santillana. No first name, he says, just Santillana. We pass the interminable hours in our hole below deck scratching for vermin and telling each other lies. About the towns we grew up in. The trouble we got into as children. Women. Monumental binges. Santillana must be twenty years older than I am, maybe more. His beard, as best I can tell, beneath the grime is white, and his hands and arms are covered with the spots that come with age. I don't know how many times I've asked him to tell me what he did to land him in this stinking ship's hold, but all he ever answers is, "We're all sinners, aren't we? One way or another. The Devil's children." On his left hand, where the index finger used to be, is a gnarled stump, but he won't talk about that either. Sometimes, when I ask him yet another question that he will not deign to answer, he'll say to me, "You talk today, Diego. I don't feel like it. But I love your stories. Tell me whatever you like: I won't rat you out. It's not in me to spread gossip." And then he gives a wheezing laugh, the way so many miners do, their lungs choked with dust.

So I talk, my back against the creaking hull and my legs braced against a barrel to keep the leg irons from rubbing off another layer of skin every time the ship pitches or rolls. Stories to fill the hours. Some of what I tell him is the truth, and some . . . I've told so many tales in my life, to so many people, that I'm no longer sure that I know the difference between what is a lie and what is the truth. As if that matters now.

There aren't many men who can say they have been tried three times by the Inquisition and escaped with their lives. One time, yes, and with luck they let you go with a slap on the wrist and a fine and a program of penance, prayers, and candles. And your moment of fame in the auto-de-fé, don't forget that. Twice, maybe: with a flogging, a stretch in jail, and the loss of every peso the Holy Office can squeeze out of you. But a third trial, that almost guarantees you a date with the garrote or the flames. I must be one of the lucky few. Or maybe not, seeing what lies ahead for me. I can still hear that friar's nasal whine:

> He shall be paraded through the city streets on the back of a donkey while the town crier reads out his crimes; then, stripped to the waist, he shall be given one hundred lashes with a whip. He shall be taken to Spain where he shall be made to serve as an unsalaried oarsman for eight years in His Majesty's galleys. When his service is complete,

he shall be remanded to the Inquisition prison in Sevilla. He shall be banned from the Indies for life. He shall forever wear his sambenito in public. And for the rest of his life he shall hear mass every week and take communion at least three times a year.

Well, the stripes on my back are nearly healed, and where there's life, there's hope. Only God knows what the future will bring.

"Amen!" echoes Santillana with that scratchy laugh of his.

I was born into an old-Christian family in the Spanish city of Segovia. My father, Diego de Acosta Alburquerque, had moved there from Braganza, in Portugal, for business reasons. We were related to the illustrious dukes of Alburquerque, which gave us a certain elevated status, although not a lot of money. Since you can't get anywhere in this world without the proper credentials, my brother Juan went to Madrid and had papers drawn up attesting to our purity of blood and our condition as *hidalgos*. After my first trial here in Mexico, I went to Puebla and paid a notary to draw up another set of papers just for me, in case I ever needed them: fancy paper, an official seal, and all the relevant particulars. Set me back thirty reales.

How does that sound, eh? That's the family story I always told people. The truth? Well, Father was from Braganza. As was my mother, Beatriz de Acosta. And my grandparents, too, the whole family. Sometime way back they went there from Spain. But as far as I know my parents never set foot in Segovia. Instead, once they left Portugal they went to Bordeaux and set up a business importing cloth. That's really where I was born, in Bordeaux, around the year 1600. They told me I was baptized there, too, in the Church of the Holy Cross. And here I am, crossing the water again.

My earliest memories are the Bordeaux harbor: the ships' masts as tall as trees, the wharfs along the Gironde River, the crowds of merchants and sailors, the dizzying smells of leather, dyed cloth, and spices rising from the barrels stacked alongside the warehouses. I can't have been more than four or five years old, but those masts and barrels etched themselves into my brain. At that age I didn't see the garbage, the drunken sailors passed out in the alleys, the rats: just the wonder of those enormous masts against the blue sky. That's what I remember most from those years. That and the fact that my father was never home and my mother smelled of lavender.

Like all great ports, Bordeaux attracts the plague, and it struck the city hard in 1605. Anyone with money moved away. My parents took me, my

Diego Pérez de Alburquerque

older sister, Isabel, and my two baby brothers, Luis and Juan, to Toulouse. During the six years we lived there my sister Beatriz de Acosta was born. She lives with her husband back in Bordeaux. I think she must be eighteen or nineteen by now. Isabel's in Bordeaux, too.

My father had enough money to send me to the Jesuit school. At first my mother went with me every day. As a woman she couldn't go into the school, of course, but she waited at the street door until I had crossed the courtyard to my classroom and been herded inside with the other six-year-olds. She was there when they let us out, too, and she would walk me home in the afternoon.

What I mostly remember from that school was how hard the benches were. And how the schoolmaster's black cassock swirled behind him as he paced back and forth droning the rudiments of Latin into us. Any seat softer than those benches, and we all would have fallen asleep. Over and over we would recite for him the Latin conjugations and declensions. By the time we left Toulouse I had almost finished the third level and could read most Latin texts without much difficulty. My favorite was the *Wars*. My friends and I used to act out the battles, chasing each other with stick swords, arguing about who would get to be Caesar, and shouting out our battle cries in Latin. When we weren't pretending to be at war, we played tag or threw a ball around. Most of my schoolmates were from families like mine, just off the boat from Spain or Portugal. We all spoke Spanish or Portuguese at home, and we played in those languages, too. The few French kids at that school used to get angry with us, but most often we ignored them, unless we needed them to fill out some team, in which case we switched to French.

What else did we study? Numbers, of course. We had to know basic arithmetic to be admitted to the second level. That wasn't hard, though, since at home most of us were surrounded by business talk. Our fathers, almost all of them textile merchants, insisted that we master the rudiments of keeping accounts. We learned religion, too. Besides hearing mass every morning in church, we had an hour of catechism every day. And when we weren't reading the classic Latin authors, we got a steady diet of the lives of saints. Most of us could recite the *Flos sanctorum* by heart. I could, anyway. I hear something two or three times, I remember it. Word for word.

I think those were the happiest years of my life. I often went with my mother and our kitchen servant, Paola, to the great open-air market behind the Jacobin church. After the day's shopping, Mother sometimes bought me a small toy or a sweetmeat. If the baskets of vegetables were too heavy, Mother would pay one of the market boys to help Paola carry them back to our house. Sometimes she bought a live goose or a chicken, and my father cut its throat with a knife in the small yard behind our house. On special days when there was no school, my brother Juan took Luis and me hiking up in the wooded hills outside the city. In the high pastures there were cows and sheep and horses; lower down we often stopped to watch peasants leaning into their plows, their massive yoked oxen billowing great clouds of steam in the early morning air. Later in the summer, when the fields turned brown, we would watch the lines of farmers scything down the stalks of wheat or barley and tying them into neat sheaves that they forked onto carts to take to the threshing floors. On clear days we could see all the way to the snow-covered peaks of the Pyrenees that form the border with Spain. We had relatives over there, in Madrid, and my brother Juan would talk about one day going to visit them. On Sundays we all trooped to mass together as a family.

Another lie. No, not what I'm telling you: how we were living. It was all a sham. I'm not talking about the happy times. Those were real enough. My father was gentle with us, letting us do pretty much as we wanted, and never raising a hand to us. But in one way he terrified us. And that was by warning us, over and over, that we must never, ever, tell people what we did behind the closed doors of our house. When he said that his eyes grew as hard as flint, and he lowered his voice so that we had to strain to hear him. There were certain things that we must not share, not with our friends at school, not with our Jesuit teachers, not with our confessors when we grew old enough to make confession. Not one word, ever.

And what was this terrible secret? At first, I remember, I didn't have the faintest idea. I saw things through a child's eyes: whatever was, was. But gradually I picked up hints about how we were different. When the family sat down to eat, my father blessed our food with some mumbled words in a language I did not understand, words I never heard at school. Nobody in our house ever crossed themselves the way my school chums were always doing. I knew all the important Christian prayers, thanks to the Jesuits, but when we were in our house I never once heard my parents pray the Our Father, the Ave Maria, or any of the others. At home we had no woodcuts of saints, no holy water font. At the market my mother never bought sausages. We rarely ate beef, and when father brought some home my mother covered it with salt and washed it two or three times, but not until she first closed the kitchen shutters. We fasted on the days the priests told us to, of course, but we fasted on other days, too. When I was old enough to ask why we did all this, my parents began to explain things to me. The Christians in France kept one Law, my father said, but we came from Portugal, so we had a different Law with different customs. Ours was the Law of Moses, not Jesus. That's why we washed our hands before and after we ate, and why we tried not to do any work on Saturday, and why at home we never crossed ourselves. Our kitchen maid, Paola, was Portuguese, too, so naturally she did all those things with us. But we weren't allowed to let anyone else in Toulouse know because if anyone saw what we were doing, they might report us to the authorities. And it could be dangerous for our relatives in Spain.

To the world outside we were good Christians. Alburquerques, members of the Portuguese nobility. That's what we wanted everyone to believe; that was the face we showed our non-Portuguese friends. So naturally, when I was arrested the first time in Mexico, that's what I told the friars who questioned me. A family of good Christians, through and through. One hundred percent.

We lived in Toulouse for six years or so and then went back to Bordeaux because my father thought he would have better business opportunities there. But since the plague was still raging, we took the ferry across the Garonne River to Libourne, where we lived in a small rented house. I didn't like Libourne very much. It was a small town, and after Bordeaux and Toulouse it seemed pretty dull. There were hardly any other Portuguese kids to play with, and I had few friends. I mostly sat around our house and dreamed about the day we would go back to Bordeaux.

I soon discovered that in this life you have to be careful what you wish for. After two years in Libourne my father judged that the plague had abated sufficiently for us to return to Bordeaux. He was wrong. Right after we moved into our new house he got sick. We buried him a week later and my brother Luis shortly after that.

Then the hard times began.

What with all the moving around, my father had left us very little, and what there was, mostly unsold cloth, the creditors took. Childhood was over: it was time for us all to go to work. 'All' meant the three women and me. Beatriz, who must have been five or six when my father died. My mother. My sister Isabel had married Luis de Acosta when she was sixteen, but eighteen months later, still childless, she was a plague widow and back living with us. My brother Juan had already left the family, gone south to seek his fortune in

Spain. In the two rooms we now rented in Bordeaux, Isabel and my mother spun thread and tatted lace every day from sunup to sundown. That's what we lived on, thread and lace that my mother sold to a couple of clothiers in the Place des Carmes. I left our rooms every day before sunup and went to the market where I earned a few sous helping unload the produce wagons or toting peoples' purchases home for them. As for Paola, within a week of my father's death my mother realized that we could no longer afford her, so she had to go.

I was thirteen or fourteen and, like all boys that age, proud of the thin fuzz on my chin. One afternoon my mother came home and told me that one of her Portuguese customers, a Senhor Horta de Silva, with whom she had begun keeping company, had a brother in Rouen who was a shopkeeper and needed a cashier who was good at languages and numbers. Would I go?

Would I go?! What do you think? I jumped at the chance to leave home. Horta put up the money for passage, making clear that I would have to repay him, and I was also expected to send half of my wages back to my mother and sisters in Bordeaux. Two days later I found myself sailing up the Atlantic coast to Honfleur, from which a riverboat took me up the Seine to Rouen. The world was mine. I felt as free as the terns swooping all around our boat, their eyes searching for the flash of minnows in the gray water. As I watched them, I could see myself in a boardinghouse with a window that overlooked the roofs of the city; or exchanging confidences with my new friends in some great plaza while we stuffed ourselves on sugared fruit and flavored ices; or in the back pews of a dark church, in intimate conversation with one of the beautiful girls I felt certain abounded in Rouen.

Soap bubbles, all of it, going pop-pop in the breeze. Reality turned out to be one airless room over the stable behind Horta's house. I had no time to make friends: Hernando Horta de Silva worked me from dawn to dusk, and I feel certain he would have worked me half the night, too, if it weren't for the price of candles. And as for girls . . . the only female I talked with was Horta's wife, Lucrecia, who weighed two hundred pounds if she weighed an ounce and had more pockmarks on her face than there are flies in a slaughterhouse. There was nothing sweet about her. She was a busybody, too. She and her husband may have been of our Nação, but the reek of fried salt pork in their house made it clear that they had put all that business behind them.

Senhor Horta's accounts were so simple that I quickly mastered the bookkeeping. I kept his shop neat, too, and alerted him when he was about

Diego Pérez de Alburquerque

to run out of some fast-selling item. Before long he had me writing out the orders for new stock. When I found him someone who would sell him buttons for only half of what his current supplier charged, he put me in charge of buying. Most of the time Horta just sat looking out the window or ogling the women who came into his shop. After a few months I could see that Senhor Horta had come to depend on me, so I screwed up my courage and told him that if he wanted me to continue working for him I needed more free time to myself. He harrumphed for a while but finally agreed to let me break off early a couple of times a week, providing, that is, that I got all my work done.

About this time I met Juan Carvallo, who had a business provisioning ships on the quay. Carvallo was a dozen years older than I, a strapping, red-headed fellow with muscles that bulged from years of lifting heavy barrels. He knew his way around, too. Among other things, he looked out for the Portuguese newcomers in Rouen. One Sunday as I was heading home from mass, he struck up a conversation with me in the street. I thought it was a chance meeting, but I believe now that he had been looking for me. Anyway, what with one thing and another, we soon became friends. The upshot was that he invited me to observe the Kippur fast with him and his family. Although some vague memories of fasting with my parents when I was a child came back to me, lots of what the Carvallos did was completely unfamiliar. For one thing, after the evening meal before the fast they all took off their shoes. They dressed up in their finest clothes—I remembered that from when I was a child—but the men all put on hats, even though we were indoors, and that was new to me. We had gathered in an inside room, so the only light came from the dozen large new candles that Carvallo's wife lit after chanting a few words that I didn't recognize or understand. And then they began to pray the Penitential Psalms in Portuguese and some other long prayers in a language that I now know was Hebrew. They prayed the whole night and the entire following day. I thought I would die from boredom. The only thing that kept me awake was figuring how I would explain to Horta why I had missed an entire day's work.

When I got home Lucrecia de Horta lit into me. Where had I been? What had I been doing? I told her I'd been having a good time with my friends, that we'd drunk too much, and that I'd been sick the whole next day. She didn't believe me for a minute.

"It's that Jewish fast. That's what you've been doing. Don't you know that you are condemning your soul to Hell?"

CHAPTER 8

Well, I knew that's what Christians believed, but since I'd been friends with Carvallo I had been thinking of myself more as a Jew. Obviously I couldn't tell Senhora Horta that, so I just nodded my head, as if I was agreeing with what she was saying. She rattled on about how the mercy of Christ would save me if I would have faith and follow his Law. I nodded again, but she insisted that I swear to her that I would. Since I wasn't inclined to do that, I told her I wanted some time to think it over. She forbade me from leaving the house, insisting that she was caring for my soul the way she would for her own son's, and said we would talk some more in the morning.

Sure enough, no sooner was I awake than she called me to the room that served the Hortas as an office. I didn't see any point in arguing with her, so I told her that she had truly convinced me to be a Christian. I thought that might be the end of it, but she straightaway took me to the Monastery of San Agustín to talk with her confessor, whose name I have long since forgotten. For the next two months he fed me a steady diet of Christian doctrine. Eventually the friar's arguments made such perfect sense to me that I resolved to commit myself with all my heart to the Law of Jesus Christ and to live and die under that Law. And from that day to this I have been a true and faithful Christian.

Santillana gave one of those wheezing coughs that were his idea of laughter. "A true and faithful Christian, eh? So that's why they put you on this stinking ship, to show us what a model Christian was like. No need to worry about your soul: if we sink, it will float." He laughed again. "I'm too old a dog to jump at that bone."

All right, then. So it's not precisely true; but it's a nice story, isn't it? The Mexican Holy Office believed it, at least for a while. The real truth is that the whole Horta family brought the Law of Moses with them from Portugal and followed it just the way I did. That's why my mother sent me to them. Later, back in '15, when King Louis booted the Jews out of France, the Hortas moved to Flanders. That's where they are now, safe and sound, so I can tell you this without any risk to them. Lucrecia Horta never tried to convert me to the Law of Jesus; she was too busy keeping the Sabbath herself. And as for the friar teaching me to love Jesus Christ and the Blessed Virgin . . . Lord knows the friars have tried often enough. But in those days I was too certain of myself to entertain the thought that what I knew might be wrong. My

Diego Pérez de Alburquerque

parents had drummed into me that their Law was the true one, and that was good enough for me.

I don't think that any of my close friends from those days was Christian. I mean not a true Christian. In fact, most of them were ten times more Jewish than I was, though unless they knew you well enough to have confidence in you, they would never let you see it. It was Juan Carvallo who gave me my first detailed lessons about how to keep the Law of Moses, things that I still remember as clearly as the day he instructed me. The laws of the Sabbath. The great fasts. Shevu'ot, Sukkot, and Tisha b'Av. The Passover seder. Reading the scroll of Esther on Purim. I learned to call those days by their Hebrew names, too, just the way they did. For each festival they made me memorize everything I had to do. *Roshanah*, the first two days of the new moon of September: you can't work, you have to wear your best clothes, and you have to give charity to the poor members of the Portuguese community. *Hanucah*, in memory of Judas Maccabee's victory over the Gentiles: the first day you light one little candle and hang it up on the wall, the second day two candles, and so forth, up to eight. Or maybe it was only seven. Something like that. I learned by heart half a dozen prayers, too: the first prayer of the morning; the prayer for washing hands; all kinds of things. In Spanish, most of them, but a few in Portuguese. A couple of short ones in Hebrew. I memorized the words, though I can't tell you exactly what they meant. The one I said most often began . . .

Santillana interrupted me. "So, is there any sex in this story? Or am I going to have to listen to you praying the whole damn afternoon?"

" Hold your water," I said. "I'm getting to that." The old fart only wanted to hear about women. Well, all right. I hadn't even scratched the surface of the things we did in our prayer group in Rouen. But it really didn't matter which direction my story took. We were just passing the time.

Here it is, then: how I fell in love. At least I guess it was love. It was at Carvallo's house, and her name was María de Acosta. No relation to my mother's Acostas. She was slim as a willow wand, with black hair and eyes the color of coal. She was a widow, they said, whose husband, João, had died on his way to Salonica. The Carvallos had taken her in when her husband went away in return for María's helping out with the two Carvallo children. When nearly three years had passed without their hearing one word from João, they had presumed him dead. Under Catholic law, of course, which demands concrete proof of widowhood, María could not remarry, but nobody I knew cared much about those things. If João wasn't dead, then he had abandoned her, and that was enough for the Carvallos. If María took a new husband, Rouen's Portuguese community would not object. At first, in my innocence I assumed that the Carvallos had their eyes on me as María's potential new husband, although since I was just fourteen I realize now that was hardly likely. In those days I was visiting the Carvallos' house once or twice a week—I tried to spend at least part of the Sabbath with them when I could—and before long María and I grew close. Well, one thing leads to another, and despite the fact that she was eight or ten years older than I was, we became confidants, spending hours together sharing our thoughts and dreams. We began to touch hands, and our eyes began to reflect more than just friendship.

By December the weather in Rouen turns cold and dank, and two can heat up a bed far better than one. That first night—my very first, to tell the truth—, as our hearts slowed and the sweat dried on our exhausted bodies, she asked me to call her by her real name, Miriam. Our daughter, Clara Margarita, was born just after the Great Fast of September. She was just learning to walk when I left Rouen eight years ago. I have had no news of them since; nor they of me, I have to say. I pray that they are still alive and happy and getting on with their lives. It wouldn't be right of me to go back to them, not after all this time. María's bound to have found someone else by now. Even if I survive the galleys, I don't think I will ever go back to Rouen.

So why did I leave them? Time passed, the way it does. I got older, and as my eyes opened wider to the world around me, Rouen seemed to shrink. María's honey voice began to sound shrill and demanding. The cashier's job was a dead end, the salary was lousy, the prospects . . .

"And you're a bastard at heart, just like all of us men." Santillana smiled. "Don't forget that."

"All right. That too."

"And a liar."

"Only when it suits my purpose."

Santillana snorted. "Only then?"

"Do you want me to go on, or not?"

"Mmmmm." Santillana at his noncommittal best.

"Yes or no?"

Diego Pérez de Alburquerque

"Have you got something better to do?"

I didn't, but now I was angry, so I sat silently and glared at him, even though I knew he could not see my face in the dim light of the hold. Minutes passed.

Finally curiosity got the best of him. "You were fed up with your life in Rouen. So then . . . "

So from Rouen I went back to Bordeaux for a while to see my family, but I didn't find any employment that fit what I was certain were my extraordinary talents. I began to think about going south to Madrid, where rumor had it my brother Juan had become very rich. I think I told you before that he had left the family to go seek his fortune. But the other reason he left was that he had already decided that the Law of Moses was wrong and that to keep his new faith strong he had to put some distance between himself and the family. If I was going to join him in Spain, I figured I'd have to do the same thing. The Spaniards . . . well, we know all about that, don't we? Keep your mouth shut and your eyes open. In France you have to be careful, but in Spain . . . Our French friends have been so beat up by their religious wars that for the most part they let the sleeping dogs of ancient sins lie undisturbed. Besides, I'd been living in a Catholic world, and every day the things my parents had taught me seemed much less meaningful. I still had doubts, but I was increasingly convinced that the Law of Our Lord Jesus Christ was the only path to the salvation of my soul. Luckily, in France the procedure for clearing my slate with God was simple: I just admitted all my former sins to my confessor who then, on faith, granted me sacramental absolution and welcomed me back into the bosom of the Church.

Still, I knew that to keep out of trouble I had to do more than just be a Christian in my heart. Since I am Portuguese I also had to put a public face on my religion. So I never missed a Sunday's mass. I liked to walk in a moment after the liturgy had begun, and walk all the way to the front of the church so that everyone would see me take my place in my pew. I hung on every word of the sermons, prayed my beads with a look of rapture on my face, and took communion whenever it was offered. I actually enjoyed the sermons: the stories were entertaining; some of them brought back to me my schooling with the Jesuits. I especially liked the ones about David and Moses, Abraham and Rachel, and all the other heroes of my parents' Law. But I also enjoyed the stories of the Holy Family, the martyr saints, and the founders of the orders whose monasteries dotted the cities like mushrooms in the fields. If anyone ever asked, I could demonstrate that my youthful Judaizing had been wiped away. That way I could live freely in Spain as a practicing Christian without always having to look over my shoulder.

Santillana harrumphed in disbelief.
"What makes you think that I'm lying again?"
"Aren't you always?"
"Are you saying that you don't trust my words?"
"Of course I do. Prester John of the Indies. True as a woman's kiss."

All right, then. A lot of what I just told you is true, but I can't swear that it all is. Looking back at it now, after all that has happened, sometimes it's hard for me to recall exactly how I felt, what my motives were. When the Holy Office arrested me in Mexico, I told the inquisitors what I just told you. There are some truths in it, but not everything. I never confessed my heresies in Bordeaux; that was a lie. I never received absolution. And I never stopped observing the Sabbath, at least when I remembered to, and when I thought it was safe. My complete conversion to the Law of Jesus came much later.

I told you we had heard that my brother Juan was rich, but it turned out he was nearly as bad off as I was. I remembered him from when I was small, but I hadn't seen him in nearly ten years. Someone in France had given me his address. It turned out to be two dark rooms in a house behind the Plaza de la Cebada, in a part of Madrid where it was worth your life to go out on the street at night. His neighbors were carters and fishmongers, cutpurses and whores. Juan wasn't at home, but they told me I'd find him in the Church of San Isidro the Laborer around the corner. I waited by the door until I saw him come out, tall and handsome as I had remembered him, with a brown cloak around his shoulders that made him look like a Franciscan. I planted myself in front of him. He started to step around me, but then he pulled himself up short. He took a hard look at my face.
"Diego?" he asked tentatively.
I nodded.
"Can it be?"

Diego Pérez de Alburquerque

"Who did you think it was, Saint Ignatius?"

He wrapped me in his arms and gave me a hug that squeezed the breath out of me.

"Come with me, brother. My God, what are you doing here? I can't believe it's you. Let's go have a drink!'

Arm in arm we made for the tavern below his apartment, where over a pitcher of Valdepeñas he brought me up to date on his travels and misfortunes.

When I left Toulouse for Rouen Diego had made his way south, thinking that in St-Jean-de-Luz or Biarritz he could find work carting dry goods across the mountains to Spain. This was without paying the import taxes, naturally. In other words, a smuggler. Three years, he told me, three years he risked his neck on the mountain roads. Three years he fought the sleet in the winter passes. Three years he dodged bandits and soldiers. And for three years he saw his profits disappear into the gullets of the customs inspectors on both sides of the border. So he decided to call it quits. He dug up the cache of coins he had managed to stash away, sold his cart, and made his way to Madrid, where for the past two years he had survived by hiring out as a laborer. Though sometimes he had gone hungry, he had not yet dipped into his cache, and had even added a coin or two to it. That was money he planned to use to get out of Europe once and for all and seek his fortune in New Spain.

"Gold and silver mines." He leaned over the table as he told me this, his eyes throwing sparks in the candlelight. "Cattle ranches the size of kingdoms, with Indian slaves and blacks to do all the work. Business opportunities, any kind we want. We'll work for four or five years and come back to Spain rich men.

"Like all of us," wheezed Santillana. "Rich as the Duke of Alba."

"The magic of the Indies," I said in the same sarcastic tone. "Though back then my brother and I really believed it."

By the time the second pitcher was empty, all Juan's talk of *we* making *our* fortunes had scrambled my wits. I decided to go with him.

We had the money my brother had put away for passage. Now all we needed was the papers. They won't even let you on the boat unless you have a travel permit that certifies you are an old-Christian. And we are Portuguese, which means that everybody thinks we're Jews. We had two choices: we could bribe a whole ladder of officials so they would let us embark without the necessary papers—risky business, and expensive. Or we could find a forger to draw up a certificate stating our general good character and purity of blood.

Well, Juan knew a man who knew another man who could cobble up our bona fides: Juan and Diego Pérez de Alburquerque, distant cousins of the noble dukes of Alburquerque, who in turn were related by marriage to the kings of Portugal, no less. Two spotless boys, born in Castilla, in the city of Segovia, where our parents were respected hidalgos living from their rents. Our scribbler had secured a few sheets of official paper—we had to pay extra for those—and all he had to do was render what we told him into the appropriate legal language. When we collected the paper it didn't seem quite impressive enough, so we decided to dress it up. We had an uncle who had lived for a long time in Spain, and several years earlier he had contrived to get himself an official Certificate of Purity of Blood. Somehow my brother got hold of it. At the top of the first page there was an elaborate colored escutcheon, which we cut off and hired a professional to affix to our own newly minted certificate. When he finished you'd have thought the seal had been painted right there on the page.

From Madrid, Juan and I made our way to Sevilla to have our travel papers stamped by the Council of Indies. One week, they told us. Two at the most. While we waited for approval we took in the sights. Sevilla was the richest city either of us had ever seen. We spent hours on the Calle de la Sierpe, which runs from the Guadalquivir docks past the royal Alcázar gardens to the Palace of the Council of Indies. Any hour of the night or day it buzzed with sailors, porters, ship owners, provisioners, tradesmen, beggars, whores, soldiers, and gawking foreigners. We bought meat pies filled with what only God and the baker knew; sardines grilled on dockside braziers; sausages, hot and cold, which we bought by the yard, wrapping them in bread and washing them down with a glass or two from some tavern. We spent the midday hours in the Great Church, the cathedral that Sevillanos boast is the largest in the world, along with hundreds of other people who crowded there not to pray but to escape Sevilla's hammering sun. And to ogle the young ladies brought to church by their duennas to pray their rosaries.

With each passing day the crowds swelled as Sevilla awaited the packet boats that bring up the cargo from the Indies fleet anchored in the Bay of

Diego Pérez de Alburquerque

Cádiz. Sevilla is the depot for all the gold and silver mined in the New World, or at least all that escapes the talons of the Dutch and English pirates who patrol the offshore waters. In the taverns, once we had been pegged as foreigners, every citizen of Sevilla thought it his duty to describe the bullion parade to us: yokes of oxen, their horns garlanded with flowers, hauling the bullion carts, groaning under the weight of the ingots, from the banks of the Guadalquivir up the Calle de la Sierpe to the Consejo de Indias to be counted, and taxed.

It wasn't likely that any silver would fall off of those carts for us. The procession sounded lovely, but we couldn't wait. While we were marking time in Sevilla, in Cádiz the Indies fleet was being loaded for its journey back to the Indies, and we wanted to be aboard. But first we needed our papers. Naturally, as departure time neared, the fee for expediting them went up. Our funds—Juan's, that is; my meager savings were long since spent—were dangerously low, but if we wanted to sail to Mexico we had no choice. So we paid, received our papers, and hurried to Cádiz to book our passage on the *Amaranta*, in the fleet of don Carlos de Ibarra. Six hundred maravedís each it cost us, leaving us damn little to make a start in New Spain. Ah, well, we thought, God would surely provide.

I was no stranger to ships, but I had never been out of sight of land before. The fifth day out when a stiff wind raised waves that broke over the gunwales, stinging us with salt spray, I began to fear for our lives. Like most of the other passengers, I spent hours bent over the rail, spewing the remnants of the ship's bad food into the churning water and holding on with clenched knuckles to keep from being swept into the sea. Between heaves I muttered every prayer I knew, and some that I invented on the spot, begging Jesus and Moses and the Blessed Virgin to keep us safe. But the storm only grew worse, and I was terrified of disappearing into the maw of the ocean. The crew seemed to take it all in stride, but by the third day of mountainous seas I began to wish I were already dead. Juan seemed half gone already. Green as a frog, wheezing and coughing, without enough energy even to stagger to the rail, he lay against a hatch cover, his clothing stinking of his own vomit. And he wasn't the only one.

Finally, as the sailors who had been mocking us said it would, the sun came out. The sails dried and billowed as we tacked into a gentle west wind. Our color returned, and some of us, the most hearty, began to nibble on the pieces of hardtack they gave us for dinner. Three weeks later a thin line of gray on the horizon announced that we were about to make landfall in Veracruz.

I could barely contain my excitement. I was eighteen years old, full of piss and vinegar, and a whole new world lay just off our port bow. Sure, I was all but penniless, but I had heard the stories. Mexico's mountains dripped precious metals, and two young men with a lot of pluck and a bit of luck were bound to return to Europe in a couple of years as rich as Croesus.

Little did I know.

Veracruz was like other port cities I had seen, stinking of fish and tar, filled with people on the make, as ready to knife you for a few coins as to befriend you. A garrison of soldiers to keep the peace. A swarm of customs officers to make sure the government got its share of every crate of goods moving in or out of the port. We saw half-naked Indian porters sweating under their heavy loads; black slaves, roped together like a string of pack mules, bound for the sugar plantations; flocks of young Spanish friars eager to head out to the missions. Veracruz was a city of travelers. The streets were lined with taverns serving up strong drink and cheap food. The shops sold boots and rope, wooden trunks, horse tack, water skins, and broad-brimmed straw hats. Ironmongers offered picks and shovels, pry bars, and chisels for the would-be miners like us, still uncomprehending the height of Mexico's mountains, and how the weight of iron increases league by league. On every street near the docks there were rooms and women for rent by the night or by the hour. Juan and I didn't have money for any of that; we had barely enough left for some salt meat and dried beans, and to lease a couple of mules to carry us up through the jungles to Jalapa and Puebla de los Ángeles. Juan's cough was so bad that some days he could barely keep his seat on his mule.

Puebla de los Ángeles is an elegant town in the center of a vast fertile plain surrounded by volcanoes. There was money to be made in Puebla. We just had to figure out how to make it. I didn't know anybody, at least at first, so there was nobody I could ask to fix me up with a job as a cashier or an accountant. Juan was too sick to work; some days he could scarcely breathe. So I did what I could; I used my strong back and arms to earn a few coins carrying packages, loading and unloading carts, and toting bricks and tiles for Puebla's construction crews. Indians work cheaper, but my smiling face seemed to inspire confidence. I earned just enough money left for a small, windowless room with a bed big enough for the two of us.

Diego Pérez de Alburquerque

The work was hard and the pay terrible, but at least we were eating regularly. The city was full of color, swarming with Spaniards, black slaves, and Indians speaking their peculiar languages, strung together with sounds I had never heard in Europe. But most days I was too tired to even take notice. Juan developed a fever and sweats, and when he could gasp out a few words, he talked as if we were back in Sevilla. I began to cough, too, so that some days I could only work until noon. Juan began to beg me to take him back to Spain, and that began to seem like a good idea to me, too. I sold our few possessions to pay for space for us both on a wagon to Veracruz, trusting that somehow God would provide the means to get us onto a ship. But it wasn't to be. Juan was so sick when we reached the coast that I called a priest to give him the sacraments. Juan took the wafer. The next afternoon my brother breathed his last, may he rest in peace.

As if it were a miracle, Juan's death seemed to give me energy. My cough cleared up, and within a month I had returned to the world of the living as strong as I had ever been. I went back to Puebla, determined to make a fresh start.

And my luck changed. One morning I heard someone calling my name on the street. It turned out to be Juan de Ortega from Rouen, with whom I had spent many nights in prayer. He had grown so tall that I scarcely recognized him. He invited me to share a pitcher with him, and then he showed me where he lived, not far from a Franciscan church. He told me that in the two years since I had seen him he had gone to Pisa and had himself circumcised. Now, he said, he felt like a real Jew. For a while he had thought to make Italy his home, but an adventure with a young lady, and the determination of her three brothers to put him in his grave, made him think better of it. Thus Mexico. Ortega had been in Puebla for nearly a year now, working in a clothing store and living in the house of Francisco de Victoria, his uncle.

I thought they were my friends until I found out what bastards they really were. Diego Gómez de Salazar, too. Another so-called friend who hung around with Ortega and Victoria.

Gómez de Salazar was part of Puebla's Portuguese circle. In fact, most of Juan de Ortega's friends were men of the Nação who had lived for a while in France before coming to Mexico. They gathered every Friday afternoon, usually at Victoria's house, and when I could, I joined them. We would pray whatever prayers we knew and talk about the Law of Moses. We all professed that our salvation could come only through that Law, but aside from that we didn't talk much about Heaven and Hell, and I don't think I ever heard anyone explain Moses's role in saving our souls. Instead we talked about the rules: what we could or couldn't do on the Sabbath; what we couldn't eat; how often we had to fast; how to determine when the festivals were. Things like that. Since we had all learned the Law of Moses in different ways, we knew things differently. Frequently we spent more time arguing than we did praying. We often ended up recalling our gatherings in Rouen or Bordeaux, and how even though the Law of Moses was illegal in France, no one there bothered us very much. We blessed the wine, and drained the bottles, and dreamed together of a day when we would take ourselves to a country where we could meet freely as Jews in a room with windows that opened onto the street.

Victoria's house was not huge, but it accommodated the dozen or so of us who gathered there most Fridays. Juan de Ortega was always there; in fact, we usually walked to Victoria's together. The wealthy merchants—Francisco de Acosta Silva and Luis Alvarez de Acosta, Diego Váez—came from time to time when their business obligations permitted. Lots of other people shuttled from Puebla to the mining towns and prayed with us only when they were in the city. I think that half the Portuguese in France must have family in Puebla. Most of these people I had never seen before, but I knew their uncles, aunts, and cousins back in Toulouse, Rouen, or Bordeaux. Every new ship brought letters from their friends and relatives. They even got news from Amsterdam, though what with the Dutch war the correspondence had to be routed through some member of the Nação in Antwerp.

All my friends were Portuguese. I got to know lots of women, too, more than I would have in France. I think that at least half the people coming to our prayer meetings were women, mostly wives or widows. And they knew what they were talking about, too. Later, when I moved to Mexico City, I found that lots of the women there knew more about Jewish customs than the men. I remember that Justa Méndez, who always brought her two daughters with her to our gatherings, instructed the men like a regular rabbi. And they listened to her, too, just as if she had been a man. When she was younger she must have been a stunner. They say that Luis de Carvajal, the martyr who was burned in 1596, used to be in love with her.

In one of those gatherings in Puebla I met Marcos de Faria, another uncle of Juan de Ortega. That is to say, he was Francisco de Victoria's brother. He remembered me from Bordeaux. Marcos had been up in the north, trucking everything from sewing supplies to digging tools to the mining towns of Pachuca, Chalchihuites, Zacatecas, and Tlalpujahua. Marcos was fifteen years older than I, thin as an acacia thorn, with brown hair and beard, and skin that had been road-toasted as dark as any Indian's. He had a good sense of humor, and the two of us quickly became good friends. I liked his son Pascual, too, who appeared to be about as old as I had been when I apprenticed to the Rouen cashier. The boy had a good head on him. He noticed things that I never paid attention to, like which *empanada* sellers had clean hands, and how Francisco de Victoria's cat snored like an old lady.

Another of Marcos's good friends was the merchant Diego Gómez de Salazar, a pot-bellied man with an inviting smile and an ingratiating laugh. His tooled leather boots looked like they had just been buffed. Gómez had grown up in Amsterdam. That man pinched his coins until they cried. Despite the fact that he had become quite rich in New Spain, in Puebla he shared a room with Marcos de Faria. As a friend he was warm and fun to be with, but as a businessman, I came to learn, he could be as cold as ice.

One of the happiest days in my life, I believe, was in September of '19 when Marcos de Faria, Diego Gómez, and I kept the fast of Kippur together near the San Diego lime kilns a league east of Puebla. On the way out there Gómez asked me if I had known his mother, Isabel Méndez, in Rouen. He couldn't believe it when I said that I knew her well and that I had fasted with her and his sisters a couple of times in their house. He was so happy that he made me feel almost like a relative.

The three of us spent the morning out by the kilns, sitting with our backs against the adobe wall of a small, half-ruined chapel, listening to Gómez describe the wonders of Amsterdam, where not only could the Jews worship openly, he said, but Gentiles who were curious about their rites could come to the synagogue to watch them pray. We had heard these stories before, of course, but Gómez put so many colorful details into his descriptions that he made us feel like he was giving us a glimpse of Heaven itself. Not once did we think of our stomachs, growling with the rigors of the fast. Eventually the sun came overhead and the heat became uncomfortable, so we walked back to Puebla. I told the people in my house that I had a thumping headache, which gave me a safe excuse not to eat and to spend the rest of the afternoon lying in bed thinking of the wonders Gómez had painted for us.

In Puebla sometimes I found work hawking pins and thread in the street from a tray. But there wasn't much money in it, and it was hard to find good merchandise to sell. I didn't have the capital for the fine stuff. I got the idea that since Diego Gómez de Salazar was bringing into Puebla precisely the sort of goods I could peddle on the street, he could set me up. So I decided to go to see him. When I got to his door, I could hear him inside talking in Portuguese with a couple of other merchants. I knocked, Gómez opened, but he didn't invite me in. Instead, there on the stoop, he asked me what I wanted. In a few sentences I told him my plan and asked him to advance me some goods from his warehouse. I said that I couldn't pay him now but that he could trust me for it, and I would pay him back punctually and with interest. Until then I had thought he was my friend, but he turned all haughty and arrogant. He told me that I was nothing but a miserable foreigner, that he had no intention of trusting his merchandise to bums like me, and that he'd had enough with the foreigners who had robbed him already. And this was a man I had prayed with on many a Friday night. I was mad as a hornet, but I tried to keep my temper. I told him he was wrong: that I was honorable, that I had no intention of making off with his damn goods. He started to scream that I was nothing but a low-class crook. I was ready to explode. If some people hadn't got in between us, I would have attacked him. One of those men, Francisco Pérez, told me I had better get the hell out of there. So I did. The next day Pérez came looking for me and advised me not to push the matter because Gómez was half crazy, in addition to being arrogant and a crook who had cheated half the businessmen in Puebla. He added that Gómez's friend, Francisco de Victoria, wasn't much better, and, truth be told, Victoria was probably the ringleader of that bunch of thieves. He said that in his view the reason people gathered at Victoria's house every week was not mainly to pray with him but to pay him homage and recognize him as the chief bandit.

After that I never went back to Victoria's house, and, except for Marcos de Faria, I never spoke to any of that crowd again. Eventually I lost touch with Gómez de Salazar, but I always wondered whether someone had stuck a knife in his belly, or whether he had gone back to Amsterdam or some other place where, while he was cheating the local business community, he could say his prayers without some priest looking over his shoulder. Much later I learned from a mutual friend that Gómez had given himself the name Diego de Oliva and had gone to Perú, where in Lima the Inquisition arrested him as a Judaizer. For all I know he is still in prison there.

By then I had taken a room with Antonio de Goitia in a four-story house on the plaza in front of the Convent of Santo Domingo. Goitia was a printer from Aibar in the Basque country. In his small shop on the plaza he cranked out copies of the viceroy's proclamations and the hundreds of different forms required by the Holy Office. He used to say that his family had all been old-Christians since the day Noah put his passengers ashore. In spite of the fact that I had to keep a great portion of my life secret from him, we became good friends, and we often went out to the taverns together for a pitcher of whatever the importers were passing off as wine. For most of the two years after my falling out with Diego Gómez, that was my life: Fridays and holidays praying with my remaining Portuguese friends and Saturday nights in the taverns with Antonio de Goitia, talking of women and what we could do to better our lives.

My favorite tavern was El Cisne, not because the wine there was any better than anywhere else, but because a girl named Luisa de Robles used to serve it to us. She had long brown locks the color of a bay mare, a smile that could light up a room, and a laugh that tickled my ear. It wasn't very long before Goitia began to rib me about Luisa's smiles being mainly directed at me. I saw he was right, so I flashed a few back at her. Before the month was out she had found her way into my bed. Goitia didn't mind, and Luisa and I always snuck up and down my back stairs so that the neighbors couldn't see us and report us to the Inquisition as fornicators. Though that's what we were, plain and simple. I don't know what love is, or whether or not we were in it, but I do know that we burned up the nights. Our son, Fernando, was born in the summer of '21. After that, for reasons that I cannot even begin to explain, the fire went out for both of us. Luisa went back to El Cisne, and the other girls there looked after Fernandico. A couple of times Luisa asked me for money for something that Fernando needed, but my street peddling was barely enough to keep me alive. So I never gave her anything. After a while she stopped asking, and I started taking my wine in a tavern on the other side of the cathedral.

"A genteel lover and a perfect father, aren't you? Like in a storybook."

"I'm not proud of it. That's just the way it was. Listen, I had to do something."

My life was going nowhere. I wasn't starving—though sometimes I went to bed hungry—, but neither was I improving my condition. Finally I resolved that it was stupid to spend the rest of my life peddling cheap nothings from a tray in the streets. Puebla had become my home, but I was convinced that as long as I stayed there I would be mired in poverty. The mansions that lined the streets around the cathedral seemed to me as remote as the moon. I needed to find myself a patron, someone with capital, a merchant who was eager to turn his small fortune into a big one. Eventually Providence brought me to the door of Martín de Oliveros, another Portuguese, who agreed to stake me with clothing to truck to the mining towns of the far north to sell. He provided the carts, the mules, and the bales of merchandise. I provided the time and the labor and—I convinced him—my substantial marketing skill. We would split the profits. I suspect that he knew that my vaunted marketing skill was a bluff; but my enthusiasm convinced him that I could do the job.

Zacatecas is not the end of the earth; it's a lot farther away than that. Or at least that's how it seemed to me during the weeks that the mules and I hauled that damn wagon over rutted roads through range after range of mountains to Zacatecas. From Puebla the road took me through Tlaxcala and the mines at Pachuca to Jilotepec, where I picked up the Camino Real. You know how that road is. I was rarely out of sight of other wagons like mine, piled high with bales of imported baubles; needles and silk thread; bolts of linen, wool, and cotton cloth; casks of Spanish and Portuguese brandy; sacks of wheat from the Bajío and maize from Michoacán. Food, clothing, and most of all the iron tools that the miners need to pry the veins of silver out of the craggy hills: picks, shovels, crowbars, chisels, barrel hoops, and boxes of nails to fasten their timber sluices or hold their shacks together. The heaviest carts, pulled by teams of four and sometimes even six mules, hauled barrels of mercury or ingots of lead that the miners use to extract silver from the ore. The days on the road were marked by choking dust; the icy nights, by pitchers of the fermented cactus juice that people in the north call *vino de mescal*. Like most of the other carters, after making sure that my two mules were tethered near enough to good grass to keep them going the next day, I wrapped myself in blankets and crept under my wagon to sleep. Sabbaths and Sundays were days like any other. And as for food, I ate whatever there was.

In addition to the mining centers like San Miguel de Allende, Guanajuato, and León, where I stopped for a day or two, there are dozens of small Indian villages along the road, each clustered around a monastery of gray *tezontle*, the volcanic stone that is the friars' standard building material. Each village has a market square where the Indians bring their goods. Some carters set up stalls in the village markets, but Oliveros had cautioned me to hold

Diego Pérez de Alburquerque

off selling until Zacatecas, where the merchandise would command much higher prices. Every block in those little towns holds a tavern or two, and what with the road-weary carters streaming through and the miners fresh in from their diggings with a few ounces of silver dust in their purses, I don't have to tell you that the tavern girls do very well.

My first view of Zacatecas left me speechless. The city clusters along two sides of a narrow ravine. My fellow carters told me that it houses five thousand people, and I could easily believe them. I soon discovered that every evangelizing order in Mexico has built a monastery there—Franciscans, Augustinians, Dominicans, Mercedarians, Jesuits—each with dreams of being the dominant purveyor of Jesus, every one of them scheming to see if they can be the ones to bring the most Indian souls to Christ. And mansions! I thought Puebla was rich, and Tlaxcala, but I'd never seen so many great houses in one place in all my life. The silver barons who had dug their money and their power out of the Cerro de la Bufa, the northeastern wall of the ravine, outdid each other in their display of wealth.

Even though it was my first visit, I quickly slipped into Zacatecas's Portuguese community, which numbered in the several dozens. My partner, Martín de Oliveros, had given me references, and I soon found myself regularly attending the Friday evening gatherings at the home of Diego López de Abreu. My enemy Juan de Ortega used to come, too, when he was in the north. And Jerónimo Salgado, who many years later shared my cell for a few weeks in Mexico. When we could, we kept the fast of the new moon, and the fast of whatever holiday it happened to be. In that country they eat mostly goat, but on Fridays, when López de Abreu's wife could buy a chicken, López took it out behind his house, cut its throat, and drained the blood onto the ground the way we had been taught.

Prayer for me was a city thing. Out on the roads, or selling in the markets, thoughts of Moses or Jesus almost never crossed my mind. But in the cities, in the company of my Portuguese friends, all that talk about the Law, the fasting and the praying, was a way of fitting in. It's not that I was lonely out in the world. There were always people to talk with, pitchers of wine to share, evenings at cards or, when someone at the inn had a guitar, singing the old songs. But it was only with my Portuguese friends that I felt completely at home.

I rented a room above one of the taverns that lined Zacatecas's main street at the low end of the city, just before the Indian township of the Tlaxcalans.

CHAPTER 8

The property had an enclosed corral for my two mules and a place to park the wagon. It took me almost six weeks to sell everything I had brought from Puebla. I could have sold the whole cargo right away to one of the Zacatecas shopkeepers, but the prices they were offering would just barely cover my travel expenses, with little left to divide with Oliveros. So I sold it off piece by piece in the Plaza Pública or the Plazuela del Maestro de Campo, just east of the parish church.

For the return trip south, as I had been instructed, I contracted with one of the convoys of wagons that haul silver ingots from the mines to Mexico City, shepherded all the way by a squadron of the king's soldiers. On the journey south it is worth your life to travel alone, what with the Chichimecas and other bandits who wait in the hills for easy pickings on the roads below.

That year I made three round trips from Puebla to Zacatecas, twice stopping on the return trip in Mexico City to deposit the silver in the royal treasury and collect my carter's fee before going back to Puebla to split the profits with Oliveros. Unfortunately, on the third trip my legs were in shackles and one of the things the soldiers were guarding was me. My wagon, with the last goods still unsold, sat in its corral in Zacatecas.

"They finally got you for fornication, did they?"

"Nothing as wholesome as that, I'm sorry to say."

What happened was that I had made a couple of spineless enemies, and to save their own hides they had denounced me. The worst of those bastards was Juan de Ortega, who gave the inquisitors a list of everybody he had ever seen at a Sabbath gathering.

I had been pretty careful in Zacatecas, even though I spent most of my time there with my Portuguese friends. Every Sunday I went to mass at the Mercedarians. The rosary that hung from my belt was big enough for everyone to see. I crossed myself every time I passed in front of a church, which in Zacatecas was at least once on every block. López de Abreu led his neighbors to believe that the Friday night gatherings at his house were just a bunch of business colleagues getting together, nothing with any sort of religious purpose behind it. But it seems that wasn't enough.

The Inquisition commissioner in Zacatecas was Diego de Herrera, a sour-faced vicar who believed that people would admire his sermons if he informed them, two or three times every Sunday, that he held a degree

Diego Pérez de Alburquerque

in theology from one of the best universities in Spain. Baeza, I think he said. He and a couple of municipal bailiffs arrested me on March 22, '23. They clapped me into a cell in the Zacatecas jail and then the next morning turned me over to the head cartmaster of the silver convoy for the trip back to Mexico City.

In the prison things turned out not nearly as bad as I thought they would. My cell was dank but not freezing, and the food was palatable enough. Better than in this damn ship, that's for sure. I was afraid I would be hauled off to the torture chamber—everybody has heard the stories—but that summons didn't come.

Six weeks into my stay they assigned me a cellmate because the prison was overcrowded, or at least that's what they said. It was Jerónimo Salgado, who trucked goods to the mining communities the same as I did. I had met him before, including a couple of times at a Friday gathering at López de Abreu's house in Zacatecas. Even so, I thought he might be a spy. I had heard that the Holy Office likes to give a prisoner a cellmate to draw him into revealing conversations so they can report them to the inquisitors. I showed Salgado a friendly face, but I was always careful not to tell him anything that might come back to bite me. He, on the other hand, seemed to have no such worry. He chatted openly about his case, which he said was trivial, that surely in a week or two the inquisitors would decide to let him go. He must have known what he was talking about, because long before they called me to testify he was gone.

"You're a spy, too, aren't you?" Santillana interrupted. "Trying to get me to talk. Come on, confess it."

I shook my head. "Would I be telling you all this if I were a spy? Besides, what's the point? You never say anything. And our cases are finished. Done. Closed. Sentences pronounced. You think anyone will give a damn in the king's galleys what it was that got me chained to my oar?"

Santillana giggled. "I'm a spy, you know. And the quartermaster. The chaplain is a spy; he writes it all down in his book"

"Of course they are. And the captain's a spy, too." Humor him, what the hell.

"It's not finished, you know. The Inquisition never closes its cases. Never ever." Santillana laughed again. "That fellow up there: do you think he's a spy?"

CHAPTER 8

He pointed at the sailor who was sliding the hatch cover to one side so that we could go on deck for our hour of exercise and fresh air.

"Come on, haul me up, matey." I helped him stand and shuffle over to the ladder. I lifted up his leg irons as he wheezed and coughed his way from one rung to the next. It has become a ritual for us, my holding the heavy chains. When at last he flopped out onto the deck, he turned and thanked me as he always did: "Good sir, your assistance is most gratifying and deeply appreciated."

"Think nothing of it, distinguished gentleman, I am honored to put myself in your service."

Later, back in the hold, our rags still wet with seawater, I picked up the thread of my tale.

I was telling you about what happened to me in the Inquisition prison in Mexico City. After several weeks they called me to an audience. I told them who my parents and uncles and cousins were, gave them a brief, somewhat accurate, history of my life, and then I waited for questions.

The Purity of Blood Certificate? I had only had it drawn up to keep people in Zacatecas from pointing their fingers at me because I was Portuguese. That had happened to a couple of friends of mine, and it made their lives miserable. No, I wasn't trying to deceive anyone; I only wanted to give myself a chance to compete on equal footing with the old-Christian Spaniards. None of that was true, but it is what I told them. What I didn't want to say was that I was trying to cover up being a secret Jew, which I still was in those days.

Did I observe the Sabbath and the Jewish festivals? Not me; I didn't even know what they were. Eat only Jewish food? Never: I'm a traveling merchant, I eat whatever there is and give thanks to Our Blessed Mother that I have enough to fill my belly. Pork? Whenever I can get it. Keep the Jewish fasts? I don't know anything about them.

Then they read me a summary of testimony accusing me of being a Jew. Naturally I denied it. I played the innocent, a man vengefully accused by some mortal enemy. From the details, I said, it was probably Juan de Ortega. He must be a secret Jew himself if he knows that much about what Jews do. I had to make a good case. I explained to them how in Zacatecas I was always running into Ortega. One time we had an argument in the street, and when Ortega saw that he couldn't best me with words, he picked up a rock and clobbered me on the head. I spurted blood and fell to the ground, and he would have killed me if some people hadn't pulled him off. I gave them the names of the people who saw it happen. Another time Ortega begged me to lend him

Diego Pérez de Alburquerque

300 pesos so he could settle a gambling debt. When I said I didn't have it, he tried to get me to borrow it for him someplace. I told him I couldn't, and I wouldn't, which made Ortega so mad that he started to scream at me and half drew his sword. Lots of people in Zacatecas heard Ortega say that if he didn't kill me in Zacatecas he would get me one way or another.

Well, that was the tale I told. And the friars swallowed it! They set me free, gave me a paper saying I could reclaim whatever was left of the goods they had confiscated, and sent me on my way.

I spent the next couple of months in Puebla and then, armed with my document, headed north to Zacatecas. This time I took the western road, stopping first for a few days in Mexico City to see some old friends. One of the first people I looked up was Jerónimo Salgado. He told me that before the inquisitors let him go they slapped a harsh penance on him. He had no problem with the Sunday masses and the sermons and the holy communion, but they also prohibited him from ever appearing in public without his sambenito. That was ruining him—who would want to be seen doing business with a branded penitent? Somebody told him that by giving 150 pesos to charity he could have the sambenito requirement lifted, but so far he hadn't been able to raise the money. I took pity on him and gave him 20 pesos and told him that I would back him for the rest if he couldn't raise it in some other fashion. Which he evidently did, because a few months later he whole-saled some imported incense sticks to me to sell on my next trip to Zacatecas. You know how scarce the water is up there, and how miners aren't much for personal hygiene. Incense would be an easy sell.

From Mexico City I went back to Zacatecas for my wagon and the merchandise that they'd taken from me. Most of it, of course, had been sold to pay the costs of my arrest and time in jail. But the inquisitors had left me a few shirts and trousers, some corduroy sleeves, assorted handkerchiefs, stockings, a few blankets and Rouen sheets, some cotton-stuffed mattresses, and a dozen or so bolts of cloth, including two that were silk. Over the next few weeks I sold what I could, and then I went back to Puebla for more merchandise.

You may have noticed that I am a man with a hot temper. I don't suffer insults, or fools, and when I can't think of what to say I use my fists, which is one of the reasons I am always in trouble. Well, shortly after I got back to Puebla I went into a druggist's shop to buy something to relieve the pain in my head, which still throbbed sometimes where Juan de Ortega had hit me. The druggist was too nosy for my taste. We had words, I drew my knife, the druggist lay flat on the floor spurting blood from his arm and his side, a woman started screaming that I had killed him, and then next thing you know I was running for my life. I figured I would claim sanctuary in the Monastery of Santo Domingo, down the block from Goitia's house where I had been living. And there I stayed for the next month or so, while the druggist's friends fumed outside.

I told the monks I was a good Christian, of course. They were hospitable—they fed me well and gave me a cell to myself above the cloister—, so it didn't bother me to pray with them two or three times a day. Several of them had good voices, so for the morning and evening liturgy their small church was usually full. I generally listened from the cloister gallery across from my cell since I didn't want to run into any of the druggist's friends. I didn't think they would dare to profane a church, but you can't be too careful. During the day I mostly walked round and round the cloister. Sometimes I read in one of the books that the prior had lent me. Mostly I worried about my business affairs: bills to pay, debts to collect, merchandise to protect, mules to look after. Goitia came to visit me a couple of times to report that the druggist's friends were still waiting for me. After nearly a month of this I made two decisions. I would ask one of my Portuguese friends, Martin de Oliveros, my sometime partner in the carting business, to take charge of my affairs in Puebla. And I would slip off to Zacatecas or one of the other mining towns just as soon as I could get away. I certainly didn't want to spend the rest of my life in that monastery chanting matins and nones. Or hiding in Puebla from the druggist's cronies, either. Of course the best-laid plans . . .

I was just in the process of writing Oliveros a letter when into my room walked Sargeant Antonio Marcos de Carvajal and two deputies with a signed order for my arrest. I argued with them, but it did no good: Marcos made it clear that the court order trumped the rights of sanctuary. By then my dander was up, and I was shouting at them and cursing. When one of the deputies swept up my possessions, including the small silk purse with all my cash, I screamed: "There are 47 pesos in that purse, damn it, 47! You write that down because I don't want there to be any mistakes! I'm going to want them back, every last stinking peso!" By then a crowd of monks had gathered in the cloister gallery, gaping at the four of us as we struggled. But not one of those monks lifted a hand to help me, not even the prior. So much for the sanctuary of the Church!

Diego Pérez de Alburquerque

"Why are you surprised? Not sanctuary, salvation! You can always count on the Church for that." Santillana at his most ironic. "You know why? Because it doesn't cost them anything. But try relying on them for anything else! Charity . . . sanctuary . . . a little mercy . . . What can you expect from men in skirts?"

I thought it best not to answer. Santillana shifted his legs, trying to brace himself better as the boat yawed into the swells.

"So they arrested you. Then what happened?"

What happened next was that there were more unpleasant surprises in store for me. It seems that my arrest had nothing at all to do with the wounded druggist. By that time he had recovered with only a couple of scars as souvenirs of our disagreement. No; the arrest order was not from the criminal court; it was from the Inquisition!

The three bailiffs took me back to my rooms in Goitia's house, where I hadn't been in over a month, to seize the rest of my belongings. They took my clothing, my bedclothes, and my comb. They rolled up my sleeping cushions into a bundle. They opened the box where I kept my small library, and before they closed it and nailed it shut, they jotted down the titles. I made sure they got them right: Pineda's *Celestial Monarchy*, a *History of the Popes*, the *Life of Christ*, and a small *Book of Hours*. They'd cost me a lot, and I wanted that stuff back. They even got the 200 pesos I had wrapped in paper and hidden under a loose floorboard.

When they marched me out of the house I got my next surprise: they had already arranged for the sergeant and two soldiers to take me from Puebla back to Mexico City. The guards rode horses, but for me they had rented two mules, one for me and the other to carry my belongings. They were in no hurry, so the journey took us four days. We put up at an inn every night, and we all ate pretty well, I can tell you. We drank well, too. What soured the journey, in addition to the fact that I was their prisoner, was my knowing that sergeant's bill for the journey—I saw the written accounting: 70 pesos—would be paid by me, automatically deducted from the 200 pesos they had seized. Bastards!

"Bastards . . . Maybe. You know it's nothing personal. Wouldn't you do the same thing if you had the chance? Good food, good wine? It goes with the job."

That stopped me. "I suppose so, but still . . . "

"But still nothing. You want to change the color of the moon? Go on with your story. So, you're off to jail again?"

Not directly. In Mexico City the sergeant swore me to silence, threatened me with unspecified mayhem if I should try to escape, and took me to the home of Juan Ortiz de Castro, a bootmaker who gets a small stipend every year for the privilege of housing prisoners of the Holy Office when the jails are full. I had bought boots from Ortiz before. We'd shared a pitcher of wine six or eight times, and twice I'd had dinner at his house. He was a decent enough fellow and his wife, doña María del Hoyo, had always been pleasant with me. Her kitchen maid was a good cook. Good-looking, too. So being confined to their house was no great hardship.

Evidently the word was out, because the day after my arrest I had visitors. I was napping in my room when I heard Ortiz's black slave tell doña María that two men were looking for me. They turned out to be Alonso Salgado Molinero and Francisco Pérez, old friends of mine. Doña María and her friend Juana Ramos were sitting by the upstairs hall window sewing when the slave announced them. Doña María jumped up and went to the head of the stairs to tell them that they must not come up because her husband wasn't home, and what would people say. And besides, her husband was the Inquisition familiar, not her, so she didn't have the authority to let them talk with me. I could hear them shouting, doña María saying that they must not take one more step, and Francisco Pérez answering that he didn't have any secrets, that she could listen to the conversation if she liked. "All right," she answered, "say what you have to say." And this with me still in the other room where I couldn't see them. I heard their footsteps on the stairs, and then Salgado trying to distract doña María so that Pérez could talk to me alone. They were all making so much noise that Pérez decided to leave before it turned into a public scandal.

"Diego," Francisco Pérez shouted at the closed door, "listen to me. I've only come to tell you that it's time for you to entrust your soul to God." And then they were gone.

You can imagine the state that left me in. How Francisco Pérez found out why the Inquisition wanted me I have no idea, but he clearly knew something, and it didn't sound good.

A week later I was back in my old cell again in the Inquisition prison. I knew the sounds, the smells, the routines: bread and water at first light; empty the slop bucket into the wheeled barrel sometime mid-morning; a thick porridge or some runny stew late in the afternoon; while away the hours cracking lice.

Diego Pérez de Alburquerque

It was beginning to feel like home. At my first hearing the friars asked what they always ask: why do you think you are here? And I gave the answer that people always give: I have no idea, unless some enemy has made up a terrible tale about me. Then they sent me back downstairs to worry over the matter for a few weeks.

At my second audience they read me the charges: I had been observed eating festival meals with known Jews; I had been heard making disparaging comments about the Law of our Lord Jesus Christ; I had been seen keeping Jewish fasts. And it wasn't just one enemy who had spoken out against me. They had dozens of credible witnesses. So what did I say to that?

I know a corner when I've been backed into one. I had been expecting this. I knew it was time for me to stop denying those things and to start trying to explain them away. As to my making disparaging remarks, I told them, that was absolutely false. I never did, and I never shall. The Law of Jesus is my Law, and I love Jesus and his Holy Mother as I love my life. I admitted that the other charges were true, but they all happened a long time ago, and since then God had illumined my soul so that I no longer had anything to do with Jews or things Jewish. And that really was true, or at least I believed it as I was telling it to them.

"If that's the case," the chief interrogator continued in a tone that suggested he didn't believe one word of what I was saying, "why didn't you confess all this a year ago?"

I figured this question would come eventually, and I had rehearsed in my cell the answer I would give them. The real answer was that a year ago I was still uncertain which Law I wanted to follow. But it would be stupid to tell them that. So I told them that back in Bordeaux I had been misled by my Portuguese Jewish friends into believing that the Law of Moses was the true one but that I had gradually come to see the light. I said I had confessed all those sins to a priest in Rouen, and he had absolved me of them and assigned me a penance of prayer, so that my slate had been wiped clean and I had no reason to confess it all again.

"Even if that should be true," the friar went on, "what about the Jewish fasts you were seen keeping here in Mexico? Why didn't you tell us about those in your first trial?"

That, too, I expected. "When I came to Mexico," I told them, "it is true that most of my friends were Portuguese, and some of them persuaded me to return to the Law of Moses. But I never believed it firmly in my heart, even though it is also true that for a while here I considered myself a Jew. I know that in my former testimony I took an oath to Jesus Christ to tell only the truth and to hold nothing back, but I thought that since at that time I was still partly a Jew that oath did not bind me. Also I considered that since Your Worships released me after my first trial and returned all my goods to me, then what I had done in the past was no longer of concern." "Besides," I told them, and this was the point that I thought would tip the scales in my favor, being that it was the one that made the most sense, "I was afraid, afraid that I might lose my honor, and my property, and even my life. That's the main reason I kept quiet when I talked with you before."

That was a bouquet of reasons, all the ones I could think of. They were all true, up to a point, or at least I believed they were as I was listing them for the inquisitors. Let them take their pick, whichever one they liked, so long as they would absolve me and set me free again.

I spent the better part of three years in that prison, my boredom relieved only by bouts of terror. I don't know which was worse, waiting there in the dark for the next audience with my interrogators, or wondering after an audience whether I had told them anything that might lead me to the torture chamber or the stake. In my cell I prayed for strength: sometimes to Moses, sometimes to Jesus, sometimes to them both. Whatever might help.

At first I was always hungry. The slop they doled out in that prison hadn't improved since my earlier visit. But this time, fortunately, I had good friends on the outside who once in a while brought the jailors food to give me: fruit preserves and crackers, raisins, almonds, or what I missed the most, chocolate for my breakfast drink. I presumed most of these things were gifts from my old cellmate Jerónimo Salgado. Though they might have been from somebody else. Who knows? The jailor who brought them to my cell wouldn't tell me. Another time, just about when the weather was turning chill, someone sent me two shirts and a sheet, some leggings and a pair of socks. Much appreciated, seeing that almost all my clothing had disappeared in Zacatecas. And just as warm as the clothing was the knowledge that I had friends who cared about me.

Even so, the damn jail was miserable, and I spent entire days slumped against the damp stones in the darkness without finding the strength to open my eyes. By that time the wheat gruel and the half-rotted stews and the cold

Diego Pérez de Alburquerque

tortillas disgusted me so that I rarely finished what they brought me. And except for the gifts from outside, what I did eat never stayed with me long. I had always been strong as an ox, but now my ribs stuck through my flesh like on those skeletons the priests hang up to frighten us with the horror of our mortality. Nothing but a few graying wisps was left of the thick brown beard that I had sported ever since I arrived in Mexico. I had an open ulcer on my neck, too, as big as a silver peso. There were times I thought I would die in that cell. The jailors must have thought so too, because twice they got the friars to send a surgeon to bleed me. I was so thin that I didn't have much blood to spare, but what I had they took, and that left me feeling even worse than before.

Eventually, though, the ulcer healed. I put on a little weight. Then the audiences began again. Are you a Jew or a Christian? Where did you begin to Judaize? How did you learn? When and why did you change? What other Jews do you know? Where are they now? Who can confirm what you say? Now let's go over it all again. No surprises.

Out in the world we talked about these things sometimes after the Friday evening prayers. If, God forbid, the day should ever come . . . People who had been in the Inquisition's audience chambers gave their best advice to those of us who had not—yet—had the pleasure of being interrogated. What people said was mostly common sense. Keep it simple. Tell enough truth to be persuasive. Protect your friends.

Easier to say than to do. Every audience pushed me a little further. Every audience went back over what I had already said to see if they could trip me into some contradiction, some lie. If I slipped up, I knew they would clarify the inconsistencies in the torture chamber, which I had managed to avoid so far. But let me tell you, the thought of what they would do to me down there haunted my dreams. When I talked with them I tried to keep the fear out of my voice, but it was difficult. There were always new witnesses for me to respond to, and there was the real possibility that some future witness might let slip a name or a detail that I had neglected to include, even though I had sworn to hold nothing back. Against this dripping acid that was wearing away my defenses a little at a time, there wasn't much I could do. I could play the enemy card, and I did, denouncing Juan de Ortega over and over again. I told the inquisitors that he hated me not only because he owed me money, but because he still followed the false religion of Moses—I knew the inquisitors knew this already—while I had accepted the saving power of Christ's grace, making me a traitor in Ortega's eyes. I told them Diego Gómez hated me because I had accused him and all his family in public of being thieves and scoundrels who cheated other people out of their property. I figured that Francisco de Victoria was probably telling the inquisitors things about me, too, so I accused him of hating me because I had told people that in Rouen he had cheated his own brothers out of their inheritance and because back in Spain I had taken up with Victoria's girlfriend, the one he later brought over to the Indies.

I also figured I could play the contrition card. I admitted to them that sometimes I had wavered between the two Laws. I confessed that once in a while I had accompanied my Portuguese friends in celebrating Friday nights or observing one of the Jewish holiday fasts. But I insisted that even while I was doing those things, deep in my heart I loved Jesus and knew that my soul could only be saved in His Law. That is why I went to mass so often. It was proof that even while I was sinning, I knew it was wrong and was sorry for it. I asked Jesus to show me his mercy, and, on my knees and with tears in my eyes, I asked the inquisitors to do the same.

It took three years, but eventually that is what they did. This time they made me appear in a public auto-de-fé and tell the world I had repented all my sins and accepted with humility whatever penance the Church saw fit to assign me.

Let me tell you, freedom never tasted more sweet. When they released me from prison in Mexico City, I hit up my friends for travel money and went back to Puebla. My rough plan—I hadn't yet worked out all the details—was to sell off everything the inquisitors had left me. With the money I would go back to Bordeaux for my sisters. Though I hadn't heard from them in several years, I felt certain they were still alive. Then I would take them with me to Padua, in Italy, where we could all start a new life together under the Law of Moses, which people have told me is practiced freely there. As you can see, when they let me go I decided to be a Jew again. Moses had given me the strength to resist their pressure, and that was enough to convince me.

In Padua I had an uncle: Alonso de Valencia Alburquerque, one of my father's brothers. Several friends of mine from Bordeaux and Rouen, who had also gone there, had sent me word, once by letter and several times through mutual acquaintances who had come to do business in Mexico, that they would find a nice bride for me there in Padua. A Portuguese woman, or maybe

Diego Pérez de Alburquerque

an Italian girl, with enough income to support us both, or at least enough to get me started in my new life. I hadn't written them back, but I would just as soon as my travel plans were fixed. Just one more trip to Zacatecas, I told myself. Or maybe two. Enough for me to put some money together. I would live frugally, stay out of the taverns, and when my pockets were full of silver I would go back to Veracruz. The ship would take me to Cádiz. I wouldn't spend much time in Spain, of course; I'd head straight north. Then before I went to get my sisters in Bordeaux I would go to Rouen for a few days to see if any of my old friends were still there. Maybe I would catch a glimpse of my daughter, Clara Margarita. From the street, or in the market when she and her mother went to do their shopping. I wouldn't speak to them. I wasn't part of their lives. But maybe a glimpse, so that I would know that she was well.

Good intentions, like the ones that pave the roads to Hell. But those years in prison had taken something out of me, some of the fire, the willingness to break out of the web of routine, to strike out for new lands with new dreams and no guarantees but my belief that God would provide, that tomorrow I would have a roof over my head and enough food to fill my belly. I had every intention of going to Italy, but . . . but there you have it.

Why didn't I go? Maybe it was because I was tending to feel more like a Christian again. And besides, I told myself, as long as I lived faithfully as a Christian I was safe in Mexico. Every time I told myself this, I would hear mass every day for a solid week or two. But then one day I would find a reason not to go. It was raining; I needed to see a man about some merchandise; the mules needed taking out to pasture; or maybe I just didn't feel like it. There were days when waves of despair overcame me and I feared for my soul, and those feelings drove me to church. But most of the time I only heard mass to keep up appearances, to make certain my religious fervor was well noted by people whom I someday might have to call as witnesses.

It seems strange to me now, but during most of that time I also felt myself to be Jewish and that to save my soul I had to live in the Law of Moses. Did I keep the Sabbath? Sometimes, when I could. But what with buying and selling, and all that time on the road, I couldn't afford to take the day off. And as for food, in those roadside inns I ate what was put on the table, just like everyone else. If I didn't, I would call attention to myself. Not to mention go hungry. Hardly a week went by that I didn't resolve to do a better job of keeping the Jewish festivals, but I rarely knew when they were, and, even if I did, business got in the way. What I could do, and what I often did on the road, was to pray all the Jewish prayers and the psalms that I had learned by heart. With my rosary in hand, of course, counting off the beads as I silently intoned the name of Adonai. But as for all the rest . . .

For nine months I soared as free as a bird. Life on the road was hard, but I had the mountains to lift my spirits, the sky as blue as the Virgin's mantle, the perfume of pine trees and wild flowers as thick as incense. I couldn't bear to remain indoors. And I was making money. In Puebla and Mexico City and Zacatecas I was reconnecting with old friends and making new ones. I didn't think much about women, although I didn't always sleep alone. Instead, as the silver dribbled through my fingers in the inns and taverns, I dreamed about Padua and the life I would lead there when I finally put together enough money.

This time they arrested me in Mexico City. Same prison, different cell. No window this time. The only light was what leaked in through the barred opening in the door. In the morning, if I sat on the stone floor with my back against the planks, there was just enough light for me to read in the book that one of the jailors had given me for the benefit of my soul.

I was no novice. I knew how they would deal with me, wear me down: the appeal to my soul, my conscience, my yearning for peace of mind, for freedom. Likewise, I knew that the strategies I had used during my first two incarcerations to win my release wouldn't work this time. The inquisitors had more, they knew more, or I wouldn't be here. This time I saw no advantage in holding back. I would tell them everything I knew, everything that could be checked and verified by witnesses. I clung to the hope that my inner world still belonged to me. Once again, like so many times in my life, I had under-estimated my enemies.

In the first audiences they made me go through my whole life story once again: my parents, my travels, my business ventures, the people I had known and loved or hated. You'd think they knew that story better than I did by now. Whenever I faltered they spurred me on with questions drawn from the papers piled in front of them. In Toulouse, hadn't you also known X or Y, and weren't they Judaizers just like your other friends? Where did you stay in Veracruz? Who helped you get the Purity of Blood Certificate in Madrid? Who attended the Sabbath gatherings in Puebla? And in Mexico City and Zacatecas? In Rouen? Here: take these sheets of paper back to your cell and write down the names of everyone you knew in those places, and how you knew them. And

Diego Pérez de Alburquerque

which Jewish customs they kept. And which ones you yourself celebrated with them. And who else was present. I went over my answers a dozen times, each time adding a name or two that I thought I had long since forgotten. They seemed especially interested in my friends from Rouen and Bordeaux. They must be sending the files to Spain so that the Inquisition there can watch out for the new-Christians who dare to come back across the Pyrenees.

They made me go over every Jewish custom I had ever practiced, or seen practiced. I told them as much as could about the fasts we observed in Rouen: Purim and Tisha b'Av, and the Great Fast of Kippur. Every scrap of prayer that I could remember went into their files. They asked me if I knew Hebrew, which I didn't. In France we had always prayed in Portuguese or Spanish, with only an occasional word like *Adonai* in Hebrew. Those were the prayers that I had recited when the storm hit us on our crossing from Cádiz and that I mumbled into the air, my rosary in hand, on the streets of Puebla and the dusty Camino Real through Querétero to the north.

But naturally I didn't tell them that.

What I told them instead was that once I had been converted in France to the true Law of our Savior Jesus, I never put Him out of my heart, even when I was with my Portuguese friends, keeping the customs that they kept just to be sociable, to be part of their group.

This time the inquisitors didn't believe me. During my three trials I had said far too much. My life must have seemed to them like a tangled ball of yarn with no beginnings, no endings, no clear strands connecting one piece with another. A tale more concerned with appearance than reality. I had seen miners do that when they were looking for a buyer for their claim: a flash of ore here, a little sparkle there, carefully placed to reflect the light, promises of deep veins and fabulous riches at bargain prices. God knows, the strategy had worked for me for the past eight years.

When they told me they had voted to send me to be tortured, my blood turned to ice. Of course, they said, if I had anything to confess before they took me downstairs . . .

I was in shock, even though I had been expecting it. My brain and my tongue were frozen. "No, nothing," I managed to stammer. "I've told you everything. All the truth. There is nothing I can add."

Two bailiffs escorted me—it was more like they dragged me, since my legs would no longer hold me up—down two flights of stairs and along a short stone corridor to the torture chamber. There were no windows; it was lit by torches stuck into sconces on the wall. To the left of the door were a table and four chairs: one for the scribe, two for the inquisitors who ask the questions and apprise my answers, and one for the doctor to ensure that I suffered no serious injury. All this my chief interrogator explained to me in quiet, measured tones, as if he had conveyed the information so often that he found it boring. I confess that I was only half listening to his words, since my eyes were riveted on the room's other piece of furniture, a low table affixed with ropes and pulleys, cranks and levers. Next to it stood two burly men awaiting their orders. I thought I might faint.

As I sagged between the two bailiffs I heard the inquisitor say, "This is Dr. Ríos. He's going to examine you now." The doctor, a tall, thin man who smelled of some odd tincture or potion, walked around me. He had me bend my legs and lift my arms over my head. I had a running sore on one arm—I'd had it for a month now, and it wouldn't heal—and he probed at its edges with a wooden scapular that he took out of his pocket.

"Note this," the doctor said, as the scribe dipped his quill. "The prisoner has an ulcer on his right arm; it is covered with a thin scab, and the flesh around it is hard and unyielding. It is likely to bleed if pressure is applied to his upper body. It would be much less risky to apply the ropes to his thighs or calves."

He walked back to the table and sat down.

The chief inquisitor admonished me to tell the whole truth, warning me of the danger to my eternal soul if I held anything back, and then he asked me if I had anything more to confess.

"I have nothing to add," I said, my resolve still firm.

"Strip him."

While the bailiffs held me up, one of the torturers tugged at my ragged shirt and scraps of trousers.

The inquisitor repeated his admonition, and again I said I had nothing to add.

The two torturers tied my hands, affixed them to a ring at one end of the table, and stretched me flat.

Again the admonition. Again my silence.

They looped a rope tightly around my upper legs, and with a lever tightened it until I could just begin to feel its pressure.

Again the admonition. My brain told me to keep silent, that whatever I might say would only make things worse. But my tongue played me traitor, and I began to blubber.

Diego Pérez de Alburquerque

"Stop! Please stop! I was lying. I confess that I was lying before. I have much more to tell you. Only stop. You don't need to go any further."

The inquisitor nodded to the torturers, and they loosened the ropes and sat me up on the edge of the table. I was shivering so badly that they brought me a blanket to wrap around myself. When I'd secured it, I fell on my knees and begged them for mercy. I was crying, babbling.

"So . . . begin." The inquisitor's voice was calm, soothing, encouraging.

"I have so much to confess, so much to tell you," I said. My wits were returning. "It is not the torture; it is my fear for my immortal soul, and my love for our Savior Jesus. I need to tell you how all this has come about, but it is going to take a long, long time. More than . . . " Without wanting to, I shot a glance at the apparatus in the center of the room.

"Take him upstairs," the inquisitor said. The bailiffs helped me to my feet.

And so it began. I was down to my last defense: my honest confusion. I knew that what they wanted to hear was when and why I had finally, truly, and completely accepted the Law of Jesus Christ. In Rouen? In Madrid? In Puebla? Because it seemed to them that I had practiced the ceremonies of Judaism right up until the moment I had been arrested.

I had embraced Jesus in Rouen, I told them, but I had Moses in my blood, and my family and my friends followed his Law. So what could I do? My friends told me my soul could only be saved under the Law of Moses, and the priests told me exactly the opposite. They both had good reasons, I know, but they both told me that my salvation did not depend on reason but on faith. I knew I would have to choose one Law or the other, but I never could. Not completely. It is as if there was always a battle raging in my head for possession of my soul: the Law of Jesus or the Old Law, which I knew now was the Devil, the enemy of the Law of our Lord and Savior. I told them that even though Jesus always reigned in my heart, I did not always know which way to turn.

I told them that it was only there, in the Inquisition prison, that it had all finally made itself clear to me. It wasn't the fear, even though I was always afraid. It was the books that the jailors had put into my hands. It was Alonso de Villegas's *Flos sanctorum*. His sermon showing how the infant Jesus was truly the Messiah prophesied by the Old Law had convinced me that only Jesus could be my savior. And his sermon on the Last Judgment had brought home to me how fragile and fleeting life is, and how the only purpose of this world is to prepare the soul for the next. It was Purim when I read these sermons, and even though I was keeping the fast of Esther, I knew that God had finally illumined my soul once and for all.

"I suppose I was lucky." I shifted my back against the bulkhead, trying to get comfortable again. The pitching and yawing had abated somewhat. I had been wedged here so long that my muscles were beginning to cramp. Or maybe it was my recollections of the torture chamber, still raw although more than a year has passed since then. I could hear outside the soothing whoosh of the waves cut by the ship's prow and the occasional sharp snap of a sail recovering from a momentary loss of wind.

"They could have sent me to the stake and been done with me instead of condemning me to a slow death in the king's galleys. Still, I'm only thirty; I have my whole life in front of me. And while there's life, there's hope, don't you think?"

"Mmmmmm," said Santillana.

Diego Pérez de Alburquerque

9

The Barajas Women

MADRID, 1634

It was almost midnight, and I had just gone to bed when we heard pounding on the street door. In those days my parents, my older sister, Francisca, and I lived in Calle San Bernardo in a four-story house. Francisca is twenty-nine, but she looks a lot younger than that. My brother Diego had moved out the year before: too many arguments with Mother, I guess. Our family rented three small rooms on the third floor. Our front room has a window on the street. One of the panes was broken so we could hear the woman's voice at the door pretty clearly:

"Beatriz Álvarez; I need to talk with Beatriz Álvarez."

"I recognize her voice," I said to Mother. "It's María, María Rodríguez." Back in those days María was one of my closest friends. We sewed together at her house or at mine almost every afternoon.

"Let her in while I get dressed," my mother said, disappearing into the bedroom that she shared with my father. Mother is a short woman with a dark complexion and hair that she wears in braids; some people say she looks like a gypsy. Her nightshirt had a big tear down one side, so she was hardly decent to receive a visitor. I was covered from head to toe with my long white nightdress. I could see my father through the door, lying in their bed, his head propped on one elbow. His wheezing was always loudest when he first woke up. Father disapproved of mother's nighttime errands, but since she was supporting all of us and he was sick, there wasn't much he could do.

As mother pinned her wimple to her hair she turned to me. "You dress while María and I talk."

To my father she said, "Pedro, it's all right. Go back to sleep. I may have to go out." He nodded to show that he understood, as Mother added: "I'm taking Beatriz."

She meant me, of course. The fact that we both have the same name confuses a lot of people. When my parents lived in Portugal, Mother used to be called Violante Suárez, and some people still know her by that name. Here in Spain, though, most people know her as Beatriz. Sometimes they call me Beatricica, little Beatriz. I don't mind being called little, although I am already fourteen and taller than she is. But most of the time they just call us the Barajas women.

I took a candle stub over to the banked fire, picked up an ember with the fire tongs, blew on it, and touched it to the wick. I drew a blanket over my shoulders and went down the narrow stairs to unbar the door. María stood on the stoop in the dark, her mother's black cloak wrapped tightly around her. The flickering candlelight made the tear tracks on María's cheeks glisten. I gave her a hug.

"It's my father."

I should have guessed. About a week before the night I'm telling you about, my mother came back to our house carrying a bundle of clothes. There was a black cassock—it looked like the kind that priests wear—and a flannel cape. She said that she'd been to visit Luis Rodríguez in his family's rooms on Calle del Carmen. He was very sick, and he had asked Mother to fast some Jewish fasts for him so that he would get better. He had given her those clothes as a kind of payment. My mother was always bringing home something or other from her errands, so I wasn't all that surprised. Now I guessed that María's father had taken a turn for the worse. I couldn't imagine why else they would allow María to brave Madrid's streets at night.

María followed me up the stairs to where Mother was waiting. "Señora Beatriz, please, we need you to come to the house. It's my father. He's dead. One minute he was coughing and gasping for breath, and then he rolled over on his side with his face toward the wall and stopped. He just stopped." María began to sob again, wiping at her eyes with a corner of the cloak. "My mother says you're the only one who can prepare him to be buried."

CHAPTER 9

My sister Francisca continued to snore quietly in the bed that she and I shared in the tiny room next to where my parents slept. Mother bustled around, stuffing her scissors, a razor, and a spool of linen thread into her market bag. I quickly slipped into my daytime clothes.

"Beatriz, put on your snood, and make sure you wear your scarf. You know how cold the March winds can be, and if you take chill . . . "

She handed me her bag. "María, you have the shroud at home?"

"Yes, we have everything," María managed to choke out between her tears. "It's in the trunk, clean and folded and ready."

"And your mother has put a kettle of water on the fire?"

"Yes, our biggest one."

"Then off we go." Mother's matter-of-fact tone was meant to cheer María, but it seemed to have no effect, for she continued to sniffle as we made our way out to the street.

I, on the other hand, was excited. This was the first time that my mother had taken me with her on what she sometimes called her "missions of mercy." My brother Diego never went out with her: this was women's work, not men's. For a long time Francisca used to go with her, after her husband disappeared and she moved back with us, but for the last year or two mother went out on her missions alone. Francisca always told people she was a widow, but the truth is that her husband had run off to the Indies when Francisca was only sixteen, and Francisca had never heard from him again. Once, when I asked her why she always lied about it, she said that as a widow she had hopes of remarrying.

"But if he's still alive," I objected—I must have been nine or ten years old then, and I was very idealistic—, "and he comes back and he still loves you . . . ?"

"Fat chance of that," she snapped at me. "No, I'm sure he is dead. He never gave me anything when he was with me, not even children, and he is not likely to come back here with a kiss and a pot of gold."

"But even if he doesn't come back, and you get married again, and somebody finds out that he is still alive, and the Inquisition accuses you of having two husbands?"

"If, if, if . . . Leave it alone, Beatricica. It's my business, not yours."

Francisca is sixteen years older than I am. I hope that when I get bigger I'll be as pretty as she is. My hair is mousy brown, and not jet black like hers, but we have the same delicate skin, pug nose, and turned-up eyebrows. I love

The Barajas Women

Francisca very much. From the time I was a little girl she was almost as much of a mother to me as my real mother. When I was little we lived in a village not far from Madrid called Barajas. It had a wall around it, and on a low hill behind the village was the castle of the noble who owned that place, Count . . . Zapata, I think his name was. Francisca used to take me for walks in the vegetable fields outside the walls. Diego never went: it was just us two. Sometimes she would bring a piece of cheese or a sausage and some bread, and we would eat our lunch together in the shade of one of the poplar trees that grew along the irrigation ditches. She would tell me stories as her drop spindle rose and fell and the hank of wool on her lap turned steadily into yarn. She knew lots of stories from the Bible about people who lived in far-off times, and how God had created this beautiful countryside with its cooling breeze, and shade, and icy water just to make us happy. But I liked best the stories about dragons, and princesses who lived in castles like our village castle, only taller, with many more towers, and windows that looked out on the road from the distant mountains along which the handsome prince would come to claim her love and carry her off to his kingdom. We could see mountains from Barajas, too, in the west where the sun set. But nobody ever took me to see them close up. I think they were a long way off.

Francisca and I used to chatter about almost everything, but we never talked about boys. She especially didn't want to talk about her husband who ran away. Or how she was going to find that new husband of hers. That was a closed subject. I was too embarrassed to ask her how she and Mother would go about finding a husband for me one day. One day not so far in the future, I think. Lots of girls my age are married already. I wanted one of them to bring up the subject, but they never did.

Now that I'm old enough to help Mother around the house, Francisca seems to spend more time away. Mother and I do most of the spinning and sewing the collars. The ruff collars that gentlemen wear. Mother irons the pleats, but she's teaching me how to do it, too. Francisca has mostly taken over the selling. She takes the orders for collars and delivers them to the majordomos or the house managers of the fancy people who buy them. When there are no deliveries, she loads up a tray with thread and makes the rounds of the markets: La Cebada, Puerta Cerrada, the Plaza Mayor, wherever she thinks she'll find customers. She must have some other business, too, though she won't tell us what, because sometimes she brings home a handful of silver reales, or a basket of fresh fruit.

CHAPTER 9

She and Mama used to fight about it. "Where have you been, all dressed up like that?" Mother would ask, with that dark scowl that meant she was really angry.

"I'm a grown woman, Mother. A widow."

"A widow, my ass. A married woman, who ought to know better."

"My business is my business."

"Well, you're still my daughter, and you're living in my house, and you'll speak to me in a civil tone or you'll find yourself out on the street."

"I was just with some friends of mine, Mama; just some friends. Leave it alone."

"Of course, friends."

The way they looked at each other, the air had that thunderstorm smell about it. I would sit on my stool by the window, sick to my stomach from the shouting, hoping they wouldn't notice me. Usually Francisca would stomp out of the house, but sometimes she would smile and apologize, and the room would fill with sunlight again.

After a while Mama stopped asking. She would take the fruit basket or whatever Francisca had brought and set it in the middle of the table, and they would both go on as if there had never been any tension between them.

In the last year Mother has been spending more and more time on her errands of mercy. Everyone in Madrid's Portuguese community knows that Beatriz Álvarez is ready to help them, no matter the hour. She is always businesslike, and she seems to have a knack for mixing cheerfulness and compassion. At least that's how she is when people call on her for help. But when she thinks people are taking advantage of her, like in the market, or when she thinks somebody has been less modest than she ought to be, then her tongue can be sharp as a knife. I'd say that everyone who knows Mother considers her either a friend or an enemy: there is no in-between.

Mother never asks for payment from the people she helps, but they always give her something. Whatever they can: sometimes money, sometimes food or clothing, or things that we can sell. She'll accept anything. It's always a struggle for her to pay the rent and keep us all from going hungry. After my father could no longer work, these missions of mercy became one of our mainstays. For months I had been nagging Mother to teach me that business, so that I can help the family, too, and so that I will have something of my own besides my sewing to rely on when I get married.

The Barajas Women

It was usually only a ten-minute walk from our house on San Bernardo to Calle del Carmen where the Rodríguez family lived. But Mother first turned right to Calle Hortaleza, where her friend Águeda de la Parrilla lives with her husband, Julián the Shirtmaker, in a room next to Blas's Tavern.

"This will just take a minute," she reassured María.

She knocked quietly at the door: three taps, one tap, and another three. "Águeda," she called in a loud whisper, "get dressed. We have work to do."

Señora Águeda must have been wearing her day clothes, for in less than a minute she was with us in the street, a knitted wool cap pulled down over her ears, her gray cloak wrapped tight against the March chill. "Águeda, you know Beatricica. And this is María Rodríguez: it's about her father."

That night Calle Hortaleza, like almost all of Madrid after the sun goes down, was inky black, and if it weren't for the faint moon glow we would have no idea what we were stepping over. Or in. There were enough oil lamps lit at the Rodríguez apartment, though, that we had no trouble making out which was their house.

María's mother was ready for us. Her washday kettle, two-thirds full of water, was bubbling on the fire. A large linen cloth and a stack of clothing, neatly pressed and folded, rested on one of the family's trunks. María's two younger sisters were dressed, and stood mutely by their mother, their reddened eyes wide open.

After a brief "We're so sorry," my mother was all business. "Where is he?"

Luis Rodríguez lay in his bed where he had died. A sour, nasty smell of sweat, feces, urine, and burning lamp oil filled the room. I felt I might retch at the sight of the dead man, and the stench, but I managed to choke it back. His family seemed used to it by now, and Mother behaved as if this were her everyday workplace. A wooden table in the middle of the room had been cleared off. The bed that the Rodriguez daughters slept in had been made.

Mother took charge, sending the daughters to the front room with instructions to keep the water hot. She closed the door. With Señora Águeda's help, she lifted Luis's body onto the table. Mother stripped off his soiled bedclothes, leaving his body face up and naked on the oak planks. She said to me: "Strip the bed, and take these things. Tell María's mother that they'll need two or three good washings with soap and hot water before she'll want to use them again. For now, have her put them someplace where we won't see them or smell them. And have María give you a bucket of hot soapy water. A pitcher would be better. Bring it back here with a couple of clean cloths."

When I came back with the pitcher—one of the cloths was linen and the other a square of white broadcloth—, Señora Águeda closed the door behind me, leaving the three of us alone with the corpse. "Now," my mother instructed, "watch carefully how we do this." I must have made a face, for she added: "Don't be squeamish. It's just a body. He's not a person anymore. His soul is on its way to God the Creator." I couldn't help staring at the corpse. Mother smiled. "That's the way a man is; that's the equipment God gives them. Nothing's going to hurt you."

Mother soaked the linen cloth in the pitcher and wiped off the body, working from the head all the way to the toes, and taking extra care under his arms and private parts. She had Señora Águeda and me roll him onto his side. "Steady him there while I wash off his back and bottom." When those parts were clean, we rolled him onto his other side and repeated the process. Then she dried him with the broadcloth.

"Now comes the hard part." Mother soaped Luis's face and then scraped off the stubble of his beard with the razor she had brought. She had me lift each arm in turn and did the same to the hair on his underarms. "This is always at least a two-person job," she told me as we worked. "Sometimes I ask the widow to assist me. But they get so emotional. You two are better."

She smiled at Señora Águeda, and I swear I saw her wink before she turned back to me. "Now, Beatriz, hold this up so that I can shave his groin."

I am sure that I blushed as red as a beet, but I did as Mother asked. It felt odd, like a sausage that hadn't been fully stuffed.

When that was done, Mother sent me for a pitcher of clean water scented with some crushed lavender leaves. "So the soul of the deceased will appear clean and sweet-smelling before his God."

I came back with the water and the cloth and the stack of white clothing that had been on the trunk. Mother unfolded the clothing first. There were britches, a shirt, knee socks, and slippers, all of them white linen. "Well, look at that! Who'd have thought?" was all my mother said as spread them on the bare mattress of the bed.

You could tell that none of the clothing had ever been worn. The edges of each garment were ragged, as if the pieces had been torn along the bias by hand rather than cut with a scissors. "Because that's the way it's supposed to be done," my mother answered my question. "It's what the Law commands us to do."

Mother and Señora Águeda rolled Luis's body onto its side again. "Hand

The Barajas Women

me the britches first. Hurry now, we have to be quick, before the body begins to stiffen."

Between the three of us we managed to pull the britches up and tie them loosely at the waist. Then the stocking, right leg first. And then the linen slippers. Señor Águeda pushed the corpse into a sitting position, and Mother and I wrestled him into his shirt. The whole thing must have taken only ten minutes, but by the time we were done all three of us had worked up a sweat. Mother unfolded the large square of linen. "Galician," she said, testing it between her thumb and forefinger. "Very nice. Almost as good as Flemish linen."

"Now here's how we do this," she instructed me. "You fold the cloth in half the long way and then, with the fold on your left, roll up the top half as tightly as you can. We'll get him onto his side again, and you push the rolled cloth tight up against him. Then we'll rock him onto his other side, and you can unroll the rest of the cloth."

It turned out to be easier in the doing than it is in the telling.

"Now we close it, like a bag," my mother said. She threaded her needle, slipped onto her thumb the battered old thimble that I'd seen her use so many times, and with neat overhand stitches closed the shroud, first in the middle and then at both ends. "It's time to call in the family. They are going to cry, but don't let that bother you. You can cry, too, but there's no need if you don't want to." She gave my hand a squeeze. "Beatricica, you did a good job tonight."

The Rodríguez family filed in, and my mother asked them to stand quietly while she said a few words. Mother only knew a couple of prayers, and she said them so often that in a week or two I could say them, too. We had a book of prayers somewhere—I'd seen it once or twice—, but since Mother couldn't read or write, it wasn't much use to her. Now she put her hands together and said:

"God of Creation, accept the soul of this good man, Luis Rodríguez, who has always been your faithful servant. Admit him to the abode of the righteous. Amen."

Mother gave Señora Rodríguez a hug. "He was a good man, and you have been very brave. And so well prepared. I don't believe I have ever seen a better suit of grave clothes than the ones you made."

"It's what he wanted," Señora Rodríguez managed to croak out.

"Now listen to me, there are things to be done." Mother's tone had completely changed. "You have to cover your mirrors, and pour out all the water from the basins I have been using and anything else that you use to store water in your house. Every drop. You can send the girls to bring in fresh water, but if you keep what you have, your husband's soul will not want to undertake the journey that is God's reward for him."

"I understand."

"Your neighbors, they will bring you something to eat?"

"Yes. Some of the Portuguese people we know said they would help."

"Remember: fish is all right, and vegetables. And there have to be some boiled eggs. But no meat: no beef, no chicken, no lamb, nothing. For at least a week."

"We understand."

"Last, Señora Águeda and Beatricica and I want to thank you for allowing us to perform this small mercy for you in your time of need." With that, which Mother had alerted me was our cue to exit, we headed for the stairs.

"Wait, we want to give you something for all your, for your . . ."

"There's no need," Mother assured her. "It is just something we are proud to be able to do. But if you insist, have María bring whatever it is around to our house when she can."

"All right. But please take this for now. We're so grateful." She handed Mother a small folded piece of cloth.

A moment later we were in the street. Mother unwrapped the cloth and found six silver reales. She gave Señora Águeda two and put the rest into her purse. It had already grown light, and the food vendors were setting up their tables along the street from the Carmen church down to the Puerta del Sol, one of Madrid's old gates. It was Saint Joseph's day, so there were lots of yummy pastries piled on the tables. But Mother hurried us past them to the Puerta del Sol fountain, where we washed ourselves: face, hands, arms, legs—at least the parts that weren't covered by our clothes—and our feet. We had touched a dead man, my mother told me as we splashed ourselves, and we couldn't touch food or go into any Portuguese house until we had washed. That was the custom, the Law. We shook ourselves to dry off. Then, as we headed back to Calle San Bernardo, Mother bought us each a cinnamon bun.

Though we have shared lots of experiences since, I don't believe I've ever felt closer to my mother than I did at that moment.

That was the first time I went with Mother on one of her errands of mercy, but it was far from the last. When we got the call—night or day, it didn't

The Barajas Women

matter—Mother would drop everything and hurry to the dead person's house. If the person who died was a baby, or a young child, the two of us could manage the job between us. But if it was a grownup, or someone whom mother knew was unusually fat, she generally took Señora Águeda with her, too.

I knew that Madrid's Portuguese community was big, but I didn't know how big until I began going out with Mother. Over the last year we must have helped twenty or thirty grieving families prepare their loved ones. Mother wasn't the only woman doing this kind of work, of course, but she must have been the best. People thought that she knew everything there was to know about these things. One time the brother of some widow asked Mother how she knew so much about all this if she had never been to France where our people don't have to hide how they are burying someone. Mother smiled knowledgeably and said that an old circumcised Portuguese man had been her teacher. She didn't tell this man his name, though.

Mother and I always spoke Portuguese with the older people; in fact, when there were grandmothers or grandfathers in the family they rarely spoke any Spanish. And most of us spoke Portuguese at home. But the people my age had mostly all been raised right here in Madrid, and with them we were more comfortable in Spanish.

After a while, all Mother's errands of mercy began to blend into one another in my mind, and I truly can't recall which dead person belonged to which family. A few of them stand out, of course. Not six months after María Rodríguez's father died, her sister Blanca, who was one year younger than she was, took ill with a fever and was gone within a week. They had to call in the parish priest, of course, because everyone in their building knew that Blanca had died, and not to bring in the Church created a danger for the whole family. So the priest came in and sat by the bed, and mumbled his words, and took out the jar of holy oil from his bag, and smeared a little on Blanca's face and hands and feet, the way they do. Señora Rodriguez gave him a tip—it was expected. But as soon as he was out the door my mother and Señora Rodríguez took a kitchen knife and scraped off all the oil. "It's not right for Blanca to go to her maker dabbed with Church oil," my mother said. And Señora Rodríguez answered, "Amen." They did the same thing when María's four-year-old cousin died. Lots of times Mother and I helped scrape off the oil. I would never do that now, of course, not since I have become completely Christian.

Another part of our family business in those days was fasting for the souls of the dead. It always earned us a gift. I remember one night we washed and shrouded the father of a Portuguese woman who lives in Calle Arenal—her name escapes me right now. After she had given us a large hank of wool and two liters of olive oil for our trouble, she stopped us at the doorway. "Señora Beatriz, I want you to fast for him, too, you and your precious daughter." And then she handed Mother a pair of the dead man's shoes in payment. As if any of us could wear them. The next day Mother had me take them to a shoemaker to repair and sell, and he gave me three reales and six maravedís for them. Cardoso, that's what her name was.

Portuguese women sometimes had Mother called in when they were about to give birth, too. Mother really wasn't a midwife, but she was good at giving comfort, and she knew a prayer that would make the woman in labor believe she was in good hands. They had confidence in her, that's what is important. Sometimes—I couldn't believe it the first time I saw her do it—, Mother would take down the image of Our Lord that hung over the bed, or the woodcut of Our Lady, and she would put it in a box, if there was one, or behind the door: someplace where it couldn't observe the birth and where the new mother wouldn't have to look at it. She did that when Beatriz Navarro was in labor.

We had to be careful about who we allowed to come into the room where the woman was giving birth. No servants, of course, and no family members who were not committed to doing things in our Portuguese way. And no men. Beatriz's uncle Gaspar Navarro was in the house that night, but she made him stay outside. When the baby came out it was pretty mangled, and they all thought she might die. When Gaspar came in and saw it he snatched the baby away from my mother and took it straight to the Church of Saint Martin to be baptized. No one in that family liked Gaspar very much. He was completely churched, going to mass three or four times a week. He never missed a procession or a saint's day celebration in any of Madrid's parishes. The family did what they could to keep him out of their affairs, but that night he was there at the house, so they had no choice.

The baby died a couple of months later, and mother and Señora Navarro scraped off the chrism the way they always did before we wrapped the infant for burial. What I remember most about that time was that some people in the family wanted to shroud the baby in an old piece of linen that had been used to cover a window. But Señora Navarro wouldn't hear of it. Nothing but

The Barajas Women

brand-new linen would do. "We're never going to give that poor thing any dowry but this," she told the family in a tone that no one dared to challenge, "so I want her to have the best."

Back when my father could still work, he brought a little money into the family. My brother, Diego, contributed nothing. He was fifteen back then, a year and a half older than I was, but he looked older than that. He had broad shoulders, and he was built solid, with thick arms and legs like my father must have had before the cough wasted them away. His hair was black, like Francisca's, and his beard, which was coming in strong, was the same color. His eyes, though, had a blue tinge, like mine. Diego should have been employed at something by then, but he mostly spent the days in the street with his friends. I think that's the main thing he and Mother used to argue about. She thought Father should have gotten Diego an apprenticeship somewhere, as a weaver, maybe, or a dyer. A tailor. Lots of Portuguese men did that kind of work. One of Papa's friends could have taken Diego—I overheard Mama complaining about that to Francisca. But I don't think Papa had any friends. He never talked about any, and no one ever came to the house to see him.

The major source of our family income was my mother. In addition to her errands of mercy, she always had a dozen little schemes going to make a few maravedís for the family. A lot of them had to do with thread: spinning, buying, selling. We didn't do our own weaving—looms were expensive, and heavy—, but we would buy linen cloth and make ruff collars to sell to the fancy gentlemen. We had a flat iron and a board that we put on our table when we crimped them. Mother's hands were always busy, and she never let any of our hands rest idle either. I remember that there was this woman, her name was Beatriz Navarro, and she used to come to the house sometimes to card the raw wool that Mother had bought to spin. The three of us, and sometimes my sister, Francisca, too, would sit in the front room by the window and spin and card and talk for hours. The Navarro woman loved to gab, and she drank in everything that we said, but I could tell she wasn't very bright. She was only with us for a few months because, she said, every time she went home her husband scolded her for having anything to do with us.

What brought things to a head with her, I think, was that one day the conversation turned to religion, and which church we went to, and which preachers we liked the best. My mother told her that we usually went to the Atocha church, and that she liked it because it was always so full of people and noise that she couldn't hear the preacher at all. Mother tried to pass if off as a joke, but it scandalized the Navarro woman, who pushed her to explain herself further. So after a while Mother explained that our family followed the True Law, the Law of Moses, and not the Law of Jesus Christ, because we had been taught that the Christian Law was wrong and that you could only be saved under the Law of Moses. She told Beatriz that she ought to do that, too.

Beatriz was dumbfounded! "How can you ask me to abandon the Law that my mother and father taught me when I was a child?"

My mother had an answer for everything: "I'm sure your parents meant well, but they probably didn't know that what they were teaching you was very wrong and that it is blindness and error for you to go on living under that Law."

I think the Navarro woman must have looked up to Mother—after all, Mother was Navarro's employer, and a good deal older, and knew a lot about a lot of different things. By the time the sun faded and we had finished our work for the day, Mother was explaining to the poor woman how for her soul to be saved she had to fast three times each week for her sins and that she must never do any work on Saturdays, and all sorts of other things that we do in our family. Diego came home in the middle of all this—one of his rare appearances—, and he told the Navarro woman that everything my mother said was the truth and that if she knew what for she would do as Mother instructed. They made the Navarro woman swear never to tell any of this to her husband, or the landlord of her house, or her confessor, or anyone at all, because it could be very dangerous for her and for all of us. When she left our house she walked like she was in a daze.

I couldn't believe what had just happened. After warning me time and again that I must never discuss family business—not religious matters any-way—with a stranger, here Mother had let our secret cat out of the bag. And if the Navarro woman talked . . .

Beatriz came to card wool with us a few more times, but she never seemed as jolly as she had been before. She always complained how her husband called her a dummy and a spineless ninny for believing without question everything anyone told her. Mother tried to shore her up, but she wasn't very successful. They never talked about religious things again, and eventually the Navarro woman stopped coming. Mother had to trust that Beatriz would guard her confidence, or that the incident had passed through her sievelike mind without leaving any incriminating trace. And, of course, Mother had to find someone else to help card our wool.

The Barajas Women

Mother was like one of those summer winds that blow down from the mountains: hot one minute, cold the next. One thing was for sure, you never wanted to argue with her. Mother was always right, and anyone who didn't agree with her was wrong. She herself was no saint, but the people she crossed words with were always immoral, or stupid, or both. She never missed an opportunity to criticize someone else's behavior, especially when she thought they had been whoring around. I'll bet there were a half dozen women on our street alone whom Mother considered her mortal enemies. The one I remember most clearly was María Vizcaína, because she carried a big knife in her apron and when I was little I was afraid of her. She used to sell mattress covers and straw or wool to stuff them with. You could always find her on the corner of Calle Montera, dirty and reeking of wine, her uncombed hair spilling from the corners of her wimple, with her wares spread out on the ground around her. Well, one day, when her daughter was there working with her, Mother taunted them by congratulating them for having finally gotten honest work where they could sit up and not spend all day on their backs. By the time the Vizcaína woman had pulled out her knife, Mother and I had scampered away. I never went up Calle Montera after that; I always took the long way around to get to our house on San Bernardo.

Another time, in the vegetable market, Mother picked a fight with Francisco García's wife because she said that the García woman had slept with half the men on her block—and not just the Portuguese men, either. "Your poor husband," she shouted at her across a cabbage stall, "everybody laughs at him because he thinks all those squally brats are his, when they could be anybody's at all. Just look at them!" Mother ducked as the cabbage just missed her head. After that, whenever she passed the García woman in the street, she would hiss "Whore!" under her breath. But García's wife got back as good as she gave, because she hissed back at her: "Beggar bitch!" It was all Francisca or I could do to hold Mother back, or I am sure there would have been more vegetables in the air.

We could toss off "bitch," but "beggar" hurt. You couldn't argue with the fact that we were poor. No matter how hard we stitched and spun, no matter how many collars we crimped or bodies we wrapped for burial, no matter how many times we fasted for the good of someone's soul, there was always more money going out than coming in. When Papa got sick it was worse, of course, because he couldn't work and he ate a lot. When he died, and then Diego moved out, we three women managed a little better. But it

CHAPTER 9

was still a rare day when we could pay the rent and also put enough on the table to fill our bellies.

Were we actually reduced to begging? Not really, although we sometimes did borrow a little food from one or another of our neighbors, and I can't recall that we ever paid any of it back. Or were expected to. Sometimes Mother would have me run over to Fernando de Montesinos's house to see if his wife had any extra eggs. A couple of times she gave me a whole chicken to take home, claiming that she had bought too much at the market, that it would spoil before they could eat it, and that it would be a sin to let it go to waste. We could always count on Isabel de Santillana, too, for a cup of olive oil or a handful of carrots. María Báez and her husband, Enrique, were usually good for a half loaf of bread and, every once in a while, a piece of salt cod.

The Lord may have rested on the seventh day, but we Barajas women didn't. I remember once when Uncle Tomé came to our house he scolded Mother for not keeping the Sabbath the way he had taught her. "If I don't work on Saturday when my customers are in the street," Mother complained, "how do you expect me to be able to feed my children? The Sabbath was made for rich people. Me, I think about the Sabbath sometimes, and God will have to be content with that."

Uncle Tomé wasn't happy, but there wasn't much he could do about it. He couldn't support our family.

The funny thing is that our downstairs neighbors, who were Castilians, used to nag Mother the same way about working on Sunday. "You ought to be taking your daughters to church, you know, not sitting at home sewing. It's not right."

"We do go to church," Mother snapped back, "the Atocha church. And I don't recall seeing you at mass there very often. Besides, how we honor the Lord's Day when we get home is our business, not yours."

All the same, conversations like that made Mother nervous. There was far too much Inquisition in Madrid. So from then on, on Sundays she made us sew our collars far enough away from the window that we couldn't be seen from the street.

I was born in Spain. In fact, all of us kids were. My mother moved here from Portugal when she was only thirteen. She came with her brother, Tomé, and Pedro Álvarez, my father. They were already married by then. They didn't have a mule or anything, so they could bring with them only what they carried on their backs. Mother said that they had to cross a lot of mountains, too. My aunt Catalina, mother's older sister, had come to Spain the year before and found a job making collars in the village of Barajas. That's why our family settled there and why they still call us the Barajas women.

My father never ever talked with us about Portugal, but every once in a while, especially in the winter when we were all huddled around the brazier with a blanket over our knees, Mother would talk about Freixo de Numão. That was the village near Torre de Moncorvo where she grew up. "It was always so green there," she would say. "There were flowers everywhere, all seasons of the year. It never got as cold as it does here. I used to like going to the well at the end of the village to get water for our kitchen. There were always a lot of kids there, especially on Friday afternoons, since our mothers wouldn't let us draw water on Saturday. We would play games and chase each other around, and then try to explain to our mothers how a fifteen-minute errand could take a whole hour."

"What did Freixo look like?" I would ask her. "Was it like Barajas? Was there a castle?"

"No, no castle," Mother would laugh. "Freixo de Numão was just a tiny village, a lot smaller than Barajas. Small, but a lot of our people lived there. Your grandfather Fernando was from Mujagata; there they did have a castle, and a pretty big one, too! In Freixo the houses were all white, gleaming white. We put on new coats of whitewash twice a year, once in the spring, just before Holy Week, and once in the fall, before the Great Fast."

"And Papa?"

"Your father was from Freixo, too, but a different one: Freixo de Espada á Cinta, about a two-day walk away from our Freixo. I don't know how my parents knew the Álvarez family, but they did. Pedro was almost nineteen when we got married; he didn't have any other trade but fieldwork, but he was very good at that. The landowners always hired him first when it was time to plant or to harvest. He was always happy to work in the fields. He liked the smell of dirt, he used to say."

"But, if Portugal was so nice, and you were so happy there, why did you come to Spain?" Whenever I asked that, the stories would stop, and Mother would change the subject. So naturally I stopped asking.

It was my sister who finally told me the whole story when she got tired of my badgering. "Portugal has an Inquisition, too, just like Spain's, only worse. Well, one day some of Mama's friends were arrested because they kept the Jewish Sabbath at home, just like we do. The Inquisition took all their property, and they had to wear a sambenito over their clothing whenever they went out of their house. Some other people in Freixo were tortured, and some were burned! It sent all Mother's friends into a panic, at least that's what Mother told me. They were afraid of the sambenitos, and they were afraid of being killed. That's why our parents left everything they had and snuck across the border into Spain. And since Mother knew that Aunt Catalina lived in a village near Madrid . . . "

It was about three years ago when Francisca told me all this, when I was eleven. I thought then that she had answered all my questions, but in fact all she really did was open up a lot of new ones. Mainly about why our people had to be so different. Why couldn't we just go to church and worship Jesus and Mary and work on Saturdays the way all our Castilian neighbors did? Jesus was going to take their souls to Heaven, at least that's what the priests said when they came and dabbed their oil on the people who were dying, so why wouldn't he take our souls, too? I was afraid to say any of this to Mother or Francisca or any of my Portuguese friends. So I kept it to myself.

I think my conversation with Francisca about the move from Portugal must have opened a door in our house that until then I did not even realize had been shut. Francisca and Mother began to talk openly about things without first sending me out of the room on some long errand. Mother began to teach me how to cook: what foods we couldn't eat, and how to prepare them in the Portuguese way. It's not that I didn't already know most of that stuff; but she made the rules clear, and explained how doing things in a certain way, in the way of the Law of Moses, would ensure the salvation of our souls.

As I said, Aunt Catalina was the first of our family to come from Portugal, and my parents and my uncle Tomé were the next. I don't have memories of Uncle Tomé from when I was little. He didn't come to our house much, and when he did, that's when they would send me out on errands. But after I got bigger and Francisca and I had talked, they began to let me stay. Uncle Tomé wasn't very tall—he was shorter even than Mother—, and he had long, bushy white eyebrows. He always had a donkey smell on him, probably because he made his living transporting goods from villages like Barajas into Madrid. My uncle had a way of speaking that made him seem like the biggest person in the room. No matter what anybody asked him about the Law of Moses, he always knew the answer, and there was something in his voice that told you that what he said really was true. I was a little

The Barajas Women

afraid of him, even though there was always a sugared almond in his pocket for me. He was married, but I never met his wife, and I don't even know her name, and I'm pretty sure they never had any children. That was a long time ago; Uncle Tomé died the year that Princess María got married to that Austrian prince, Fernando.

My brother, Diego, was Uncle Tomé's favorite—Diego still lived at home in those days—, and he seemed to soak up everything Uncle Tomé said: how we were to wash our hands before and after meals; the things we could and couldn't eat; the proper way of fasting all day until evening when the stars came out; how we were to sway back and forth when we were praying; all the things we had to do to keep the Sabbath properly; and how we had to buy all new dishes in the fall at the time of the Great Fast—or maybe that was the spring fast, I'm not exactly sure. Uncle Tomé taught Diego a lot of prayers of the Law of Moses, too, and Diego taught them to the rest of us, although now I don't remember any of them, except the one that says "God of Creation, thank you for this food." We always said that prayer before we ate. Sometimes I still do, out of habit, even though I'm completely Christian now. When Uncle Tomé died, Diego took over as our main teacher. Those last years in Barajas and the first year that we lived in Madrid, Diego was our main authority, really our only one. When Diego moved out to live with his friends we didn't have anybody to tell us when the special days were.

When I was little I never asked questions about God or the Law of Moses. If Uncle Tomé said all that stuff was right and proper, and Diego said so, too, and Mother, then there was no reason for me to have any doubts. My father didn't count. He never ever talked about those things, and if Diego or Uncle Tomé got after him to keep some fast, or put on a clean shirt on Friday afternoon, Father just said, "You do things your way, and I'll do them mine. Just leave me out of all that." Father didn't go to church much, just the required festivals and Sunday mass and confession a couple of times a year.

As I got older I began to realize that although Father was Portuguese, he wasn't our kind of Portuguese. He was kind but silent, and when he still had his health he was a hard worker. He used to say that his father and his father's father were farmers, and that was good enough for him. They didn't have any land of their own, but they always found enough work doing this or that, and they never went hungry. Still, I couldn't imagine why Mother's parents picked him out as her husband. I tried to get her to talk about it once, but she just changed the subject.

CHAPTER 9

I'm pretty sure now that my father's family didn't do any ceremonies of the Law of Moses the way we did. I think they were old-Christians, and that he believed what the Church told him to believe. He was a doer, not a thinker. He didn't question things. If he thought about it at all, he probably decided that his way was a simpler way, without all those rules that made our lives so difficult, and without all those fasts that made my stomach growl all day. Jesus was powerful: you couldn't look at the huge churches on every street corner without knowing that. And if the Church said that living according to the Law of Jesus was the way to get your soul into Heaven, well, maybe they were right. Certainly there were more of them than there were of us. And they didn't have to hide, the way we did.

But of course I didn't say anything to anyone in the family. I liked my warm, friendly mother better than the sharp-tongued one.

Of all my memories of Barajas, the most vivid is the day we left for Madrid. We didn't own a lot of things, but we had accumulated more than we could carry by ourselves. So Uncle Tomé came out from Madrid with a cart and a strong brown mule to pull it. He helped us pack our last few things, and then, after a cold supper, we caught a few hours of sleep.

We got up with the first light. Mother, Francisca, and I brought out all our things. Father hobbled down the stairs and sat on a stone bench in the sun, his cane balanced in his lap. He said he had to supervise the loading, but in five minutes he was asleep. Really, there wasn't that much to load. Four bed rolls with their wool covers. Mother said we could get fresh straw in Madrid to stuff them. A box with Mother's sewing supplies, and another with Francisca's. I wasn't old enough to have all my own tools yet: I mostly used Mother's. Five or six large bags of wool that we still had to card and spin. Some iron cooking pots. A half-dozen clay water jugs. A polished wooden trunk with all of our good clothes, and another box, knocked together from some boards Diego had found, that held our other clothing. A bag with the oil lamps. I brought out my rag doll, Melisenda, that Mother had stitched for me when I was little. I didn't play with her anymore, but it didn't seem right to leave her behind. Somewhere in all of the clothing there was a book, too. I don't know what it was, but I had seen Uncle Tomé or Diego with it once or twice, and I know they always kept it hidden. Uncle Tomé and Diego loaded it all on the cart and lashed everything tight with a length of rope that our uncle had thought to bring.

The Barajas Women

Mother asked Uncle Tomé to wait with the cart for a few minutes, because there was something that she had to show her children first. She took me by the hand, and we went out the village gate and walked all the way around the wall, through the vegetable gardens—the peas were in bloom, the smell of their blossoms overpowering—, by the threshing floor where the flint-bottomed threshing sleds were leaned up against two huge live oaks, and all the way to the hill where the castle gleamed in the clear light. It was one of those March days that feel more like May: the sky was deep blue, the blackbirds were piping out love songs from every bush, and the bees were buzzing back and forth, sniffing out the best wild flowers for their honey. Francisca and Diego—they were still talking to each other then—walked behind us.

"I want you to remember this," Mother said. She almost never got sentimental, but I heard the catch in her voice. "We've been happy here in Barajas. We'll be happy in Madrid, too; but the Madrid sky is never this color blue. Too many cooking fires, too many people. Lots of good work for us, though, and lots of the right sort of people for Beatricica to meet. And you too, Francisca," she said, without glancing behind her to make sure that Francisca was listening.

A grunted "Unh huh" let her know she hadn't missed the hint.

"And Diego can learn a trade in Madrid and make something of himself." This time there was no answer at all.

"But it won't be like Barajas," she said. "Barajas is like Freixo, a place where your soul can fly."

By now we had circled all the way around to the village gate that led us back to our house. We hadn't been gone but about twenty minutes. Uncle Tomé was waiting with the cart and the mule. He made a place between the bedrolls for Father to sit. Diego and Uncle Tomé lifted Father into place. Diego took the mule's halter, and off we went to our new life.

Uncle Tomé had found us an apartment on Calle Caballero de Gracia, not far from the Puerta del Sol. It was three small attic rooms above a fish shop, and the smell was so bad that it stuck to our clothing and, even worse, to the collars and the thread that we were spinning to sell. After a few weeks, Mother found us some rooms in a house owned by a Portuguese woman she had met, Señora Damiana de Robles, in Calle San Antón. The Robles family had done well by themselves in Spain. Mother said that when they came from Portugal they were just as poor as she was, but what with buying and selling, and this and that, they had managed to acquire several properties. Damiana's widower brother, Antonio de Robles, lived with his daughter, Catalina, on Calle Hortaleza. I was friendly with Catalina's daughter, Isabel, for a while, before she died of the pox. Señora Damiana's sister, María de Robles, had a nice house on Calle San Bartolomé. She is the one who taught us how to make pleated collars to sell. For a while we sewed them for her, and then we started selling collars on our own.

Señora Damiana and Mother got along pretty well. When one or the other of them was not out doing business, they would sit together near our front window spinning or stitching and gossiping about their mutual friends or talking about the Law of Moses. They tried to keep their voices low so that Father couldn't hear them, but he always knew what was going on. Father didn't like the way the Robles family was so open about not working on Saturday, and never going to church, and never buying pork. Sometimes at night I could hear him arguing with Mother about it. He didn't much care what we did, he said, as long as we kept it secret. But this openness was dangerous. He kept nagging Mother to have nothing to do with the Robleses, but Mother was stubborn about it.

One night she actually shouted at him: "This is my business, Pedro, not yours. You're not supporting this family, I am. I'll decide where we live, and who our friends are. If you don't like it, haul yourself out of here. Find something to do with yourself." Father tried to answer back, but the effort sent him into a spasm of coughing, and by the time he had recovered it was pretty clear that we kids were awake and hanging on every word. So the argument ended there.

What Mother said wasn't fair. She knew that there was no way that Father could get around on his own, and he was far too sick to work. But anger makes you say things you shouldn't, and Mother was never very good at controlling her temper. Francisca and I pretty much kept out of our parents' fights, but Diego would wade right in. And it seemed like he always took our father's side. The morning after all the shouting, Diego cornered Mother by the hearth and demanded that she apologize.

"Apologize?! Who are you to tell me when to apologize?"

Diego stayed right in her face. "You know how sick he is. He can't even get out of bed without help. How can you expect him to go out and find work? Besides, all he knows is farmwork. Have you seen any fields here in Madrid?"

The Barajas Women

"Don't you talk to me like that, young man! I know what's what. But if he isn't going to help support this family, then he can damn well keep his mouth shut about the things I have to do to put a little food on our table."

"Yes, but since he . . ."

"And that goes for you, too. Let's see a little more work, young man, a little more money coming in. And a little more respect for your elders."

Diego got that tight look on his face that he sometimes gets. I could see that he wanted to scream something hurtful back at Mother, but he didn't dare, not when Señora Damiana in the next room undoubtedly had her ear pressed to the wall. So he just clenched his teeth, slammed his felt hat onto his head, and stalked out.

He didn't come back home that night, or the next night either. When he showed up for breakfast on the third day, Mother told him to help us pack up our things because we were moving to Calle San Bernardo.

That's where we've lived ever since, in three rooms on the third floor. Once we got Father up the stairs and into bed he never left the house again. Not while he was alive. It was tight for a while, but after Diego moved out and Father died, the apartment was more than enough for Francisca and Mother and me.

Diego never did tell us where he was living, or with whom. Though one of our neighbors said he had taken a room up at the other end of Calle San Bartolomé with two brothers who sold goatskins. I don't know their names, but I would see them around sometimes, struggling up the street with a huge pack of half-cured hides on their backs. The "Goat Guys" was what everybody called them. Anyway, a couple of times each week Diego would come by our house and put a few maravedís, or sometimes seven or eight reales, on the sewing table and talk for a while with Francisca and me. I think he must have kept an eye on our house, because he usually showed up when Mother was out. If she walked in during one of his visits they were civil enough to each other, but their conversation never got much beyond a few pleasantries, and Diego didn't stay long.

We heard from some friends that Diego was mostly hanging out at Madrid's markets helping move merchandise or carrying a morning's heavy purchases home for someone. Francisca would run into him sometimes. She always told us that he was looking fit. Diego was smart, smarter than the rest of us, I think. His couple of years of schooling in Barajas taught him to read and write, and he remembered every detail of what Uncle Tomé explained about the ways of the Law of Moses. To Francisca and me, it seemed a shame that Diego was having to rely on the strength of his back rather than his mind. But then, Madrid was chock full of people with lots of education and no job. Whenever we went out we saw them clustered on the steps of some church, or in the great courtyard in front of King Felipe's palace, or on the steps of one of Madrid's theaters, trying to look purposeful, even though their thin faces, their empty hands, and their threadbare clothing in last year's style always gave them away. Francisca and I thought they looked pathetic.

One day Diego came by to tell us that he had found another job as a night guard at the Fuencarral Gate, a few blocks up the hill from Calle San Bartolomé. "Two other guys and I register everyone coming through the gate to make sure they have paid their city import tax. People are always trying to smuggle in clothing to sell, or sacks of flour. But mostly it's barrels of wine, because they're taxed the most. What we have to do is stop them and make them wait outside the gate until the tax collectors come in the morning. Sometimes, if it's just a small barrel or two, we let them through, as long as they leave something in our cups and something in our pockets. I get a regular salary, too, but it isn't much. I think the city expects us to pick up a little extra on the side. Certainly our boss does: we have to give him a third of whatever people pay us."

Diego carried himself differently than the last time he had stopped by our house: he stood straighter, with his shoulders back, and a smile played on his face. It's clear he was proud of his new position. I was proud for him, too. And worried: it sounded like rough work to me.

"Isn't it dangerous, stopping people at the gate?"

"Well, it can be." Diego puffed himself up even more. "But usually the three of us can handle it. There was one night last month, though . . . "

Francisca and I could see he was itching to tell the tale. "Go on," I said.

"It must have been a little after midnight, and we had already let four wine carts through, so we were feeling a little tipsy. I was jingling the coins in my pocket when somebody hit me on my shoulder and my head with a heavy stick. As I was falling I could see that it was a gang of ruffians. They were so completely wrapped up in their black capes that you could barely see their eyes in the lantern light. I was groggy, and they soon emptied my pockets of their jingle. They wore swords, too, so I guess we were lucky that they didn't use them."

By then I had sat down on a cushion with my hand over my mouth. "They could have killed you! What did you do?"

The Barajas Women

"We didn't do anything," Diego said. "The night watch came by and picked us up and checked to see that we didn't have any wounds or any blood on our weapons—we don't carry swords, but we all have big knives—, and then they went about their business and we went about ours."

Francisca's voice showed her disapproval. "You're a lucky fool, Diego."

"Well, we couldn't very well tell the night watch that the thieves had stolen our 'tip' money, could we? We just offered them a little wine and off they went."

"You've become a regular Castilian, haven't you?" Francisca said.

"What do you mean by that?"

"These new buddies of yours, don't they suspect anything? What about the Sabbath? What about our fast days? What is going to happen when your so-called friends remember that you're Portuguese, and see that you won't share the meat pies they've brought for their midnight snacks? Won't they make the connection?"

"Don't worry about it. It's not a problem because I don't do any of that anymore. I eat anything I want. That stuff that Uncle Tomé taught us, that was before. It doesn't suit me now. I think Uncle Tomé and Mother are just plain wrong."

"Are you serious?" Francisca was scandalized. "Aren't you worried about the salvation of your soul?"

"Of course I am; everybody is. I just think I was wrong, that's all. What we used to do is wrong. The Law of Moses is the dead law; the Law of our Lord Jesus Christ is the law my soul will be saved in. Uncle Tomé and Mother mean well, but they've got it wrong, that's all. They taught us wrong. That's why I go to mass with my friends now. That's why I always cross myself when I pass a church. And why I make regular confession. And you should, too, if you want to save yourselves."

I was speechless, even though by then I was beginning to suspect in my heart that he might be right. But Francisca wouldn't let it lie. "So now you're a Castilian, like the rest of them. I assume you still know how to keep your mouth shut, though. You know that whatever you tell anybody about us is only going to hurt you more."

"Don't worry. I'm not going to tell anybody that you still follow the dead Law; and I would never say anything about our family at confession. I may be a Christian now, but I'm not stupid."

Francisca glared at him. "Well, you'd better keep your mouth shut, because . . ."

She broke off at the sound of someone coming up the stairs.

"I'm not going to tell. But don't you say anything about this to Mother either. That goes for you, too, Beatriz."

Mother was huffing as she came through the door. The market basket on her arm was piled with chard, shiny white onions, carrots, a quarter of a great round loaf of barley bread, and a piece of dried salt codfish. "I heard your voice, Diego. Everything all right? What were you all whispering about?"

"Nothing, just keeping our voices low." I couldn't believe that I was already covering for Diego.

"You'll stay for dinner? Fish stew . . ."

"Maybe another time, Mother. There are things I have to be doing."

Castilian. That's what Francisca had called Diego. "Castilian" had always been a dirty word in our house. It meant everybody who was not Portuguese, everybody who was not our kind of Portuguese. It was a codeword for people we didn't want to be like, for people we were afraid of, and had to be careful around. When Mother and I would go to prepare some dead Portuguese person for burial, Mother always warned me to be wary of the Castilian servants. She always asked the grieving family to send the Castilians out of the room. If the family had hired a Castilian wet nurse, the woman had to take the baby somewhere else while we worked. There were Portuguese women like Francisca de Matos whom we pitied because their husbands were Castilian, so they couldn't follow the Law the way they were supposed to. By then I understood that that was at the heart of the bitterness between my mother and my father. Sometimes when they were fighting, I heard my mother muttering to herself, "Why did they have to marry me to a Castilian?"

I remember that once we were working at someone's house when a Castilian neighbor woman—I think her husband had a business making chairs—came in with a piece of blood sausage for the widow.

"When we heard about your loss my husband bought you this *morcilla* because he thought it might cheer you up. We know the person who makes it. It's really good."

As soon as she had left the room my mother said: "Just look at these bitches. You can see how much these Castilians hate us when they bring us this garbage to eat."

The widow nodded her head in agreement. "This can't stay in the house. It's dirty. God punishes the soul of anybody who eats this crap." "Here," she handed it to her daughter, "go throw it into the street."

She made such a funny face when she said it that we all had to laugh, even though her husband's body was right there on the table in its shroud.

Once when we first moved to Madrid I asked Francisca how she could tell when she was all grown up. She said that you were grown up when you stop believing that the world is going to stay the same forever, and you realized that everything changes and there is no way to stop it. When Father died I thought I knew what she meant, but to tell the truth, he hadn't played a part in our lives for so long that when he was gone nothing really changed, and it was as if he had never been there at all. And when Diego moved out—well, he wasn't physically in the house, at least not at night, but we still saw him from time to time. He was still my brother, and I still loved him. Then early last month, five weeks ago now, everything in our lives really truly changed, and I wasn't a little girl anymore.

Mother and I were sitting at the table, shelling the first peas of the season when Francisca burst in. It was May 19.

"It's Diego! They've arrested Diego!"

"Who arrested Diego, the night watch?" Mother was thinking of Diego's scrapes at the Puerta de Fuencarral and the "tip" money he was taking.

"No, not the night watch. The Inquisition!"

My mother turned white. "God help us."

The Inquisition was always there but in the background. We were afraid of it, but we took precautions. The things we did to honor the Law of Moses, we tried to keep secret. We kept our mouths shut around Castilians. If we had to talk about anything even remotely connected with the Law of Moses, we talked in Portuguese. We went to mass and marched in the processions where everybody could see us. We could all recite the Four Prayers and count the beads on our rosaries. We knew of people who'd got arrested, of course. Even as large as the Portuguese community is, word gets around pretty quickly. Those were the people who made an outward show of being Jewish, we thought, the ones who didn't take any trouble to hide; they were the ones the inquisitors came after. And the rich people, of course, because the Inquisition always took away everything they had. If they came after what our family had, they wouldn't get much beyond a sewing box, a couple of iron pots, and a pair of scissors.

We always knew we were at risk, of course, but it didn't affect our daily lives very much. Sometimes I would hear the grownups talking about how the king's prime minister, Count Duke Olivares, would never let the Inquisition come after the Portuguese. Whenever anybody said that, an argument was sure to follow.

"Maybe that was true when Olivares was in control. But look at how bad things are, how things cost more every day, how much we're spending on all the wars. The count duke is slipping. He can't protect us the way he used to."

"But he still has King Felipe's ear. The king does what Olivares tells him to. Always has; always will."

"Even if that is true, which I doubt, the Church doesn't do what Olivares wants."

"Yes, but that doesn't matter. Spain needs us. If the country wants to be rich again, they have to leave us alone. Spain needs our Portuguese wealth, and it needs our skills in business." Whenever I heard that I wanted to laugh because nobody we knew had any money. We all worked hard, but our business skills just barely kept our heads above water.

"Need is one thing; powerful enemies are another."

I didn't care about Olivares. Our brother, Diego, was in jail. We sat in stunned silence for a while, the bowl of peas on the table entirely forgotten. We wanted to do something, but it didn't seem that there was anything we could do. Mother had never been at a loss for words, but now she kept opening and closing her mouth, and nothing came out.

"We're all going to have to testify," Francisca said. "You know they are going to call us in. "You, too, Beatricica." She must have seen the frightened look in my eyes. I had heard the stories.

"Maybe we should just . . . " Mother's voice trailed off.

"We have two choices, as I see it," Francisca went on. "We can wait until they call us, or we can go in voluntarily, all contrite, and tell them as little as we can."

I didn't say anything, because I had already decided what I was going to do. I would go in and make a full confession. For the last two months I had

The Barajas Women

been living as a secret Christian anyway, praying silently to Our Lady when I went to bed, and always sneaking a little food when I was supposed to be fasting. I would tell the inquisitors that I had lived by the Law of Moses, because that was how I had been raised, but that Jesus had helped me see the light and reject the Devil, who had made me do all those things. I could never tell Mother or Francisca that, though. They would have my hide!

I was running through this plan in my mind, what I would say to convince the inquisitors that I was a Christian, when all of a sudden Francisca stood up and cried, "Oh my God, the book. I forgot about the book!"

We had all forgotten it.

I think I mentioned that Diego knew how to read and write but that the rest of us didn't. If we wanted to pray something in the Law of Moses, we had to memorize it first, and help each other get the words right. Uncle Tomé knew how to read and write, of course, and Mother said that back in Portugal her parents had both learned their letters. Her father owned one book, and she brought it with her to Spain. When I was little she would sometimes take it out and let us hold it while we prayed. It had tiny print, so small that you could hold it in the palm of your hand. She didn't know exactly what it was, except that it was from the Law of Moses. I don't know where she hid it in our house in Barajas—I could never find it—, but when we moved she brought it with her to Madrid. For a while she kept it in the box with our clothing, wrapped in a piece of white linen.

Both Diego and Francisca had tried to let Mother know how dangerous that book could be. "If a Castilian neighbor found it, if it ever came into the hands of an inquisitor, that would be the end of us."

Mother wouldn't throw it out, but she finally agreed to hide it in the attic, still wrapped in linen, in a hole that Diego cut into one of the walls and plastered over. Then for some reason, when we moved to our house on San Bernardo, we forgot about it.

"We have to get it back." Francisca was pacing the floor. "Listen, we can't leave it there. They know where we have lived, and they'll search everything."

Mother didn't move. She sat at the table, her head in her hands, staring at the wall.

"Mother, are you listening?" Mother looked up at Francisca, but it was clear that she was not focusing on what my sister had just said.

CHAPTER 9

"All right, then, Beatricica and I will go. Come on, Beatriz, we have to hurry."

We ran back to our old house on Caballero de Gracia and told the landlord, whose name was Garrabalde, that we had forgotten something in the house and needed to get it. He must have thought it was odd, but Francisca spun him a convincing story. He led us up the stairs and told the current tenants to let us look.

"It's a keepsake of my mother's," Francisca told them. Their names were Jusepe Something-or-other and his very pregnant wife, María Ordóñez. From the looks of things they were even poorer than we were.

"We may raise a little plaster dust," Francisca told them, "so it might be better if you wait outside. We'll only be a couple of minutes."

Francisca knew exactly where the hole was, and she hacked off the plaster with her sewing scissors. The linen packet was still there, apparently exactly as we had left it. To be doubly sure it was the book, Francisca unwound the cloth. But just as the last fold dropped away, María Ordóñez came into the room.

"What's that in your hand? Don't tell me you've found a book? Let me see."

With that she snatched it out of Francisca's hand and carried it over to the window to show her husband.

"This looks to me like heretic stuff," he said. "Let's see what our downstairs neighbor says. He knows how to read."

"It's not heretic stuff," Francisca said, snatching it back. "It's a *Flos sanctorum*, a book of saints' lives. See what it says here?" Holding it tightly, she opened it up to show him a page. How she came up with that story I'll never know. For all that any of us could read, she could have been holding the book upside down. "Our mother will be delighted that we found it again. Our grandfather used to read to her about the saints."

The skirmish won, we beat a strategic retreat and took the book home with us. Whether Jusepe would tell his neighbor about it, or their parish priest, or maybe the Inquisition, we had no way of knowing. But at least we had found the book.

"What are we going to do with it?" The fear must have been strong in my voice, because Francisca stopped right there in the street and gave me a hug, the way she used to when I was little.

The Barajas Women

"Don't worry, Beatricica; we'll take it home and burn it. Nothing bad is going to happen, you'll see."

What more can I tell Your Worships? I was arrested on June 8 of last year, and I have been sitting in this jail since then. I know that at first I didn't tell you everything. You can understand; I wanted you to know how sincerely I follow the Law of Our Lord Jesus Christ, and that must be the reason why I did not recall all the details of how our family followed the Law of Moses during all those years.

There is no need to have me tortured again. Please, I beg you. That one time was more than enough to jog my memory, and since then I have been completely frank with you. I have told you everything that I can remember. And when something else occurs to me, I always ask for another audience so that I can report it to you.

My sister, Francisca, my mother, my brother, Diego, my uncle Tomé, and my aunt Catalina, they are the ones who persuaded me to live by the Law of Moses. Yes, I know that it was wrong. I know that the Church forbids any Christian to stray from the Law of Jesus Christ. Yes, I knew it then, too. But they were my family, and I was just a little girl. You can't blame me for believing what they told me and doing the things they instructed me to do. It was only when I got older that I began to see how wrong I was to let them influence me, and how they had put my soul in great danger.

When did I draw away from all that? It's exactly what I told you, several times: it was about three months—maybe it was two months—before my arrest. I never told my sister or my mother how I felt. I kept it to myself. But I came to see what a great sin it was to believe in the Law of Moses. All those people told me that's what I had to do to save my soul. And like a ninny, I believed them.

La causa que movio a ser Cristiano fue porque . . . sucedio una tormenta muy grande, y todos los marineros y pasajeros que Venian en la dicha nave . . . invocaron a nuestro Señor Jesucristo que los ayudase, y a San Nicolas, visto lo cual ofrecio en su animo volverse Cristiano si Dios le sacaba de aquella fortuna.

—AHN Inq. Leg. 165, Exp. 11: 63r

10

Carlos Mendes: Turkish Jew, Spanish Christian

MADRID, 1622–1623

October 31, 1622. The afternoon audience.

Inquisitors Gonzalo Chacón and Fernando de Sandoval. The prisoner was brought in and asked to identify himself for the record.

Your Worships, I am called Carlos Mendes, though the name I was given when I was born was Joseph Binán. My father's name, Carlos Mendes, is the same as mine. He went to Constantinople from Lisbon long before I was born, and there he met my mother, Deborah, who is a native of Constantinople. She was still alive when I left there three years ago.

Why did my father leave Portugal? Why do Your Worships think? Because he was a Jew. What other reason could there be? So was my grandfather, Abrão Mendes "el Grande." No, I don't know why he was called that. I always assumed that he was very tall or very fat; though, come to think of it, if he'd been fat he'd have been called "el Gordo." Maybe he was important: my father used to say that back before the Inquisition his father wore the habit of the Order of Santiago. I don't know if that's true, but it doesn't matter anyway. I was born in Istanbul, and my grandfather never left Portugal, so I never met him. Or my paternal grandmother either. In fact, I don't even

291

recall her name, though they told me she was born somewhere in the Portuguese Indies. Brazil, maybe. I don't know where.

Istanbul: that's what the Turks call Constantinople.

Uncles and aunts? A few. My father's brother Benjamin also married a Constantinople girl, doña Juana something. They had one daughter, Sarah, but she's dead now. On my mother's side? Who knows? They were all Greek Jews, so we didn't have anything to do with them. Our people only marry the daughters, not the whole family. Me? I married a Greek, too. My wife, Bienvenida, comes from a Constantinople family of Jews that must go back as far as Abraham. We have three children, two boys and a girl. Why do you ask me for their Christian names? They're all Jews, never baptized, so the only names they have are their Jewish ones.

I can tell by your expressions that you are surprised that I confess all this so openly. Well, why shouldn't I? I have nothing to hide. I was a Jew then too, the same as they were, back before Our Savior brought the light to my soul and showed me the error of my ways. There is no reason for me to be embarrassed about it. I was a Jew, a good Jew. I was even a rabbi. I studied Hebrew in my home city and in Jerusalem, where I was certified by rabbis from Venice, Fez, and the Holy Land. And I led Jewish prayers in Constantinople and in Ancona, too, when I was in Italy. The Jews there praised me for my voice and my knowledge of Torah. You see: I'm not embarrassed. I'm a learned man, and I'm proud of it. I studied with the best scholars in Jerusalem, real sages. I circumcised infants, too. That? That I learned from my father: he wasn't a rabbi, but he had a good hand with the knife. My other duties as a rabbi? I preached at the minyan on Mondays, Thursdays, and Saturdays. I chanted the Psalms. Of course without the "Gloria patri," what did you think? When I was in the synagogue I covered my head with a tallit—yes, that's like a towel, with some Hebrew writing on it. I talked with people about Torah; I studied Talmud with them. Things like that. What rabbis do, I did.

My father, my uncle, they were both merchants. Buying, selling, traveling with their goods from one port to another. Scissors, needles, thimbles, things like that. I began to go with them when I was eight. I know the streets of Rhodes, Cyprus, and Salonica as well as I know the streets of Constantinople: where the synagogues are, the markets, which taverns cater to Jews. The languages, too. You want to make money in that world, you have to speak Greek and Turkish. Arabic doesn't hurt either, especially with the deckhands. Among ourselves, of course, we speak Spanish, or sometimes Portuguese.

And Hebrew for the prayers. My father kept his accounts in Hebrew, too; well, really in Spanish, but using the Jewish letters. I used to do the same thing. I'm still not comfortable with your backward alphabet. I can read it, slowly, with some difficulty, but I can't write it worth a damn.

Let me tell you, we met some wealthy merchants on those ships: silks, fancy furs, cabins to themselves. We couldn't afford that. Because we were Jews, we gave the quartermaster a little something to make sure no one bothered us. We slept in hammocks in the hold during the winter, and in the summer, when the weather was nice, up on deck. Our business was strictly small change. My father could never put together enough money to buy high-class goods to trade. He dreamed and schemed, but nothing came of it. If wishes were fishes . . .

No, I wasn't always with them. On one trip, when I was eleven, we put in at Jaffa, and my father decided to take me up to Jerusalem so I could pray at the Temple wall. The three of us—my uncle Benjamin went, too—stayed in one of the Portuguese hostels in the Holy City, and over dinner, what with one thing and another, my father fixed it for me to study in one of the Portuguese *yeshivot*. Yes, that's a school, a religious school. It was run by a famous rabbi who had come to the Holy Land from Holland. We only had about half the money for the tuition, but somehow my father persuaded him to take me as a pupil. I think he convinced him that I was such a bright lad that it would be a sin against the Jewish people if I were not well educated. Of course he also promised to pay the rabbi the rest of the money when he came back for me in a year. That turned out to be two years, not one, and when he finally came for me he had only part of the money. The rabbi raised a ruckus, but what could he do? He took what my father offered and sent me on my way.

What did they teach me at that school? Talmud, Mishnah, the different holiday chants, how to settle disputes by finding the precedent texts. What Jews study.

Anyway, as I was saying, on the way back to Constantinople from Cyprus my father died of the coughing disease. The captain ordered him buried at sea, even though we protested that was against the Jewish Law. My uncle Benjamin tried to keep things going, but it turns out he was even worse at business than my father, and after another couple of trips my uncle called it quits, leaving me to make a living on my own. My father left me only debts. And my mother's family was no help. I took whatever jobs I could find: unloading ships on the quay, carrying packages for people shopping in the markets, cleaning tables in the portside taverns. Living by my labor and my wits with

Carlos Mendes: Turkish Jew, Spanish Christian

my friends who were doing the same thing. No, they weren't all Jews. Most of them were Turks, or Greek Christians, and there were some Armenians, too, as well as a few Russians. They used to call me "Bushboy" because my beard was so heavy. What we all had in common was that none of us knew where our next meal was coming from.

December 18, 1622. The morning audience.

Michael de Tricala, age thirty-five, a Greek.

Yes, I know this man Carlos, but I don't think I ever heard his last name. Since I've been in Madrid I have seen him two or three times in the great courtyard in front of the palace. He's a medium-sized man, dark faced, with a thick black beard. He has a bald spot on top of his head like a cleric, even though he was born a Jew. How do I know he's a Jew? Because he himself told me so two or three times.

I used to live in Epiro; that's a Turkish city on the Vointza River, near where the Albanians live. That's where I first saw don Carlos. He was dressed like a Turk, with a huge turban, and they were leading him along on a red horse that was all decked out with fancy trappings. He was surrounded by Turks, several of them holding out silver begging bowls, and they were crying: "For Allah's sake, open your purses for this poor Jew whom Allah has moved to become a Turk." I saw him dressed like that several times, always with the same crowd of Turks. That begging must have collected a lot of money because they were always at it. One day, I was in the shop of a Greek named Jorge Casacas, I saw them coming down the street the way they always did, and this Greek storekeeper said to me that he would never give money for a Jew to become a Turk. Now, if he wanted to become a Christian instead, then he would have been delighted to open his purse.

Anyway, that's why I was so surprised ten days ago when I saw don Carlos in Madrid dressed in a black cassock like a priest. I asked him about it, and he said he had recently been ordained in Rome. He told Fray Gabriel Malara that, too, and that Cypriot priest, Salome Santino. I assume he was lying, since he had told me earlier that he was a priest of his own law and that he used to circumcise young boys.

December 20, 1622. The morning audience.

Carlos Mendes was brought from his cell, reminded of his oath, and informed of the specific charges against him.

If that's what some witness told you, that he saw me in Constantinople or some other city dressed like a Turk, then he's lying. Or he's mistaken. But even if it were true—and it isn't—, what difference would it make? It's not important, and it's no reason to put me in prison. Haven't I freely confessed to you that back then I was not a Christian? I was a Jew. I was baptized only two years ago, so I couldn't have been sinning in any way against the Law of Jesus before that. As for that business about circumcising, though, that is true, as I have freely confessed: I was a Jewish priest, and I did circumcise young boys. But that was long before I was baptized and accepted the true faith.

I can't believe that someone said that I claimed to be a priest. Tell me how that could be. A brand-new convert ordained as a priest?! When I can't even read or write Latin? I am surprised that you even listened to such foolishness. And they accuse me of having celebrated mass! Well, if I was a priest I would have, wouldn't I? But I'm not; and I didn't.

What did I do after my father died? Like I said, a bit of this and a bit of that. Whatever I could find. Manual labor mostly. And circumcising. I was good at that: gentle with the baby, quick with the knife, and with all the formalities and decorum you could wish. People looked for me, sought me out. They didn't care what my other jobs were. People do what they have to do. They respected me for what I know.

Circumcising is a profitable business because they always serve a good meal after the ceremony and people usually tip you really well. It is competitive, though. All the rabbis in Constantinople want to do it, especially for the rich families. You get your clients by word of mouth. Or when you pray with the different minyans around the city you can let it be known that you are available. You can't make a living exclusively from circumcising, but it helps. And it is steady work: people will have babies, no matter what.

That was how I lived for more than ten years. A little of this and that. I even earned enough to take a wife. I think I already said that. Bienvenida and I lived in a little apartment in Balat, up the hill from the Ahrida Synagogue. From the roof you can see the harbor and the bridge that takes you across the Golden Horn to Galata, where the rich Jews live. When our children were small—we have three of them, two girls and a boy; I think I already told you that, too—, well, when they were small and we had enough money, we'd go for walks along the quay by the bridge and lunch on sardines fresh from the fishing boats. They grilled them right there on the quay, on charcoal braziers. Octopus, too; though we didn't eat that.

Carlos Mendes: Turkish Jew, Spanish Christian

Unfortunately, the good times didn't last. It was the competition. The days when we had enough money for grilled sardines became few and far between. To supplement my income I started to travel out to the small towns where there were only a few Jews, to perform circumcisions there. Some were in Turkey, but I did better in the towns in Greece. The big cities like Monastir, Kastoria, and Johanina had their own rabbis, of course, but the villages . . . The rabbis didn't like to ride out there for just one or two circumcisions. Me, I would go anywhere. I'd enter a town, find out where the minyan was praying, and then ask who had recently given birth. I had a regular circuit, and even though the parents had to wait longer than the eight days prescribed in the Talmud, they would hold their business for me. When I traveled, sometimes I'd be gone for weeks at a time, even months.

There were nights I went hungry, but most of the time I did all right. Bienvenida? I brought home what money I could, but it was never all that much. Her family sent her things sometimes. If it hadn't been for them and for the aprons she stitched and sold, there were times when I think that she and the children would have starved to death.

Finally, about three years ago, I decided that I had to find a way to do better. Greece, at least in the villages, was growing poorer year by year. And in the big-city minyans all the men talked about was how the Turks had let things get so bad, and how good life was for Jews in Italy. We Portuguese all had some relative or other there, in Venice or Ancona or one of the other port cities, and the news filtered back. It's not that the Italian streets were paved with gold, but everyone said that there was money for the making if you were clever and had a little luck. That was good enough for me. A couple of years earlier my wife's father, Isaac Aboasijo, had moved to Venice, and I made up my mind to go look him up. I told Bienvenida that I would be gone for a while but that I would soon be sending her more money than she had ever dreamed of. And in the meantime, if things got really desperate, she should go back to her family. Or ask the Widows and Orphans Society for help.

That's really all there is to tell. I came to Venice. I looked for my father-in-law, but he'd moved away. I decided to become a Christian. I was ordained as a priest in Rome. And here I am.

Why are you looking at me like that? You don't think I am a priest? Well, I've said what I've said.

🕱

CHAPTER 10

October 18, 1622. The morning audience.

Constantino de Constantinopla, a Greek, age thirty-one.

I've known don Carlos for nearly three years. When I met him in Constantinople, I was called Ali. He wasn't called don Carlos yet: that was the name they gave him when they baptized him in Aragoza. Aragoza? It's just outside of Venice; it's where the Franciscans give you lessons about how to become a Christian. Anyway, don Carlos's name in Constantinople was Ibrahin, which the Jews say as Abraham. Since I was on my way to Italy as well, the two of us decided to travel together. My intention all along was to become a Christian; but don Carlos only decided to convert along the way.

When we got to Venice they directed us to Aragoza. The brothers gave us beds, they fed us, and for forty days the monks taught us all about the Christian faith and how to pray the Christian prayers. When they finished the sessions they took Ibrahin to the Church of San Francisco and baptized him and gave him his new name. I decided to wait to get baptized in Rome. I don't know why; it was just a dream I had. So after a couple of days we left together to go there. Carlos was wearing Christian clothes by then, but I was still dressed as a Turk. Anyway, we traveled along together, begging for alms as we went. When people learned that I was on my way to Rome to accept Jesus, they opened their hearts and their purses, so we ate well and we always slept indoors. When we got to Ancona, Carlos told me he wanted to be on his own in Ancona for a few days. Then he would look for me again and we would go to Rome. There are a lot of Jews in Ancona, and Carlos knew some of them from before. He took off his Christian clothes and put on Jewish ones that his friends gave him and went with them to the synagogue. He didn't use the name Carlos there either, only Abraham.

As it turned out, we both stayed in Ancona for a month and a half, and after that we went to Rome. I was still dressed like a Turk, and Carlos was wearing his Jewish clothes. "Alms, give us alms," Carlos would say to everyone we met along the way. We used to stand in the street with the saddest expression we could muster on our faces and in a little sing-song voice cry out: "Help this poor Jew and this poor Turk go to Rome so they can declare their love of Jesus to His Holiness the Pope and be welcomed into the bosom of the Church." It was a miracle: not only did we earn enough to eat, but we both had money in our pockets when we got to Rome.

So, as I said, in Rome I was baptized and I got my new name, Constantino. Carlos persuaded me to hide the fact that I was now a Christian so that

Carlos Mendes: Turkish Jew, Spanish Christian

we could keep on begging. After a few weeks, though, I grew tired of playing the would-be convert; also I was ashamed. Besides, we weren't making as much money as we had on the road. So I left Italy for Spain in the company of some soldiers. I don't know how long Carlos stayed behind in Rome. I didn't see him again until just a few weeks ago in the palace courtyard.

October 20, 1622. The morning audience.

Carlos Mendes was brought from his cell and read the summary of the evidence against him.

It has to be one of my enemies who told you that story about Aragoza and Ancona and begging on the road. It's all a pack of lies. I swear it. I have lots of enemies, as I've explained to you. They are angry with me because I accepted the Law of Jesus, so they make up these stories to damage my character. As for Aragoza, I've never even heard of such a place. In the Duchy of Venice? I don't think so. Have they told you the name of the monastery? Or said who it was who baptized me, and who witnessed it? There isn't one word of truth in it. Not one!

October 21, 1622. The afternoon audience.

Clemente Icatina, a Greek from Monte San Basilio, age forty-one.

I met Carlos Mendes in Madrid about two months ago in a tavern near the courtyard of the Royal Palace. When he heard my accent he came up to me and asked me if I was from Salonica. Well, we got to talking, and since we had traveled to some of the same cities and since we both knew some of the same people, we became friends. Carlos told me that he'd been baptized twice, once in Rome and once in Florence, where the Great Duke of Florence himself served as his godfather. I don't know whether to believe that or not, but you could ask the Nuncio. I know that he knows don Carlos, because Carlos has been asking him for money. Unsuccessfully, I think, to hear the way Carlos talked about him, calling him a God-cursed dog and a hypocrite to his faith. Carlos is like that. He gets angry and forgets to watch his tongue. Another time he brought back a letter from the Escorial authorizing somebody here at court to give him some money—it was charity, don Carlos told me, not some debt that he was owed—and when Carlos went to collect it the man wouldn't cough it up. Carlos cursed him, too. He said that if Christians were going to be this tight-fisted he would just as soon go back to Constantinople to live as a Jew again with his wife and children.

October 26, 1622. The morning audience.

Carlos Mendes was brought from his cell. The prosecutor read him the summary of the accusations.

Another pack of lies. Ask the Nuncio. He'll tell you. The only truth in all that is that they treat us Greeks very shabbily here in Spain. There is no sense of hospitality, and no sense of charity at all. It's worse even than in Greece. I was talking one day with Pablo Ríos, he's a Greek Christian who lives here in Madrid, and he was complaining that no one would help him here in Spain, even though when foreigners go to Constantinople the Greeks shower them with hospitality. I told him that was a crock of shit because Greeks and Turks were just as stingy as Spaniards, and he shouted at me to keep my nose out of it, that if I didn't shut up he would see that I was burned. So if you've heard any of this slander from him you should forget it. He would say anything to get me in trouble. Sagria the Cypriot is another one, and that friend of his who makes rosaries. Just because I tell the truth and I don't support their mistaken ideas they hate me and pursue me and want to destroy me.

October 28, 1622. The morning audience.

Captain Pablo Paterno, age thirty-six. He resides in an inn on the Cava de San Francisco, in a new house with a tower. When he is in Sicily, he serves the Inquisition as an interpreter. Deposition taken in the Office of the Inquisition in Madrid.

Of course I know don Carlos Mendes: I brought him here to Spain, from Ostia to Valencia. That's where my ship is now, in the harbor, having some work done on the hull. I've been here on business in Madrid for about four months.

I saw don Carlos here at the Nuncio's house, where he'd gone to ask for money. We left together, and when we got outside I could see that he was very upset. He began to curse the Patriarch in a loud voice because he hadn't given him anything. He said that the Patriarch's faith was false, his soul was cursed, and other things like that. He said the Patriarch had sold him out and that his soul would end up where Judas's was.

When Carlos gets worked up, he says things that would scorch the ears of a saint. He could give the Devil himself a lesson in cursing. He'd bellow that all Christians were hypocrites. The Holy Trinity was a joke, and so was the sacrament of the Eucharist. "Take me back to Constantinople," he'd say. "I'd rather live with Jews and Turks. At least they're honest about their faith!"

Carlos Mendes: Turkish Jew, Spanish Christian

When he wasn't angry he was quite a pleasant fellow. Actually I saw quite a bit of don Carlos. We sometimes took our evening meal together at the same tavern. He used to say that Salonica was the best city in the world for Jews and Turks, because they were there in equal numbers and got along very well together. He told me that his father was from that city. He said that his father—no, I think it was his grandfather, or his great-grandfather—had come there from Spain with his son on account of certain problems he had with the king. He told me that when he got to Constantinople, he converted to become a Jew. But I don't believe that he converted. He was probably a Jew all along. Most of the Spaniards and Portuguese in the Ottoman cities are; that's why they went there. Don Álvaro de Mendes, he said his name was. He indicated that he was related somehow to the duke of the Infantado.

I assume that the Nuncio asked you to arrest don Carlos because of all the slanderous things he said about him. I myself have heard the Nuncio say more than once that he holds don Carlos in low opinion.

January 23, 1623. The morning audience.

The prisoner Carlos Mendes was brought to the chamber and reminded that he was still under oath.

I keep telling you: it has to be one of my enemies who told you all these slanderous things. I would never curse the Eucharist or deny the Holy Trinity. Why would I? I had become a Christian, freely, of my own free will. Nobody forced me to convert. I recognize the truth of the Law of Jesus, and I fear for my soul. I know that Jesus is my only Savior. There is no way I would have said such things.

Could I have been drinking? Well, to that I won't say no. Sometimes I have a glass or two in the afternoon, maybe three or four in the evening. And it's possible that sometimes when I get angry and have maybe one or two glasses too many . . . Yes; then I do tend to say things that I would never say if I was in my right mind. But show me a man who doesn't do that, and I'll show you a man who is already long dead.

And as for going back to Turkey . . . Never. I am a Christian now, and I want to live in a Christian kingdom with my fellow Christians. If I can put together enough money, then what I will do is send for my wife and my children so that they can come here and learn to love Jesus and save their souls as I have.

You know I'm telling the truth about being a Christian. Haven't you tested me? The Our Father, the Ave Maria, the Apostles' Creed? You heard me say them all perfectly. You saw me cross myself exactly the way all Christians do. I know there are lots of false converts here in Spain. I know that from personal experience. But I am not one of them.

For example who? Well, Domingo de Acosta, for one. He came here from Lisbon, but he tells everybody that his family is all in Africa, and that he wants to go back there so he can live like the Jew that he has always been because he's tired of being a Christian. No, I don't know if anybody else can attest to that. He told me those things in Arabic, and not everybody understands that tongue. What does he look like? He's fat and short, with straggly white hair.

I'll name you another one, too. There's a Greek Christian here in Madrid called Estéfano. I knew him back in Constantinople. His parents were so determined that he should become a priest that he renounced them and became a Muslim. He lived near my family in Balat so I saw him going into the mosques to pray. He dressed like a Moor, and he practiced all their customs, right out in public, so he could drive his parents crazy. Finally he got fed up with the life in Constantinople and went to Algiers. But he didn't stay there either, at least not for very long, because I saw him in Madrid just before I was arrested. He must have had a run of bad luck because now he's the slave of a widow woman who lives near the Church of San Francisco. He says he's a Christian—well, he has to be if he is living in Madrid, right?—but he still dresses like a Moor, and he calls himself Hassan. You can find him if you look: he's about forty years old, thin as a toothpick, and he cloaks himself in a black jelaba like the Moors wear in Africa. Wears a gold chain.

June 9, 1623. The morning audience.

Inquisitors Bernardo de Quiroz and Gonzalo Chacón. The prisoner Carlos Mendes was brought in. He was advised of the formal charges against him. To wit:

- that after his baptism in Aragoza he had reverted to Judaism in Ancona;
- that after being baptized in Aragoza he was baptized a second time in Rome;
- and a third time in Florence;
- that he blasphemed against the sacraments;
- that he expressed a wish to return to Constantinople to become a Jew again.

Carlos Mendes: Turkish Jew, Spanish Christian

The prisoner, having denied the truth of these allegations, was taken to the torture chamber and shown the instruments of torture. He was admonished to tell the truth for the sake of his soul and to spare himself the rigors of torture. The prisoner fell to his knees, kissed the inquisitors' feet, and, groaning and sobbing, begged that the inquisitors deal mercifully with him. At don Gonzalo Chacón's request, the bailiff raised the prisoner to his feet, loosened the bonds on his wrists, and brought him a chair.

Your Graces, it's true: not everything I told you before was completely accurate. The real truth of the matter is this. I did leave Constantinople for Venice with the intention of finding my father-in-law, Isaac Aboasijo. But along the way I resolved to become a Christian as soon as I arrived. The reason I changed my mind was that while I was on shipboard we were swept by a great storm. All the crew and all the rest of the passengers were Christian, and together they prayed to Our Lord Jesus Christ and to Saint Nicholas of Bari to help them survive the storm. I was frightened to death, and seeing their faith, I swore that if God saved us from that storm I would become Christian, too.

Well, we survived. And as soon as I got to Venice I sought out the chief catechist to ask him where Jews went to become Christians. That was in Aragoza, with the Franciscans. He said he would baptize me, and he did. I don't remember his name, or the name of the man who stood up with me as my godfather, except that it was something Romano. The name they baptized me with was Joseph. Carlos? No, that name came later.

After that I remained in Venice for a month and a half, living completely as a Christian. From there I went to Ancona, and I stayed there for eight days or so, maybe two weeks. I found my father-in-law, Isaac Aboasijo, who had moved there from Venice. In Ancona I dressed as a Jew, because I had a lot of friends there and I wanted to see them and be with them and go to the synagogue with them. If they'd known I was a Christian they would not have had anything to do with me. After all, I know all the Jewish prayers, all the customs. I had been a rabbi, I had studied in Jerusalem, so it was not difficult for me. Why did I do that? I suppose that the Devil deceived me into going back to my former Law. And I wanted to please my father-in-law. He thought I was going back to Turkey so he gave me some money to take to his daughter.

But instead I used it to pay my traveling expenses. I know I never should have pretended to be a Jew again. I felt bad about it at the time, and I still do. Did I tell my Jewish friends that I had been baptized? Certainly not. Why would I do that? They didn't have the slightest suspicion that I had done it.

When I left Ancona I put on my Christian clothes again. I spent a couple of days in Loreto and then headed for Florence. When I got there I asked where I could learn more about Christianity, and they took me to the Jesuits at San Giovaninno who instructed me and baptized me in their parish church of San Giovanni Battista. No, I don't recall the name of the priest who performed the baptism, but he's the one who gave me the name Carlos. Carlos of the Most Holy Sacrament. Why did I do it, if I had already been baptized in Venice? It was because of a dream I had while I was traveling, that if I didn't become completely Christian, the next time I went out on the sea I would surely drown. That's why I did it, to persevere in the Law of Christ. But if I had known then that a person cannot be baptized more than once, then I never would have done it.

As I said before, after Ancona I went to Rome. The Papal Nuncio in Florence had given me letters of introduction to Cardinal Montalvo and Cardinal Burgesio, asking them to find some employment for me and to present me to His Holiness the pope, which they did. His Holiness in turn gave me a letter for Our Lord King Felipe, which I gave to don Baltazar de Zúñiga when I got to Madrid so that he could give it to the King. Don Baltazar gave me a suit of clothes and arranged for me to take my meals at the Nuncio's palace. He also found me a job with don Diego de Guzmán, the king's chaplain and almsman. Do you know him? He's the man who distributes the charitable donations that the King wishes, including some to me. Sometimes, when he didn't follow through with those gifts, it's true that I got angry with him and cursed him and said that I'd rather go back to Constantinople and be a Jew with my wife and children than to serve such people. When I was angry I'd say things like I didn't believe in the cross that he wore on his breast or in the sacrament of the Eucharist that he celebrated in mass. But I don't believe those things. It's just that when I get so worked up I can't control my tongue.

Did I ever claim to be a priest? I knew you would get around to asking me that again. I think I told you once that I had been ordained. I'm sorry: I shouldn't have said that. That wouldn't be possible; you and I both know that. The truth is that sometimes when people saw me wearing a cassock and asked me if I was an ordained priest I said I was. But I've never been ordained,

Carlos Mendes: Turkish Jew, Spanish Christian

and I've never professed in any religious order. That's the whole truth. I'm sorry that I misled you. I didn't mean to deceive you, but my tongue got away from me. I beg you to have mercy on me.

I'd be pleased to answer the rest of your questions. Whatever I can. But couldn't we go upstairs, where it's more comfortable?

No, no, Your Graces; it's all right, I'm fine right here.

Do I know that the Law of Moses is contrary to that of Christ? Of course I do. That's why I resolved to leave it, and to follow the Evangelical Law to save my soul. Do I go to confession? Yes, of course, and take communion, too. Six or seven times in Italy, and even more than that here in Spain. But as I said, I never confessed all my baptisms, or the time in Ancona that I went back to being a Jew. No, that's not accurate. I did confess it once, last year in Florence, to a Father Agapito. I told him I'd been baptized two times.

Three times? No, Your Graces: twice. Once in Venice and once in Florence. Did I say Rome, too? No, the priest in Florence told me to go to Rome, but I wasn't baptized there. What happened was that Father Agapito told me that being baptized twice was highly irregular, and that I should go to Rome to ask His Holiness for a dispensation. Not to baptize me again, to pardon me. But when I got to Rome the pope was sick, so I couldn't speak to him. And as for taking the sacrament when I hadn't been absolved of my double baptism, I didn't think that was so important. I mean, when I was passing through Zaragoza on my way to Madrid I asked a priest there if it was all right, and he told me to go with God. No, I don't recall his name.

Why didn't I confess all this when you first arrested me? I think the Devil must have blinded me and persuaded me that the safest thing was to keep quiet. But now God has opened my eyes and freed me to tell the truth, the way I have today.

Your Graces, I am a good, God-fearing Christian. I have a clear conscience. Since I converted I only associate with good Christian people, virtuous people. I have received so many favors from the hand of God. He has brought me the knowledge of his Holy Law. He has shown me the light, and taught me the true path to salvation. And if that was not sufficient, he has sustained me in my quest to live purely in accordance with his Christian Law. I was born a Jew, and I was taught to follow all its mistaken doctrines. But now I am converted, and I know that now my soul will be saved.

I beg you, Your Graces, have mercy on me.

Notes and Sources

Chapter 1. Beatriz Núñez

In Guadalupe Ferdinand and Isabel's ad hoc Inquisition tribunal operated throughout 1485. This was one of the first rounds of show trials, designed to put a dread of nonconformity into the converso community. Mercy could come later. As result of their proceedings, seven autos-de-fé were held in the monastery's cemetery that year. Twenty-five conversos who had had the foresight to run for their lives before the inquisitors could take them were burned only in effigy. Another 52 conversos were burned alive at the stake, among them, on July 23, Beatriz Núñez and her stepson, Manuel González. The bodies of another 48 conversos convicted of Judaizing were exhumed and their bones burned. The Inquisition confiscated the property of all 125 victims, amounting to 7,286 ducats, enough money to construct a palatial royal residence to house the king and queen during their visits to Guadalupe.

In the course of the inquisitorial purge of 1485 many townspeople testified that numerous monks inside the monastery were observant crypto-Jews. Subsequently the Jeronymite order conducted an internal inquisition, which led to the imprisonment of many monks, the burning of the most blatant Judaizer, Fray Diego de Marchena, and a policy change that resulted in the order rejecting membership by any new-Christians.

This chapter is based on two trials preserved in the Inquisition section of Madrid's Archivo Histórico Nacional:

Legajo 164, Expediente 2. Beatriz Núñez, vecina de la puebla de Guadalupe

Legajo 154, Expediente 371. Manuel González

Additional material is drawn from the following sources.

Fita y Colomé, Fidel. "Proceso de Beatriz Núñez, natural de Ciudad Real y vecina de Guadalupe (13 enero–31 julio, 1485)." *Boletín de la Real Academia de la Historia* 23 (1883): 289–341.

Longhurst, John Edward. *The Age of Torquemada*. Lawrence, KS: Coronado Press, 1964.

Sicroff, Albert A. *Les controverses des statuts de "pureté de sang" en Espagne du XVᵉ au XVIIᵉ siècle*. Paris: Didier, 1960.

———. "The Jeronymite Monastery of Guadalupe in 14th and 15th-Century Spain." In *Collected Studies in Honour of Américo Castro's Eightieth Year*, ed. M. P. Hornik, 397–422. Oxford: Oxford University Press, 1965.

Starr-LeBeau, Gretchen D. *In the Shadow of the Virgin: Inquisitors, Friars, and Conversos in Guadalupe, Spain*. Princeton: Princeton University Press, 2003.

Chapter 2. The Arias Dávila Clan

Diego Arias Dávila's tower house is today the second tallest building in Segovia, exceeded in height only by the cathedral's spires. The memorial inscriptions on his wives' graves have disappeared.

Bishop Juan Arias is fondly remembered as one of Segovia's most distinguished bishops and one of the initiators of the Renaissance in Spain. The cathedral museum displays some of his resplendent embroidered ceremonial capes. The street leading from the tower house to San Martín Church is named for him.

Diego and Elvira's grandson Pedrarias Dávila, perhaps because of his treatment of Balboa, is today remembered in Central America as one of the cruelest and most ruthless conquistadors.

The only member of the vast Arias Dávila clan to end his life at the stake was Elvira González's nephew Jerónimo de la Paz, burnt sometime between July 1487, the date of his last deposition, and October 1489, when his wife, María de Paz, reported him dead.

The witness testimony is drawn from AHN, Sección Inquisición, Legajo 1413, Expediente 7. This dossier—containing excerpts of 245 separate depositions that were logged during a seven-year investigation—was published by Carlos Carrete Parrondo, *Proceso inquisitorial contra los Arias Dávila segovianos: Un enfrentamiento social entre judíos y conversos*, Fontes iudaeorum regni castellae, vol. 3 (Salamanca: Universidad Pontificia de Salamanca / Universidad de Granada, 1986).

Additional material is drawn from the following sources.

Bernáldez, Andrés. *Historia de los Reyes Católicos don Fernando y doña Isabel.* Crónicas de los Reyes de Castilla, III, vol. 70. Madrid: Biblioteca de Autores Españoles, 1953.

Contreras Jiménez, María Eugenia. "Los Arias de Ávila: Consolidación de un linaje en la Segovia del siglo XV." In *Arias Dávila: Obispo y mecenas. Segovia en el siglo XV*, ed. Ángel Galindo García, 99–114. Salamanca: Universidad Pontificia, 1998.

Echagüe Burgos, Jorge Javier. *La corona y Segovia en tiempos de Enrique IV (1440–1474): Una relación conflictiva.* Segovia: Diputación Provincial de Segovia, 1993.

Galindo García, Ángel, ed. *Arias Dávila: Obispo y mecenas. Segovia en el siglo XV.* Salamanca: Universidad Pontificia, 1998.

Gini de Barnatán, Matilde. "Mujeres sefarditas y criptojudías, herederas del universo español." In *Los caminos de Cervantes y Sefarad: Actas del II Congreso Internacional*, 183–204. Zamora: Asociación Caminos de Cervantes y Sefarad, 1994.

Gitlitz, David M. *Los Arias Dávila de Segovia: Entre la sinagoga y la iglesia.* San Francisco: International Scholars Press, 1996.

González Novalín, José Luis. "Juan Arias Dávila, obispo de Segovia, y la Inquisición española." In *Arias Dávila: Obispo y mecenas. Segovia en el siglo XV*, ed. Ángel Galindo García, 181–99. Salamanca: Universidad Pontificia, 1998.

Marqués de Lozoya. "Los sepulcros de los Arias Dávila." *Estudios segovianos* 9 (1957): 25–26, 67–81.

Rábade Obradó, María del Pilar. *Los judeoconversos en la corte y en la época de los Reyes Católicos.* Madrid: Universidad Complutense, Facultad de Geografía e Historia, Departamento de Historia Medieval, 1990.

———. "Religiosidad y práctica cristiana en la familia Arias de Ávila." In *Arias Dávila: Obispo y mecenas. Segovia en el siglo XV*, ed. Ángel Galindo García, 201–20. Salamanca: Universidad Pontificia, 1998.

Romero de Lecea, Carlos. *Sinodal de Aguilafuente.* Vol. 1. Madrid: Joyas Bibliográficas, 1965.

Chapter 3. The Doctor's Daughters

On April 18, 1574, the San Juan sisters learned their fates at the auto-de-fé celebrated in Córdoba, whose Inquisition by then had assumed jurisdiction for Baeza.

Leonor de San Juan, the eldest sister, whose knowledge of the law had been insufficient to clear her, and Juana de San Juan, the youngest and with Leonor the least repentant of the sisters, were condemned to wear the sambenito, the cloak of shame, in the auto-de-fé. They were sentenced to jail for life without possibility of parole, and their property was confiscated.

Elvira, who had indoctrinated her husband, Francisco de Écija Zayas, Isabel "the Weather Vane," and Bernardina de San Juan, whose husband, Dr. Juan Infante, had set the chain of arrests in motion, were also condemned to wear the sambenito in the auto-de-fé. Each was sentenced to jail for life and her property confiscated.

María de San Juan, the sister who had been so moved by the Holy Thursday processions, was also condemned to wear the sambenito. She was sentenced to jail for two years or more at the discretion of the Inquisitor General and members of his council. Her property, too, was confiscated.

In this same auto-de-fé three other members of the family were reconciled with the Church.

Elvira's husband, Francisco de Écija Zayas, was twenty-nine when he was arrested in June 1573. Like the sisters, he had an old-Christian father and a new-Christian mother. Although he admitted to having read some Jewish books, like the story of Joseph, he denied having actively Judaized, and he attempted to discredit the sisters' testimony by declaring them his enemies. None of this struck the inquisitors as credible. Then, under torture, Francisco apparently came clean. He recounted how when his wife tried to induce him to Judaize, he was furious with her and for several days would not even talk to her. But then he agreed to give it a try and soon was Judaizing enthusiastically with Elvira and her sisters. When the girls were arrested, Francisco decided to flee. He gathered his funds and the merchandise he planned to sell along the way and was about to leave Baeza when the Inquisition's bailiffs came for him. At his audience he told Fray Pedro that he had planned to go to Rome to ask the pope to pardon him and give him a document that would say that he had made his penance and was absolved of his sins. Francisco was condemned to wear the sambenito and was sentenced to jail for life, with the first three years to be spent rowing in His Majesty's galleys without salary. As was common practice, his property was confiscated.

The girls' aunt Catalina Gutiérrez, widow of the doctor Hernán Rodríguez from Jaén, was arrested in December 1573. She told Fray Pedro and Fray Teófilo that her main Judaizing activity was fasting. They did not believe her. Under torture she confessed that she had been Judaizing for twenty-six years. Her sentence was similar to the others: sambenito, life imprisonment, and confiscation of all her property.

Elvira Gutiérrez, the sisters' other aunt and widow of the spice dealer Hernando de Baeza, was fifty-seven years old when she was arrested. She also said that her main Judaizing activity was fasting, to which she had been induced by what she called the "bad company she kept." It turned out that the bad company was her own sister and her six nieces, especially Isabel and Juana, who talked to her about the coming Messiah, told her which foods were forbidden to Jews, and cautioned her about getting too caught up in the worship of images because they were only "wooden idols made for Gentiles." While she was being held in prison pending further interrogation she took sick and died. At the auto-de-fé she was reconciled to the Church in effigy and granted permission to be buried in sanctified ground. Her property was confiscated.

We know nothing about the daughter mentioned in Leonor's testimony, or whether any of the other married daughters had children.

The surviving records of the Cordoban Inquisition cover another hundred years. Not one person named San Juan or Gutiérrez appears among the lists of people accused of Judaizing. If the San Juan sisters were paroled and returned to society, as was generally the case even when people had been sentenced to life in prison, they seem to have successfully assimilated into the Catholic mainstream, for although the Inquisition undoubtedly watched them closely, they were never again charged.

The documents on which this chapter is based were published by Rafael Gracia Boix, *Autos de fe y causas de la Inquisición de Córdoba* (Córdoba: Diputación Provincial, 1983), 131–42.

Notes and Sources

Chapter 4. The Rojas and Torres Women

In 1591 inquisitors in Granada became aware of a large group of third- and fourth-generation conversos still showing evidence of Judaizing practices. Their investigations led to trials in which 88 individuals—14 men and 74 women, among them the 6 Rojas and Torres women—were convicted of heresy.

The documents are mute about the three sisters' ancestry. If indeed they were conversas, it appears that their parents had successfully assimilated into mainstream Christian Granada. The sentencing document makes clear that the Portuguese housemaid was the principal Jewish influence in their lives and that the nieces learned their Judaizing from their three aunts.

Catalina de Rojas, Leonor de Rojas, and Leonor's daughter Costanza Vázquez were each made to wear the penitential sambenito in the 1593 auto-de-fé in Granada in which they were reconciled to the Church, and each was sentenced to one year in prison.

Juana de Rojas changed her story several times under questioning, alleging that she had been so upset during the early sessions that she didn't know what she was saying. She, too, was reconciled to the Church while wearing a sambenito, but her inconsistency was interpreted as willful evasion, and she was sentenced to two years in prison.

Catalina de la Torre was likewise reconciled while wearing a sambenito, and that was the extent of her punishment.

Inés de Torres, the other niece, became seriously ill when she was in prison. The inquisitors never finished questioning her but instead sent for a priest to hear her confession. The last document in the dossier says that after heated debate the inquisitors gave permission for her to be buried with modest ceremony in holy ground in the Church of Santiago in Granada and that masses should be said for her soul but without, however, mentioning her name. At the auto-de-fé at which the other women received their penance, a small statue of Inés, dressed in a sambenito, was symbolically reconciled to the Church.

This chapter is based on the summary data recorded in the Inquisition section of the Archivo Histórico Nacional in Madrid: Legajo 1953, Expediente 29. Additional material is drawn from María Antonia Bel Bravo, *El auto de fe de 1593: Los conversos granadinos de origen judío* (Granada: Universidad de Granada, 1988).

Chapter 5. The Three Fonseca Miners

The three miners were not the only Fonsecas living in the mining towns and Mexico City in those years, and having the name Fonseca was not in itself indicative of Jewish or even Portuguese ancestry. Among the Mexican Fonsecas in the early seventeenth century were three individuals named Pedro de Fonseca: one was a gatekeeper for the Inquisition, one an Inquisition notary, and the third a nuncio of the Holy Office. Antonio de Fonseca served the Inquisition as notary of confiscations. Juan de Fonseca was a member of the Viceregal Council.

This chapter is based on documents preserved in Mexico's Archivo General de la Nación.

Audiencia Mercedes. Vol. 10, folios 100v–101r. Disputa sobre un herido de agua para ingenio.

General de Parte. Vol. 4, Expediente 304, folio 87v. Reparto de azogue a Héctor Fonseca.

Indiferente Virreinal. Caja 4383, Expediente 007. Jorge de Almeida debe al Real fisco 6,535 pesos.

Inquisición. Vol. 1A, Expediente 38. Héctor de Fonseca contesta petición de divorcio.

———. Vol. 127, Expediente 1. Causa de Tomás de Fonseca Castellanos. 1589.

———. Vol. 156, Expediente 4. Causa de Tomás de Fonseca, mozo. 1595.

———. Vol. 158, Expediente 1. Causa de Héctor de Fonseca, minero de las Minas de Taxco. 1596.

———. Vol. 158, Expediente 3. Causa de Tomás de Fonseca, vecino de Talpuxagua. 1596.

———. Vol. 158, Expediente 4. Proceso contra Antonio Díaz Márquez. 1596.

———. Vol. 271, Expediente 1. Duarte Rodríguez contra Héctor de Fonseca y otros. 1604.

———. Vol. 276, Expediente 14. Manuel Gil de la Guardia: Información sobre Héctor de Fonseca. 1605.

———. Vol. 1489, Expediente 1. Luis de Carvajal: Información sobre los Fonseca. 1595.

———. Vol. 1490, Expediente 3. Causa de doña Mariana de Carvajal. 1600.

———. Vol. 1527, Expediente 1. Causa de Tomás de Fonseca Castellanos, mercader tratante en las minas de Taxco. 1589–91.

Real Fisco. Vol. 6, Expediente 5, folios 257–330. Secuestro de bienes de Tomás de Fonsca. 1596.

———. Vol. 8, Expediente 11, folios 280–318. Demanda sobre los bienes confiscados a Tomás de Fonseca el Viejo. 1601.

————. Vol. 9, Expediente 3, folios 73–81. Inventorio de los bienes confiscados a
Tomás de Fonseca el Viejo. 1604.
Regio Patronato Indiano: Capellanías. Vol. 269, folios 393–93 bis. Capellanía que
fundó Felipa de Fonseca. 1591.
Tierras, Vol. 91, folios 1–59. Disputa sobre un herido de agua. 1577.

Additional material is drawn from the following sources.
Adler, Cyrus. *Trial of Jorge de Almeida by the Inquisition in Mexico*. Baltimore:
Friedenwald, 1937.
Cohen, Martin A. *The Martyr Luis de Carvajal: The Story of a Secret Jew and
the Mexican Inquisition in the Sixteenth Century*. Philadelphia: Jewish
Publication Society, 1973.
Liebman, Seymour. *The Jews in New Spain*. Coral Gables, FL: University of
Miami Press, 1970.
Reynoso, Araceli. *Judíos en Taxco*. México: Gobierno del Estado de Guerrero /
Instituto de Investigaciones de José María Luis Mora, 1991.
Toro, Alfonso. *La familia Carvajal: Estudio histórico sobre los judíos y la
Inquisición de la Nueva España en el siglo XVI, basado en documentos
originales y en su mayor parte inéditos, que se conservan en el Archivo General
de la Nación de la ciudad de México*. 2 vols. Mexico: Patria, 1944.
Uchmany, Eva Alexandra. *La vida entre el judaísmo y el cristianismo en la Nueva
España: 1580–1606*. Mexico: Fondo de Cultura Economica / Archivo
General de la Nación, 1992.

Chapter 6. Francisco Gutiérrez: A Man of Three Faiths

On Sunday, May 10, 1615, Francisco Gutiérrez, wearing his yellow sambenito
with the large red X of the cross of Saint Andrew and carrying a wax candle in his hands, marched with the other penitents into Toledo's Plaza del
Zocodóver. A reviewing stand had been set up at one side of the plaza because
this was a very special auto-de-fé. In the royal box sat King don Felipe III, his
French wife, doña Margarita, and their son Crown Prince don Felipe IV, as
well as Prince don Carlos and Princess doña María.

This chapter is based on the data recorded in Legajo 156, Expediente 4, of the
Inquisition section of the Archivo Histórico Nacional in Madrid.

Chapter 7. Jerónimo Salgado

Salgado's seven-hundred-page trial dossier contains fascinating information
about his legion of friends and debating partners, both in Nicaragua and in
Mexico. Much of the testimony was recorded in Mexico City, but the file

includes witness depositions taken in a number of other cities in Mexico and Central and South America. Spies within the Inquisition's Secret Prison recorded dozens of Salgado's jailhouse conversations. These records also provide information about the prison's routines and the methods the prisoners used to communicate clandestinely with each other. Salgado was held in the prison for nearly four years. A separate file includes an itemized list of Salgado's confiscated goods that were auctioned off in Nicaragua from February 25, 1624, through April 3, 1625, to pay his prison expenses.

On Palm Sunday, April 3, 1626, Jerónimo Salgado, cloaked in his sambenito, received his penance in an auto-de-fé in Mexico City's Santo Domingo Church across the street from the Palacio de la Inquisición and the prison. The relatively light jail sentence—two additional years—suggests that the inquisitors believed that Salgado's long philosophical journey had indeed brought him to accept the Catholic faith.

This chapter is based on documents preserved in Mexico's Archivo General de la Nación, as follows:

Inquisición. Vol. 344, Expediente 1. Causa de Jerónimo Salgado. Granada, Nicaragua. Judaizante. 1624.

Real Fisco. Vol. 17, Expediente 4, folios 68–101. Secuestro y almoneda de los bienes de Jerónimo Salgado, Portugués, en la Ciudad de Granada. 1624.

Chapter 8. Diego Pérez de Alburquerque

Diego Gómez de Salazar, Juan Pérez de Alburquerque's enemy in Puebla, did indeed emigrate to Perú in 1622. Arrested there as a Judaizer, he provided his inquisitors with hundreds of damaging details about the crypto-Jewish communities in Rouen, Puebla, Mexico City, and Lima. He reported having Judaized with Diego Pérez de Alburquerque—among many others—in all four cities. He was assigned penance in an auto-de-fé in Lima on December 21, 1625.

Juan de Ortega was arrested in Lima in 1624 and assigned penance in 1630.

Among the prayers that Diego Pérez de Alburquerque dictated to the Inquisition scribe were lengthy versions of the morning and evening daily prayers, the Amidah—taught to him by an Italian Jew who had come to Bordeaux—and the beginning of the Shema in Hebrew, words that Diego claimed not to understand but were transcribed by the scribe as follows: *Semah ysrrael, adonay, heloeno, Adonay / hehath. Baruch sem keboth malcutoth, leonan haheth.*

Data for this chapter are found in the following sources.

Inquisición Vol. 348, Expediente 5. Causa criminal contra Diego Pérez de
    Alburquerque por judaizante. 1629.

————. Vol. 370, Expediente 2. Relaciones para enviar al Consejo en la Armada de
    1631.

————. Vol. 823, Expediente 1. Causa criminal contra Francisco Pérez de
    Alburquerque. Natural de la Torre de Moncorvo en Portugal y vecino de la
    ciudad de la Puebla de los Ángeles, por judaizante. 1629.

Bakewell, R. J. *Silver Mining and Society in Colonial Mexico: Zacatecas, 1546–*
    1700. Cambridge: Cambridge University Press, 1971.

Chapter 9. The Barajas Women

Every member of the "Barajas" family was called by the Holy Office to testify, some merely as witnesses, some as defendants in their own trials.

Diego Suárez, Beatricica's brother, held nothing back as he detailed to the inquisitors the family's Judaizing customs: what they did, when, and with whom.

Francisca Álvarez, Beatricica's sister, initially claimed that all the charges were the result of lies or malice. But once the weight of the testimony against her sank in, she, too, held nothing back, at one point cursing her mother for influencing her to Judaize: "She wept and sighed and said her mother belonged in thirty hells for what she had done."

Beatriz Álvarez, Beatricica's mother, related several conflicting versions of events. But when threatened with torture if she did not confess fully and unambiguously, she claimed that her previous statements had been the result of her fear and confusion. Since her subsequent testimony was also judged unsatisfactory, she was forced to undergo two sessions of torture.

And Beatricica . . . ? When she was arrested on June 9, 1633, all her good intentions went out the window. At first she denied any Judaizing activity. Then, confronted with witness statements, she confessed dribs and drabs of Jewish observance. At last, in January 1634, after one session in the torture chamber, she confessed everything. And, surprisingly, her efforts to convince the inquisitors that she had become a sincere Christian worked.

Dozens of witnesses testified in the three trials, both for and against the accused. As is often the case, many of the people appearing as defendants or as witnesses were known by multiple names. Five separate women, for example, were called Beatriz Álvarez:

Beatriz Álvarez, the mother of "las Barajas"—aka Violante Suárez, Violante
Ferreiro, and Violante Suárez de la Sierra
Beatriz Álvarez, her daughter—aka Beatricica
Beatriz Álvarez, a sixty-year-old Portuguese widow
Beatriz Álvarez—aka Beatriz Navarro
Beatriz Álvarez, daughter of María Álvarez and sister of Isabel Álvarez

The daughters of the "Barajas" mother used the surname Álvarez, but her
son was called Diego Suárez. The extended Suárez and Navarro clans were
similarly labyrinthine.

Despite the rock-solid evidence about the family's long history of Judaizing
and their apparent commitment to the Law of Moses, they were given relatively light sentences. Beatriz and Beatricica were required to abjure their
errors in an auto-de-fé. They had to wear a sambenito over their clothes
whenever they appeared in public. They, and whatever offspring they might
have, were prohibited from wearing fancy clothes, carrying a weapon, riding
a horse, entering a university, or holding any government or church-related
job. And their property was confiscated.

In addition, Beatricica's mother was ordered to be confined for life in
the Inquisition prison. As usual, after some relatively brief prison time, this
was reinterpreted to mean house arrest. She also was required to attend
Madrid's Church of San Pedro Mártir every Sunday, with the other penitents,
to hear mass.

Beatricica was sentenced to two years of confinement, one to be served
in the Inquisition prison.

The sentences of Francisca and Diego are not recorded.

This chapter is based on three trials preserved in the Inquisition section of
Madrid's Archivo Histórico Nacional.
Legajo 133, Expediente 10. Beatriz Álvarez, vecina de Barajas. 1633–34.
Legajo 168, Expediente 4. Beatriz Navarro Álvarez, vecina de Madrid. 1633–34.
Legajo 184, Expediente 17. Violante Suárez de la Sierra, vecina de Barajas. 1633–37.

Chapter 10. Carlos Mendes

In the main, the inquisitors seem to have believed Carlos's story, noting in
the preamble to the sentencing document that "he showed signs of contrition and repentance in asking God to pardon his sins." He was condemned

to appear with a sambenito in an auto-de-fé to publicly abjure his sins, to receive one hundred lashes, to serve four years in prison where he was to undergo instruction in Catholicism by a competent priest, and, for the rest of his life, to hear mass every Sunday and festival day and to confess and take communion three times a year. As usual in such matters, he was banned from holding any public employment.

Data for this chapter are found in Mendes's trial dossier preserved in Madrid's Archivo Histórico Nacional: Legajo 165, Expediente 11. Carlos Mendes, vecino de Constantinopla. 1622–23.